Dear Reader,

I've spent my entire life immersed in music and books.

I'm not kidding. My mom taught me to read at age four and I begged my parents for my first album at age five (John Denver, if you must know). Throughout my childhood, I can't think of a time where I wasn't either holed up with a book or obsessing about music.

My obsession even morphed into several career iterations—first as a band manager and rock promoter and now as a media attorney and romance author.

Which brings me to the *Hope & Harmony* Anthology. As you might imagine, I'm beyond thrilled to fuse my two passions together and I anticipate these stories will resonate with you as much as they have with me.

Before you dive in, please join me in thanking some key individuals without whom this anthology would not be possible.

First, a round of applause to the brilliant authors who've infused these pages with inspiring, uplifting words—thank you for stories which show how profoundly music impacts our lives and hearts.

Second, I'm incredibly grateful for the support of Meredith Wild at Page & Vine (author and publisher), Stephanie Phillips at SBR Media (literary agent), Dani Sanchez at Wildfire Marketing (marketing and PR) and Regina Wamba (cover designer). This anthology would not be possible without the support, dedication and expertise each and every one of you have brought to the table.

Finally, I'd like to give a special shout out to Willow Yanarella, my "right arm," who wrangles my literary dreams into reality.

With heartfelt thanks and musical cheers,

Kaylene Winter

Founder and Creator of the *Hope & Harmony* Anthology

HOPE & HARMONY

HOPE & HARMONY

CHELLE BLISS   STACEY MARIE BROWN   MARI CARR
JAINE DIAMOND   HELEN HARDT   JILLIAN LIOTA
KAT MIZERA   LAYLA REYNE   M. ROBINSON
BECCA STEELE   RACHEL VAN DYKEN
MEREDITH WILD   KAYLENE WINTER   JULIA WOLF

PAGE
&
VINE

Page & Vine
An Imprint of Meredith Wild LLC

A Music Romance Anthology supporting MusiCares.

Helping the humans behind music because
music gives so much to the world.

TABLE OF CONTENTS

CHORDS
OF
DESTINY

KAYLENE WINTER

About the Author

Kaylene Winter is an Amazon best-selling author of steamy, contemporary romance.

Each character-driven novel is filled with snappy dialogue, pop-culture references and enough steam to make you fan yourself. Kaylene weaves authenticity, emotion and angst into a turbulent rollercoaster ride of love, passion and soul-searing romance always ending with a delicious HEA.

Kaylene lives in Seattle with her amazing Irish husband and gorgeous Siberian Husky. She loves creating art of all kinds.

www.kaylenewinter.com

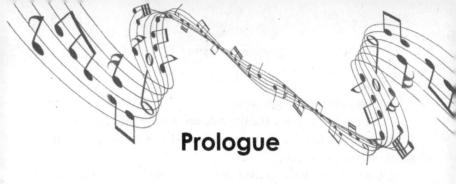

Prologue

HOPE

Present Day

Icy chills skate up my neck.

My eyes dart around the crowd at the sea of faces watching me.

I feel exposed.

Putting myself out here is nerve-racking on the best of days. A gig's a gig, though. At least, that's what I told myself when I added this afternoon busking shift at Pike Place Market. I'm used to the lunchtime crowd and my regulars who stop by to see me every day.

This crowd is unfamiliar. The vibe is just...different.

Determined not to let fear get the best of me, I take a deep breath and belt out the last note of the melody. Holding...holding—allowing it to linger until the song fades like vapor into the late-afternoon air.

When the accumulated audience bursts into applause, I hold back tears of relief. Dozens toss money into my open guitar case. A few say the sweetest things as they pass by.

"My coworker told me not to miss your performance." A woman in a navy business suit hands me a twenty. "I'm so glad I came. You're going to be a big star."

An elderly man wearing a fedora drops a dollar on top of the other bills. "Sweetheart, you're a balm to my soul every day."

Wait, what? Did these people actually make an effort to come see me play this afternoon?

Wow.

Maybe I'm on the right path.

Gratefully, I observe the tips pile up in my guitar case while I chat. Nod my thanks. Shake a few hands. I guess the power of music means something.

A dude wearing a quilted gray jacket shyly offers me five dollars. "Quite the haul."

"Uh, yeah. Not bad for February." I take the bill. He's quite handsome. Untamed black hair flops over kind, brown eyes framed by trendy, square glasses. I dig his snazzy green Puma sneakers.

He blushes. "I usually listen to you at lunchtime, but I heard you were playing again today. I was wondering..."

A quick glance at the clock on the Market sign freaks me out. I'm gonna be late for my bartending shift if I don't skedaddle right effing now.

"I'm sorry, but I've gotta jet." I hurriedly stuff the tips in my crossbody bag and pack my old Gibson J-45 in its worn, duct-taped case, taking a millisecond to run my thumb over the frets. The sunburst finish is faded and scratched, but the guitar holds a cherished place in my heart.

It's all I have left of my mother.

To save a couple of minutes, I take a shortcut. Dart down a narrow alley hemmed in by aging brick buildings. A musty, damp odor clings to the old, uneven cobblestones worn by time and weather. The dim light from a flickering street lamp casts a twisted shadow against the gum wall. It's quiet except for an occasional drip of water from a leaky gutter. The scuttle of a rat in the shadows. A horn honking from the ferry line. A distant clank of a dumpster lid.

Tamping down the involuntary shiver creeping along my spine, I pick up the pace.

Only three more blocks.

Seconds later, the bustle of the waterfront comes into view, and I sigh with relief. I can see my car, its blue paint dulled by years of sun and rain. Pulling the keys out of my pocket, I'm about to unlock the door when I'm yanked back with a force that steals my breath.

Fear grips me, glacial and sharp. My guitar, slung across my back, becomes the center of a violent struggle. I cling to it fiercely, wrapping my arms around the case.

"Let go!" I scream, though my voice is lost in the chaos.

My assailant, whose face is hidden under a ski mask, jerks the strap of my crossbody bag. Holy crap, he wants my tips. I desperately scream, kick, and thrash, trying to hold on to what's mine.

A horrific blow to the side of my head catches me off guard.

Pain explodes. The world spins.

In slow motion, my body crumples to the ground. I try to get up, but it's useless. A sharp kick in the gut renders me helpless. I watch as the guy takes off with my bag and guitar.

You needed the money for rent.

Darkness claims me.

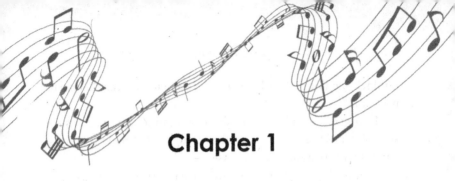

Chapter 1

ALEK

One Week Earlier

Her name's Hope, and seriously, she's a goddess out of my dreams.

I'm here again, sneaking glances at her between the chaos of the Pike Place Market crowd, feeling like a ghost.

Hope, on the other hand, is a vibrant, magnetic nymph holding court at "The Clock," situated at the market's entrance in front of the famous fish vendor. With a beat-up guitar cradled in her arms, she captivates everyone who passes by with her commanding presence and rich, emotive voice.

Effortlessly edgy, she rocks a faded and patched-up vintage denim jacket. Her jeans are ripped at the knees, with black tights peeking through. She stomps one sturdy boot, scuffed and worn, on the cobblestone street to the beat of the song.

I usually find myself here on my lunch hour. Her talent is unquestionable, but there's something about the way she throws her whole self into her art. Like she's telling stories straight from her soul.

She's authentic. Stunning.

Out of my league.

I've memorized everything about her. How her eyes shut tight when she's reaching for those impossible notes. Or the way her hands effortlessly know their way around the strings of her guitar. When she sings, it's like she's weaving magic—every note, every word, feels like it's just for me.

Oh, how I want to know her. Like, *really* know her.

Except, every time I even *think* about talking to her, I freeze. She's out here living her dream, confidently performing for thousands of people in the middle of the hustle, while I spend my day in a cubicle, coding away at Hungry Llama Games.

A faceless dude in the crowd who longs for a chance...

Except, what would I even say to her? *"Hey, I think your music's awesome?"*

Nah. I'd probably just trip over my words. Make a fool of myself.

She's everything I wish I could be confident, full of passion, totally free.

Hope wraps up her performance. People gather around, snapping pictures and dropping compliments. She navigates it all with ease, handing everyone who asks a slip of paper. Before I can talk myself out of it, I shuffle up to her and take one.

Hope flashes me a smile. Time stops for a second when she offers me an elegant business card with *Hope Kristiansen* printed in a swooshy script. There's also a phone number and a QR code.

I can't believe it. I've got her contact info.

Taking it from her dainty fingers, I ease into the crowd and return to work. Back at my desk, I scan the QR code like it's a treasure map. It leads to her bio, her busking schedule, and I learn she works as a bartender at The Mission, Seattle's hottest rock venue.

The thought of seeing her in a club vibe is both thrilling and terrifying.

What do I have to lose? Maybe it's time to drag my coding crew out and, for a change of pace, do a little peopling. If I step out of the shadows and move a bit closer to Hope's world, who knows?

It could be the start of something new. Or at least a break from the usual routine.

Either way, it's on.

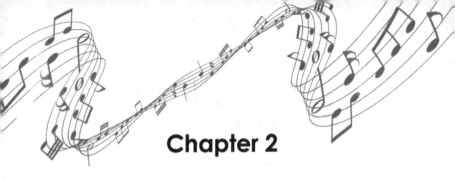

Chapter 2

HOPE

Later That Night

The Mission is pulsing with life tonight, a mash-up of clinking glasses, laughter, and the low hum of excited conversations.

Lake Lyon, an up-and-coming alternative songwriter, is playing, so it's packed. Every corner bursts at the seams with an eclectic mix of Seattle music fans celebrating the next big artist to break out of Seattle.

As usual, I'm behind the bar, pouring drinks and soaking in the energy. This legendary club has become my second home over the past couple of months.

Zane Rocks, the bad-ass guitarist of Less Than Zero, the last big band to break out of Seattle, co-owns the club and the restaurant next door with his wife, Fiona. With wild hair and frenetic energy, Zane may be young, but he's Seattle music royalty. His father, Carter Pope, is the guitarist for the legendary grunge band Limelight. Fiona's father, Gus, owned the original Mission Club before he died.

The two of them are, well...most def #couplegoals.

Amidst a blur of orders, Zane approaches me. "Hope, please do me a solid. The opener is stuck at the Canadian border. Could you fill in?"

"Uh..." I'm tongue-tied and excited all at the same time. Playing any slot at The Mission is a dream come true. "Um..."

"I'll have someone cover the bar." He places his hands

together like he's praying. "*Please*."

I shake my head sadly. "I didn't bring my guitar."

"Shit." Zane scrunches his nose.

I realize it's now or maybe never. He's giving me a shot, I need to take it. "Do you have an acoustic I can borrow?"

"Uh...yeah! Absolutely. Come with me." Zane takes off, gesturing for me to follow.

My heart skips a beat. The Mission's stage is a world away from the lunch crowd at Pike Place Market. Can I do this?

"You've got half an hour to get ready." Zane hands me a gorgeous Breedlove Tobacco Burst acoustic. "I'll grab you a few minutes before you go on."

Quickly, I run through a couple of songs on the unfamiliar instrument and scribble out a set list.

Zane pops his head in. "Ready?"

"Uh...yeah." I squeeze out a smile and follow him down the back hallway. "Thank you for the opportunity."

We arrive at the side of the stage. "From what I'm hearing, you've earned it. Try not to feel any pressure. Enjoy yourself, you'll be great!"

Onstage, I glance out at the audience, desperate for a familiar face to anchor me. It's futile, the stage lights are blinding, and the room seems to stretch on forever. Gulping down my nerves, I adjust the microphone and take a deep breath. My fingers tremble slightly when I poise them on the frets.

Well...this is it.

My moment.

I strum a chord and begin. My voice is a little shaky at first, then stronger as I feel more at ease. By the second verse, I'm flying, lost in the performance. Music fills the room and finds its place amongst the murmur of the crowd.

When I finish, there's a moment of silence before the crowd erupts into whoops and cheers. Encouraged, I close my eyes and launch into the rest of my set. These are my songs. My stories. The music flows through me until, before I know it, my time is up.

I did it. I faced my fear. Took the stage. Sang my heart out.

"I'm Hope Kristiansen, thank you for listening." I wave.

The enthusiasm is deafening. Placing my hand over my heart, I take a moment and let it wash over me. My legs may feel like jelly, but my heart is soaring. One of my biggest dreams has just come true.

I can't help but grin.

This is just the beginning, I can feel it.

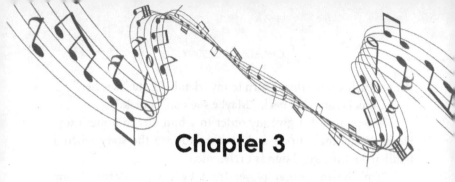

Chapter 3

ALEK

The Same Night

Tonight's gonna be epic if I can just calm myself down.

I've gone through with it—I'm at Seattle's hottest live music venue, though the thought of mixing it up with the cool kids gives me hives. Probably because of the years of bullying I endured before finding my tribe of programmers in college.

I'm sucking it up, though.

All in the name of Hope.

Daniel, Jamie, and I hold our wrists out for the doorman to stamp, and then we're granted access.

Holy crap.

With an eclectic mix of rock memorabilia and a thumping state-of-the-art sound system, this place feels worlds away from the algorithmic puzzles and code lines defining my day-to-day life at Hungry Llama Games.

"Dude." Daniel looks around in awe. "I can't believe we're here."

I stand tall and try to muster some confidence. "Yeah, well, believe it. Maybe I'll even talk to Hope."

After a shot...or two.

Except I've never had a shot in my life.

"There's the bar. She's the bartender, right? Let's get a drink." Jamie gestures to the back of the room.

"Yeah, okay..." My stomach seizes as we head in that direction.

We're nearly there when I turn to my friends. "I don't see her."

Daniel cranes his neck. "Maybe she's on a break."

Disappointed, I give my order to a buff guy in a mesh top. He hands us three beers and we turn toward the stage when a familiar-looking guy bounds to the mic.

"Isn't he the guitar player from Less Than Zero?" Jamie nudges me.

I shrug, distracted. "Maybe?"

All I see is *Hope.*

Not where I expected, though. She struts on stage, new guitar in hand, commanding attention through the sheer force of her presence. There's something different about her. Gone are the flowing bohemian clothes. Tonight she's a rock star wearing tight black jeans and a low-cut black tank top.

She's even more beautiful under the spotlight.

My friends' conversation fades into the background as I watch, transfixed.

Hope begins her performance. Within seconds she pulls the room into her orbit with her voice, which fills the space, soulful and passionate. The audience is rapt with attention, hooting and cheering after each song ends.

She belongs up there.

"Man, she's incredible." Daniel stares at her, slack-jawed.

Hope finishes her set to thunderous applause. She disappears behind the curtain for a bit, but fifteen minutes later walks right past us and takes her position behind the bar.

Jamie nudges me. "You're up, Romeo. Go talk to her."

I hesitate, my previous bravado shattered. She's laughing with the two burly bartenders. One of them picks her up and twirls her around. I'm frozen in place.

"I can't," I finally murmur. The two words taste like defeat.

Daniel claps a hand on my shoulder, understanding. "It's alright, Alek. There'll be other nights."

We quickly finish our beers and leave. The drive back is quiet. Ten minutes later, I'm lying alone in bed, crushed because I've let my shyness and insecurity define me. *Again.*

Sure, I managed to step beyond my comfort zone tonight. But, in the end, I choked.

I'm disappointed in myself. Living like a scared rabbit won't get me anywhere.

Not if I want a shot with an exquisite woman like Hope.

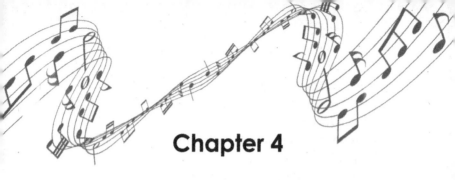

Chapter 4

HOPE

Later That Night

Mood: Confused.

I'm riding a weird high-low combo. It's become my life's soundtrack lately.

Back at my studio apartment after an electric night at The Mission, I drop my keys on the counter and flop onto my threadbare thrift-store couch that's seen better days. My mind's still buzzing from tonight's unexpected gig.

I wish I could enjoy it, but my heart sinks at the sight of my pile of unpaid bills cluttering the coffee table.

Reality bites. *Hard.*

I'm about to spiral into a full-on freak-out when my phone buzzes. A text from my BFF Lissa. Without thinking, I hit FaceTime.

"Girl, you won't believe the night I had," I blurt out, skipping formalities when I see her face fill my screen. Lissa's been my rock since...well, forever. Even more so after Mom passed last year.

Fucking cancer. It took more than her life, which is an unbearable loss—she was my best friend. Greatest cheerleader. Biggest fan.

One terminal diagnosis and our support system disappeared. Treatment wiped out her life savings. She had to sell the house and most of her possessions to ensure I wasn't saddled with medical debt when she passed. There was just enough left over to keep me going for a few months, but it's mostly gone now.

I glance at my guitar. My most-prized possession.

Just knowing it's close by makes it feel like she's here with me. My one remaining comfort.

Lissa cuts through my haze. "*Hope*. Snap out of it and give me the scoop. Let me guess, Zane and Fiona want to adopt you?"

"God, I wish." I bat my eyes at the screen, then dive into the tale of my impromptu performance and how Zane promised more gigs at the club. "It was terrifying and amazing. Playing on a real stage for a crowd who loves music? Incomparable. It's what I was born to do. For a minute, I forgot all about the mess I'm in."

She beams at me. "I wish I could have been there, it sucks I live two thousand miles away. I'm sorry you're struggling."

"Yeah, I'm in my destitute era, big time. Rent's due, and I'm short. Like, 'eating-ramen-once-per-day' short. Bartending and street performing don't cover my basic bills. Seattle's so crazy expensive."

The weight of adulting presses down hard on my shoulders.

I can practically hear Lissa's brain ticking. "Okay, so here's the short-term plan. This week, you're gonna busk during every open spot you can slip into. Milk it and then some. Secure your bread."

Huh. It's simple but genius. I should have thought of it sooner, but I haven't wanted to seem greedy. There's a certain protocol to follow until you've paid your dues, which I have, so I'm already mentally scheduling myself. "You think it'll work?"

"Absolutely." Lissa's confidence in me means everything. "You're talented, and people love you. Plus, it's Seattle. Tourists eat an indie music vibe up with a spoon."

Her enthusiasm buoys my spirits. By the time we hang up, I'm armed with a game plan and a sliver of optimism. Sure, the next few days are gonna be a grind, but I've faced worse. Mom's guitar seems to hum in agreement from its stand by the window.

By the time I crawl into bed, I feel better.

I can do this.

I'll busk my little heart out, make rent, pay some bills, and keep chasing my dream. It's what Mom would have wanted.

Honestly, it's what I want, too.

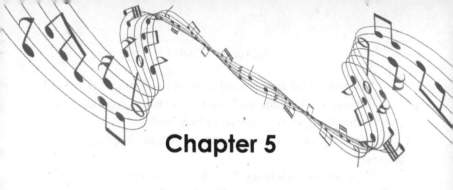

Chapter 5

<u>ALEK</u>

The Next Evening

Keeping it 100, something's gotta change.

Lost in thought at my folks' place on Bainbridge Island, I poke at my dinner. Even my mom's legendary lasagna can't lift the fog I'm in. I'm so tired of being a slave to insecurity. It's like carrying around a backpack full of bricks. All the effin' time.

Facts: I'm killing it in the adulting department. The company I work for is bussin'. I make decent money. My downtown apartment is fire. I'm not the same kid who was bullied in high school.

Also facts: I've caught feelings for Hope, and I've got to find a way to harness some main-character energy. Skulking out of a nightclub like a defeated loser isn't going to cut it.

Dad breaks the silence. "You're quieter than usual, Alek. What's up?"

I take a bite of cheesy, noodley goodness to buy time. The truth is, a girl I can't muster the courage to talk to is living rent-free in my head. Admitting this to my parents seems...pathetic?

"Ah, it's just some work stuff," I mumble.

"You know you can talk to us, right?" Dad gives me a look that says, *"Nice try, kiddo."*

Ahh, eff it. "Fine. It's not work. There's a musician I've been following. Her name is Hope, and she performs at Pike Place Market at lunchtime. I, uh...um..."

"*Ohhhhh.*" Dad leans in, all ears and wisdom. "Let me tell you a little secret. Confidence is something you can build, it's not always something you're necessarily born with."

I frown. "How is your astute platitude helpful? I need *tangible*."

"Fine, let me spell it out. I think the kids today call it a 'glow up.'" Mom sets her fork down. "You're still wearing the clothes you had in high school. Same glasses. Same haircut. I know you had a hard time back then, but you're a grown man now. You'd be amazed at how much better you'll feel when you change things up."

My mom's a genius, but I'm skeptical. "It's that simple?"

"No, of course not. But it's a step in the right direction." Dad nods at me.

Mom stands and hugs me from behind. "Go to Nordstrom. They have personal stylists who'll work with you to figure out what you like without radically changing your aesthetic. Unless you want to, of course. Afterward, make an appointment at a real hair salon instead of those cheap barbershops you usually go to."

"I guess it couldn't hurt." I tap my finger on my chin. "She's probably used to guys who spend time thinking about this stuff."

Dad shakes his head. "C'mon now. Upgrading your game isn't about her, it's about you and feeling more comfortable in your own skin. When you bolster your confidence, nothing will stop you from talking to your musician crush or anyone else who catches your eye."

"You think?" I tilt my head skeptically.

He nods. "*I know.* Besides, either way, if you keep it simple and ask her for coffee, the worst possibility is she'll say no."

My parents exchange grins.

"I said yes." Mom reaches for my dad's hand.

He takes it and brings it to his lips. "Best decision I ever made."

That's it. I'm taking their advice.

On the ferry on my way home, I book an appointment with a

stylist and research salons. Taking these steps is like a promise to myself—face your fear and reap the rewards.

Because maybe, just maybe, it will help.

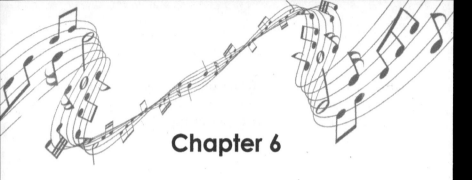

Chapter 6

HOPE

Present Day

What the eff just happened?

Sprawled across the cold, unforgiving pavement, I gaze at the sky as my world spins out of control in a blur of pain and confusion. A distant sound of sirens cuts through my brain fog—a stark reminder of the devastating reality crushing me like a bug.

Squeezing one eye open, I see the quilted-coat guy from the market waving frantically. "Wha...what's going on?" I manage to eke out, though my voice comes out so faint I'm not sure if he hears me.

"Hope?" The guy crouches next to me and grips my hand. "Hey, you gotta stay with me, okay?"

I'm startled he knows my name. "How..."

"*Shhh.* Please don't worry. The ambulance is coming." He tenderly brushes a strand of hair from my face. "You're gonna be okay."

Easy for him to say. Everything hurts. Worse, the panic and fear bubbling up threatens to overshadow my physical pain. "No. Send it away. The guy took my money. I can't afford to go to the hospital."

"Please don't worry about anything right now," the guy reassures me, his voice a steady presence in the turmoil. "Just focus on breathing."

Breathing?

As if air could fix the mess of my life.

I make a feeble attempt to sit up, driven by a desperate need to escape, but he gently pushes me back down. "Stay still until they check you out. The guy knocked you on the head pretty hard."

Tears leak from the corners of my eyes as the sirens grow louder. Closer. In this vortex of dread, his calm is literally the only thing I can latch on to. The ambulance screeches to a halt beside us, and he stands to speak to the arriving paramedics. For a moment, his body is a welcome barrier between me and the rest of the world, and my mind floats away...

Suddenly, he's next to me again. He leans in close, his voice barely a whisper. "Hope, my name is Alek Bozic." His eyes lock on to mine with an intensity that anchors me. "Follow my lead, okay? I've got you."

I try to nod, but it hurts too bad.

"Her name is Hope Kristiansen. She's my wife." He gestures to the paramedics. My heart stutters at the audacity of the lie, a declaration he makes with such conviction it almost feels true. "She's on my insurance."

His words promise safety when I feel so exposed. Part of me wants to protest with the truth. Insist we're strangers. But there's a look in his eyes—a plea for trust. Somehow, deep in my soul, I know this stranger is my protector and advocate in the midst of such intense vulnerability.

When the paramedics load me into the ambulance, Alek is by my side. His hand finds mine again, a lifeline in the chaos. Once inside, the doors close behind us, sealing off the life I knew just moments ago.

Through the haze of pain and fear, I relax and catch glimpses of the city lights speeding by—a kaleidoscope of colors against the burgeoning nightfall. Alek's grip never wavers. His presence is a steady, comforting force as reality slips in and out of focus.

As I slide back into unconsciousness, I can't help but wonder...

Is Alek a beacon of light?

Or just another shadow?

Chapter 7

<u>ALEK</u>

Present Day

What was I thinking?

Hope looks so small and helpless on the stretcher. Nothing like the fiery, talented woman I've watched owning the crowd at the Market all these months. Nothing like the beautiful, confident woman I've been so reluctant to approach.

"Her name is Hope Kristiansen. She's my wife. She's on my insurance."

The words just flew out of my mouth. No filter. No second thoughts. In the moment, it felt like the only solution to get her the help she needed, fast.

The EMTs didn't question it, they were too busy trying to stabilize her. I even sat beside her in the ambulance holding her hand as we zipped toward the hospital.

Once we arrived and hit a stonewall of "family only" on the way to the examination room, I doubled down on the husband bit. They let me through, and I've remained beside her for hours with my fingers threaded between hers as she rests.

My heart races like crazy, though. I've made a promise to Hope that everything will be okay. Any minute I'll need to sign off on her paperwork, the thought causing the gravity of what I've done to sink in.

We're not married. She's not on my insurance. How in the hell will I pull this off?

I've got to figure it out. Luckily, her care team arrives, giving me the chance to step out and phone a friend.

"Dude, I need you to do me a solid," I blurt out when Jamie answers my call.

After I recount the afternoon's events, he gives me good advice. "Call HR. Hungry Llama might cover her, but you need to get on top of it before she racks up hundreds of thousands of dollars in charges."

Shit. I didn't think about the ramifications of my impulsiveness. Now it makes sense why she wanted me to send the ambulance away. I can't imagine not having health insurance.

No wonder she was so freaked out.

*　*　*

An hour later, I'm fighting the urge to nod off when Hope wakes up, confused and vulnerable.

"You're here?" she rasps when she sees me sitting beside her. "I don't even know you. Why would you say you're my husband?"

Man, how do I even start? The truth, I guess. There's no turning back now. "I'm Alek. I've watched you perform at the Market at lunchtime for the past few months and always wanted to...I don't know, connect with you somehow? I'm crap at social stuff. Today, when you mentioned you'd be playing another set, I came back and gave you a tip under the guise of asking you for coffee. You were in a hurry, though, so I aborted the mission. On my way back to work, I saw some sketchy guy follow you and I couldn't just do nothing. I felt compelled to protect you."

Her eyes widen. Almost like she doesn't believe me. Or maybe she's not used to people going out of their way for her. Either way, she's clearly trying to figure out if I'm for real. "You didn't have to do what you did. This could come back and bite us in the ass."

"I know. Honestly, though? I'd do it all over again if it helps you." Somehow, my words flow effortlessly today. "I called work, and there's a way...but it's out there. Probably too weird..."

Hope cracks a small smile, and it's like a ray of sunshine breaking through clouds. She reaches for my hand, her grip surprisingly strong. "Thank you for everything. Tell me how we'll get through this."

I fill her in on the plan and, shockingly, she seems to be on board.

How did my lie turn into the most real thing I've ever felt?

This will be one heck of a story for our grandkids if we ever get there...

Whoa.

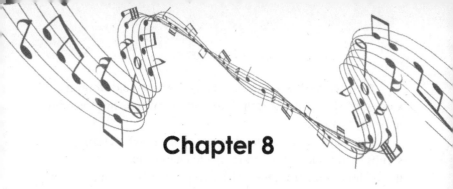

Chapter 8

HOPE

Two Days Later

Good God, make it stop...

Lying here in this too-bright hospital room, my head pounds like it's trying to keep beat with the annoying buzz of the overhead lights.

Every time I open my eyes, it feels like I'm stuck in limbo between the life I was living and what's waiting for me on the other side of this headache.

It's terrifying.

Through my haze, I hear Dr. Felix discussing my care protocol with Alek. "Hope's responsive, her memory's intact, and the swelling's gone down." He's so calm as he delivers bombshell after bombshell. "No brain injury is the same, and recovery will be different for everyone. I have high hopes for a full recovery as long as she rests and heals for the next couple of months. We'll get her set up with physical therapy and counseling. Regular checkups, of course."

"I understand. I've got her covered—I'm working from home until she's back on her feet." Alek is so sure of himself. He's a take-charge kind of guy.

"Great. I'll get the release papers prepared." Dr. Felix glances over to see I'm awake and listening. He takes a step toward me. "Hope, remember, just because an injury isn't visible doesn't mean it isn't real."

Alek beams down at me like he's been by my side forever, not some guy who willingly placed himself in my mess by pretending to be my husband.

Not until after the doc leaves—who placed a clean pair of scrubs on the end of the bed for me to change into—does it really hit me how crazy this all is. Alek being here is legit amazing, but also super stressful.

We're strangers bound together in a huge lie. And now I'm about to move in with him so we can officially be domestic partners.

"I'll need some help getting dressed." I squeeze my eyes shut as he adjusts the bed so I can sit up. "I'm still so dizzy."

He coughs nervously. "Are you sure there's not a friend I can call? I'm happy to help, but I don't want you to think I'm taking advantage..."

"It's fine. My friends are all in Bozeman. Mom and I moved to Seattle for her treatment when she got cancer." I tug at the hospital gown. "I decided to stay after she died. Better music scene."

Alek reaches over hesitantly to assist. "I'm sorry to bring it up, I remember you mentioning it. I just meant...if you're not comfortable with me, I can always call my mom to help."

I'm not stupid. Most men wouldn't offer a seemingly helpless woman this level of financial support without some ulterior motive. My vulnerable condition is like a magnet to predatory assholes.

But Alek? He's like an angel. I don't get any creepy vibes at all. Plus, he seems to genuinely like me.

Besides, it's nice to have someone looking out for me for a change. What comes next scares me. I never paid rent on my apartment, so I'm going to be evicted any day. My injuries won't allow me to work so I have no way to make money. The Mission is holding my job open, but I'll lose my coveted location at the Market, if I haven't already.

Please let him be legit.

A tear trickles down my cheek.

Alek's hand finds mine. "Don't worry. We're in this together."

Oh, I'm worried. *Terrified, more like it.*

A man, who was just another face in the crowd two days ago, is now my knight in shining armor.

This can't possibly end well.

Can it?

Chapter 9

<u>ALEK</u>

Three Weeks Later

It's funny how my life changed in an instant.

One minute I couldn't fathom saying hello to her, and now Hope is living with me in my apartment.

Time's zipped by since Hope got out of the hospital. We're slowly figuring out how to navigate...whatever this is. On a positive note, she's no longer dizzy and can get around on her own. On the other hand, the brutal headaches are still an issue. Day by day, she's getting stronger.

Our routine's settled into a fairly comfortable pattern. I work from home and take care of feeding us both. She rests and listens to soft music while I work. If she has an appointment, I go with her because she's not cleared to drive for at least a few more months. At night, after I make dinner, I read to her. She's still on a strict no-screen routine while her brain heals.

Tonight, we've just enjoyed delicious takeout dumplings from my favorite Chinese restaurant in the ID, and finished three chapters from our current book, *To Kill a Mockingbird*. Her feet are in my lap as she reclines against the pillows on the couch.

It's weird how something as simple as reading out loud can feel so intimate. So right.

I close the book. The silence wraps around us for a moment.

"You know." I take her foot in my hand and press my thumb into her sole. "Hungry Llama's come through for us. I'm glad everything worked out, and my health care policy covers significant others. Your hospital bills and medical care are paid for."

Hope's eyes blink open. "Well, my *'significant other,'* thank you again for everything you're doing for me. Please let me know when I wear out my welcome and you want to kick me to the curb."

"That'll never happen." The words escape before I can stop them.

Her face pinkens. "Well, I know I say it a lot, but all of this... It's...really kind of you. And your mom popping by so you can work...I owe you so much."

"No. You owe me nothing." I feel a bit awkward because Hope living with me is a dream come true. She's everything I thought she'd be and so much more. "I truly love having you here. My mom thinks of you as the daughter she never had."

We fall into a brief silence, the comfortable kind. Not strained in any way.

"You know, I wanted to talk to you for months before you were assaulted, but I was such a coward," I admit, laughing at myself. "I spent each day trying to psych myself up. Right before your attack was the first time I found the courage to hand you a tip."

Hope's laughter joins mine, light and easy. "I remember thinking you were handsome, but I was late for work. Little did I know you'd come to my rescue minutes later."

I shake my head. "Guess I'm not exactly the hero type."

"No, you're *exactly* the hero type." The mood shifts slightly as a shadow of sadness crosses her beautiful face. "I miss singing so much. It's like part of me is missing when I can't perform."

Instinctively, I sit up, and my hand finds hers. "You'll find your way back once you're feeling better."

Our eyes lock, and the world pauses. Lost in the moment, I lean in and press my lips against hers. It's a soft, hesitant kiss, but it's charged with all the unspoken feelings I've bottled up, combined with the growing affection we've shared over the past weeks.

Hope moans and kisses me back. Threads her fingers through my hair. It lights a spark between us. An undeniable connection where everything else fades away, and there's only us.

Eventually, Hope pulls back and gazes at me, her blue eyes sparkling. "Alek. Wow."

"Yeah." I smooth her dark hair away from her face. "*Wow*."

Though there are a million questions still hanging between us, for now, this is enough.

It's like we're on the edge of something new. Something exciting.

I can't wait to see where it leads.

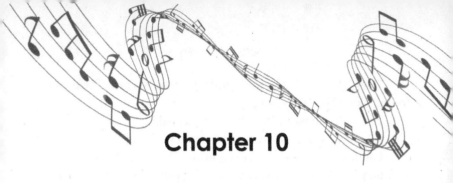

Chapter 10

HOPE

Three Weeks Later

If there were a blueprint for the perfect boyfriend, it would be Alek.

It's three weeks post-kiss, and we've shared many more beautiful, intimate moments. Our dynamic has subtly evolved from strangers to friends to lovers in a short span of time, which is...confusing. Throughout it all, Alek's been my sanctuary. Not only has he provided unwavering support, but he makes me laugh and accepts me for who I am without judgment.

So, on one hand, adapting to life together has been unexpectedly wonderful. Yet, as I piece myself back together, I'm tangled in a myriad of emotions. As irresistibly drawn to Alek as I feel, my dependency on him—both financially and emotionally—freaks me out.

In other words, falling for him has been easy, but my reliance on him shakes me to the core.

At least my health's on the upswing, even the lingering headaches don't hit as hard. The brain fog, however, is a stubborn reminder of the night I was brutally attacked. Not to mention the loss of my cherished guitar.

I try not to think about it much because when I do, it feels like I'm going to start screaming and never stop.

The problem is, I *do* think about it. All. The. Time.

Tonight, as we enjoy delicious Chicken Tikka Masala, a weighted silence hangs between us.

"Hey." Alek, intuitive and gentle, furrows his brow. "Are you feeling okay? You seem...off."

I puff out a breath. "*Um*. It's complicated."

"Tell me." He reaches over and clasps my hand.

I squeeze his fingers between mine. "This...us. I'm into you. So much, but it's also scary. I lean on you. Rely on you. Not just for recovery but also emotionally. It's overwhelming."

"Oh." His eyebrows raise in surprise.

"You have to admit, the past few weeks have been intense. It's hard not to feel like I'm losing myself." My attempt to clarify has the opposite effect, as evidenced by how wounded he looks.

Damn. The last thing I want is to hurt him.

He pulls his hand away. "I'm sorry if I'm smothering you. I never wanted to push you into anything."

"You haven't. I promise. It's just...I don't know how to do this." My voice is raw with confusion and fear.

Just like that, I see the depth of his feelings laid bare. His brown eyes reveal a vulnerability that makes my heart twist. "Hope, I'm in love with you."

"I'm falling for you, too, *but*..." My words, meant to reassure, have the opposite effect.

I can't say the words. Not yet. It's too soon.

He stiffens as he processes my words or lack thereof.

"I thought we were...in the same place." His voice is laced with pain. Immediately, I want to reach out and erase the distance I've carelessly created.

"We are. It's also a lot very quickly. I've never been this dependent on anyone, and it's hard to not feel like I'm losing myself in the process," I try to explain, my heart aching at the confusion in his eyes. "I'm going to my room. I need to lie down."

Alek's sorrowful gaze follows me, yet he doesn't hold me back. Though my guilt of deepening his distress is crushing, I wasn't lying. My head is pounding, and I have to rest.

Lying in the dark room, I'm torn between my developing feelings for Alek and my need to reclaim some independence.

This feels like a crossroads.
When all I want is for our paths to merge.

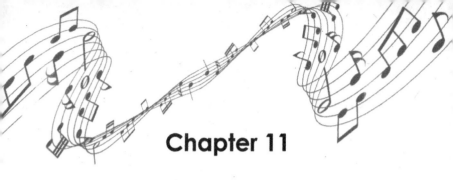

Chapter 11

ALEK

Five Days Later

God, I miss her.

It's been a tense five days since Hope expressed her need for space. She and I have barely spoken or addressed our conversation. We're not fighting, no. Instead, we tiptoe around each other with pleasant smiles and polite words.

The effortless chats and laughter are gone. There's been no physical affection. No stolen kisses. No making love.

All the good stuff has been replaced by a strained cordiality that's wearing me thin.

I'm a mess.

Plus, my brain's stuck in a worry loop. She's catching Ubers to her doctor's appointments instead of riding with me. Don't get me wrong, her steps toward independence are exactly what I've hoped for. I'm happy she's piecing her life back together because I never wanted her to feel like a caged bird.

I just want to be along for this part of her journey, and it feels like I'm being iced out.

So yeah, I'm proud but also panicked of becoming irrelevant in Hope's colorful world.

And now, apparently, she's got the green light from her neurologist to start working again—with conditions. Zane's wife, Fiona, offered her a gig as a host at her fine-dining restaurant, Gus. It's perfect, really. She'll earn some money in the high-end establishment and won't be subjected to The Mission's sensory overload.

Tonight's her first shift.

As Hope's about to head out, looking gorgeous in a black, fitted dress, I muster up a weak, "You look beautiful. Good luck tonight."

God. My attempt at normalcy feels so forced. Even to my ears.

She pauses. "Thanks, Alek. I... Do you think I'll be okay?"

Hope wrings her hands, clearly anxious. I hate that she doubts herself.

"Absolutely." I paste on a smile. "You're going to be great. Fiona is lucky to have you."

Her grateful smile permeates her entire being, and she visibly relaxes. That's when it hits me. The distance between us is as much my doing as hers.

"I'll see you later?" She sounds almost hopeful as she reaches for the door.

My heart lightens a bit. "Yeah, see you later."

After she's gone, the silence in the apartment is deafening. I can't imagine living like this ever again. Needing to fill the void, I dial my dad. I let it all spill out: my fears, my insecurities, everything.

"*Alek*," Dad finally interrupts my rant. "You've got to remember, healing happens in layers. Hope needs to return to her own definition of normal. Your job? Whether you're her friend or her significant other, always be her anchor, not her chain."

"But what if she moves on? Realizes she doesn't want to be with me?"

There's a long pause before my dad speaks. "Son, relationships aren't static. They're tested, stretched, reshaped. If you survive this? You're set for the long haul."

"And if we don't?" I pinch the bridge of my nose with my fingers, trying not to cry.

His voice is soothing. "Then I'll help you pick up the pieces and move on."

Dad's words echo in my mind.

I pray that, on the other side of this struggle, Hope and I will have a stronger, deeper bond.

Only time will tell.

In the meantime, I'll stay the course.

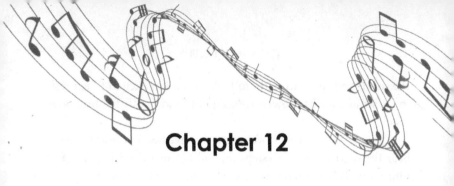

Chapter 12

HOPE

Three Weeks Later

I look around the apartment in awe.

How and when did this happen? Somehow, my stuff is no longer confined to boxes. I'm fully unpacked, and everything I own is interspersed with Alek's things.

His apartment is now our shared space.

Despite the crunchiness of a few weeks ago after I insisted on reclaiming my independence, things have settled down. My life with him has blossomed into a vibrant and unexpected journey. There's no question. I want a future filled with shared dreams and the simple joy of waking up beside each other every morning.

The hosting gig at Gus has been a Godsend. This is the most I've felt like myself since the attack. Alek's been nothing but supportive. He's given me the space to find my footing. Our relationship has stalled, though. Probably because of the distance I inadvertently created in my quest for autonomy.

I'm ready to bridge the gap once and for all and show Alek how I feel about him.

Earlier on our weekly phone call, Lissa sensed my determination and suggested a grand gesture. "Now, I haven't met him, but he seems like a unicorn. Why not surprise him with dinner? He's taken care of you for months, turn the tables a bit."

The spark of an idea turned into a whole thing. I'm all in. Alek should be home soon. My mom's favorite roast chicken is in the oven, and the dining room table is set. I'm excited to express my gratitude for his unwavering support and finally tell him how I feel.

I'm in the midst of preparing the mashed potatoes when I hear the door open. Alek steps in, and the surprise I planned for him is nearly forgotten when I see he's not empty-handed.

I'd recognize the worn, old case anywhere. My hands fly to my mouth when I realize he's carrying my beloved guitar.

"I found it." Alek's voice is tinged with excitement and something deeper. More meaningful. "I tracked it down and found it at a pawn shop in Tacoma. I know you miss your music and were planning on buying a new one, but I thought..."

Tears prick my eyes as I take in the sight of my long-lost companion. This guitar is more than an instrument. It's a piece of my soul. My link to a past I thought was gone forever.

Alek, in his quiet, thoughtful way, has managed to return a piece of myself I feared was lost.

I melt into his arms. "I love you. I really, *really* love you. You have no idea how much this means to me."

His warm, genuine smile is like a cozy blanket. "I love you too. No matter what, I want you to be happy. To see you whole again, with or without me."

"With you." The sentiment behind his words, the selflessness, only deepens my feelings for him. I press a kiss to his sweet lips. "*Always* with you."

Dinner can wait.

Any remaining space between us is now filled with happy tears, laughter, and soft touches. Expressions of love and forever. Urgent kisses. Bodies pressed together.

I lead him to the bedroom to assure him, once and for all...

Our love isn't a shackle, it's my foundation.

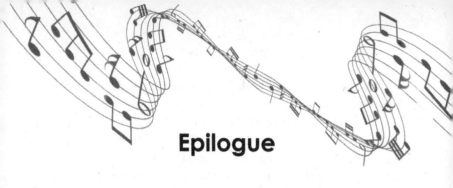

Epilogue

<u>ALEK</u>

Two Months Later

Times sure have changed.

Nowadays, I confidently walk into The Mission every Thursday as a VIP, surrounded by my friends.

It's Hope's night. Her standing gig has become the highlight of my—and many of her fans who missed her—week. She's transitioned from the whimsical, unpredictable life of busking to a more established presence here.

Her journey hasn't been all hearts and flowers. Beyond her music career taking a significant turn for the better, she's navigating all aspects of her recovery with grace and resilience. Her physical symptoms have all but resolved. She's added therapy sessions to her routine. A necessary step for her to heal from the assault's lingering shadows.

It's a testament to her strength, watching her tackle these challenges head-on. Hope's unwavering determination to move forward is an inspiration.

Before she steps onstage, I make my way to her dressing room, eager to steal a kiss before her set. Knocking softly, I enter and find her in a state of focused preparation. She strums her battered guitar, playing a melody I haven't heard before. "Hi, my love."

Flipping her dark hair over her shoulder, Hope smiles at me and puts down the instrument. "Hey, baby."

"Feel ready?" I sit beside her and tug her close.

She blinks up at me. "Yeah, I was feeling inspired. I'm writing a song about fate."

"Oh yeah?" I kiss her temple. "Tell me."

Hope nestles into my side. Strokes my bicep. "Therapy's been tough, but it's making a difference. Do you know, I wouldn't change anything that's happened. Meeting you feels predestined. As weird as it sounds, especially given how hard my recovery has been, I really believe we were in the right place at the right time."

"Well, I'd take the part of you getting hurt away any day." I squeeze her to me. "I'd have figured out a way to talk to you eventually."

She laughs. "Oh, you'd probably still be watching me from behind the flower vendors. Tell the truth."

"Probably." I chuckle.

"And now you've received a promotion, and I'm working at Gus and playing here. After tonight, the real work begins—auditioning my band..." She strokes my cheek. "If the creating music for the games thing works out, it'll be a whole new world."

Her resilience in the face of adversity and drive to reclaim her narrative—it's nothing short of remarkable. "All of it is cool and all, but you're the only thing that matters."

"Same." She smiles. "*Same.*"

A knock on the door signals it's time for her to perform. I offer a supportive smile. "I love you. You're going to be phenomenal. I'll be in the front row with the guys, cheering you every step of the way."

"I love you, too. So much," she whispers, and we share a sweet kiss before she steps into the spotlight.

As she heads to the stage, her silhouette is framed by the backstage lights. I can't help but feel a surge of pride. She's right. Our journey, marked by its trials and triumphs, has led us here.

She strums the first chord, and her music fills the room. "I'm Hope Kristiensen, and this song is dedicated to Alek."

"Dude!" Jamie nudges me, and I can't help but beam.

"It's brand new." She gazes out into the audience, looking like an angel on earth. My angel. "It's called *'Chords of Destiny.'*"

SING
FOR
ME

CHELLE BLISS

About the Author

Chelle Bliss has dedicated her life to education before unleashing her creativity on the romance book world. While teaching did give her a creative outlet, she yearned for something more. Writing has given her that, no longer about just creativity, it became a journey beyond her wildest dreams.

She's a *USA Today* and *Wall Street Journal* bestselling author of spicy romantic suspense focused on family sagas. Chelle's an avid reader, consuming contemporary romance, dark reads, young adult, and fantasy reads.

www.chellebliss.com

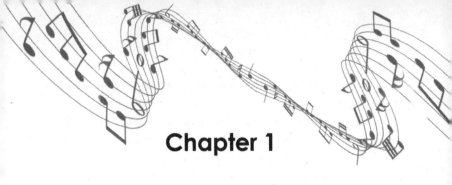

Chapter 1

LUCCA

I stare at my phone, reading the text from my brother repeatedly in disbelief.

Rocco: We're pregnant…again.

I'm overjoyed for him and Callie after years of battling cancer and complications from the treatment. They are the best parents, but I remember not so long ago, they said they were done having kids.

I feel behind the ball. They are on kid number three, while I haven't even found someone who can stomach me and my creative mood swings for longer than a few months.

Not that my brother is easy. There is no person more intense than he can be, especially when he feels there is danger nearby. And his life is riddled with bad guys and life-threatening situations. I don't know how my sister-in-law deals with the knowledge that he may not come home from work someday.

Everything about us is different—always has been, and I assume it always will be. I'm creative where he's calculating. I was always carefree and silly where he was always plotting and planning. But even with our differences, we always got along and loved each other. That had more to do with our parents and the importance of family than the two of us having much of anything in common.

"Need anything else?" Caleb asks as he wipes down the bar to my side. "It's last call."

"Nah, man. I'm good," I tell him, ticking my head toward the glass of whiskey I've been nursing for over an hour.

I grab my phone, sending a quick text to my brother because I have had no greater joy in my life than being an uncle to his children.

> **Me: Congrats, brother. I hope it's twins.**

He's quick to reply, no doubt glaring at the phone, wishing he could crawl through the screen and choke me for even whispering those words.

> **Rocco: I don't care if they're triplets as long as they're healthy.**

His words cause me to jerk my head back and blink a few times in disbelief. "Wow," I whisper to myself in shock.

I shouldn't be surprised. I'm not sure I've ever seen a more loving father than him. He dotes on his children as much as he does on Callie. My brother loves deep and hard, leaving no doubt about how he feels for those closest to him.

There is a sudden movement at my side as a leather bag is thrust on top of the bar. "Hit me with a double, Caleb. I've had a long night, and I have a feeling it's about to get even longer."

My heart picks up its pace at the sound of her voice. Madeline Hart. She could make the strongest man weak in the knees.

Madeline is well-known in the New York City bar scene as one of the premiere local singers who performs original compositions instead of covering other musicians' songs. She not only has a killer voice, she is also stunning, with big green eyes, wavy red hair with hints of brown sprinkled throughout, long legs, the perfect lips, and just as beautiful as any popular musician out there today.

. She has everything and yet...she hasn't hit it big. I've asked her a few times if I could share her music with the industry people I know, but she's always turned me down. She wants whatever happens to happen organically and not because she knows someone who knows someone.

But the thing she doesn't seem to understand is almost everyone knows someone who knows someone. I wouldn't have gotten my start if it weren't for my brother. He made a few calls, cashed in a few favors, and things have never been the same for me.

I'm now one of the most sought-after songwriters in the pop music industry today, with a specialty in lyrics that could shred even the most black-hearted.

Madeline tosses her long red hair over her shoulder before she turns toward me. "Hey, Lucca." Her gaze dips to the notepad in front of me. "Writing your next smash hit?"

I give her a wry smile. "Something like that," I mutter.

She taps her fingernails against the polished wood as she raises her other hand to her cheek, resting her face in her palm and her elbow on the bar. "Must be nice. I don't know where you get your inspiration from, but I wish you'd send a little my way."

She doesn't know it, but she is my inspiration.

Her beauty.

Her voice.

Her smile.

The way the energy changes when she walks into a room.

"It doesn't always come easy," I lie, hoping to make her feel better.

Madeline's lips flatten. "You're a bad liar, Lucca."

I give her a smile, knowing I've been caught.

"How do you do it?" she asks, reaching for her drink that Caleb set in front of her a few seconds ago.

"I honestly don't know. Sometimes the melody isn't as easy,

but the words just come to me."

Madeline lets out a loud sigh as her shoulders sag forward. "I'm jealous, Lucca, and that's not an easy thing for me to admit. I've been struggling with the same song for a month now, and I'm about to give up."

I stare at her profile, wishing I could console her in some way. For over a year, we've danced around each other, talking whenever we're together at this bar, but she's never thrown so many hints that she'd like my help. If I waste this opportunity now, I'll be kicking myself forever.

"I can help," I tell her, knowing this is my shot and I may not get many more before someone else snaps up the red-haired beauty.

She turns her head, her eyebrows high and green eyes wide. "You'd do that?"

I want to tell her that I'd do anything for her, but I keep that to myself. "Of course."

She's quick to her feet, and before I know it, her arms are wrapped around my shoulders and her cheek is against my face. "You're a lifesaver, Lucca Bruno. I could almost kiss you."

She could almost kiss me.

Sigh.

I take a moment to enjoy the feel of her warmth against my skin and the way her hair smells like the sweetest vanilla I've ever inhaled.

She pulls her face away but stays tethered to me by her arms. "Are you sure? I can pay you, but I know you make more money on one song than I make in a decade."

"Friends help friends."

She stares at me, blinking rapidly in disbelief at my words as she finally separates her body from mine. "I'm your friend?"

I've always thought of her as one. For a year, we've been together a few nights a week, chatting at the bar, and sharing our war stories from the music industry.

"Well, yeah."

"I always knew you were a good egg, Lucca, but this favor is so huge, it leaves no more doubt."

"And if I can't help you?" I ask, reaching for my drink because having Madeline so close has left me feeling out of sorts.

She playfully swipes at my shoulder. "You're a musical genius. If you can't help me, nobody can."

That's a tall order to live up to, even for me. While I've been successful and do know I have talent, I can't always retool someone else's work with the same clarity I can work on my own.

"Your songs are beautiful, Madeline."

"Not good enough to hit it big, though," she says, but not in a sour voice. "At least not yet."

Caleb slides the key to the building across the bar. "Once the last guy is out, so am I. You two know what to do."

Six months ago, Caleb offered us the place after hours to practice without the interruption of others. Here, we don't have to worry about waking anyone up in the late hours of the night with our songs. Although this is New York, neighbors only have so much patience, especially in buildings with thin walls.

"I'll make sure things are buttoned up tight," I promise him.

Caleb gives me a nod before he smiles at Madeline and makes himself busy again, trying not to hover over the last customer who's been nursing a beer for longer than anyone would think is humanly possible.

Madeline slides her stool over until I can almost feel her body heat against my arm. "Do you have a specific process?" She peers down at my notepad, but all it holds is a bunch of illegible scribbles. "I don't think I've ever asked you."

I push the notebook toward her. "Not really. I start a new page when the vibe of the lyrics shifts."

She turns one page, her eyes scanning the lines. "You must go through a lot of notebooks."

I have more stacks of them than I care to admit. They are everywhere in my loft, and eventually, they became more of a part of the décor than they should. "I can't seem to go digital. I've tried, but it kills my creativity. There's something about paper and pen that I can't shake."

"Writing words by hand gives your mind time to process and move forward. Typing is too fast."

"You haven't seen me type." I laugh, almost embarrassed at how slow and awful I am at it. "I peck at the keys at an excruciatingly slow pace."

"I amend my statement, then... You're too busy trying to find the next letter instead of thinking about the next word."

"Something like that," I tell her before taking another sip of my drink.

She reaches into her purse and pulls out a well-worn piece of paper. "Do you want to see what I have?"

I take the paper from her hand and gently unfold it because it looks like it'll disintegrate in my hands if I'm too rough. I scan the page, reading over the words that are beautiful but slightly disjointed. "What's the melody?"

"Do you want me to sing it for you?"

I'm envious of her ability to stand up in front of a crowded room and belt out a song. I've never been able to. It's the one thing that's kept me a songwriter instead of a performer. I'm a behind-the-scenes guy with my name as the writer of more than one hundred hit songs over the last decade.

"If it's not too much trouble."

She touches my bare arm with her soft, warm fingertips. "It's no trouble. You're the one helping me. I'd stand on my head if you thought it would help."

"While the idea is entertaining, it wouldn't help at all, which is a shame."

She laughs, and the sound is more beautiful than any ballad I've ever heard. "You're ridiculous sometimes, but it's part of your charm."

Is Madeline flirting with me? I want to believe she is, but I've never been the smartest person when it comes to romance.

I turn around on my stool as she heads toward the stage with her lyrics still in my hand.

I watch her intently as she adjusts the microphone, raising the stand higher to be closer to her lips.

She clears her throat, the sound echoing in the mostly empty bar. "Don't judge me too harshly," she says, her eyes pinned on me.

"Never," I promise her.

A beat-up guitar is near the left side of the stage, and she grabs it, lifting the strap over her shoulder. Her fingers move over the strings, and when she's satisfied with the tuning, she steps up to the microphone again.

I can't take my eyes off her as she begins to sing. The sound coming out of her lips sends goose bumps scattering across my skin, and the hairs on the back of my neck to stand on end. There's no one else in the music industry with a voice like hers.

I close my eyes, trying to concentrate on the words instead of her pretty face. The lyrics and melody flow beautifully throughout the first verse and chorus, but I can tell she falters with the second verse because her voice becomes quieter and less sure.

The song is slow and emotional, bringing the listener along on the journey of heartbreak after a long and deep love.

The words tug on my heartstrings, something that doesn't happen easily because I've been told I'm not good at explaining and exploring my feelings, even though most of my songs are about love and heartbreak.

I open my eyes when the stool down the way slides against the tile floor. The man stumbles in my direction and pauses right in front of me. "Don't be an idiot. That girl likes you," he mumbles before he shuffles toward the door.

I turn my gaze back toward Madeline as she sets the guitar back down on the stand. "Well," she says while she walks down the few steps from the old stage. "See what I mean? Got any ideas?"

Thanks to the guy, I have more ideas than I ever thought possible.

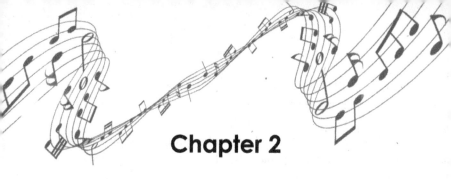

Chapter 2

LUCCA

Madeline plops down next to me and takes the lyrics from my hands. "I can't seem to get that second verse right. I've tried a million things, and nothing makes it better. What did you hear?"

We turn around to face the bar, and I grab my pen, ready to jot down a few ideas. "The song is amazing. I felt every bit of the emotion in your voice. There are two things we can do."

"We," she whispers, giving me a smile when I peer up at her.

"I'm in this with you. There's no turning back now," I tell her before I return my attention to the paper instead of allowing myself to get sidetracked by her pretty face and plump, pouty lips.

"What makes you tick?"

I peer up at her again. "What makes me tick?"

She nods. "We've talked on and off for over a year, and I don't know much about you except you're successful and write some of my favorite songs. I want to know who Lucca Bruno is—the man, not the songwriter."

I set down my pen and turn toward her on the stool. "I'm a pretty boring guy, Madeline."

"Maddy," she corrects me and touches my arm, sending shocks throughout my system. "I think we've known each other long enough to get rid of the formalities."

"What do you want to know?"

"Where are you from?"

"I was born and bred here. You?"

"Same," she says.

"My parents are up in Watkins Glen now, but they used to live here when we were younger," I reply.

"We?" She raises her eyebrows in surprise. "Who's we?"

"I have a brother and two sisters."

"Nearby?"

I nod. "My brother and sister-in-law live here in the city along with their kids."

"You're an uncle?"

I can't stop myself from smiling. "I'm the best uncle ever, or, at least, I try to be."

"I bet you are. I'm an aunt, and it's the best thing in the world. I get to play with the kids, give them lots of hugs and kisses, and then send them on their way back to my sister. I get to avoid all the hard stuff."

"Do you want kids of your own?" Even I am taken aback by my question. Maybe it was too forward and sounded like I was fishing, and maybe somewhere in the back of my mind, I know I am.

"I do someday. I'll have to give up my career, though, which is hard for me to imagine."

"Not necessarily," I tell her, knowing plenty of successful musicians with children.

"It's hard to play the bar scene at night with little ones at home." She shrugs. "But that'll require me to find a man first, and that hasn't happened either." She snorts. "A struggling musician doesn't seem to be a sought-after partner for many. You know my schedule. It's not conducive to dating."

"If someone likes you, they'll find a way to make it work, Maddy."

"Maybe," she says, not sounding convinced.

"Don't settle for someone who wants to change the things you love doing the most. Music isn't like anything else. It's rooted deep in your soul. It's part of you and not a simple hobby that someone can easily give up. The only person who would be happy about that would be your partner, not you. You'd be miserable."

"Sounds like you know from experience."

"Someone wanted me to give up music a long time ago, and I decided to end the relationship instead. She said I'd regret that decision, and not a day goes by that I don't think about how ridiculous her statement was, especially with all the success I've had. I can't imagine what I'd be doing if I had stayed with her. I know I'd be unhappy and probably working a desk job somewhere."

"That sounds awful."

"Right?" I shake my head. "I love the freedom this work allows me. Heck, I wouldn't even call this work. When you get to do something you love, there's no work involved."

"Well, I love music, but it's still work for me. I think success and money allow you to feel more like it's a hobby in a way. I still grind every single day to try to pay the bills."

The thought of her struggling makes my heart hurt. I have more money than I know what to do with anymore. I never thought I'd be this lucky, but people throw money at me to try to get their song written sooner than others.

"Things will change for you soon."

She pats my arm softly. "That's sweet of you to say, but we both know that isn't true."

"I meant what I said before..."

"No," she interrupts me. "I want to do this myself. It's how I'm built, Lucca. If I'm not good enough to make it big on my own, I don't want it to happen."

"I didn't get where I am by myself, Maddy. It's rare and doesn't mean anything if someone makes a few calls to their friends. We all need help sometimes."

"I don't know... For now, I need to do it this way."

"Okay."

"I didn't mean anything negative. No matter how you got your big break, you're successful."

"I know."

"Can I ask you something?" she says, her hand not moving from my arm.

"Anything."

"Why don't you sing your songs yourself?"

I stare at her green eyes, hating that I must tell her what a scaredy-cat I am. "I get stage fright."

Her mouth drops open. "Really?"

I nod again. "I tried everything, but I couldn't get over it. It's why I focused on songwriting. I love music and creating lyrics, but I've never been able to make it all the way through a song onstage in front of even a single person."

"Wow. I wouldn't have guessed that. It's such a rush, though. There's nothing like singing in front of a crowd that's swaying to your music, and when they cheer and clap at the end...it's so exhilarating."

"I feel that way when I hear one of my songs recorded. When someone brings it to life in the perfect way, exactly how I heard it in my head... It's the greatest."

"Do you sing when you're alone?"

"Sometimes," I admit, never having told anyone that. But then again, no one's ever asked me that question before.

"Interesting..."

"Why is it interesting?"

She shrugs. "I don't know. It just is."

"My voice is similar to fingernails on a chalkboard."

She stares at me without saying anything for a solid minute. "If you help me with my lyrics, I'll teach you how to sing. Everyone has a beautiful voice buried deep inside themselves. It just takes more to dig it out of some people than others."

"I'm fine with mine buried down deep, Maddy. It's where it should stay, too."

She gives my forearm a squeeze before she pulls her hand back to grab her drink. "The offer is always there, Lucca."

Am I an idiot? She's offering to teach me something that most likely will take a lot of time, which would give me an in with her. It'll at least give me the ability to spend more time with Maddy, and there's nothing I want more right now than that.

"Let's tackle your lyrics, and we can talk about my voice another time."

"Your speaking voice is dreamy. I can imagine your singing voice as something deep and soulful."

"If deep and soulful sounds like a dying animal, then yes, that's exactly how I sound."

Maddy tips her head back and laughs. "Stop it," she says through her laughter as she waves her hand between us. "It can't be that bad."

"Not even my mother likes my voice, and she loves everything about me. She doesn't have a mean bone in her body, but I'm forbidden from even singing 'Happy Birthday'."

Maddy gasps. "You're lying."

I chuckle. "My mother is the only person in the world who says I have a nice singing voice. She's lying, of course, but she was never able to say anything negative to her children."

"She sounds lovely," Maddy breathes.

"What about your parents?"

"They don't talk to me anymore. When I dropped out of college to follow my dream of becoming a musician, they said they washed their hands of me, and I haven't heard from them since."

I wonder if that's where the heartbreak in most of her songs comes from. I can't imagine my parents disowning me and never speaking to them again. They're an important part of my life and have supported every stupid idea and decision I've ever made.

"I'm sorry."

She waves me off. "I've come to terms with it. It's fine." She has a sadness on her face when she speaks.

But I don't believe the words she's saying. There's no way a person can be okay with their parents forgetting they exist.

"What do you do at the holidays?" I ask her, genuinely interested.

"I usually work. All the bars are open, and since I don't have a family, my availability is wide open, which makes most bar owners very happy."

"You shouldn't work on a holiday, especially Christmas."

"It beats sitting at home alone, watching old Christmas movies about happy families."

"That's it. This Christmas, you're going to come with me to my parents. I refuse to let you be alone, Maddy."

"You don't need to do that."

"I thought we were friends, and as soon as I tell my mother, she'll insist."

"I'm sure the last thing she wants is one more mouth to feed."

"You don't know my mother."

Maddy stares at me, a soft smile on her face. "Is your family as nice as you?"

"For the most part."

"Who isn't?"

"My brother can be intimidating."

"I think I know who he is. I've seen you in here with him a few times. He is intimidating."

"He's a big teddy bear, though. He looks tough on the exterior, but he's a cinnamon roll on the inside."

"To everyone?" she asks.

"To those he loves."

"And to the others?"

"Depends on who they are and how they treat him." And then I remember she has a sister. "Why don't you go to your sister's house on the holidays?"

She shrugs, dragging her drink closer to herself across the bar. "She typically goes to her in-laws' house and sometimes to my parents. I'm fine with it."

"Not the next holiday. Christmas is with the Brunos."

"We'll see. I don't want to impose."

I pull my phone between us and tap the screen, dialing my mother's cell. She's a night owl, and I know she's up doing whatever she does in the late hours of the night.

"What are you doing? It's late. Don't bother your mother," Maddy says, her voice laced with panic.

"She's up."

"Lucca, are you okay?" my mother asks as Maddy drops her head onto her arm, practically throwing her upper body onto the bar.

"I'm fine, Ma. I had a question."

"Shoot, honey, you about gave me a heart attack. What's up?"

"Kill me now," Maddy whispers into the polished wood.

"I have a friend who doesn't have any family in town. I was wondering if they could come home with me for Christmas and spend some time with us."

Ma gasps before letting out a little squeal. "You're so sweet, Lucca. Of course. The more, the merrier. Does this friend happen to have boobs?"

"Jesus, Ma," I mutter.

"Oh my goodness. You're bringing a girl home for Christmas, aren't you?"

"This is so embarrassing," Maddy mumbles as she raises her head to glare at me.

I give her a wink, ignoring the look of death on her face. "A woman, Ma, and yes. She's my friend, and I don't want her to be alone, eating takeout."

"No. No. No one should be alone at Christmas."

"That's all, Ma. Go back to whatever you were doing. I was just sitting here with her working on a song, and I wanted to make sure it was okay with you before I invited her."

"I was just working on a Christmas present. I've become very crafty lately."

"Just don't chop off a finger or anything else."

"No promises, baby," she says with a light chuckle. "Night."

"Night, Ma. I love you."

"Love you too," she says before she disconnects the call.

"Man, you hit the jackpot in all aspects of life, didn't you?" Maddy shakes her head. "Great job, even better family. I'm way beyond jealous at this point."

"Don't be jealous until you meet them. They may be a little much at times."

"A little much is better than nothing at all," she says softly.

It's my turn to reach out and place my hand on her arm. "I'm sorry, Maddy. That was insensitive of me to say."

"Lucca, if there's one thing I know about you, it's that you have a tender heart."

"There're plenty of people in my past who would say otherwise."

"They're idiots."

"Anyway, I have a few ideas for the song."

She straightens her back and leans in my direction. "Whatcha got?" she says, the sorrow of our earlier conversation vanishing in an instant.

I jot down a few lines and add a few that she had in her previous verse. "I think if you do something like this, it'll flow better."

She starts to sing the song softly, starting at the chorus and heads into the verse as I wrote it. It sounds good. Not perfect, but better than it was before.

"What if we..." She takes my pen and crosses out two words, replacing them with something softer. "What do you think of this?"

I read over it, singing it in my head, where I can carry a tune. "I think it's great."

Maddy hops off her stool and snatches the paper from in front of me. "I need to do the entire song to make sure it's right."

I turn around, watching her as she walks up on the stage, grabs the guitar, and starts to sing. I'm envious of how easy it is for her to do it, too. She doesn't have a moment of hesitation about singing in front of me. The very thought of me doing the same sends a cold shiver across my skin.

But when she hits the second verse, it's better than the first time, but it's still not the best it can be.

She stops playing the guitar, and her gaze meets mine. "Is it me, or is something still off?"

"You're right."

"Do you think it's the words or the melody?"

I stand up, needing to stretch my legs. "Sing it one more time," I request, knowing we're so close to getting it right.

She starts over again, putting her heart and soul into every word and note that she belts out, with only me as her audience. She doesn't hold back as she sings, and I could watch her every day of my life and never get bored.

This time, she sings through the second verse and heads into the chorus, giving me a longer chunk of the song to make a decision. When she stops, the silence in the bar is deafening.

"Well..."

"What if you changed the note of the last word in the second verse."

"To what?"

I explain the change, but she just stares at me, blinking like I've said the wackiest thing in the world.

"How would that work?"

"Trust me."

"Come up here," she says, dipping her chin to the stool at her side. "It's weird singing to you out there."

If it were anyone else, I'd say no. But this is Maddy. A woman I've had a secret crush on for months but didn't think she felt the same. The way she's been with me tonight, with the small touches and sitting close to me, I think I've missed earlier clues and she is now doing her best to make her feelings clear. Even the drunk guy at the bar could see what was between us, despite the fact that I was too dense to do the same.

My shoes feel like they're filled with cement as I walk toward the stage. "Only for you," I say as I climb the stairs, and my stomach begins to flutter.

"Man, your fear is strong. You look like you're about to pass out, and it's only the two of us."

"I haven't been on a stage in years." I swallow down the overwhelming desire to run off the stage, back to the safety of my stool.

I can do this. I can do this for Maddy.

"I promise I won't bite." She smiles at me with a wicked gleam in her eyes. "Unless you want me to."

Somehow, I chuckle, fighting the fear that's clawing at my insides.

Maddy holds out her hand, and I take it, needing the extra encouragement to keep myself moving forward. I slide my palm into her hand and am shocked by the electricity again.

"I'm proud of you," she says, giving my hand a light squeeze. "Sit there." She ticks her head toward the stool, and without a second thought, I plop down before my knees have a chance to give out on me. "Now, how do you want me to change the song?"

I hum the few lines, the closest to singing I can do without sounding like I'm killing an animal.

"I can tell by your hum that there's a beautiful voice inside you like I thought."

"Maybe your ears aren't as good as you think," I tell her, adjusting myself on the stool because my ability to sit still is nonexistent.

Maddy takes a step forward and places the guitar on the stand next to me. "Sing the chorus," she asks, moving between my legs.

I crane my neck back, staring up at her. "What?" I swallow hard, the fear and excitement of this moment mingling.

"Sing for me, Lucca," she begs as she places her hands on my legs, sending a wave of excitement and hope through my body.

"I really want you right now, Maddy, and I know my voice will kill the moment," I croak out, barely able to catch my breath as I speak.

"Your trust will mean more to me than the sound of your voice. Sing, baby," she whispers.

I stare into her deep green eyes, and for the first time in my life, I'm unable to say no. I start softly to dull the off-key sound of my voice.

Maddy smiles down at me as I sing, looking happy with the sound of my voice instead of horrified. Maybe I misjudged myself or, as I've aged, my tone has changed.

When I finish, she moves her hands from my thighs to palm my cheeks. "That was beautiful."

I lift my arms, placing my hands on her hips, drawing her toward me. "No, it wasn't," I whisper, wanting her now more than ever.

She leans into me, pressing her body against mine. I dig my fingers into the material of her jeans that sit snugly against her luscious hips.

I raise a hand, sliding my fingers around the side of her neck, and pull her face down to me. "Is this okay?" I ask, always wanting to check before I act.

"Yes," she whispers, her eyes soft and lazy.

My heart beats faster as the anticipation of kissing her gets more intense. I lift my face, staring into her green eyes before I close my eyes and press my lips to hers.

Fireworks explode, sending tiny shocks across my skin and throughout my entire body. Never have I felt this when kissing anyone else.

Her lips are soft and warm as I kiss her gently at first, testing the waters. She pulls back, staring down at me with even softer eyes.

"What was that?" she asks, sending a moment of panic through me.

"I'm being gentle."

"Don't," she says firmly before she leans in, taking my lips in a hard and demanding way.

That's all it takes to make my gentle side fade away. The kiss is long and deep, filled with all the hope and longing I've felt for her for months.

I could get lost in her. Get lost in this moment. Months of wanting her have led to this very spot, with her in my grip and lips pressed against mine.

I'd sing in front of a sold-out stadium if it meant I could kiss her again and hold her in my arms.

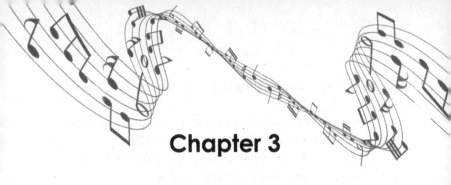

Chapter 3

L U C C A

"Maddy," my mother says, opening her arms before we're fully in the house. "It's so good to finally meet you."

Maddy's eyes are as big as saucers as my mother wraps her arms around her, giving her a long hug. "It's nice to meet you too."

My mother pulls back, keeping her hands on Maddy's shoulders. "You're stunning."

Maddy's cheeks turn a bright shade of pink. "Thank you," she says, sounding uncomfortable.

"Ma, go light," I say, reminding my mom that she can be a bit much for strangers, especially those who aren't used to a hands-on mother.

Ma turns her gaze toward me with her smile still firmly planted. "I am being light."

Maddy laughs. "It's okay, Lucca. It's nice."

I smile at the easiness of Maddy with my mom. She doesn't seem overwhelmed in the slightest.

"Are you hungry, doll? I made some food, and I'm sure you could use some after that long road trip."

"Ma, it wasn't even five hours."

"Anything over an hour is a haul and requires a meal," Ma says, making me sound like I'm ridiculous.

"I could eat," Maddy tells her, making my mother happier than I've seen her in a very long time.

A moment later, the door opens, and Callie walks in, looking more than a little pregnant. "Oh my goodness," Ma says, rushing away from Maddy and heading right toward Callie. "Look at you and my new grandbabies."

"Twins," Callie mutters to us over my mother's shoulder as Ma hugs her harder and longer than she did Maddy.

"You're right in time, baby. We're just about to eat, and we must feed those babies and keep them healthy."

Maddy comes to my side, sliding her arm into the crook of mine. "I can't even imagine having twins."

"Right?" I breathe, horrified at the thought of all the sleepless nights and constant feedings.

"Baby brother," Rocco says as he walks in behind Callie, carrying two other children in his arms like they're light bags of groceries.

"Whoa," Maddy whispers as she tips her head back, taking in the enormity of my brother. "Why does he look so big here?"

"It's the lower ceilings." I assure her that he hasn't grown larger since the last time she laid eyes on him.

"And with the kids," she says in disbelief.

"He's a sucker for his littles," I tell her before turning my attention to him. "Congrats on the twins."

He lets out a long exhale.

Callie smacks his chest with the back of her hand. "Don't let him fool you. The man is over the moon about two more kids."

"I'd have ten kids with you if you'd let me, baby," he says to Callie.

Maddy slides her hand into mine, intertwining our fingers.

"This is going to be the best Christmas ever," Ma says, clapping her hands together softly.

"The best ever," Maddy repeats with a squeeze of my hand.

I lean over, kissing her temple and knowing there's nowhere I'd rather be than right here with my girl and my family.

SONG
IN
SILENCE

STACEY MARIE BROWN

About the Author

USA TODAY Bestselling author Stacey Marie Brown is both a PNR and Contemporary Romance writer of hot cocky bad boys and sarcastic heroines who kick ass. Sexy, cheeky, and always up to no good. She also enjoys reading, exploring, binging TV shows, tacos, hiking, writing, design, and her fur baby Cooper. Loves to travel and she's been lucky enough to live and travel all over the world.

www.staceymariebrown.com

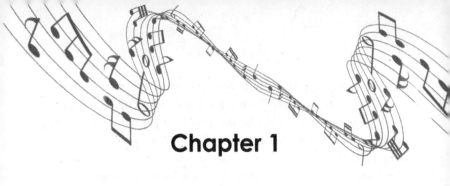

Chapter 1

Vibrations thrummed through my bare feet, traveling up into my bones. Every note, every pulsation sang in my body, written out in my head. The beat of the drums crashed and resonated in my chest, my arms whirling two hickory drumsticks. Music wasn't just a love of mine; it was my blood, my air, my connection to this world.

My eyes closed, strands of my long purple and black hair falling onto my face as I pounded out my last solo, the song coming to a crescendo. Perspiration dampened my pierced brow, my frame swaying, feeling with my entire body.

The final beat pulsated up my arm, and I sucked in a gulp of air. Twirling the drumsticks, my breath heavy, I pried my eyes open, a smile of pure joy tugging at my lips. This was the only place I felt part of the world, not having to fight for everything. This was where I was supposed to be: my happy bubble.

Then the bubble popped.

Four heads were turned at me; it was obvious they had cut out earlier in the song. The lead singer, Ames Isley, had his normal frown of impatience on his face, while the lead guitarist, Tobias, the keyboarder, Geo, and our manager, Emmit, all stared, waiting for me to realize no one was playing anymore.

Chagrin bloomed in my cheeks at their gazes, my eyes automatically peering at the spot where our bass guitarist, Ziggy, always stood. The position to my right was now empty, reminding me he was gone and filling me with grief. My link to my cues, the one who kept me in the loop of changes, was no longer here.

"Sorry," I muttered, but I wasn't sure if anyone heard me, their attention already snapping back to Emmit. Ames's head wagged, his arms flying dramatically, twisting the nerves in my stomach.

"Now, hear me out." Emmit's hands went up, his mouth moving quickly, telling me he was trying to get out whatever he needed to say before Ames stomped out. Whoever said women were the emotional, dramatic ones had never met Ames. He owned the cliché of temperamental rocker as a badge of honor. While moody, sensitive, and ego-driven, he was incredibly talented and hardworking. I had known Ames since my late teens, and he had always been this way, though the more our star rose, the more those diva qualities came out in him.

Ziggy had been the only sane one. The one who kept us grounded, especially Ames. In his absence, we were off-kilter and not clicking as well. His death was an abyss in our group. One we couldn't seem to fill.

Ames's back was to me, his head shaking. I could feel his agitation growing and sense it in the body language of the others. I glanced over at Tobias and Geo, trying to see what I missed, feeling even more isolated without Ziggy next to me. Over time, he and I had developed a great connection. He was a true legend and my touchstone in every way.

So many in this business were incredibly talented and loved music, but if you didn't have it in your bones, written into your DNA, this lifestyle could break you. It could destroy those who breathed music even more. Too many legends were dead because the music industry was a demon who consumed you, and if you didn't find a way to survive the drugs, alcohol, imposter syndrome, and burnout would swallow you whole.

Ziggy was swallowed whole.

"No! Absolutely not!" Ames turned my way, about a beat away from throwing down his microphone stand and striding off stage. He paced on the stage, running his hands through his long blonde hair, loosening the braid he had down the middle like a mohawk. Ames could be cast in the next Viking show, though he was too lean for war.

"What choice do you have?" Emmit replied, a twitch in his

cheek, which I knew was a sign he was frustrated with Ames. "Ziggy is gone; he has been for six months! You need the spot filled now, and you know it!" Emmit motioned to where Ziggy usually was, but his eyes drifted to me before jumping back to Ames.

I felt the underlying accusation. They felt the need to fill it faster because of me. Being the only woman in a rock band already came with a lot of pressure, but I felt it even more because of who I was.

"We'll open it to auditions," Ames retaliated.

"You already did, and you rejected them all!" Emmit's arms went up.

"They all sucked."

"No one is going to be Ziggy." Emmit took a deep calming breath, which he did a lot around Ames. "You guys have been together for a long time. I get it's hard to imagine anyone else in his place." He motioned to the blank space, wrenching my heart. My lids filled up with tears and I quickly blinked them away. It never got easier. "But you are no longer those kids practicing in a burnt-down warehouse. You were nominated for Best New Artist and Best Song of the Year last year."

"Which we lost to *them*!"

Them, meaning our nemesis, The Velvet Kings. A band the industry had pitted against us since the beginning. People said our sounds were similar, which only pissed us off more.

The Velvet Kings were hacks. A bunch of pretty boys who had no heart or soul in their music. Fans didn't seem to care. At one time, they might have been more original, but now they were produced and formulated to be a hit. They caved to the music industry and whored out for money.

They were a bunch of assholes, who I heard barely tolerated each other either, which didn't surprise me. A long time ago, when we were all starting out, I had auditioned to be their drummer. Let's say it didn't go well, though I was glad now it hadn't worked out.

We crossed paths at events and award shows, but I stayed as

far as I could from them.

Mental Breakdown was my home, my family, my brothers. Even if they weren't in blood, they were in every other way. It was not as if I knew who my blood family was anyway. Ziggy and I had been in the foster system together. Music was our way to stay out of trouble and have a reason to keep going when things got dark.

"No fucking way that asshole will take his place!" Ames swung back for Emmit, putting his back to me again, his frame dramatically flailing about.

What? Who was he talking about? Someone was taking Ziggy's spot? I hated not knowing what was going on. I hit my stick on the ride cymbal with irritation.

With a heavy sigh, Ames curved his body to face us all. "We all agree, right?" He motioned to the rest of us, Geo and Tobias nodding in agreement. I seemed to be the only one who was clueless.

"What is going on?" I set down my sticks, conveying my frustration.

"You don't have a choice," Emmitt continued on, not noticing me. "You guys are a mess. Missing cues..." Emmit peered at all of us, though once again I felt this was about me. "You've been off without him, and I get it. His loss was a shock. But you are at the cusp of being the next big thing, and I won't let you throw it away! I understand it must be difficult to go on without him. But you didn't work this hard, *he* didn't work this hard, for you to throw it all away. And don't tell me Ziggy wouldn't want this for all of you. You know he'd be screaming at you guys right now," Emmit challenged us. He was right; Ziggy, of all people, would be telling us to get our shit together. He was our rock, while we didn't notice he was losing his way in drugs. "As your manager, unless you want to fire me, I'll make this decision. I'll be the bad person and fill Ziggy's spot. "

Ames snapped to him as though he was about to speak, but Emmit held up his hand.

"At least give him a chance. Okay? You can at least do that

since he came all the way here."

"What?!" Ames sputtered, making it hard for me to understand. "He's here? Now?"

"Yes."

"Are you serious?" Geo's pierced mouth hung open, his shaggy reddish-brown hair falling over his forehead.

"Fuck this!" Tobias ripped the guitar strap over his head, his movements irritated, his curly black hair tangling in the fabric.

"What is going on?" I asked, frustrated, as no one seemed to be paying me much attention, too caught up in their own anger. "Who's here?"

"Stop being babies!" Emmit's chest lifted, his tone humming through the floor. "You're about to have everything you've wanted if you just put your egos away!"

"Mental Breakdown are not sellouts!" Ames scrubbed his hands through his scruff as his long, lean, fit body, covered in tattoos and piercings, paced in a circle.

"Mental Breakdown will not be selling anything if you don't get out of your own way!" Emmit's button-down shirt stretched across his chest, his arms swinging. His brown hair was styled and had a hint of salt and pepper, which he blamed on us. "'Scotch Tape Hole' is starting to fall in the charts, and this business is fleeting. One minute, you're the hot thing; the next, you're not. We have to strike while the iron is hot. And he is the best thing to happen to you right now." Emmit struggled to stay facing me. "Think about it. One of the best bass guitarists from the top group in the world right now joins Mental Breakdown? The fans will go apeshit, and the press alone will be insane!"

Dread tricked down my throat into my stomach, sensing the world about to collapse. Intuition told me what was coming, yet my head shook in denial.

No. No way. Emmit would never do this to us. Plus, there was no way he would come here. Join our band. It had to be someone else.

He was the best guitarist. Even if the group were sellouts, you couldn't deny his talent. He carried the band and had ten times more charisma than the lead singer or anyone in his band. He always did.

Emmit swung away from us, his arm motioning for someone to come in.

My gaze darted to Geo and Tobias, hoping to see something in their expressions that told me I was wrong, that who I thought was about to walk in wasn't going to.

Their eyes met mine with the same dismay.

Heavy black boots shuddered across the wood stage, all our heads darting to the entrance.

Holy. Fuck.

Air sucked out of the room, and time stopped like it couldn't handle this man's energy either. Even as a teenager, when our paths first crossed, he had an effect on me.

But then I learned what kind of man he was, and I vowed to avoid the base guitar of The Velvet Kings at all costs.

Hendrix (Drix) Decker.

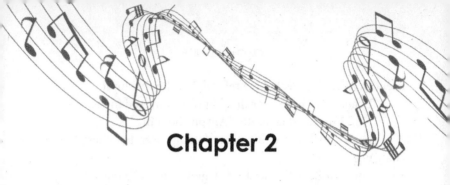

Chapter 2

No one moved and no one spoke. All eyes were on the famous bass guitarist. The tension in the room flourished, tasting bitter on my tongue. He seemed immune to it, his expression unintimidated by the hostile energy. Always cool, always unflappable.

And it pissed me off.

He was the epitome of a rockstar god. Probably most of the reason The Velvet Kings were so popular. Women fell to their knees when he entered a room or walked onto the stage, and men bowed to him as if he were a legend.

Drix Decker was over 6'3" with a ripped body. His broad shoulders had my 5'4" size self feeling like a flea next to a lion. Dark brown hair hung to his shoulder on one side and shaved on the other. A nose and eyebrow ring adorned his face, and tattoos went up his neck and covered his torso, arms, and hands. His amber eyes always felt as if they were hunting, tearing into your flesh. The man was drop-dead gorgeous and held such brutal, raw energy it caused fluttering in my chest.

I loathed him for causing that sensation, especially as my irrational mind told me otherwise.

Cognac-colored eyes slid around the room, stopping on me. My teeth gritted. His attention was overwhelming, and he oozed so much confidence that it was like staring at the sun.

"I assume everyone knows everyone?" Emmit nodded at all of us. "We can jump straight into practice?"

"No." I heard the word cut up my throat, my legs pushing me up, my head shaking.

A smirk twisted Drix's mouth, but it was anything but

friendly. As if he expected my refusal. Was hoping for it.

"Echo, we've been over this," Emmit conveyed to me.

"No," I repeated fervently. "Anyone but him."

Drix's smirk grew, his arms folding over his chest like a challenge.

"I'm with Echo," Ames huffed, glowering at Emmit.

"Me too." Tobias and Geo nodded.

"Guess what?" Emmit's face reddened with frustration. "I don't give a fuck! I'm done dancing around this. You need a new bass guitarist. He is one of the best. There is no more discussion."

"No more discussion? This is *my* band!" Ames's timbre pulsed off the walls.

"So you're going to let your ego stop the band from making it?" Emmit's tone matched his.

"Why are you here?" Ames stepped around to call out Drix. "Why aren't you with your own band? You can't play both."

"He won't be playing bo—"

"I quit." Drix cut off Emmit, sending a rippling wave of confusion through our group.

"Quit?" Geo stepped away from his keyboard. "You weren't even hired, and you already quit?"

"No. I quit The Velvet Kings." The rumble of Drix's voice wrapped around my vertebrae, feeling it from across the room.

My head reared back in shock. "What?" He quit the biggest rock band in America? Why? They had sellout concerts and songs topping the charts. None of this made sense.

"Why?" I regripped my sticks, which gave me a sense of security. The wood was damp and heavy in my grasp, my knuckles clenching them tightly.

His head tilted, and his eyes slid back to mine slowly, zeroing in on me as if I were prey. It felt like a pulse against my skin. "Not important." He spoke clear and precise.

"Not important?" Tobias laughed. "You walk out on the number one band and come play with your competitors?"

"Funny." Drix stayed facing me but let his gaze jump to

Tobias. "I never thought of you as competition."

Holy fuck. He didn't just say that. Our group's shoulders rose in sync, a snake about to strike.

"Whoa." Emmit stood between us and Drix, his 5'11 frame comical-looking as he guarded the beast of a man behind him. "Enough." Emmit only gave us his "threatening" look when he was about a hair away from ripping up our contract. It would never happen, but he threatened to daily when Ames was being pig-headed and running on ego. "I've had enough of the whining. Drix is no longer with The Velvet Kings, which is all that's important right now. Especially when you're supposed to be going on tour. You are opening in New York to thousands of people in a week."

"Exactly! He doesn't know our playlist. He can't learn the songs in time. We are better off just keeping it us," Ames interjected.

"Better off?" Drix scoffed. "I heard you guys. You are not better off."

"Excuse me?" Ames marched up to Drix, chest all puffed up. Ames was at least 6 feet tall, but his thin body seemed insignificant next to the bass guitarist.

Drix's arms stayed across his chest as he leaned into Ames, his expression empty. But I could see fire glint behind his eyes.

"You're dropping notes, and the entire band is out of sync." His cognac eyes flashed to me before jumping back to our lead singer. "And without a bass guitarist, your music lacks any depth. You sound like shit, Isley, and you know it."

"Fuck you!" Ames lurched for him, with Emmit in between, while Tobias grabbed for Ames, pulling him back. "Get the hell out of here."

"You know, I think I will." Drix dropped his arms, curving for the door. "I want to be in a band who *wants* to be the best."

"Stop!" Emmit's arms went up in the air, pointing to Drix. "You are not going anywhere." His finger slid to Ames. "And you need to get your head out of your ass. I am trying to help you. I am trying to give this band a sellout tour, which you currently do not have. So, all of you need to check your egos and realize this is the best for the band. You have a contract and a record label who want to see results, not hear you throwing tantrums." He swung back to Drix. "Grab your guitar, you are next to Echo."

My mouth parted in horror, knowing Emmit was right. But I still couldn't get over the thought that this was happening, and the one person I fucking hated more than anyone was taking Ziggy's spot. I wondered if he even remembered what he did to me. Or cared about anything at all. He didn't seem like the kind of guy who thought much outside himself.

"But—" Ames started.

"Hear what he can do, Ames," Emmit warned. "He knows his shit."

Tobias was the first to hook back up his guitar, giving in to Emmit, causing Geo to head to his keyboard.

Ames huffed and sighed, his jaw still tight with anger, but he moved to the microphone.

"Remember what we talked about?" Emmit turned to Drix privately, though I could still understand. "Your position here? What you need to do?"

"Yeah." Drix made a point of fully facing me before responding. He pulled the strap over his head, his stare heavy on me, cutting under my skin. "I'm Echo's babysitter."

Aghast, I blinked at him, my knuckles cracking against my sticks.

"Let's start with 'Scotch Tape Hole.'" Emmit clapped his hands together, heading to the front of the stage as Drix strolled up to the exact spot Ziggy had stood for so long, plugging into the output jack. His long fingers fiddled and tightened the tuning pegs on his guitar, his head cocking to me.

"Better sit down, Echo." He nodded at my stool, a smirk upping the side of his mouth in his notorious bad-boy expression. "Looks as though you and me are going to be working close together." He lifted his hands from the guitar and signed in perfect ASL,

"Looks like I'm your new ears, drummer girl."

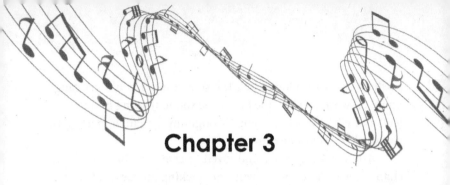

Chapter 3

Being a girl drummer in a world of men had always been an uphill battle. Most rock bands were men, most managers and agents were men, and sadly, most music labels were run by men. Not to say things weren't changing, but it was still extremely hard to be taken seriously in rock.

You had to be ten times better than a male counterpart to even be seen.

And I had double the challenge.

At 24, I was tiny, with a heart-shaped face, huge onyx-colored eyes, and long, naturally dark brown hair, which I streaked purple. I didn't necessarily look like a rock drummer in one of the most popular bands, but one fact had driven a lot of attention and reservations to me.

I was deaf.

One of the few who, with unrelenting determination, pushed through the stereotype that a drummer couldn't be deaf. Most assumed that because we couldn't "hear" music the same way as "normal" people, we couldn't play it. Especially not well.

Music, to some, was only sound, something you listened to on the radio to fill the silence.

Silence.

That word was different to me.

Music was something I felt. It was an entire-body experience, sweeping through me like I was the instrument of sound. The vibration of my drums would pulsate my body, throbbing into my skin, digging into my bones. I could see every note, feel every lyric, and disappear into another world where music was my entire existence, and I no longer felt the separation. I could get caught up in my world, feeling the beats, the sound floating into my bare feet, and vibrations thumping through my system, forgetting the real world existed sometimes.

Ames was impulsive and loved to chat with his audience or change the order of our playlist. So, picking up cues and shifts in a performance when the band's backs were to me was difficult, especially if I was lost in a performance and didn't know Ames went in another direction.

Even though I had worked hard to read lips, Ziggy became my "ears." He would sign to me of alterations in our song set and cues for when things were off script. He was placed close, where I could see his face, read his lips, and notice his signals.

We had become good friends since junior high when Ziggy and I met. Family. A mutual bond of being in the foster care system together, we protected each other. Or more, he protected me. We found our mutual love of music, playing and auditioning for every band we could.

He was asked to join most of them, his talent obvious. A deaf drummer girl...yeah...not so much. No matter how many times they heard me play, when I could outbeat all the other men auditioning, they didn't want me. Ziggy wouldn't leave me behind. It was us as a package or nothing.

The rejection was brutal. One was from someone I thought I could trust. I was wrong, but it burned a fire in my belly. I wanted it more. And I wouldn't stop until I was the best.

Until he regretted his choice.

A year after that dismissal, Ziggy and I met Ames, Tobias, and Geo. It was like finding family. The one I never had before. At the very center of the nucleus had been Ziggy.

That shattered when his demons won out, taking him from us, fracturing this group in a way we couldn't seem to recover from.

Now, I felt the familiarity of the bass guitar vibrating through me again. The notes of "Scotch Tape Hole" throbbing against my chest, the deep chord tingling my skin gutted me. As if I looked up, Ziggy would be there.

It was not Ziggy who stood next to me, though. It felt wrong. Yet, I couldn't stop the way my body responded. My gaze was captured by the man who stood in his place. His long hair flipped to one side, his huge physique, his hips curved into the guitar like it was his lover, while his fingers skillfully strummed at the strings. I could sense the passion in every note, the genius in his talent. He moved with certainty, a confidence and ownership of the instrument, a talent very few could challenge. And a promise that his proficiency would go way past playing music.

If rumors were true, his off-stage talent exceeded expectations, with multiple women at a time. At one time, I might have been just another one.

For a moment, I understood as his tune moved up my body, thrumming through my thighs, pulsing similar to a heartbeat. Drix Decker played with a primal passion. He didn't show much emotion in everyday life, though he laid it all out on stage, giving insight to the raw power behind the man. The command he would have over you if he treated you anything like he did his guitar, just with his fingers alone.

There was no denying the man was sexy as hell. Carnal in a way that drew you to him no matter if you liked his music or if he was your type. He oozed visceral confidence and pure unadulterated sex. A true rock god. I hated to admit it, but Hendrix had the talent to back it up and the looks to drop you to your knees in reverence, which made me despise him more.

But what the fuck? He knew ASL...

I knew he didn't when I first met him. When he found out I was deaf, his reaction was callous, cutting me deeply. Yet now, he signed to me so fluently that I would think he had signed all his life. When did he learn it? Why?

Drix finished his riff, eyes on me, my own beat syncing as if his gaze kept me in a trance. His boot tapped at the floor, and I picked up on the rhythm, counting the beats, the change in tempo.

He strummed at his guitar. His chin lifted before it dipped to me, his finger raised from the strings pointing at me, telling me it was time for my solo.

It was similar to what Ziggy used to do for me. It took us months to reach a place where our signals and prompts were second nature. How did Drix pick it up so quickly?

A burning rage seized my chest as my arms pounded down, my bare feet hearing the music, crashing the ride, my right foot hitting the bass drum. We shouldn't have this kind of rapport so soon. It felt like a slap in the face to how hard Ziggy and I worked to create the exchange between us.

He shouldn't have known those signals. It felt intimate and way too comfortable, as if we had been doing this for years together when he was nothing but an outsider. One who none of us would let into the band, nor did I believe he truly wanted to be. Why was he here and not with Velvet Kings? Was this some trick?

Ames cupped the microphone as the song ended, crooning out the final heartbreaking lyrics. It was a song I had written right after Ziggy's death. The song mirrored what I felt, the fake smile I had to put on, pretending my world wasn't falling apart.

Emmit jumped back on stage, his hands clapping together in excitement. "Holy shit!" He purposely faced me so I could see him. "That was the fucking best I've ever heard you guys play!"

The insinuation cut went deep: we never played this well with Ziggy.

A scowl puckered my mouth, my aggravation shooting over at the man a few feet from me, then to the men I considered brothers.

Tobias and Geo had smiles on their faces, their heads bobbing in agreement. I could tell Ames was fighting a smile, his mouth thinning. "It was pretty good." He shrugged one shoulder. "But can you keep up with 'The Devil Takes Me?'" Another hit we had with complex cadences and one of the toughest bass riffs.

Drix's fingers strummed the first cords, a smugness twitching his lips before he let loose.

The melody of "The Devil Takes Me" struck from the soles

of my feet to my scalp. I could feel every cord, taking me with him through the highs, touching the sky, to the lows, where the devil awaited. Air caught in my chest, my eyelids wanting to close, wanting to fall into his resonance.

Drix did what very few musicians could—took you to another world. Another dimension.

Music was just another way to tell a story. To capture people and take them on a journey. It was heartbreaking, healing, joyful, and angry. It captured human emotion, no matter what creed, race, or sex you were. Music could unite with a note or rally with a war cry.

Music didn't discriminate. It just found another way to seduce and take hold of your soul.

It was why even those of us who couldn't hear the lyrics still found a home within the beats and rhythms. We heard it differently than others, but because other senses were more developed, I think we felt it even deeper.

Drix's fingers skillfully thrummed the song's bridge, running a shiver up my spine. His notes hit deeper, more soulful than anyone I'd ever heard before. Even more than Ziggy, as if Drix bargained with the devil to take his soul in exchange for otherworldly talent.

His amber irises lifted to me, his chin dipping twice, already knowing how to cue me in to start playing with him. Twirling my sticks, my arms moved automatically while my brain told me to flip him off. The pull to play always overpowered my logic. I jumped in on the bridge, our beats syncing instantly. His gaze stayed on me as we finished the last crescendo, making me feel like we were the only ones on earth, a connection only music could build.

The song came to an end, but his focus stayed completely on me, a smile hinting at his mouth, our gazes locked, the air hitching in my lungs, fluttering in my stomach.

"Fuck man, you guys were insane!" Tobias peered between us in awe. "Never heard that take on that song, and never heard Echo play that way either." He stepped toward him, breaking our connection and forcing the air back into my lungs, jolting me back to reality.

Did I just get butterflies? What the hell was wrong with me? I *hated* him.

But when he looked at me, it felt magical. Like no one else could touch our level.

Grow up, Echo, you're not seventeen anymore.

I had learned long ago that it was just a party trick, an act to make those around him feel special and seen. I stupidly fell for it once until I learned what he was really like.

"Yeah, fuck. I say bygones be bygones." Geo laughed. "That made me fuckin' hard."

"Which is not difficult for you." Tobias chuffed.

Ames was the stereotypical lead singer manwhore, though he was particular in wanting models, actresses, and Playboy Bunny types. Tobias took all the ones Ames didn't, but Geo subtly outdid them both because he had no preference. He was open to anyone who was hot and flattered his ego. Though they might all have to bow down to Drix if rumors of his endless stream of women running through his bed were even partially true.

"Whatever bullshit you guys had." Emmit stepped in. "Forget it. You want to be the best out there?" He gestured to Drix. "This is the key."

"I'm in." Tobias and Geo both agreed.

I was not.

All eyes went to Ames. Though it was a mutual band decision, Ames always seemed to have a little more weight in his vote.

Ames rubbed at his blonde scruff, a debate raging across his brows. Then his head started to bob, his shoulders easing down. "Yea—"

"No!" My revolt danced through my vocals, producing enough vibration to turn their heads my way. "No!" I shook my head, dropping my sticks, my hands reconfirmed my vote.

Drix's gaze burrowed into me, peeling at my skin, but I kept my attention on my band. "*He* will not take Ziggy's spot." Ziggy fucking hated him. Probably because of me, but I still couldn't stomach the thought of Hendrix Decker standing in his spot, creating a bond with me only Ziggy and I should have.

"Echo..." Emmit signed my name.

"NO!" My throat cut over the word, and I knew it was extra loud. Ziggy was the one to help me with speaking, from how to measure the vibration in my throat to how clear and loud it came out. While we were kids in foster care he became my everything. Yet, somehow, I missed all the signs he was struggling. That he didn't come out of what happened to us unscathed. He was good at hiding his demons, keeping the focus on me, being my big brother and best friend.

Geo started to open his mouth, his countenance speaking before his mouth did, and I could see the empathy to my struggle, but they did not feel the same. Ziggy had been a friend, but clearly, his memory would go to the wayside.

Even Ames looked at me with the same expression. They were all on board with Drix joining us. How easily they all flipped. Their principles yesterday no longer mattered in the face of fame and fortune today.

My head shook harder, my glare sweeping over the brothers I thought would feel the same about Drix.

"It's three against one." Ames shrugged. "I'm sorry, but he's in."

Disgust and hurt wrapped around my gut, burning the back of my throat.

My fingers spoke what my mouth could not.

"So much for honor and integrity. I guess Ziggy's memory can't hold up to your need for fame." I whirled around, stomping out.

I couldn't hear but could feel someone call out my name. Being deaf meant we listened with our whole bodies, intuition guiding us when other senses failed.

And mine took me to the only person who had ever really heard me.

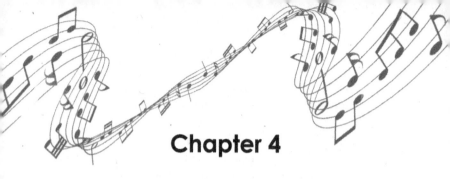

Chapter 4

Pictures of our band hung on the wall of our rehearsal studio, a hodgepodge of us from the beginning to more recent, though not one picture was taken in the last six months.

My attention zeroed in on my favorite. It was taken here, all of us looking utterly exhausted, but elation had smiles on our faces, a fire behind our eyes. Ziggy's arm draped around me, my head on his shoulder, while the other guys surrounded us. We had just finished lining tracks for our first LP.

It was before we made a name for ourselves, before our record label started to really put demands on us. We were free to make music, find our sound, and be creative, and when we laid "The Devil Takes Me," we knew we made magic.

It was before you realized your dreams, and the best time in your life was not the marker you set but all the stuff before it. There is a disappointment when you achieve all you've ever wanted and find it didn't fill the hole you thought it would. Success didn't make you happy. The process is where creative people thrive.

It was where Ziggy was the happiest. He was just another incredible talent, a spark in this industry, who went out too quickly.

My finger glided over his face, heart-wrenching agony yanking a sob up my throat. I missed him so much. I felt so lost without him. *Ziggy.* A fissure cracked my chest, the tips of my fingers tracing his lazy smile.

I sensed a presence behind me before I felt a touch on my shoulder. Whipping around, a gasp hitched my lungs, my head craning back, surprise pooling anger through me.

I expected Emmit or one of the boys. Not him.

"I'm not here to take his place." Drix signed, nodding at the wall to Ziggy.

"Good, because no one *ever* will. Especially you." I spat back with my hands.

"I don't know what the fuck I've done to you." Drix's mouth moved with his fingers, fury stepping him closer, looming over me. "But I'm not here to play games."

The fucking audacity.

"Are you kidding me?" My hands fired back. I also verbalized, but my emotions were bubbling over too much to care if I was enunciating clearly. "You don't know what you did? Oh, right, you probably don't remember. Just another pathetic girl you messed around with."

He sucked harshly through his nose.

"Are you seriously talking about our little hook-up *seven* years ago? We made out. That was it." His mouth moved faster than his hands, dropping some of the sentence. "We were kids. Plus, you were the one who walked away from me."

"Did you think I would stay? Waiting for you on your bed like a groupie?" I fired back. "After what you said about me?"

"What the fuck are you talking about?"

"I was there!" My arms expressed my fury. "I 'overheard' what you and Corey said about me." Corey was the lead singer of Velvet Kings and probably one of the most arrogant assholes I'd ever met, besides Drix. Maybe it was why he left; their egos couldn't fit in one band. "What was it you said? Having not only a *girl* drummer in your band would weaken any chances of making it, but she was also a deaf bitch on top of that!"

Drix stepped back like I slapped him, which I really should have. I should have hit him back then. But I was seventeen, so young and insecure, I ran instead of fighting back. It took me a long time not to believe what they said. That I *was* good enough. Back then, when we were all just starting out, I had this major crush on Drix. I thought we had this deep, magical connection when we played together. I wanted to be part of their band, played my ass off when we all got together, drinking and hanging out.

Drix finally took notice of me one night after we played together. He told me how amazing I was. Our kissing quickly heated up, and he left me on his bed to get condoms.

Fifteen minutes I waited until I snuck out looking for him. I found him with Corey and the rest of the band, still just in his boxers, a condom package in his hand.

* * *

"Dude, you're seriously gonna fuck that deaf bitch?" Corey laughed. He was facing in the direction where I hid behind a wall. "It's obvious she has such a crush on you, but how hard up are you?"

"Shut the fuck up." Drix's eyebrows furrowed, his profile harder to read.

"I mean, she's smokin' hot, but still. Won't it be weird? I guess she'll sign when she calls out your name." The rest of the band laughed at his hurtful joke. "Well, go ahead and bang her, get something useful from her. She's not joining this band." Corey peered over at the other members, their heads bobbing in unison. "I mean, a girl drummer in a rock band? No fucking way we want some deaf bitch part of us. A cockblocker when we're gonna have swarms of women on us." He stalked over to Drix, slapping him on the shoulder. "Models and celebrities will be begging to suck our cocks. We don't want some girl with us. Especially a deaf one."

"You can't deny she's pretty good." Drix shrugged one shoulder like it was an afterthought.

"You want pretty good, or you want amazing?" Corey asked. "I want this band to make it big. Do you really trust a girl drummer to play with us? Seriously?"

I could feel the air holding in my lungs, my hope pinned on him. The guy had me so smitten it was like I was one big fluttering drunk butterfly, and I wasn't known to be girly or swoony over any guy.

"Drix?" Corey said his name, an eyebrow curving. "You getting *a crush on the deaf girl?"*

"Fuck, no." Drix shook his head. *"She's just an easy fuck. Nothing else."*

* * *

In one sentence, my heart and confidence splintered into pieces.

I took off and never went back. At that moment, my hatred for The Velvet Kings began, along with my drive to be the best.

They splintered me, but I didn't break. And I can't deny they pushed me to work harder. I practiced relentlessly, never leaving the studio until I had it perfect. And perfection wasn't something an artist ever found. Ziggy helped me develop a system where I was so in tune with everything that no one could say I was good for a "girl" or a "deaf drummer."

No, I was just fucking brilliant, period.

"You don't remember telling him I was just an *easy fuck* and nothing else?" My hands moved so fast and violently, his forehead creased, trying to keep up. When my statement registered, I watched his frame stiffen, his expression walling up.

"You were there?" He stopped signing, his voice vibrating against my skin.

"Yes. I was there to learn that behind my back, you all thought I was just a pathetic deaf girl who had no business being a drummer."

"That's not—"

"Shut. Up." I cut him off, rage raking through me. "Now it's me who doesn't want you here. Who gets to reject you!"

"Echo—"

"No! Get the fuck away, Drix." The shout hummed in my vocals, my hands aching at how fast I was signing. "Why are you even here?"

"Because..." He shifted on his feet, turning his head away from me. I hated when people did that, cutting me off from their facial reactions. Frustrated, I reached up, grabbed his chin, and yanked his face back to me to read his lips. The feel of his beard between my fingers, his mouth so close, and how his cognac eyes looked at me took me back to his bed so many years ago. I recalled the way his mouth felt on mine, his hands touching my body, the skillful way his tongue twined with mine. It was the same magic when we played together, but it exploded even more in the bedroom.

I sucked in, dropping my hands away as if he burned me. "Actually, I don't want to know," I spoke with my hands. "Just go back to where you belong." I turned, starting to stride out of the room.

Fingers wrapped around my arm, yanking me back, my spine hitting the wall, knocking a few pictures off, firing heat between my thighs. My nipples hardened as Drix's physique pressed into mine. His huge hand slid up my neck, forcing my head to look up at him.

"I'm not going anywhere, drummer girl." He spoke so close I could feel the heat from his lips brush against my own, stealing the air from my lungs. "Get used to it."

His gaze dropped to my mouth. Slowly, he slid his thumb over to my lip ring, tugging on it. A primal need for him to kiss me, to pick me up, slide my pants down and fuck me against the wall overpowered me. A yearning so deep I felt both disgust and desire.

As if he had read my thoughts, I could feel a vibration coming from his chest. His jaw crunched down, a nerve in his cheek twitching before he pushed away.

Shoulders hunched forward, he ran a hand through his hair as he stomped out of the room. The door vibrated the wall when he slammed it.

Oxygen heaved into my lungs, and my wobbly legs dropped me down the wall, shocked at my own reaction.

After seven years of despising him, he could walk into the room, touch me, and I was legless on the floor. Going against everything I was.

I was known for being a badass. For being the one the men crawled to, not the other way around. But there had always been something about Drix. Something that pulled me to him like a magnet, and I couldn't seem to fight no matter what my brain told me, even after this long.

Outvoted, Drix Decker was now my bandmate, someone I would have to communicate with the most.

My eyes caught on a picture that fell, my shaky fingers picking it up. Liquid blurred my vision, a sob barking in my chest.

Broken glass cut across Ziggy's face, like he knew we were moving on. Drix's face would start replacing these pictures, and slowly, Ziggy would disappear.

From the band, the wall. And my memories?

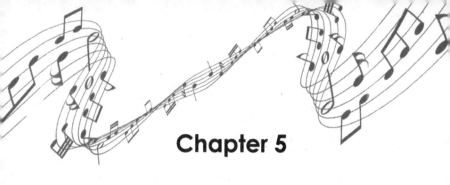

Chapter 5

"It's been two months since you joined Mental Breakdown." The journalist's flirty, red smile pointed to Drix. His chair sat so close that his arm was pressed into mine, his warm skin making my body restless and hot. But it was the camera lights and the fact we were on our *fifth* interview, not him.

Drix and I were put together a lot while Ames, Geo, and Tobias did the other circuit loop. Though I could read lips, Emmit made sure an ASL interpreter was behind the reporter, knowing after the eighth or ninth one, I would start to get exhausted and miss questions.

"The rumors surrounding your move to leave The Velvet Kings have stirred up *quite* the media storm." That was putting it lightly. The news exploded across social media the day after his so-called audition. His silence on the matter created so much hype that the rumor mill was churring up conspiracies and fan-fiction level stories.

Especially about us.

"'Scotch Tape Hole,' 'The Devil Takes Me,' and 'Vertigo' are all topping the charts, and this tour you're on has sold out with more shows being added."

She stared at Drix, her lashes lowered as though she was waiting for him to respond, waiting for him to pick her up and carry her off.

One thing about Drix most didn't know, besides Ames, was that he hated being in the spotlight and didn't talk just to hear himself talk. His enigmatic, rocker vibe wasn't a facade. He was that mysterious puzzle everyone wanted to figure out. His grumpy silence was catnip to fans and reporters, the world more intrigued and desperate to know him. To have the privilege to peek into the man underneath all the tattoos, piercings, and intensity.

Unfortunately, I didn't get his silent treatment. He now seemed to be signing more than he actually spoke to others, and he lived to torment and challenge me. Over the last two months, our cues had become so tight, so in sync, he would just look at me and I would know what to do.

I hated it. I tried my best to ignore him, just taking his prompts on stage and avoiding him off. It wasn't working so well.

The twenty-something blonde reporter shifted in her seat at the silence and intensity of his gaze.

"I was just wondering if you credit yourself for that?"

He tilted his head, his arm pressing more into mine, and I could feel his irritation growing, blooming over into my own veins.

"No." His hands lifted to sign like it was the most natural thing to do now, but he stopped himself. "The songs were hits before. I had nothing to do with it. Maybe you should acknowledge the one who actually wrote the songs, not me." He nodded toward me, his bobbing leg nudging into mine.

"Oh." The reporter turned to me, a blush on her cheeks, looking like Drix had just called out her integrity. "You wrote them?" If she had done any research, she would have known that. "Really? You can hear the music and the ballads when you are writing?"

A growl shuddered from Drix as the translator finished the reporter's ignorant assumption tied up in an "innocent" question.

"What the fuck is that supposed to mean?" Drix's timbre was low, dragging across my skin, his hands once again signing his thoughts. He did it so naturally, I don't think he even knew he was doing it.

"I mean, since she's..." The woman's cheeks pinked even more, afraid to say the word deaf, as if some politically correct police would jump out the moment she suggested it.

She wasn't the first reporter today to hint at this, and she wouldn't be the last. Usually, the male reporters came with the misogyny of me being a woman drummer as well. I was used to it by now.

"You mean because she's deaf?" Drix sat up, leaning into her with a challenge. "Music isn't just about your ears. There are different ways to hear music. It's a feeling. An emotion, a depth you can't reach with your normal senses. You can't literally taste, touch, or see music either, which doesn't take away from the experience. Music is in here." He tapped at his head. "And here." He knocked a fist into his chest, his combative energy filling the room. It was the most passion I had seen from him off stage. "Her talent speaks for itself, but I promise you, Echo experiences music far more than the rest of us do."

Seeing the pure horror and embarrassment on the reporter's face, my hand pressed down on his thigh, trying to calm him down.

His head jerked at my touch, his gaze catching mine. Without even having to do anything more, his eyes read mine, his shoulders lowering, slumping back in the chair. He looked away from me as if he needed to regain himself, but his hand slid over mine, curling around it like it was his only anchor.

The reporter's attention went to our hands, tracking how we touched, how he held my hand against his inner thigh. Intimacy only a couple would have.

Suddenly, I became very aware of my hand, his warm palm cupping around my fingers, holding on like we did this all the time. Oddly, it felt natural. But I mean, we were bandmates. We knew each other better than anyone.

Would you do this to Ames or Tobias? Geo?

No. I would've elbowed or hit them with my knee, the same as if they were my brothers.

A shot of fear flooded my veins, and I tried to tug my hand away, scared of how comfortable it was to touch him. To have such a deep familiarity with him that I didn't even have with my other bandmates.

His hand clamped down tighter, not letting me pull away.

The journalist's gaze brightened, an *ah-ha* glint caught in her eyes. Taking in this evidence, the way he stood up for me and held my hand in such an intimate position against his thigh. I could see the puzzle she was putting together in her head, coming to an incorrect conclusion.

She sat up, her chagrin replaced by the scandalous story she thought she was getting an insight into.

Drix caught the shift, his eyes going down to where he held my hand, and quickly pulled his hand away.

But it was too late.

"The rumors before, from sources, said you two *hated* each other prior to Drix joining the band..." She led us, hoping one of us would jump in and pick up. We both stared, cross-armed and defensive. "Is there any truth to that?"

"No," Drix lied. There was *a lot* of truth to us hating each other. At one time, I laid on his bed, my pants on the floor, his fingers exploring my body, before fate stepped in and thankfully deterred the biggest mistake I could've made.

"So...is there something going on between you two?"

"No." My fingers responded harshly.

"Because fans are convinced there is. There are already hashtags and websites dedicated to you two, dissecting every look and touch. There is no denying there is intense chemistry between you guys. On stage, you are so in tune with each other, the connection so combustive you pull all the attention. It is the only thing anyone can talk about." Ames's ego would love to hear that.

"We have to be in sync." Drix was short and curt. "She relies on me for cues and changes."

"Not the same as way she did with Ziggy. What you two have is explosive."

When I saw her lips utter his name, my spine went rigid, fury blooming in my chest.

"Don't you dare compare Ziggy with anyone." My fingers hissed, fury fueling me. "Don't ever lessen what Ziggy was to me and this band in a need to concoct some juicy made-up story to get views. There is nothing going on between us." I stood up, ripping off the mic the sound people hooked onto my top. "This interview is over!" I didn't care how angry Emmit would be for walking out on an interview. I was done with the dumb, insensitive questions about being deaf or, even worse, a girl. The salacious inquiries about Drix and me, and the outright insulting comments about him being behind all this fame we had.

Did his arrival come at a time when we happened to be on tour? Yes, but we had talent and fans before him. He just added an extra layer.

And did fans want a budding love affair between us so bad they saw things? Fuck, yes, they did. I got a dozen tags a minute with our names linked. #EchoDrixLove and #DrixEchoship. But it was all in their heads.

Drix was just a bandmate. Nothing more. A knot braided up from my gut, pumping more adrenaline into my body.

Right?

Slamming out of the room and stomping down the hall, I felt him behind me, his boots thumping the floor. I was so hyperaware of him that I even recognized his weight behind me.

My legs started to run. Anxiety pushed me through doors, zigzagging down corridors and through rooms, trying to get away from him.

Trying to outrun what I knew deep down.

A hand wrapped around my arm, whirling me around.

"Let me go." The protest hummed in my vocal cords.

"Goddamit, stop." Anger and frustration hardened his features, his nose flaring. His frame leaned over me.

"I don't want to talk to you." I signed furiously.

"Tough shit." His lips curled. "I'm tired of doing this your way."

"My way?"

"Yes, this whole avoidance thing."

"What are you talking about?"

His head slanted, giving me a look. "Like it's not obvious that you get the farthest you can from me the moment we are off stage. What are you running from, Echo?"

"I'm not running from anything!"

"That's all you do!" He let go, exclaiming with his hands too.

"Excuse me?"

"You run from dealing with what happened to Ziggy. You run from me."

"From Ziggy?" I sputtered, feeling my face flaming in ire.

"You still haven't dealt with his death. You blame me for being in his spot, but he's the one you are mad at. Because he left you. It's okay to be mad at him."

"I'm not mad at him! I can't be because he's dead, and I don't blame you for being in his spot. I blame you for being an asshole!"

"Why? Because I fucked up seven years ago?" His fingers shouted back. "Yeah, I'm sorry. I fucked up."

"Fucked up?" I shoved at him. "It's because you *hurt* me! I thought of all people you would have my back. That you didn't think the worst things about me, too. Just a laughable deaf girl who thought she could play drums with the likes of the great Hendrix Decker."

"I *never* said that!" He shot back. "Corey did."

"You didn't deny it!" My hands could barely keep up with my emotions; the box I kept tucked away with all my pain popped open, spilling out. "I thought you were different. That there was something there. When we played together, it was special. But I was the fool, thinking so highly of you. You are no different from any other ignorant, insensitive person out there." I motioned in the direction of the reporter. "Actually, you're worse because you couldn't even say it to my face." I began to turn around, needing to get as far from him as possible.

Hands clutched my arms, his body shoving me back into the door. And then his mouth crashed down on mine. Every thought blanked from my mind, every reason I had to keep us at arm's length disappearing. All the justifications I had for hating him vanished as his lips met mine. Hunger claimed me, desire pumped through my veins, and I swallowed back a moan. Hunger exploded between us, a line between rage and desire licking through me, making the fire between us explode like a storm.

He pulled back just as fast as it began, his hands gripping my face, leaving me breathless and dizzy.

"Was I a young, stupid eighteen-year-old who was too afraid to admit how he felt?" He trapped me against the frame of the door. "Yes. I will own that. You scared the hell out of me. And I wasn't man enough to defend you, to speak up and say I really fucking liked you." A gasp hiccuped in my throat at his claim. "I will fully admit I was too young to know how to handle you being different. But there hasn't been a day I haven't regretted it. Fuck, I even learned ASL because of you!"

"You what?" I gaped.

"But I never thought you were a pathetic deaf girl." His hands clasped the sides of my face. "You blew me away then and even more now. Your talent, the music you write, how hard you work. I am in awe of you. And yes, when we played together back then, it was fire..." His grip tightened. "And even more now. Everything people see on the stage between us is true. And I can't keep my fucking eyes off you."

"What?" I don't know if any noise actually came out of my throat, my heart thumping in my head like a drumbeat.

"And I was jealous."

"Jealous?"

"Yes. You guys are like family. You make music from your soul. I wanted that. It's part of why I came here. But in all honesty, the main reason is I came for you." His mouth brushed mine, his eyes locking on mine.

"You are my song in silence."

WILD
HOPE

MARI CARR

About the Author

Virginia native Mari Carr is a *New York Times* and *USA TODAY* bestseller of contemporary sexy romance and romantic suspense novels. With over three million copies of her books sold, Mari was the winner of the Romance Writers of America's Passionate Plume award for her novella, Erotic Research. She has over a hundred published works, including her popular Wild Irish and Italian Stallions books, along with the Trinity Masters series she writes with Lila Dubois.

www.maricarr.com

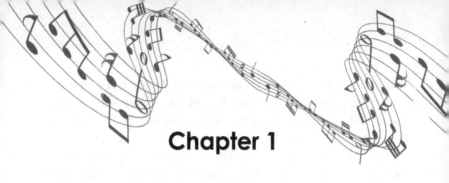

Chapter 1

"After you."

Andi Jennings smiled at the attractive man, who waited to hold the door for her at the Stop and Go convenience store. "Thanks."

The man nodded, and the two of them entered together. He walked toward the coffee pots while she headed around the checkout counter.

"I'm here," she said to Barbie, who gave her a grateful smile before reaching under the counter for her purse, rooting around for her car keys.

"Oh, thank God. I'm so sorry to do this to you, Andi, but my husband is absolutely useless when Eleanor is sick. He can't stand the sight of vomit. Makes him gag, and he always has to leave the room."

Andi crinkled her nose, recalling Robbie, who seemed to have a similar aversion to poopy diapers. She got the sense Barbie's husband had discovered the best way to get out of dirty jobs was to protest too much. "I'm not sure anyone enjoys cleaning it up."

"Yeah, well, Robbie is the worst. He's called three times because he moved her from her bed to ours to the couch and she got sick on all three. He's out of places to put her, and I swear I'm going out of my mind with all his play-by-play texts about how she's crying nonstop and how he's got every window in the apartment open to air it out. He's twenty-five, for God's sake. You would think he could deal with a sick kid for a few hours without being such a drama queen."

In addition to being coworkers, they were friends, so Andi

had met Barbie's husband countless times. Barbie had a running joke about being the mother of a beautiful four-year-old girl and a man-child. Andi didn't have the heart to tell her the joke was less funny and more accurate.

Barbie looked miserable. "I'm so sorry to dump this on you. I know you just got off at the pub and you have to go to the hotel right after this. I hope you managed to get a little bit of sleep before I called."

"I'm fine," Andi reassured her. "Go take care of Eleanor. Craig will be here at six, so it's only a few hours."

Andi didn't add that, even though it was three a.m., she hadn't been to bed yet. She'd closed Pat's Pub at two and just gotten back to her apartment when Barbie called asking her to cover the last part of her shift. Today was going to be one long-ass day.

"You're an angel." Barbie gave her a quick hug and scurried out the door.

Andi slid on her name tag and stashed her purse under the counter.

The handsome man who'd come in with her still stood near the coffee pots, perusing the packaged pastries. She took a moment to study him, curious about what brought someone like him into a place like this.

They got all sorts of people in the convenience store, though they didn't get many hot guys in tuxedos. While he'd dumped the bow tie somewhere, unbuttoning the first couple of buttons on his dress shirt, he was still way overdressed for this place. Even in profile, she could see just how good-looking he was with his chiseled jaw, dimples, and five-o'clock shadow. His hair was dark brown with just a sprinkle of gray at the temples.

When he looked at the coffee pots and sighed, she called out, "Can I help you?"

The man turned around, his expression turning serious when he saw her standing there. He looked displeased about something.

"Are the pots empty?" She walked around the counter and down the aisle where he stood. "I can make a fresh pot if you'd like."

He glanced around the store as if looking for someone, then shook his head. "There is coffee. I'm simply debating between a cup of it or a bottle of water. Coffee sounds better, but..."

"Keeps you up at night?"

He nodded. "It does."

"It does the same to me." She lifted the pot and poured herself a cup. One of the perks of the job was that they could help themselves to the coffee. Andi would need a jolt of caffeine if she hoped to stay awake. "But I'm still many, many hours away from bedtime."

The man watched as she added a dash of cream to her cup. "I suspect coffee is a must if you work the night shift," he said before glancing at her name tag, "Andi."

"This isn't usually my shift. I'm just covering for my friend."

"So the other woman left?"

Andi nodded. "Sick kid."

"I see." She got the feeling he didn't like her answer, though she couldn't figure out what she'd said wrong.

Andi took a sip of coffee, then set the cup down so she could clean up the counter, pitching empty sugar packets and coffee stirrers in the trash can. Barbie was typically on top of keeping things tidy, which just proved how much Robbie had been annoying her with his constant texts and calls.

"It's nice of you to help her out."

"She's a friend, and I know she'd do the same for me."

Not that Andi had ever asked. Money was too tight for her to give away her shifts. Every penny counted these days.

"You're out late," she said, making small talk. She much preferred her day-shift hours because there was always a steady flow of people in and out to keep her busy. Working these wee hours of the night was the equivalent of watching paint dry.

"It's been a long night," he confessed.

"Oh?"

"My business partner was supposed to attend a charity gala

in New York this evening, but his flight got canceled, and he's stuck in L.A., which meant I had to go. So I've spent three hours driving up to Manhattan, four hours of making small talk, and now three hours back down here," he explained.

"Ouch. That does sound like a long ten hours. Are you from Baltimore?" she asked.

He shook his head. "No."

Andi wasn't sure why she found that disappointing. The odds she would run into this guy again were basically nil, but a tiny part of her would have liked a better chance of it happening.

There was something about him that felt dangerous yet not threatening.

Yeah...like that's a thing, Andi.

Regardless, her instant attraction to him was off the charts, which wasn't something that ever happened to her. She was too busy to be horny. It was a simple, if painful, fact of life.

"I'm actually from New York, which is why today felt like adding insult to injury. Any other weekend, it would have been a simple thing to pop across the city for the event," the man continued. "But, of course, thanks to Murphy's Law, I'm in Baltimore this week for work. I got into town a couple of days ago. I would have spent the night at my apartment in the city, but I'm meeting a client for brunch here in Baltimore tomorrow, so I decided to come back tonight rather than in the morning. It was all going fine until the car got a flat."

Andi glanced out the window. "Oh. Hey, wait. Are you riding in that limo parked across the street?" She'd seen it on her way in and wondered if someone famous was sitting inside.

He nodded. "While the driver is dealing with the tire, I offered to buy us both a bottle of water."

"That's very nice of you, um..."

"Joel," he replied, introducing himself. "Joel McKenna."

She took the hand he offered, shaking it. "Andi Jennings. Nice to meet you. Have you always lived in New York City?"

"I have," Joel responded.

"I've never been, but I'm hoping to visit there someday. My brother wants to move to Manhattan after he graduates from high school. He'd like to go to college there."

"Oh? What school?" Joel asked.

"NYU." Her response triggered the response she expected.

Joel tilted his head. "That's a great school, but tough to get into."

"Dylan knows that and he's got a list of backup choices. But NYU is his dream school. I'm not too worried about him not getting in because he's working so hard to make it happen. He's valedictorian of his class, and he scored fifteen hundred on his PSAT."

Joel's eyes widened. "Wow. Impressive."

She smiled, pleased by the compliment. She was so proud of her brother she could pop. "I'm hoping he'll get some help from scholarships. He's the brightest, sweetest kid on the planet, and I know he's going to do amazing things in the future."

"What does he want to study?" Joel asked.

"International Business and Global Management. He's tried to explain to me what kind of jobs he could find with that degree and what he'd be doing, but I'm not sure I fully understand it all. To be honest, it sounds kind of boring." Andi realized she was prattling on too much. Her little brother was her favorite subject, so she tended to go on and on about him.

Joel chuckled. "Sounds like he's on the right path if NYU is his plan."

Dylan had only been a few weeks into his freshman year of high school when he started talking about college, buckling down and getting good grades, and building a well-rounded portfolio of community service, academics, and clubs. She'd been impressed by his plan and his determination. Of course, that was when Andi realized he wasn't the only one who needed to buckle down.

Andi was the sole provider for her family...most of the time. Her father had left her and her pregnant mother when Andi was nine. Andi's mom did her best to keep a roof over their head and food on the table, but as time passed, she grew more and more depressed, drinking too much. Their mom's alcoholism made it hard for her to hold down a job for any length of time, so Andi had learned a long time ago to stop relying on her to pay the bills. By the time Andi was a sophomore in high school, she was working full-time hours stocking shelves at a local grocery store from the moment she got out of school until eleven at night.

"How old is your brother?" Joel asked.

"Sixteen. He's a junior. If Dylan gets into NYU, he'll be the first in our family to go to college."

Andi wanted that for her brother as much as Dylan did. So when he'd told her his plans for after high school, she had kicked it up a notch, taking on a third job in order to save as much money as she could to help him achieve his dream. In addition to working here and at the hotel, she'd started waitressing at a local bar a couple of years earlier.

When she'd originally been hired at Pat's Pub, it had been as a dinner shift waitress, the hours working in conjunction with her other jobs. One night after the bar closed, the bartender, Padraig Collins, had heard her singing quietly to herself, and he'd convinced her to perform on stage. To her amazement, the patrons liked listening to her. Since then, Padraig paid her to perform a couple nights a week while she waitressed the other evenings.

Joel crossed his legs, still leaning against the counter. He was seriously one of the most attractive men she'd ever met, though probably too old for her.

She did an internal eye roll because this guy was not flirting with her, and he never would.

"You didn't have any interest in furthering your education?" he asked.

Andi shook her head. "It wasn't in the cards for me. Not enough money, and my grades, while passing, weren't anywhere near as good as Dylan's." Writing papers and studying for tests usually happened on her work breaks or on the bus ride to school, neither of which allowed much time for her to do more than the bare minimum.

"How old are you, Andi?"

She was surprised by the question even though she was curious about his age as well. "I'm twenty-six."

"Twenty-six," he mused aloud.

"How old are you?" she countered with a grin.

For the first time, he smiled. "I'm ancient. Thirty-nine."

She laughed. "Wow, yeah. A total relic."

He narrowed his eyes good-naturedly.

She should probably get back to work, but there wasn't anyone else in the store, and there were only so many rounds of solitaire she could play before boredom kicked in and her hand cramped from holding her phone for so long. "So, how was your gala? Must've been bougie as hell considering the tux and limo."

He grinned, shaking his head. "It was mind-numbingly boring. Making small talk with self-important snobs and raging narcissists is a tedious thing. This is the most interesting conversation I've had all night."

She made a face. "If this is a winning conversation, you're obviously running with the wrong crowd."

"As I said, it was a meet and greet deal tied to work. I was only there an hour when I began to suspect my partner probably canceled the flight himself just to get out of attending."

She started to ask what Joel did for a living, but he glanced out the window, speaking first. "Looks like the tire's changed."

Andi followed his gaze and saw the limousine pull into the parking lot, claiming a space right in front.

"I need sleep, so I'm going to skip the caffeine." Joel walked away from the coffee, heading to the cooler to grab two bottles of water, while Andi picked up her cup and returned to the register.

She rang up Joel's purchase, and he paid.

"Are you safe here by yourself?" he asked, concern in his tone.

"Oh, I'll be fine." She was no stranger to working after dark. A job was a job, and unfortunately, she couldn't afford to be afraid of every shadow.

Joel didn't look convinced.

"Honest," she tried to reassure him, though she was touched by his trepidation.

She wasn't accustomed to someone worrying about her. Her mom was typically too drunk to know whether or not she was home, and Dylan had spent his entire life with a sister who worked too much. This was the norm to him because it was how things had always been. He had offered to get an after-school job to help with bills on more than one occasion, but she'd put her foot down, telling him that getting good grades and getting into college was his job.

Then, she always joked that he could start paying the bills when he was a rich businessman living in Manhattan, after which she could put her feet up and eat bonbons all day. They would laugh, and then Dylan, bless his kind heart, swore he would take care of her when that day arrived.

Not that she would ever let him, of course, but it was a sweet promise all the same.

Joel sighed, clearly not convinced. "Okay, if you're sure," he said at last. "It was nice talking to you, Andi."

"You too." Most people who came in treated her like she was invisible, simply grabbing whatever they wanted, paying, and leaving. It was nice to have someone help her pass a few minutes of what was bound to be a very long three hours.

He hesitated for a moment longer before turning and heading for the door. "Good night."

She waved as he left, then perched on the edge of the stool, watching as Joel climbed into the back of the limo. She wished they'd had longer to chat because her curiosity—okay, and libido— had kicked into overdrive.

What did he do for a living?

Did he always travel around in a limo?

Did he have a girlfriend?

What would it be like to kiss him? Would he be gentle and sweet? Or rough and hungry?

She scoffed at the last questions because it wasn't like the answers mattered. Men like Joel McKenna did not go for girls like her. He was older, sophisticated, more experienced, well-spoken, and rich.

But none of those facts stopped her from running her finger over her lower lip, imagining those hard kisses. Or from fantasizing about what it would be like to lie down underneath him on the backseat of that limousine while he had his wicked way with her.

She let the images play out for too long, then sighed because now, it wouldn't just be a long night.

It was going to be a lonely one, too.

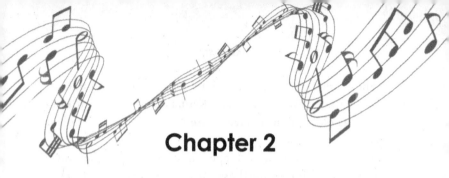

Chapter 2

Joel looked up from his computer when there was a knock on the door to his hotel suite.

"Housekeeping," someone called from the hallway.

He rose and opened the door, prepared to say he was okay for towels, but stopped when he saw Andi's smiling face standing next to her cart.

Her eyes widened when she realized it was him.

"We need to stop meeting this way," she joked.

"Andi." He could tell she was surprised he'd remembered her name.

The truth was he'd been thinking about the petite blonde ever since he walked out of the convenience store a little after three a.m. Leaving her had been harder than he might have expected, considering the woman was a stranger.

However, it went against his nature to leave someone in what he believed to be a dangerous situation. And as far as he was concerned, a young woman alone in a convenience store in the middle of the night was asking for trouble.

Joel would like to think he'd feel protective of anyone in the same situation, but something about Andi had caught his attention and held onto it. He was no stranger to beautiful women, and while she was charming with her wavy blonde hair and big blue eyes, that wasn't what drew him in.

It was her personality. She'd gotten called in to work someone else's shift in the middle of the night and showed up with a smile on her face and a cheerful attitude. She was friendly and bubbly, and he got the sense that what he saw was what he got with Andi. It was refreshing, given the fact he spent too much time dealing with people who were fake—inside and out.

Then something else occurred to him, and his pleasure at seeing her again morphed into anger. Dark circles under her eyes indicated she hadn't gotten much sleep last night, and he frowned. "Did you come straight from the convenience store to work here?"

"Yep," she replied, oblivious to the irritation her response sparked.

Where was this woman's family? Why was she working two jobs back-to-back like this? Didn't she have anyone to help her?

She mentioned her brother but no one else.

He reached out before he could think better of it and ran the tip of one finger under her eye. "You're tired." They certainly didn't know each other well enough for him to touch her, but Andi didn't shy away.

Instead, she lifted one shoulder casually and gave him another dose of that gorgeous smile. "It's okay. You're one of my last rooms. I'm actually getting off a little bit early today. I had a lot of rooms with Do Not Disturb signs." As she said that, she waved jazz hands to celebrate. "There is definitely a nap in my plans for this afternoon."

"Good," he said, though her reassurance didn't make him feel much better. "You can mark this room off your list as well. I'm good on towels."

"How was your brunch?" she asked, peering around him as if she wanted to make sure he really was okay without her cleaning his room.

"Successful," he answered succinctly.

"That's good. I know you said you're here for business, but have you had a chance to do any sightseeing?"

He shook his head, pleased that she seemed as anxious to keep the conversation between them going as he was. If he'd been smart, he would have asked her to clean the room just so he could be with her a few minutes longer.

Joel had never been so overwhelmed by such an immediate

attraction. He was definitely succumbing to lust at first sight, where Andi was concerned. "I'm afraid there won't be time for that on this trip, though I have been trying to hit some good local restaurants at mealtimes rather than ordering room service. Got any suggestions?"

Her eyes lit up. "You absolutely have to go to Pat's Pub. It has the best food and ambiance, and the waitstaff is top-notch, second to none in the entire city." She giggled, then confided, "I wait tables there."

"Are you fucking kidding me?" Joel didn't even bother to hide his dark scowl, and her smile wavered.

She worked three jobs?

"Um," she stumbled, taken aback by the vehemence in his voice.

"I can't imagine working such long hours is good for you, Andi." Joel was fighting hard to keep a lid on the part of him that was compelled to swoop in and take charge of this woman's life. It was a foolish notion, considering they'd just met, and he had no right to do so. The problem was it appeared no one else was doing it, and...well...goddammit, he wanted to. He'd have to analyze that compulsion later, or maybe he should pretend it wasn't there.

He was well aware of his overly dominant personality, and while that trait had served him well in his career, it had never crossed over into his personal life.

Not until Andi.

"What's that saying?" She was clearly trying to put them back on more steady ground. "No rest for the wicked."

Joel took a couple of deep breaths, his impulse to help her suddenly overridden by a more powerful desire. One that was ignited by her comment. He leaned against the doorjamb and crossed his arms. "And are you wicked?" he asked in a deep, dark tone.

He didn't think she meant the smile she gave him to be one of pure seduction, but damn if it didn't nearly bring him to his knees.

"I'd like to be," she confided with outright honesty. "But

there's not much time in my schedule to be naughty."

"Jesus," Joel breathed.

She blushed as if she hadn't meant to cross that line. "Well, if you're good to go," she said, turning to her cart.

"When do you work at Pat's Pub?" he asked, anxious to see her again before he left town.

"Tonight."

It was the best and the worst thing she could have said because while he looked forward to seeing her, there was no question in his mind now that he was about to become a part of Andi's life. God help the woman.

He stood straighter. "Tonight?"

"Yeah," she said cautiously, as if she could tell the tide had turned, but she didn't have a clue why. So the clever girl decided on a quick escape. "I have a couple more rooms to take care of. Will I, um, see you tonight?"

Joel nodded. "You will."

Wild horses wouldn't keep him away.

* * *

Joel glanced around Pat's Pub, and he could instantly see why Andi had spoken so highly of it. The place was inviting, and from the camaraderie shared by the patrons sitting around the bar, it was clear the pub was popular with the locals. He could imagine large groups gathering here on Sundays in the fall to watch football on the big screen TVs or popping in after work on Fridays for a weekend-launching happy hour.

The bartender noticed him standing by the door. "You can grab a seat anywhere," he called out with a smile.

Joel looked around for Andi, wanting to sit in her section. He hoped to entice her to join him during her break and planned to leave her one hell of a tip. Given that she was working three jobs, money was obviously a concern for her.

Joel claimed a table near a small makeshift stage, nodding his thanks when the bartender walked over and handed him a menu.

"Welcome to Pat's Pub. I'm Padraig. Haven't seen you here before. You live in Baltimore, or are you just passing through?"

"Just passing through," Joel confided. "I met one of your waitresses, Andi, earlier today, and she suggested I give the place a try. I was hoping to sit in her section," he added.

"Well, I think you're about as close to her section as you can get." Padraig nodded toward the stage. "She's not waiting tables tonight. She's singing."

Joel glanced toward the stage, noting the tatty guitar set on its stand and the lone microphone. "She sings?"

"She's got one of the most beautiful voices I've ever heard. And my aunt is Teagan Collins."

It wasn't often that someone could genuinely shock Joel, but Padraig had managed when he casually dropped his famous aunt's name.

"Teagan...Collins." Joel was no stranger to the music industry. Hell, he'd been working as a music producer for twelve years. Teagan Collins was one of the biggest names there was. She and her husband, Sky Mitchell, have owned the top of the charts for the better part of three decades.

Suddenly, a light went on.

"Pat's Irish Pub," Joel murmured. He'd watched a documentary on the life of Sky and Teagan several years ago. The pub was mentioned not only as the place where Teagan and Sky met but also as a sort of jumping board for other musicians. Hunter Maxwell had gotten his start here as a pub singer, and while she wasn't discovered here, Aubrey Summers, the pop sensation, had married into the family and was reported to drop into the pub from time to time to give an impromptu show.

"You've heard of us?" Padraig was obviously pleased by that.

Joel nodded. "I'm a music producer. This pub has quite the reputation when it comes to showcasing talented musicians."

"Yeah, well, the truth is we've just been lucky. Talent seems to find its way to our doorstep," Padraig said humbly. "You really a music producer?"

"I am."

Padraig sighed. "Damn. Looks like I'm about to lose a great waitress." He gave Joel a wink. "What can I get you to drink?"

Joel ordered a National Bohemian beer—when in Rome—and Padraig returned to the bar.

Over the next hour, more patrons made their way into the pub, more than Joel would have expected, given it was a Sunday night. When Padraig delivered his food, he confided they were all there to hear Andi, bragging that she'd more than doubled the Sunday traffic since she'd started performing that night.

He had polished off his second beer and a plateful of the greatest fish and chips he'd ever eaten when Andi walked into the pub. She made her way to the stage, stopping to greet several people along the way.

"Joel," she said with delight when she spotted him there. "You came."

He stood up and gave her a quick hug. He wasn't sure why it felt like they'd already progressed to that point, but Andi hugged him back, so the familiarity was shared. "It was a great recommendation."

She glanced down at his empty plate. "Fish and chips? Excellent decision. They're killer, aren't they? I swear the cook, Riley Collins, is the best in the city."

"Collins? She's related to Padraig?"

"Yes. The Collins family has owned and operated this pub forever. It started with Patrick Collins and his wife, Sunday. Then some of their kids, and now there's a lot of the third generation working here as well, Padraig included." Andi clearly adored the Collins family. "Are you hanging out for a little while? I'm about to start my set."

"Wouldn't miss it."

She smiled at his response, then climbed the stage, tuning her guitar for a minute before she started playing. For an hour, she sang an array of music, from popular bar tunes everyone sang along to and a few songs she'd written herself.

Joel was blown away. He'd known halfway through the first song Padraig had been right because there was no way Joel would allow someone as talented as Andi to continue working three dead-end jobs. Not when she was so obviously destined for much bigger things.

When her set ended, she rose and walked right over to his table. "You stayed."

He pointed to the chair. "Can you join me for a little while?"

She nodded. "Yeah. I usually take a fifteen-minute break. Then I'll do another set. I only do two on Sunday nights."

Padraig walked over to hand her a glass of water. "Great job, Andi. As always. I've had a couple people ask if you're going to sing 'Bigger Dreams' tonight?"

Andi lit up. "Seriously? Yeah. Of course, I'll sing it. Wow."

Padraig returned to the bar, leaving Joel to wonder about the request. "Bigger Dreams?"

"It's a song I wrote. Usually, people request the covers, so I'm thrilled they want to hear one of mine."

"You perform here a lot?"

"Just Fridays and Sundays. Then I wait tables the rest of the week."

Joel sighed. "You're going to work yourself to death at this rate."

Andi didn't seem to share his concern. "It's worth it."

"Why?" Joel asked, curious about what was driving her to work so damn hard.

"I told you why. Because of my brother. Dylan wants to go to college. That's not cheap, and there's no way I'm letting a lack of money be the reason he can't attend. He's done without enough in his life."

"And what about you?"

"What about me?" she asked confused.

"Aren't you doing without things, too?"

She waved his question away like it was ridiculous. It wasn't, and her response tweaked the alpha in him that wanted to demand she take better care of herself.

"Where are your parents?" Joel knew it was a personal question, probably too personal, considering they hadn't even known each other for twenty-four hours. Still, he needed to know what he was up against if he hoped to convince her to give up her three jobs and take a chance on a new career, recording her music.

"My dad split when I was nine. Mom was pregnant with Dylan at the time. She did the best she could...for a while. She has a drinking problem," Andi admitted.

"So you pay the bills." His statement wasn't a question, but Andi answered it as if it was.

"Mom chips in sometimes, but holding down a job isn't really one of her strengths." Andi gave him a rueful grin as if she was ashamed of herself for saying something negative about her mother.

Meanwhile, he felt the need to meet her mom and read her the riot act for allowing her daughter to not only carry the weight of the family on her slim shoulders but also put herself in dangerous situations to do so. Andi had no business working in that convenience store in the middle of the night.

"To be honest," Andi added, "the nights I sing here don't feel like work. My music is my happy place, so having the opportunity to play my guitar and sing the songs I've written for an audience feels like a gift."

"You realize you're talented enough to record. Have you never considered pursuing a career in music?"

She laughed as if the idea was preposterous.

"I wasn't joking," he said, too seriously. This woman worked too hard for her family without giving a second thought to herself. Didn't she have any dreams? "What do you wish for, Andi? In life," he clarified.

She tilted her head. "I told you. I want my brother to go to college."

"No." Joel shook his head. "That's your brother's dream, not yours."

Andi sighed, and for the first time since he had met her, that ever-present smile on her face faded. "Dreams are for people with money, Joel. I've learned it's smart to keep my aspirations smaller, more achievable. I need to get back on stage. Thanks for the chat. I hope the rest of your business in Baltimore is successful." She used the word he'd said to describe his brunch meeting. "Goodbye."

It was apparent she expected him to leave, but she didn't know him well enough to understand that their conversation was nowhere near finished. Andi thought walking away would end the uncomfortable topic, but she was about to get her first lesson in who he was. Because Joel was a stubborn son of a bitch.

He spent the next hour listening to her sing, falling more and more in love with her voice—and God help him, maybe even Andi. He found himself imagining a future *for* her since she refused to dream for herself.

When she sang the requested song, "Bigger Dreams," he didn't doubt that Andi had the potential to become as big a star as Teagan Collins.

As the last strains of the song faded away, she rose, thanking everyone for coming, then packed up her guitar.

"You're still here."

He liked that she sounded pleased by that.

"I am. Are you heading out?"

She nodded. "Yeah. I don't live too far away. I usually walk."

Joel bit his tongue as he looked out into the dark night. "You have a penchant for living a dangerous life, don't you?"

A small crinkle formed between her eyebrows as if she was confused by his comment.

"It's not safe for a woman to walk home alone at night," he added to clarify. "Would you like to share a cab with me?"

He was proud of himself for making his words a request when all he really wanted to do was tell her she was going to let him see her home safely.

"Sure. That would be nice. I'm beat. Only managed to squeeze in a three-hour nap after leaving the hotel, so I'm struggling from missing a night of sleep."

He frowned. "You didn't sleep at all last night?"

"When I got home after my shift here, Barbie called to ask me to cover for her at the store. It's no big deal. Mo' money," she joked as his scowl grew darker. "Plenty of time to sleep when I'm dead."

He didn't laugh. Instead, he reached out, taking Andi's guitar case from her, then grasping her other hand. The moment their palms touched, an electric spark traveled along his skin. His body already knew what his head was only just starting to wrap itself around.

This woman was his.

Joel was no stranger to relationships, but he was a hell of a lot less familiar with love. He'd always pushed the emotion off, claiming he didn't have time for it, too obsessed with his career.

Now, all bets were off. Because he didn't just want Andi in the recording studio, he wanted her in his bed.

They waited on the sidewalk outside the pub for a few minutes, neither speaking, just holding hands and enjoying the peaceful night air.

When the Uber arrived, they climbed in, and she gave the man her address. Joel paid attention to the route, bothered that she had walked these dark streets alone for too many nights.

That wouldn't be happening again.

If Andi's family didn't care enough to make sure she was safe, he was stepping in and taking over.

As they pulled up in front of a run-down apartment building, Andi thanked him for the ride and tried to give him cash to pay half the fare. He told her to put her money away.

"I'm in Baltimore until Tuesday afternoon. I'd like to see you again. Any chance you could take a night off to go out to dinner with me?"

Andi nodded. "Mondays are my nights off at the pub anyway. I'm finished at the convenience store by three."

"Perfect. I'll pick you up here at six?"

"I'd like that."

The two of them got out of the car together, Joel asking the driver to wait while he walked her to the front door. Once there, he cupped her cheeks in his hands and bent toward her. She was a good foot shorter than his six-three frame.

"Good night, Andi." He sealed those parting words with a soft kiss, loving the feeling of Andi's hands gripping his waist. When they parted, he rested his forehead against hers. "See you tomorrow night?"

"Yes," she whispered. "I can't wait."

He couldn't either.

Once she was inside, Joel returned to the car, pulling out his phone as he planned their date and a lot more. She worked too hard with too little time or money to do anything nice for herself.

As of right now, that changed because he intended to spoil her, to make every wild hope she'd never dared to dream a reality.

He wanted to show her the world, but more than that, he wanted to be by her side every step of the way.

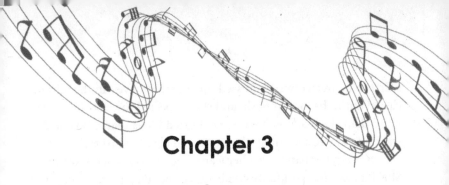

Chapter 3

Andi walked downstairs, silently loving the way Joel's hand rested on the small of her back. It was a protective gesture, something she'd never experienced before. Andi had never had a lot of time to date.

Sure, she'd gone out with guys in high school and since then... sometimes to see a movie, sometimes just for drinks after work.

Dating those guys, however, felt different from dating Joel.

For one thing, he was older than she was, a real man, mature and experienced, while the guys she'd gone out with had been her age, though they'd acted and seemed younger. Less suave, more dude-like.

Andi gasped when they reached the street and saw the limousine parked out front. The driver was standing near the back door, and as she glanced around her neighborhood, she saw more than a few curious faces—from windows and on the street—peering in her direction. Limos weren't a regular thing on her street, let alone one that was stopped rather than merely driving through after making what had to be a wrong turn.

She thanked the driver as he opened the door, climbing in and taking in the soft leather seats and the bar along one side of the vehicle. Joel followed her in.

"I've never been in a limo," she admitted, suddenly feeling slightly self-conscious about her outfit. She was wearing black jeans and a white blouse—the best clothes she had. She hadn't had time to shop for anything else, and even if she had, she couldn't have afforded anything she might consider "limo-worthy."

Joel was wearing navy blue pants and a white button-down

shirt, so he wasn't overly dressed up either. But even in the fairly casual outfit, he looked posh, and she suspected the clothing cost more than she made in a week. He looked like a man who could walk into any restaurant in the world and blend in just right.

She ran her hands over her jeans, her palms suddenly sweaty. She'd looked forward to this date all day, her daydreams running rampant as she played over his sweet, almost chaste goodbye kiss last night. She didn't have a clue how he'd managed to make a gentle kiss so damn hot, but it had triggered an arousal that had her tossing and turning most of the night—despite the fact she was tired as hell.

"Do you think," she started, before stopping. "Am I dressed up enough?" she forced herself to ask.

Joel didn't even bother to look at her outfit, his gaze locked on her face. "You look beautiful, Andi."

She'd never considered herself the type of woman who needed compliments about her looks or anything else. She figured it was good enough as long as she liked the woman looking back at her in the mirror.

But hearing those words from Joel warmed her soul and made her feel...beautiful.

"Thank you." She rubbed her hands on her thighs again, the action drawing Joel's attention.

"Are you nervous?" He plucked one of her hands up, clasping it in his.

"A little. I don't have a lot of time to date. I couldn't tell you the last time I've gone out with someone."

"I don't date much either," he confessed.

She was surprised by that. "Really?"

"Like you, my work keeps me busy." Joel lifted her hand and kissed it. "So I'm going to have to make sure this is a date we'll both remember."

"I'm pretty sure I'm never going to forget being picked up in a limo," she said, giggling.

"You deserve to be taken out and spoiled. You work too hard."

He'd said the same thing to her countless times yesterday, every time with that same thread of concern in his tone.

"I don't mind hard work," she said softly.

Joel didn't respond to that. Instead, he bent forward, pulling a bottle of champagne out of a chiller, popping the cork with an ease that told her this wasn't his first rodeo. He poured each of them a glass, then tapped his against hers.

"To first dates," he said.

She smiled, secretly loving how he called it a first date, like he expected there might be more. The pragmatist in her knew this was it—a one-off—but the dreamer couldn't help but hope he might want to see her again the next time he traveled to Baltimore.

The ride to the restaurant was pleasant. They talked about the unseasonably warm weather they've been having in Baltimore and sipped their champagne. By the time they reached the restaurant, Andi's nervousness was gone because Joel was easy to be with.

Andi was a friendly person by nature, but she'd never felt such an instant connection with anyone before.

The driver pulled up to the front entrance, and Andi's concern about her outfit crept back in as she watched two very elegantly dressed couples enter the fancy restaurant.

Stepping out onto the curb, Joel reached in to help her, tucking his arm around her waist to draw her close.

"Stop worrying. You look lovely, Andi. There's no dress code. Trust me when I say you'll be the most beautiful woman in there."

"Are you a mind reader?" she joked.

He shook his head. "Not usually, but with you..." He shrugged. "Would it sound strange to say it feels like I've known you for years, not just a day?"

"It wouldn't. Because I feel the same way."

He kept his arm around her waist as they entered the restaurant, the hostess guiding them to a cozy, private corner booth. While Andi knew of this restaurant—one of the classiest in the city—she'd never stepped foot in it. Taking a peek at the menu drove home exactly why.

"This is..." She stopped herself from remarking on the prices, uncertain if that would be rude. Joel rode around in a limo and selected this place, so obviously he could afford it. Regardless, she wasn't comfortable spending so much on a meal.

Once again, Joel seemed to read her thoughts. "Don't look at the prices, Andi. Just the descriptions of the food. Pick what you want based on what sounds good, not what it costs."

There was no way she could do that. "I'm not super hungry," she lied.

Joel got that look on his face—the one that seemed dangerous but not threatening—as he took the menu away from her. "Do you eat red meat?"

She nodded.

"Is there anything you don't like?"

She shook her head. "I'm not picky."

"Good. Then I'm ordering for you."

Her feminist inside wanted to protest his heavy-handedness, but the girl who'd been taking care of herself since birth loved the idea of handing control over to someone else for one night. It was exhausting to constantly make all the decisions for her family. It fell to Andi not only to pay for the groceries but also to buy them. She'd become very adept at meal prepping so that Mom and Dylan always had dinners prepared on nights when she had to work.

The idea of letting Joel decide what she ate tonight felt strangely freeing.

"I'd like that," she whispered.

Joel's features softened, and she sensed that she'd given him the correct response.

When the waiter arrived, Joel ordered a bottle of wine for them and their meals, which sounded mouth-wateringly delicious.

Once they were alone again, he placed his arm along the back of the booth behind her, turning so that they were sitting close.

"I have a confession to make," he murmured.

Shit. She should have known this was too good to be true. Things like this didn't happen to her. God...he was probably married or engaged or facing indictment for something horrible. Her mind went wild, imagining all the bad things.

"What is it?" she finally forced herself to ask.

"I haven't been able to stop thinking about your performance last night. Andi. You're wasting your talent in that little pub."

She breathed a sigh of relief, even as her heart swelled. "That's nice of you to say."

Joel picked up a lock of her hair, toying with it in a way that had her nipples budding and her panties going damp. "I'm not blowing smoke up your ass. I mean it. Your voice is incredible, and the songs you've written deserve to be shared with the world. Tell me about 'Bigger Dreams' because that song has been playing on repeat in my head all day."

Andi never ceased to be amazed when someone said they liked a song she'd written, but for some reason, coming from Joel, it felt like an even bigger deal.

Usually, she brushed off the question of where the inspiration for that song came from because the story was too personal. Her typical response was something generic like "the words just came to her," but tonight, she wanted to share the story with Joel. "The chorus of the song is the last words my dad said to me before he split."

He frowned, and she could practically hear him replaying the words in her head. "Andi," he started.

She cut him off, repeating the lines from the song. "My dreams are bigger than this place. Wake up every morning. Don't recognize my face. I don't mean to hurt you, but I gotta go. Gotta go."

She sang the song at the pub a couple of times a week, so the repetition had allowed her to distance herself from the emotions they evoked. Tonight, however, the feelings were crashing around her, the pain causing her chest to tighten.

"I'm sorry," he murmured, giving her a comforting kiss on the cheek.

She considered his response, expecting the pity in his tone to bother her. It didn't.

It comforted her in ways she didn't expect, encouraging her to share even more. Her dad was one of those topics she avoided like the plague because talking about him, thinking about him, hurt, but she didn't want to do that tonight. "You know, my memories of him prior to his leaving were really good. He was a loving, funny father, always attentive, and unlike some dads, he didn't mind playing games with me or taking me to the park or teaching me how to play the guitar."

"He taught you to play?" Joel asked.

She nodded. "The old guitar I use during my performances at the pub was his. It was the only thing he left behind."

Joel reached out, his finger stroking her cheek, and she was surprised to realize he was wiping away a tear.

She was crying?

She sniffled, determined to swallow the tears down. For one thing, she never cried, and for another, she was on a first date with the hottest, coolest, nicest man she'd met in...well, ever. So crying within ten minutes of sitting down to dinner was definitely a stupid thing to do.

"Don't do that, Andi."

She frowned, confused. "Do what?"

"Pretend it doesn't hurt. Hide your feelings from me."

Andi shook her head, trying to find the right response to that. "We just met, Joel. We barely know each other. I don't understand why I feel compelled to tell you all this. For God's sake, I've never even talked about Dad to Dylan, and he's my brother."

"I'm glad you're comfortable enough with me to share. I want to hear it, want to know everything there is to know about you."

She blotted her eyes with her napkin. Despite his reassurances, she took several deep breaths, pulling herself together. She was an ugly crier, and she refused to screw up this night any more than she already had. "I've sung that song enough that I didn't think it could get to me like this," she admitted.

He ran his fingers through her hair. "It's a powerful song.

That's why it speaks to people, why they want to hear it again."

"Maybe." Then, before she could think better of it, words she'd never said aloud slipped out. "I stopped dreaming after he left. You asked me the other night what I wanted. I meant what I said. My dreams are small because I don't ever want to hurt Dylan the way Dad hurt me."

Joel frowned. "You don't really believe that you'd leave your brother behind in pursuit of a dream, do you?"

She wouldn't, but sometimes fears weren't logical.

"I might not know you well, Andi, but I know you well enough to know you would never walk away from Dylan. Jesus. You work yourself to the point of exhaustion so you can make his dreams come true. Why is it okay for him to dream big but not you?"

She'd never looked at things from that perspective. "I don't know."

Joel rubbed his chin for a moment, his gaze locked with hers. She imagined this man—this veritable stranger—was the only person in the world with the ability to look into her eyes and see straight to her soul. "I asked you last night what your dreams were. I'm asking you again. And this time, I want you to put your fears aside, stop making excuses, and really think about what you would do with your life if you could choose anything."

Andi knew the answer, but years of pushing her dreams down deep was a hard thing to overcome. Her throat grew tight, and she wondered if she could speak, even if she tried.

"There's a quote I like," Joel said when she didn't respond. "From Thoreau. He said, Live the life you've imagined. I'm asking you to imagine that life, Andi. What's it look like?"

She licked her lips, then let it all spill out. "I want to sing. Want to get married and have a family. I want financial security, and I want enough money to be able to make my brother's dream come true, too."

Joel listened as Andi opened up, her answers lining up with the new list of goals he'd created ever since seeing her in that convenience store. From the first moment he saw her, he knew she was special, and when he heard her sing, it was as if her soul was calling out to his in a way he'd never experienced before.

He leaned toward her, unable to resist being as close to her as he could. He kissed her, this one lingering longer than the one he'd given her last night. Their lips parted, and he stole a taste, exploring, aware he could kiss her for the rest of his life and never want for anything more.

When they parted, he cupped her cheek in his hand. "Those dreams sound achievable to me."

She scoffed, but he didn't relent. He'd made quite a few calls today, setting Andi's dreams in motion.

"I want you and Dylan to come visit me in New York next weekend."

Andi started to shake her head, and he knew immediately why she was refusing.

"Take the time off, Andi. I'll show you around the city, and then..." This was the part he hadn't told her, the thing she didn't know. "Then, I'm taking you to a recording studio. You're going to record 'Bigger Dreams'."

"What do you mean record it?"

He gave her a crooked grin. "You never asked me what I do for a living." She tilted her head, curious. "I'm a music producer."

Her eyes widened.

"I want to help you achieve your dreams, but more than that, I want to keep seeing you."

"Joel," she began.

He placed his finger on her lips. "Don't say no. Think about it. I'm offering you a way to make all those wild hopes and dreams of yours come true."

"We only just met, Joel."

He couldn't argue with that, but he was old enough to understand that it didn't matter. "I know that. This is going too fast, but I don't care. This," he said, pointing to himself, then her. "This is powerful, overwhelming. It's also right. I knew it from the second I met you, even before I heard you sing."

Andi bit her lower lip, then said the sweetest words he'd ever heard. "I felt it, too."

"This is just the beginning of something incredible. Something perfect."

This time, Andi initiated the kiss, all shades of hesitance gone. It was a hungry kiss, full of passion and desire.

"Say yes, Andi. To visiting New York. To recording the song. To giving me a chance to prove to you just how right this thing between us is."

He held his breath as she gave him that same sweet smile that had stolen his heart and said the greatest word he'd ever heard.

"Yes."

A
DIRTY
PROPOSAL

JAINE DIAMOND

About the Author

Jaine Diamond is a Top 50 Amazon US and a Top 5 international bestselling author. She writes contemporary romance featuring badass, swoon-worthy heroes endowed with massive hearts, strong heroines armed with sweetness and sass, and explosive, page-turning chemistry.

She lives on the beautiful west coast of Canada with her real-life romantic hero and daughter, where she reads, writes and makes extensive playlists for her books while binge drinking tea.

www.jainediamond.com

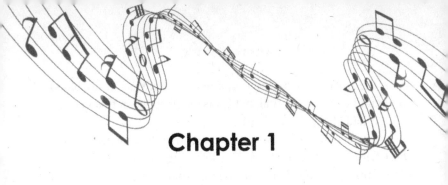

Chapter 1

JUDE

8:56 pm.

I rolled up behind the arena on my Harley and backed into my designated spot next to one of the crew access doors. I could hear the thunder of music right through the roar of my bike from a couple of city blocks away and now I felt it pounding through the concrete.

The Players were onstage, rocking out one of their biggest hit songs, "Panic Room". It was the final song on their set list for tonight.

Which meant Dirty would soon be taking the stage.

Almost time.

I took a gut-deep breath, grounding myself as I set my boots on the pavement, even as the anticipation started to build.

It was my greedy impatience to see her, to touch her, combined with the usual buzz of adrenaline. The one that accompanied every live event, every concert, no matter how big or small.

And this show would be *huge*. For many reasons.

As outwardly calm and in control as I would appear, even I couldn't help being affected by the palpable excitement of all those people—many of them my close friends. My family.

And of course, my woman.

Roni.

As I slipped off my helmet and swiped a hand through my

hair, the thrill of embarking on a new tour stirred in my blood. It would be chaos, as usual, but I was comfortable in that chaos.

It had always been chaos.

I'd devoted my life, without regret, to protecting my rock star best friends and their band. Not knowing, when we all started down this road together as little more than kids, how successful the band would become.

Nowadays, we had partners and kids and babies in the mix, but we also had more resources. More money, a bigger team.

But all that meant was the shows and the tour got bigger, too.

Tonight was the first night of the new world tour. A double bill, the Players and Dirty, rocking our home arena in Vancouver before both bands headed out on the road. I'd go wherever Dirty went, as their head of security. Wherever my best friend, lead guitarist Jesse Mayes, went, as his primary bodyguard.

That meant traveling several continents over the next year-and-a-half while Dirty rocked sold-out concerts all over the world, with the Players and with other bands.

No matter how far and wide we traveled, though, Dirty always preferred kicking off the tour as close to home as possible. The relationship they'd built with the hometown fans over the past fifteen years was sacred. It meant a lot, to all of us, to have the opportunity to keep doing what we loved with our lives. And none of us would be doing what we did without Dirty's diehard fans perpetually clamoring for more.

So, this wasn't just a night of music. It was a night of gratitude and celebration.

But this show meant even more to me, personally, than the first night on any given tour—and not just because it happened to be my birthday.

Tonight, we had something special planned.

The moment I swung my leg off my bike, though, I could tell that all those carefully laid plans had somehow gone to shit.

A petite woman with sleek dark hair had just slipped out the door to greet me like she knew I was coming, and when my eyes locked with hers, I saw it on her face. After working together for so many years, Maggie Omura and I had an almost disturbing ability to read and anticipate one another.

But maybe that was just because we were both so damn predictable.

"What is it," I said flatly.

"Happy birthday?" she hedged.

"Don't bother. Tell me what's wrong."

Maggie's pretty face twitched in a way I didn't like. She never beat around the bush with me. One reason we worked so well together.

My guts were dropping into free-fall already, because I fucking knew.

"I'm so sorry, Jude."

Maggie didn't apologize much, either. Mainly because she rarely had shit to apologize for. As co-manager of Dirty, she was reliable and professional in all things, and as wife of Dirty's lead singer, Zane Traynor, she was majorly invested.

Her face twitched again, and I realized she was chewing the inside of her mouth.

"Jesus, Maggie. What happened?"

"I'm so sorry," she repeated. Then she forced it out. "We lost the signs."

I dragged a hand over my face. This was the last thing I wanted to hear. But it was not like Maggie to fuck up. "Seriously?"

"I'm getting the crew to try to pull together some paint and plywood or something, to make new ones," she babbled, "but I don't know if they can pull it off in time. Plywood might be too heavy, it could be a liability for injury, because they need to be big enough to be visible, and the paint probably won't dry in time. We need to get everything in place before Dirty hits the stage or there's no way we can—"

"Breathe, Maggie."

She blew out a breath. "I have never felt so fucking sick. I can't believe we let you down." Her pretty gray eyes filled with tears.

This was new.

I almost didn't know what the fuck to do for a long-ass minute as we just stared at each other.

Then I slung an arm around her shoulders, tugging her to me for a hug. "Just stop it, okay?"

She sucked in a breath and nodded.

I didn't want Maggie falling the fuck apart—was that even a thing?—but shit, I felt kinda sick, too.

The door opened behind her and Jesse stepped out, dressed in his stage clothes, a ripped T-shirt that was really more rip than shirt, and black leather pants. "Jude, man. Happy birthday." I released Maggie to accept the hug he offered. My best friend gave me a tight, sympathetic squeeze. "Zane just told me about the signs. We can figure out something else, though."

"It's okay. Maybe we'll just do it another night..."

But another night wouldn't be *this* night.

It wouldn't be here, at home. It wouldn't be the first night of the tour, it wouldn't be my birthday, and Roni's mom wouldn't be here with her.

I wanted this to be as special as it could be, and tonight was the way to make that happen.

"Maybe we can play a special song instead," Jesse offered, as the door opened again and Brody Mason, manager of Dirty and the Players, stepped out, grave-faced.

"Happy birthday, brother." Brody, who was also one of my best friends, swept me into a hug, too, slapping my back. "What's the word? Maggie said the signs are in the wind."

"Yeah. Apparently so." I slapped his back and released him. Really didn't need all this *someone-just-died* energy. I didn't like being the center of attention, good or bad.

"I was just saying, we can do a song instead," Jesse put in, wearing the same gravely sympathetic look Brody was wearing. Maggie just looked sick. "You know, for Roni."

"No." I shook my head, deciding; Dirty had a show to play and I really didn't want my special birthday request to become a distraction. I also didn't want Zane doing my job for me where my woman was concerned. "Thanks, but I don't want that."

"You sure?" Brody raised an eyebrow. "That would be the easiest fix."

I glanced at Maggie. "Look—no offense, Maggie—but I really don't want a man who was once with my woman, even before she was officially my woman, serenading her on my behalf." Even if that man—Maggie's husband, Zane—was one of my best friends.

"And who could blame you," she said dryly.

"Right." Jesse rubbed the back of his neck, looking sheepish. "Didn't think of that."

"Then we'll find another way," Brody said firmly.

"I'm gonna talk to Talia again," Maggie said with determination. She promised me, "We'll fix this." Then she got on her phone and Brody opened the door for her, patting my shoulder as I followed her into the bowels of the arena.

Talia was the assistant manager of the Players. She was also Roni's best friend.

I trusted her and Maggie to do what they could.

But in all my envisioning of how this night would go down, I didn't envision any backup plan. Really didn't think I needed one, what with Maggie and Talia here to help me pull this off.

Major fucking mistake.

But maybe the whole idea was stupid anyway. Too old school.

I should've come up with something more high-tech yet simple. Something that didn't rely on so many damn moving parts and so many people, many of them strangers.

"We'll figure something out, man." Jesse squeezed my shoulder. "Do you want to just come onstage with me? Or I could sing her something?"

"I don't know. Let me think on it. Maybe this was a stupid idea, anyway."

"Brother. Don't give up. Brody and Maggie will come up with something."

Yeah. They usually did.

I glanced back, but Brody and Maggie had both disappeared. I could hear the Players onstage, muffled, shouting *thank you's* to the roaring crowd as they ended their set.

I slapped Jesse on the back. "Let me go find Roni."

"Sure, brother. I'm here when you need me."

I left him and headed deeper into the arena, checking in with Ronan, the Players' head of security. And greeting some of the guys on my crew, a mix of the clean-cut professionals we'd pulled from Ronan's VIP security company and some patched brothers from my motorcycle club, the West Coast Kings MC.

I'd always been careful to make sure that the two sides of my life, the MC and the music industry, didn't interfere with each other. They overlapped only in this way: when I hired guys from the club to work security for the bands.

Unfortunately, both sides of my life had interfered with my relationship with Roni, even when I didn't mean for them to.

Maybe because, once upon a time, I'd chosen both of them over her, when I shouldn't have.

I'd been so fucking stupid when we were young. Practically drove her into Zane's arms that one time they hooked up so many years ago. Into the arms of other men, too. I'd left her to go on tour when I didn't yet realize she was the best thing that could ever happen to me.

In truth, from the moment she crossed my path in our teens, like a black-haired Lolita sucking on her lollipop, to the first time I kissed her goodbye to leave on Dirty's first tour...to the moment I finally swore to her, years later, "You and me, darlin', we're goin' down the longest road there is," Veronica Webber had owned my heart.

There were many heartbreaks in between.

Many times I lost her.

Many times I fucked it all up.

Maybe that first time she came to kiss me goodbye before I left on tour, I should've just said *Come with me, V.*

How awesome would that have been?

Somehow, these days, it was hard to remember ever being here, backstage, without her.

When I finally found her backstage, just standing in one of the endless concrete corridors in the bowels of the arena, talking to her mom and one of Brody's managerial underlings, the sight of her sucked the breath out of me like it so often did. I'd know that sexy silhouette anywhere, the thick black hair in loose waves around her face and shoulders, the confident tilt of her chin.

As a bodyguard and a biker, I'd survived more than my fair share of dangerous situations with dangerous people. But I'd never known anyone as dangerous as Veronica Webber.

Her curves were poured into sleek black leggings and a cropped black cashmere sweater, with cherry-red high heels. She didn't wear much makeup, just a sweep of her signature black eyeliner and red lipstick to match the heels.

In skimpy lingerie or sweats, she was the sexiest woman I'd ever seen.

My woman.

The mother of my son, and if I was even luckier in the future, more children.

By the time I reached her, nodded a hello to her mom and swept her into my arms, electricity danced across my skin. When she cried, "Jude!" like she hadn't seen me in weeks—it had been a few hours—and pressed her lush body against me, her fingers digging into the hair at the nape of my neck, the electricity sizzled right through me.

"Gorgeous," I greeted her.

The faint thud of the music playing in the arena between sets and the dull roar of anticipation from the crowd underscored the fierce beating of my heart as I kissed her luscious lips, her gorgeous face, her soft neck. The last time I saw her she was in sweats, feeding our baby as she prepared to hand him off to his nanny so she could get cleaned up for work tonight. I was heading out the door, and I'd barely gotten to touch her, she'd had her hands so full.

Felt like the luckiest man in the world knowing I got to take her home tonight. And hopefully, we'd get a few sweet hours alone together while Julian was asleep.

"Happy birthday, baby," Roni purred in my ear, her lips brushing my skin. "I've got something for you."

"Mmm," I growled and gently bit her neck.

She squeezed me tighter and laughed her soft, husky laugh.

I pressed my face into her neck, inhaling deep; that goddamn sex kitten smell of hers that always did me in. I closed my eyes and savored it.

Savored *her*.

In moments like these, just luxuriating in the feel of her, her warmth and her smell and her soft breaths against my skin, I couldn't fucking believe she'd once been taken from me. While she was pregnant with our child.

Those torturous hours, when Roni was in danger, were the longest and the darkest of my life.

When she was kidnapped and held captive by the fucking Mafia.

When I didn't know where she was and I couldn't help her, couldn't protect her, trade my life for hers, *anything*.

I would've done fucking anything to save her.

My entire MC had searched for her, with my brother, Piper, our Vice President, at the helm, and I'd never felt more helpless, more out of control.

She was back in my arms, unharmed, within twenty-four hours. And here she was, still safe in my arms almost one year later. She'd had our baby, a healthy, strong baby boy, and I'd held her like this—tight, our hearts beating as one—as often as I could, every day that I'd had her back.

But it still didn't feel like enough.

I knew I could never make it up to her.

And I would never forgive myself.

My job was to protect those around me, and I'd failed the one person I loved most in the goddamn world. I'd failed to keep her safe. I'd failed to be her hero.

I'd failed to make it clear to her, every moment of every day, how much she meant to me.

She drew back just enough to look into my eyes and cupped my jaw with her soft hands. Her full lips quirked. "What is this sad vibe I'm getting on your birthday?"

I grunted. "I'm not sad. Just savoring."

She smiled tentatively. "Do you want your present?"

I gave her a heated look. "Later."

She smiled and kissed me, soft and so fucking hot, like her mom wasn't standing right there. But Cindy was distracted, chatting up one of the young crew guys; her forte.

When Roni pulled back to study me again, like she was making sure I was okay, I put my game face on. And as I looked into those gorgeous jade eyes of hers I knew, whatever it took, I had to make this beautiful thing happen tonight.

For her.

I had to make it clear—to Roni, to her mom, to the whole damn world—that she was protected. That she was loved, deeply and forever.

That she was mine.

And, that she was an integral part of the Dirty family. So the whole world would know from this night on: you do not fucking mess with Veronica Webber.

Veronica Grayson, if I had anything to say about it.

"Um, Jude?"

Maggie tapped my shoulder, breaking the heated spell. I was about five seconds from shoving Roni back against the wall and dry-humping her against it. She smirked, because she knew.

Maggie cleared her throat. "A word?"

"Better be good," I growled. When I tore my eyes from Roni to glance down at Maggie, the poor woman looked flushed, like she'd been running all over the place.

Maggie wasn't the type to break a sweat, considering she usually had all her shit under control. I almost felt guilty.

I kissed Roni's forehead and released her. "I'll be back, darlin'."

"Good." She smiled at me, her dazzling, sexy smile, and I forced myself to follow Maggie along the corridor, into a private corner.

"Good news," she told me, as soon as we were out of earshot. "Talia found the signs. She's—"

"What's this I hear about you calling it off?" Talia demanded from somewhere behind me. I felt a hand grip my bicep and nails dig in.

I glanced down into the face of a very annoyed-with-me blonde.

"I'm not—"

"You are *not* calling this off," she informed me. "This is for *Roni.*"

"I realize. So, let's—"

"She'd walk over broken glass for you, Jude Grayson. Barefoot. You don't back out on Roni. *Ever.* I won't have it."

I let her give me shit. Actually, I smiled. Roni had been fierce in protecting this girl. Nice to see it was coming back around.

When I was sure she was done, I told her, "Wouldn't dream of it, darlin'."

"Hmm." Talia frowned. "Well, then let's make this happen." She nodded at Maggie and turned on her heel. As she was walking away, she tossed back, "Oh, by the way. Happy birthday."

"Thank you."

I watched her, amused, as she strode over to Roni, and Roni smiled at whatever Talia said.

That smile on Roni's face made my insides warm. I fucking lived for it.

I was nothing but melted honey, gooey and sweet, in the woman's hands.

I wondered if she really knew how bad it was.

As the controlled chaos around me built, just before Dirty finally took the stage, I stood back to absorb it all, watching my friends and colleagues do their thing. Guys came and went, checking in with me, while my eyes remained locked on Roni.

Then I watched her lead her mom up the corridor to the stairs that would take them directly backstage and then to the side of the stage, where they'd watch the show.

At the last moment, Roni's head turned and her gaze swept the corridor behind her. Her green eyes caught mine and she hooked a questioning eyebrow at me, then lifted a finger and sassily beckoned me to follow her up the stairs.

Of course, I did.

I'd never wanted to be in the spotlight, and I didn't think Roni particularly did, either. But tonight, I was gonna shine a light on the woman I loved with an epic surprise that the whole world would see but she wouldn't see coming.

If all went according to plan, this birthday, my thirty-fifth, would be the best I ever had.

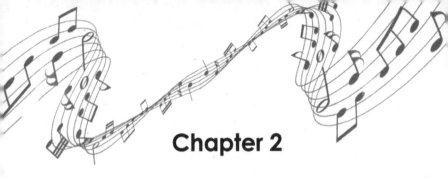

Chapter 2

<u>RONI</u>

I looked around into the dark, glimpsing the faces that flashed in and out of the shadows in the chaotic lighting from the stage. Crew members. Security. Friends and family with guest passes.

But I didn't see Jude.

I didn't feel him; his dark presence, solid and magnetic.

He'd been standing here at the side of the stage with me through the first song of Dirty's set, but he'd slipped away during the second and I wasn't sure where he'd disappeared to.

My mom stood on one side of me, beer in hand, loving the VIP treatment as she watched the show. One of my best friends, Jessa, and her husband, Brody, were on my other side. Usually, Jude would be right here with us the whole night.

Unless, of course, duty had called him away.

I had hoped there wouldn't be any security-related drama tonight.

I was thrilled about this show and the new tour, and I wanted it to be a great night for my man. It was his birthday, after all.

I wasn't sure why he was so broody tonight, but I'd sensed the tension in him. He'd tried to fool me with his stoic bodyguard-on-duty face, but I knew him far better than that. He was distracted, and that wasn't normal for Jude when he was working.

Would he tell me if something was brewing behind the scenes? Probably not until well after the issue was fixed, cleared up. He wouldn't want me to worry.

The thing he never seemed to quite understand was that I

didn't worry. Because I knew he had things under control.

Even when I was kidnapped...

A disturbing shiver ran through me as it always did at the memory of that Mafia creep shoving a gun in my back, gagging and handcuffing me in his car, and holding me prisoner. But even in that situation, dangerous as it was, especially since I was pregnant, I didn't worry. I was scared, yes. There were moments I was terrified. But I knew that Jude—and his many loyal club brothers in the Kings MC—would come through for me.

That they wouldn't rest until they got me back.

That they'd always protect me.

No matter what we'd been through, Jude had always made me feel safe like that.

It was one of the reasons I loved him so damn hard.

Because I could trust him. With my heart. With my life.

Onstage, Dirty was really revving up the show with one of my favorite songs—and one of their fans' favorite songs, "Dirty Like Me". It was heavy and hot, passionate, emotional, and had me longing for Jude.

I wrapped my arms around my waist and imagined he was holding me now.

I wondered, when moments like this—songs like this—took me back in time to our teenage years, if he really understood how madly in love with him I was.

And had always been.

Even though I'd fought it for so long when I was young and stubborn... Jude had always been *the one*.

I was scared of it back then.

But I was grateful for it now.

I couldn't possibly regret a single step on our long road here, because each step, forward and back, had gotten us to this place. Together.

I also wondered if he realized it was two years ago now that we'd bought our first house together, and what a milestone that was for me.

It was the first time I really felt like we were *family.*

Now, we literally had our own family. Our little Julian was almost six months old. Over the last few years, I'd worked my way up in my career to join Dirty's management team and for the first time, Jude and I were going on a whole world tour together—with Julian, too. No more back and forth traveling to see each other, or longing for one another long distance.

This would be our third tour since becoming a couple. But it was different now.

We were together, in every way. Colleagues. Peers. Friends.

Lovers.

Partners.

Parents.

And we were far more than any of those labels, too.

Jude Grayson was the love of my life and he always would be.

As I listened to this song that Dirty had written while I was hanging out with the band in their practice space, way back before the fancy world tours, I got crazy nostalgic. My eyes misted up.

I was not the girl who cried easily.

But how could I not feel teary-eyed right now?

Music had changed all our lives. Jessa and Brody. The band. And Jude and I, too. It gave a boy who was destined for trouble and a poor, overlooked girl a place to belong and a means to thrive.

Most of the members of the band onstage right now, idolized by so many, didn't travel an easy road to get where they were now. From losing parents too young to overcoming addiction, they'd been through some shit, and we'd been through it all with them.

I reached to take hold of Jessa's hand, and she squeezed mine. The two of us had been tight for so many years, it was still hard to fathom, sometimes, that we'd made it this far. So far from where we started.

Two girls without fathers.

One blessed with a talent for songwriting, and one armed with nothing but the determination to survive.

Together, as we watched her brother's band onstage, playing

a hit song she'd co-written, I wondered if she had moments when she felt like this; when she straight-up marveled over the beauty of it all. If she stood in awe of the fact that we'd made it all here, together.

And now we were lucky enough to have children, too. We'd come so damn far, and yet we were still *us*.

I loved being here with her.

With Jude.

And I couldn't wait to bring our kids along to these shows when they were older.

As the song ended, Zane hollered, "FUCK YEAH, VANCOUVER!" Which sent the crowd into a thunderous frenzy. Three songs in and thoroughly warmed up, it was the first time he'd addressed the crowd tonight.

I released Jessa's hand so we could clap along from the side stage.

Once the crowd had calmed enough that Zane could actually be heard over the noise again, he announced, "We're gonna kick this night off right, with a little fucking romance!" He paused for effect and the crowd went nuts again. "Strap in, kids!" he shouted. "And get ready to swoon! Jesse Mayes, do your thing!"

The crowd thundered their excitement again as Jesse grabbed the wireless mic off his stand and spoke into it. "I'll be right back. Zane, hold down the fort."

Zane looked at him like *What the fuck?* and laughter rippled across the crowd as Jesse walked off stage.

One of his guitar techs took his guitar from him, and he came straight over to me. It took me a weird delay to process that he was talking *to me*.

"We're doing a special surprise birthday thing for Jude," he said.

"Uh, okay? I don't know where he is."

"Don't worry." He held out his hand to me.

I blinked at him for a minute. Jude's rock star best friend, in the middle of his concert, holding out his hand to me. He wore leather pants, a sleeveless shirt, and shone with stage sweat, his thick whorls of dark hair a hot mess, and his brown eyes on me at once steady and sparkling.

I trusted Jesse, deeply, because he had Jude's trust.

I also knew he was up to something.

I could feel the crowd's expectations building and hear Zane laughing onstage. He'd been cracking jokes or something as Seth played a little background rhythm on his guitar. Everything was getting surreal as my heartbeat sped up and Jesse just stared at me and the crowd got louder.

"Jesse Mayes!" Zane bellowed. "Get your ass back out here! You got twenty thousand people waiting!"

Jesse raised an eyebrow at me, his hand still waiting for mine.

"It's for Jude," he reiterated.

Well, *fuck*.

I took his hand. He gripped mine, tight, and what could I do when he started walking back out onstage but go with him?

I glanced back over my shoulder to see Jessa and Brody grinning at me. "Where's Jude?" I called back to them, but my voice was lost in the noise and no one answered.

And why weren't *they* being dragged out here?

On fucking stage.

My breath caught in my throat as the awareness hit me.

Twenty thousand people...

Tingles swept through my body, from my scalp to the tips of my toes. It was knock-you-over stunning, the energy that radiated off the audience. I'd never felt anything like it.

And they were all looking at me.

Well, they were looking at the band, probably. But still.

I knew something was really getting weird when I found myself center stage with Jesse still holding my hand—and then he started talking *about me*. Into his mic. *To the crowd*.

"I'd like you all to meet Roni," he announced. "She's a friend of the band." He paused while the whole crowd made noise—for me—and I definitely felt my face grow hot.

Because now they probably *were* looking at me.

I didn't embarrass easily, but shit. I couldn't even focus on a single face in the crowd. It was just one giant, intimidating, pulsating blur of energy. I was holding onto Jesse's hand so tight, his fingers were probably turning blue.

"Not only does this lovely woman work with our management team to make all this happen..." Jesse swept his mic in a grand arc, indicating the entirety of the jam-packed arena. "But she's also the love of my best friend's life."

Oh, Jesus.

The crowd ate that up, cheering for me and my love life.

I sank my teeth into my lip and glanced around the stage, still looking for Jude. Weirdly, the rest of the band seemed to have vanished. I wasn't even sure when Seth's guitar had gone silent.

Jesse and I were standing here alone.

And I was very possibly about to pee myself.

I leaned into him. "What's going on?"

He didn't answer me.

Instead, he told the crowd, "My best friend, ever since I was a kid, is this big guy named Jude who's like a brother to me. He works very hard to look out for me and he always has. He doesn't like to be in the spotlight, but today's his birthday, so why don't we all shout 'Happy Birthday Jude' on the count of three? I want to hear ALL OF YOU, way in the back! One. Two. Three!" Jesse thrust his mic in the air and the audience shouted: "HAPPY BIRTHDAY JUDE!"

I laughed with nervous delight. This was amazing.

Where the hell was Jude?

Jesse brought the mic back around and said, "What about you, Roni? You want to say happy birthday to your man?"

Then he thrust the mic at me.

"Happy birthday Jude." My voice sounded hesitant and so *what-the-fuck-is-going-on-right-now*, the crowd laughed.

Into the mic, Jesse told me, "Now Jude has something he wants to say to you, Roni."

Me?

My knees were shaking now. Adrenaline and nerves were at war in my body as I struggled to just keep standing, keep breathing.

"You wanna let go of my hand or what?" Jesse asked me, right into the mic.

"No."

More laughter and crowd noise as Jesse pried his hand from my grip. Then he slipped behind me and said, "Just stand right there. Look out at the crowd."

I did as I was told, really fucking glad I didn't wear a short skirt tonight. There were like twenty thousand phones in the air documenting this right now, from every angle.

A shiver of something like elation ran through me.

Was this real?

"On the count of three," Jesse shouted at the crowd, "let's show Roni what Jude has to say to her. Ready? ONE. TWO. THREE!"

The split second Jesse said *three*, the lights went out. And man, that was eerie and electric. All that blackness surrounding me, and the sea of glowing phones...

Then lights shone out over the crowd.

A single spotlight shone on me onstage. My heart was thudding so hard in my chest I could barely draw a breath. I felt like I was my heart, thudding away up here, fleshy and raw, just silently witnessing this madness as I trembled on the edge of a heart attack.

The crowd noise had suddenly faded as people craned their necks to look around, to see what was going on. I watched as people halfway up the stands, in the beams of light, held up handmade signs in rows, with big letters on them—spelling out a message.

The first actual thoughts I pulled together were: *This is adorable! Jude did this? For me?*

The next one was: *Oh my god.*

The message, once it was intact, said: WILL YOU MARRY ME?

I buried my face in my hands as it hit me what was happening, and I felt his arms around me. Not Jesse. I would know the feel of my man's touch anywhere. The heat of him, his power and his gentleness, the raw silk of his skin.

I turned and fell into Jude's strong arms. He pulled me close, holding me tight as I buried my face in his chest, in the familiar scents of leather and clean cotton and Jude. I felt the beat of his heart thumping against me.

And suddenly there was nothing but me and Jude, holding each other as the lights went out again and the crowd noise thundered. But this time, it felt distant and even more unreal. We were alone in the dark.

"What do you say, darlin'," he growled in my ear. "All I want for my birthday is you."

"Yes!" I sobbed.

When I peered up, his dark eyes flashed at me in the glow of all those phones.

"You're mine, forever?"

I pushed up on my toes and cried, "Yes!" just before I kissed him.

No one could hear us over all the crowd noise but us.

And maybe Jesse, who was still standing nearby.

We melted together and then Jude swung me up in the air. I floated backstage in his arms, my face buried in his neck as I fought back the torrent of emotions that rose up, swamping me in so many feelings I didn't even know how to deal. I just gripped him tight as he swept me away.

I didn't want to cry in front of everyone.

I felt the members of the band rush past us as they headed back onto the stage and people crowding around, congratulating us, patting Jude on the back.

Onstage, Jesse announced, "SHE SAID YES!" The crowd exploded, and Dirty ripped into one of their classic hits, "Love Struck."

The song choice was perfect.

I wondered vaguely if Jude selected it, just for this moment.

He didn't even pause to absorb or enjoy the congratulations.

He just ignored them all as he carried me along the winding corridors, like I was the only person who mattered right now. One of his guys held open an exit door for us and once Jude had walked us outside, he set me on my feet next to his Harley and kissed me so damn thoroughly I would've fallen right over if he wasn't holding me up.

As always, I could just cling to his solid support and know he'd never let me fall.

When he came up for air, he dug his fingers into my hips, crushing me against him as he looked me dead in the eyes. His dark irises burned with devotion. "From now on, I'm keepin' you where you should've been all along," he swore to me. "Right by my side."

He said it devoutly, like a promise sworn with sword and blood, and I knew it meant everything to him.

That *I* meant everything to him.

I forced out the words around the knot in my throat. "I am by your side, Jude. Always."

He took hold of my left hand, which was clinging to his leather vest. He lifted it, so gently, to his lips, as my fingers shook. He kissed my ring finger, then slid a diamond ring onto it.

It appeared to be platinum. With a princess-cut diamond flanked by smaller stones.

It took my breath away.

That he'd bought this for me... Planned this for me. For us. This beautiful moment, beyond my wildest dreams.

Our eyes crashed together and he paused with the ring at my first knuckle. I could feel him holding his breath.

"Will you marry me, V?" he murmured solemnly.

I laughed softly, mostly because I was bubbling over with emotion and had no idea what to do with it all. "You already asked me that."

"No, not officially. *They* asked you. So the whole world would know who you belong to, and what that means. So the world would see how protected you are." He swallowed, and my bones turned to mush. If I wasn't still clinging to his vest with one fist and wedged between his hips and his bike, I would've melted to the ground like so much useless goo. "But I'm askin' you now. I want you to be my wife, V."

"*Yes*, Jude," I said breathlessly.

He slid the ring into place, and I felt the distinct shift in him. The resolute calm. The peace. It was in the softening of his shoulders and the way he looked at me, with such relief.

Was he actually...nervous?

After all we'd been through together already, for better or worse, did he really fear I wouldn't say yes?

I cupped his face in both hands as the gorgeous ring he'd just given me glittered on my finger. "You're nervous, baby. I never see you like this."

It was sweet, actually.

He'd told me, so many years ago, about his vice; that he drank cream soda when he felt stressed or sad. It was so rare for him to feel like that, but I'd drank it with him over the years, now and then. And even though I'd shared in his ups and downs, I'd rarely witnessed my man actually get nervous or anxious.

He made a little growly noise in his throat. "Yeah. So. I was afraid you might say no."

"Are you serious?"

His dark eyes searched mine as he cupped my face, and he stroked his big thumb across my cheek. "I love you, Roni."

"I love you, too. You know that."

He gave an uncomfortable shrug that was incredibly sweet. "It just hit me when I walked up behind you onstage. I couldn't see your face. I couldn't see into your fuckin' beautiful eyes. I could feel you shaking before I even touched you, and suddenly, I just wondered..."

"My answer is yes, Jude. A thousand times yes, and twice more just for fun. Don't you know that by now? The truth is..." I took a deep breath and sighed. "I would've married you years ago."

His eyebrow went up. "How many years ago are we talkin'?"

"Too many to admit."

I wrapped my arms around his neck and kissed him then, deep and hot, so I wouldn't have to.

But the fact was, Jude Grayson had had my heart since we were just teenagers. He'd taken it from me, piece by piece, with kisses and conversations and shared cream sodas, and never given it back.

And what I'd realized over the years?

I never wanted him to.

CATCH MY HEART

HELEN HARDT

About the Author

#1 *New York Times*, #1 *USA Today*, and #1 *Wall Street Journal* bestselling author Helen Hardt's passion for the written word began with the books her mother read to her at bedtime. She wrote her first story at age six and hasn't stopped since. In addition to being an award-winning author of romantic fiction, she's a mother, an attorney, a black belt in Taekwondo, a grammar geek, an appreciator of fine red wine, and a lover of Ben and Jerry's ice cream. She writes from her home in Colorado, where she lives with her family. Helen loves to hear from readers.

www.helenhardt.com

Warning

Catch My Heart is a romantic short story with a happy ending. However, it includes threat of violence and gunfire on the page. Readers who may be sensitive to these elements, please take note.

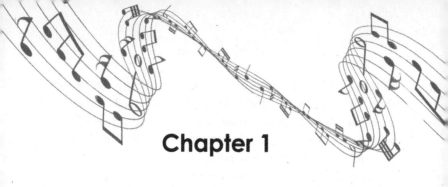

Chapter 1

GUNNAR

If only Blaire Cavileri weren't so damned *hot.*

I never asked for open mic night at the Haven to become a personal competition between the two of us, but that's what it seems to be since she showed up a few weeks ago.

I used to be the headliner here—Gunnar Healy, rock vocalist and guitarist extraordinaire, waiting for an agent or producer to walk through the door of Jamie Tyler's enterprise and give me my big break.

I wouldn't be the first. Performing at the Haven has led to stardom for some amazing acts.

Sarah Leventhal is in the audience today, and she's shown interest in me time and again, but something always keeps her from signing me.

That something today?

Blaire Cavileri.

She stands onstage singing some aria written over a century ago by Mozart or Verdi or some other classical composer.

Classical isn't the norm here at the Haven, but Blaire's voice is like a dream—as rich as the dark-red velvet of her gown. The aria she's singing has lush and seductive lines. It started with a haunting, almost ethereal melody and has slowly increased in intensity. Her voice gradually inches higher, but it never sounds shrieky. Instead it's full and sumptuous. I feel like I'm taking in a musical buffet, knife and fork at the ready.

As she sings in Italian or French or whatever—does it even

matter?—I, like the rest of the spectators sitting at the wooden tables drinking their cocktails, am mesmerized. Sarah's no exception. Despite having no interest in classical artists, she is as captivated as I am. As is Jamie, watching from the wing.

And I don't *want* to be captivated.

Because the woman gets on my last nerve.

"What were you thinking?" I asked Jamie two weeks ago when Blaire first showed up. "An opera singer?"

"Wait until you hear her," he said to me. "And if that doesn't convince you, wait until you see her. I happened to hear her at a concert last month, and I begged her to come sing here."

I'd never seen Jamie so taken with an act, but he was on target about Blaire. Her dramatic mezzo-soprano has an earthy quality that sends shivers over my flesh. Besides, she's gorgeous. Her sable hair is swept up over her shoulders with only a few strands framing her oval face. Her eyes are a warm amber-brown, and her full lips are painted nearly as dark red as her gown. I'm watching a vocal miracle unfold in front of me, and all I can think about is...

Well...things I shouldn't be thinking about, since I'm up next. My guitar will cover any boner, but it won't be comfortable.

Every Thursday night is the same—at least it has been for the last couple weeks. The Haven used to be *my* place. Sure, it's open mic night, but I was the highlight. People couldn't wait for me to go onstage. I had fans, even a few groupies.

I still have my following, but once Blaire Cavileri took the stage, she made it her own.

I look out into the audience, and—

Wow.

Sarah is hypnotized. I've never seen her so spellbound by a performer. Her gaze is fixed without interruption on Blaire. Never have I gotten this kind of attention from her.

Perfect. Just what I need.

Also in the audience is an older gentleman who I haven't seen here before. He's graying at his temples and wearing a tweed jacket. Tweed. Seriously. In a bar.

Yeah, whatever.

He hasn't taken his eyes off Blaire since she started performing.

Nothing new there. No one has.

I try to. I dart my gaze around the spectators, but I can't help myself. A couple seconds later I'm focused on Blaire again.

Watching the movement of her lips as she sings. Watching the movement of her chest as she breathes.

And what a chest it is. Perfectly round breasts with just a touch of cleavage showing.

When she finishes, every person—*every* person—in the bar rises, claps, screams, and whistles.

A few of them even shout "brava!"

And damn...

I can't fault them.

I'm next, so I head toward the stage. Blaire passes me without meeting my gaze.

"Nice job," I say to her. "Have you ever considered singing in English? That way we'll be able to tell when you mess up the words."

She turns and glares at me over her creamy shoulder. "Bite me."

I raise an eyebrow and give her a half smile. "Don't tempt me."

She rolls her eyes. "Just get onstage, Gunnar. Get onstage and slash your larynx to ribbons. Bastardize music the way only *you* can."

I exhale sharply. "I'm just glad that the guys who wrote my music haven't been dead for two centuries."

She scoffs. "Yes, and their names are still well-known now. No one will know your name a hundred years from now."

I shrug. "Guess we'll have to see. In the meantime, take a seat, Donna."

She wrinkles her forehead. "It's Blaire."

"I was referring to your last name. First name Prima, of

course."

She rolls her eyes again, but I swear there's a hint of a smile trying to force its way onto her mouth. "Aren't you clever?"

I open my mouth, hoping a retort will come to me when I'm saved by Jamie's booming voice over the mic.

"And now, ladies and gentlemen. Our next act is someone you've come to love, and he's back again at the Haven and ready to rock the place. Please welcome Gunnar Healy!"

I get the applause. Love the applause. It tingles in my ears like a thousand stars bursting.

My guitar strapped to me, I walk onto the stage, under the lights, sweat already emerging on my brow.

I stroke a few chords, and then I rock.

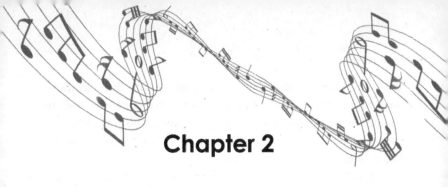

Chapter 2

<u>BLAIRE</u>

God, that man makes me want to pull my own hair out. Then pull *his* out.

And then grab him, paste our mouths together, and fall against a wall as I let him pound me.

I shake my head to get the fantasy out. Gunnar Healy is not good for me.

I've been serious about music since I was seven years old and heard opera for the first time. My grandmother took me to see *The Marriage of Figaro*. Grandpa was sick, so she had an extra ticket. I had no idea what opera was. All I knew was that I got to spend the day with Grandma, which would ultimately end with ice cream, so I was all in.

The seats at the theater matinée were luxurious, and Grandma got me a booster, but she told me I didn't have to pay attention if I didn't want to, that it was okay if I took a nap. We'd still get ice cream.

But I was mesmerized from the first note.

As I watched the singer playing Figaro measuring the floor and singing words I didn't understand, something burst inside me. I couldn't look away. From the period costumes to the comedic acting to the incredible voices, I was completely enthralled. When Cherubino came onstage, I giggled, realizing that the actor who played him was actually a woman in what I would later learn was called a pants role.

Cherubino was a nervous teenaged boy dealing with his

changing body—a comedic character to the hilt. But that didn't stop Mozart from writing him a beautiful aria called "Voi che sapete" in the opera's second act. The woman who played the role sang with a rich voice that reminded me of the plush blue velvet of the theater chair I was sitting on.

I had always loved to sing, and Mom and Dad always said I had talent and that when I was older they'd get me voice lessons.

After that opera, I begged to begin lessons. By the time I hit middle school, I was winning competitions, and when I hit high school, I was starring in every school musical. But, while musical theater was fun, opera was where my heart truly lay. I majored in classical voice at college, went straight to grad school for a Master's, and I've spent the year auditioning for the young artists' circuit, all while still working with my college professor, Corbett Morgan.

I just completed a summer program, and I'm due to begin a yearlong apprenticeship with a nearby regional company in a few weeks.

When Jamie heard me sing and invited me to open mic night here at the Haven, I was apprehensive, but the audience has been very reassuring.

Not so reassuring is Gunnar Healy. Gunnar's a rocker who looks the part. Wavy dark hair that falls to his shoulders, black stubble, and the kind of searing blue eyes—complete with long black lashes, damn him—you see on the hottest Hollywood heartthrobs.

Not to mention his body...

He always wears the same thing when he performs—dark-blue jeans that hug his ass, black boots, and a tight T-shirt that melts against his chest, showing off all his corded muscles.

And his voice?

It's a high-lying baritone with a rock-and-roll rasp that makes my knees weak.

I force myself to look away as he sings. Though I respect all genres of music, rock and roll is probably my least favorite. I've never enjoyed it much. It's too gritty, too loud, too dark.

So why am I transfixed by Gunnar's performance? Why is his music hitting me the same way Mozart's did years ago when Grandma took me to the opera? Maybe it's his sheer attractiveness. Or maybe it's his stage presence. Or his ridiculous charisma as he vocalizes. I swear he can make me feel like he's singing directly to me.

Music has always given me strength, but when I listen to Gunnar—to the depth and lushness and pure emotion of his voice—vulnerability seems to overtake me. He sings the words as if they're dripping from him like bourbon honey, as if he's stripping away my last defense and exposing everything hidden inside me. I want to hang onto every note, commit each sound to my memory, let the music take me somewhere passionate and forbidden.

His music couldn't be anything further from what I just sang. Today I debuted an aria from the *Saint-Saëns opera Samson and Delilah*. *"Mon coeur s'ouvre a ta voix,"* it's called. French for "my heart opens to your voice."

A bit on the nose, it turns out. Every single note out of Gunnar Healy's gorgeous mouth is drawing me closer and closer...

I'm jerked from my hypnotic trance when someone touches my arm.

"Blaire?" A young woman with dark hair and striking green eyes stands next to me.

"Yes? May I help you?"

She smiles. "I think I can help *you*."

I take a drink from my water bottle, trying to cool myself off. Still, my cheeks warm. "Oh?"

What's she going to do? Help me with the fantasy I'm having about Gunnar Healy?

She pulls a business card out of her purse and hands it to me. "I'm Sarah Leventhal."

I read the colorful card. *Sarah Leventhal. Talent Scout. Agent. Producer.*

I stop my jaw from dropping. Professor Morgan told me I wouldn't get an agent until I was at least twenty-seven, maybe even older because of my low voice type. I'm still considered young for a mezzo, only a year out of grad school. For the next four or five years, at least, he said I would be doing young artist programs here and there. The most I could expect for the time being would be small roles with larger companies and bigger roles in touring educational shows. Maybe I'd bite the bullet and try the European market on for size.

But representation? That was far into the future.

"Wow," I say. "It's great to meet you."

She gestures toward the back of the performance space. "Can we talk for a moment?"

"Yes, of course."

She leads me backstage to a quiet alcove. No way would we be able to talk in the bar—not with Gunnar blaring and the audience going crazy.

"Do you have representation?" she asks.

I blink. "No, not yet."

She places a gentle hand on my forearm. "I don't want to disappoint you, but that's not what I'm here to talk to you about."

My racing heart thuds. Why would she even ask if I had a manager then?

Not that I was expecting representation at this point in my career. I'm only twenty-four years old. I'm still a baby as far as the opera industry is concerned.

"I see. What did you want to talk to me about then?"

She redirects her gaze toward the stage. "What do you think of Gunnar Healy?"

I swallow. Does she want me to be honest? Because my honest answer would be something along the lines of "He's got a great voice and his body makes my knees weak, but he's a first-class jackass."

I draw in a breath. "He's...talented. For a rock and roll singer."

"He is." Sarah nods, tucking a lock of hair behind her ear. "But his career hasn't taken off yet. Why do you think that is?"

I shrug. "I don't really follow rock and roll, so I couldn't begin to give you an intelligent answer to that question."

"I can tell you why," Sarah says. "He's talented. There's no doubt about that. Every audience that hears him falls in love. He sure looks the part. Handsome, rugged, a body that rivals the best athletes in the business. But here's the truth of it, Blaire."

She pauses.

"Yes?" I urge.

"I first saw you perform here two weeks ago," Sarah says.

Okay. I'm not sure what that has to do with Gunnar Healy, but—

"Your voice is beautiful," she continues, "and there's something very special about the way you take the stage."

"Thank you."

"Have you considered singing pop?"

This time my jaw does drop. "I'm a classical singer, Ms. Leventhal."

"Please, call me Sarah." She smiles. "And I understand that. You sing beautifully. The arias come alive with your interpretations. I'm not a classical music fan, yet I can't take my eyes off you when you're on the stage. Just listening to you gives me a new appreciation for the classics."

"Thank you. I appreciate that."

She smiles. Sort of. "But let's be honest, Blaire. You're not going to make it big as a classical singer."

My brain stops working for a moment. Did this woman who doesn't know me from Eve just say something so astronomically rude?

I blink a few times and shake it off. "Why couldn't I? Classical artists have achieved worldwide acclaim and success. Talent and dedication can transcend any barriers."

"I won't argue with you," Sarah says, "but I will tell you that they are the exception rather than the rule."

"Isn't everyone who makes it big an exception? Thousands of talented singers go unnoticed. Not just classical singers. Plenty of people make a decent living in the arts without"—air quotes—

"making it *big*."

"You're not wrong." She pauses for a second. "But here's my question to you, Sarah. Do you want to be one of *them*?"

I swallow, licking my lips. "What exactly are you saying to me?"

"I'm going to suggest something that you probably haven't thought about. Something that has likely never been on your radar." She widens her eyes. "You're an incredible talent, but to get to the next level, you need to do something unique."

"All right. What do you suggest?"

"A collaboration, Blaire. A collaboration between you and Gunnar Healy."

I have to stop myself from spitting out the mouthful of water I just drank. I swallow, but it goes down my throat with a gulp of air. I stifle a burp before speaking.

"Gunnar Healy can't stand me," I say.

Sarah smiles. "I'd beg to differ. I witnessed your exchange after you left the stage."

I let out a soft huff. "You mean us tossing insults at each other? That's the only kind of exchange we've ever had."

Sarah narrows her eyes. "That was playful banter, not insults. The kind that is exchanged between two people with a heat between them. That's what you two have. And it's not something you're probably even aware of. But the two of you onstage together?" She fans herself with her hand. "That would be dynamite."

The thought intrigues me—turns me on, to be honest—but I tamp down any excitement. "I wouldn't hold your breath."

"Gunnar is the last performer tonight," Sarah says. "After that, Jamie brings out the karaoke machine."

I'm well aware that open mic night turns into karaoke night, but I'm usually gone by then. Listening to amateurs hack out show tunes and top-ten hits is kind of a professional vocalist's version of hell.

"I know. I don't stay for karaoke."

"Stay tonight," she says.

"Why?"

"Do you know the song 'Mellow'?"

"LaLa Queen? Yeah, of course. Who doesn't?"

"It's a beautiful song, wouldn't you agree?"

"Yeah. But what does that have to do with—"

She holds up a hand to stop me. "You and Gunnar are going to open up karaoke tonight. With 'Mellow'."

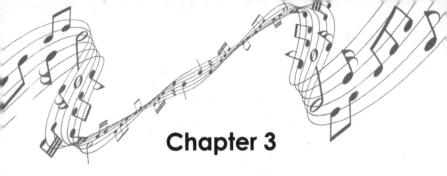

Chapter 3

GUNNAR

"Not only no, but hell no," I say to Sarah. "I'm a rocker. Not a country or pop singer."

Sarah laughs. "Man, Gunnar, you and Blaire Cavileri are cut from the same cloth."

"I hardly think so."

She smirks. "She's not a rock and roll fan, and you're not a classical music fan. But damn... Your voice and hers... The two of you could create heaven together."

"You're not going to turn me into something I'm not, Sarah."

"Did I say anything like that? I'm suggesting a collaboration of music that works for both of you. You bring your rocker charisma and she'll bring her operatic resonance and powerful stage presence. You're going to bring out the best in each other. I'm sure of it. We could even cut an album."

"Singing what? Sure, all of her classical tunes are in the public domain, but I sing mostly covers. You'd have your work cut out for you in copyright law hell."

She shakes her head. "Don't you worry about that. I've got a hungry songwriter who has written some amazing duets. Do you know how long I've been searching for the right project for you, Gunnar?"

"I know, and I appreciate it, but I just assumed when you found it, it would be rock and roll."

"Do you really want to be the next big rock and roll star?"

"Uh...yeah, I do. I thought we were on the same page with

172

that."

"I'm offering you something unique. We take two talented young singers. One rocker, one classical. We bring them together and put them into a genre where they can both shine. Soft pop rock."

"I'm not interested. Besides, Blaire Cavileri would never lower herself to sing with me."

Sarah shrugs. "Don't be so sure. She's young and hungry, just like you are."

I let my gaze wander over to Blaire, who is talking to the older gentleman in the tweed blazer. God, just looking at her turns me on. Not a great thing if I have to sing with her. Jamie's busy setting up the karaoke machine while soft rock music plays over the loudspeaker.

"I don't know, Sarah." I run my hand up and down the neck of my guitar. "Rock and roll is who I am."

She rolls her eyes. "Who you are is a man with an extraordinary amount of talent who hasn't quite found his place yet. Consider the possibility that it's not in the Rock and Roll Hall of Fame."

I shake my head. "I can't consider that. It's been my dream forever."

Sarah runs her hands through her hair and takes a deep breath in. "It can still be your dream. It can still be your goal. But there's nothing wrong with taking a diverging path sometimes."

I sigh. "Fine. I'll sing 'Mellow' with her."

"You know the song?"

"Of course I do. Besides, karaoke machines have words, Sarah."

"Great," she says. "Let me go tell Jamie it's on, and once everything is set up, he'll introduce the two of you."

"All right."

As Sarah walks toward the stage to talk to Jamie, I glance over to Blaire once more.

That guy she's with? The older one?

He's fucking *glaring* at me.

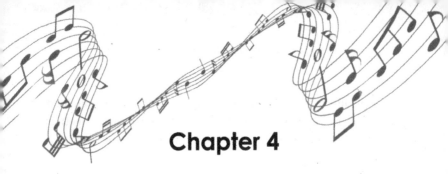

Chapter 4

<u>BLAIRE</u>

"It's just one song, Professor."

He frowns. "I've told you time and again, Blaire, you can call me Corbett now."

"And I've told you time and again that it doesn't feel right to me."

He looks back over at Gunnar. "You can't possibly be thinking about this collaboration."

I shake my head. "I don't know. I mean, I've already committed to the young artist program at Opera Livingston."

"It wouldn't look good for you to back out of that."

"I have no intention of doing so. But Sarah says she can work around my schedule."

He sighs and casts his gaze to the ground. "You're so naïve, Blaire. Do you have any idea how much work goes into cutting a whole album?"

"I minored in music business," I remind him. "I—"

He puts his finger over my lip. "That's all theory. This is practice. You'll have to learn a whole new repertoire. There will be rehearsals. Then studio time. And then more recordings. This will take time you won't have. Time you should be devoting to lessons and coachings. To molding yourself into the singer you're meant to be."

"But Sarah says—"

"Sarah isn't concerned with you," he says. "Sarah's seeing dollar signs. She's looking at the bottom line and thinks she may have discovered the next big thing. But she hasn't. She's wrong."

"Ouch."

"Don't take that as an insult, Blaire. What I mean is this." He places both of his hands firmly on my shoulders. "I've been your teacher for six years. I know what your dreams are and I'm confident you can achieve them, but this isn't the way." He brushes a strand of hair from my forehead. "I have your best interests at heart, Blaire. Don't do this."

I open my mouth to reply when Sarah rushes toward me. "Jamie's all set, It's now or never, Blaire. Come on." She grabs my arm.

I look over my shoulder at Professor Morgan shaking his head at me.

Singing one measly karaoke song isn't going to run my career off its tracks.

I give him a quick shrug and a moment later I'm onstage, looking into the searing blue eyes that can belong only to Gunnar Healy.

"Before we open up the karaoke mic tonight," Jamie says, "we have a special treat for you. If you've been here for the last hour, you've heard both of these performers sing, and you know how talented they are. Tonight they're going to team up to open our karaoke hour with their rendition of 'Mellow' by LaLa Queen and Brett Blake. Please welcome back to the stage the phenomenally talented Blaire Cavileri and Gunnar Healy!"

The applause is deafening, and I can't help but smile. How different we look. I'm dressed in my dark-red velvet cocktail gown, my hair swept up, with black strappy sandals on my feet, my toes painted the same color as my dress.

Then there's Gunnar...

Gunnar, who makes plain blue jeans look like they were made solely for him.

Gunnar, who oozes sexiness.

Maybe it's his granite-sculpted masculine beauty.

Maybe it's those corded forearms that come to life as he

strums his guitar.

But his guitar isn't strapped to him now.

And my God...

Once the applause dies down a bit, Jamie starts the karaoke machine. As the intro plays, I pick up a mic—it feels strange, as opera singers don't usually use microphones—turn, and look straight into those scorching ice-blue eyes.

And when Gunnar sings that first line...

"*Tell me what you want, girl...*"

Everything else fades away...

Gunnar is singing only to me.

"*I'll be your shooting star...*"

There's no more audience. No Jamie. No Sarah. No Professor Morgan. No stage and no karaoke machine.

Just Gunnar.

Just me.

Just music.

"*Just say the word babe, and I'll meet you where you are.*"

I can't help it. A smile creeps over my face. I stare directly into Gunnar's eyes, into his very being, as the artificial karaoke track drones under us.

Gunnar's eyes narrow, and he mouths the words "your part."

Right! The song. LaLa Queen's verse.

I come in a half-beat behind, but I make up the difference by singing the first line a bit faster than normal.

"*In the moonlight we'll dance, underneath a velvet sky...*"

I can't remember the last time I sang in this style. I'm breaking every rule that Corbett Morgan spent the last six years pounding into my skull. No rounded vowels, no big space in the back of my mouth, no...

No anything except this love song to Gunnar Healy.

"*When I'm in your arms, lover, I feel like I could fly!*"

On the word "fly," I bring my chest voice into a high belt that resonates with power and passion.

I take a look into the audience. They're eating this up.

I forgot what it's like to sing in English. There are operas in English, of course. My go-to aria is called "Must the Winter Come So Soon." But I mostly find myself singing in Italian and French. Beautiful languages, to be sure, but there's something about singing in your audience's tongue that bridges you together in a way that foreign languages can't.

Heat swirls between Gunnar and me as we answer each other in song.

We alternate two more verses, and then we reach the chorus, where we sing at first in unison, then crescendo into a harmony that can only be described as ecstasy.

"'With you, my lover, all time stands still. With every touch, my soul you fill. In our mellow vibe, we find our bliss, lost in a lifelong mellow kiss.'"

As I sing the lyrics, I can't help but wonder what a kiss with Gunnar Healy would be like.

I have a feeling it would be anything *but* mellow.

And then, just as quickly as it started, the song is over... I drop my hand holding the microphone to my side and tilt my head back.

When the applause is so thunderous—more than I've ever heard—I lift my head, meet Gunnar's gaze, and slowly...

Ever so slowly...

I move toward him as he moves toward me.

Until only an inch separates us, and his lips come down on mine.

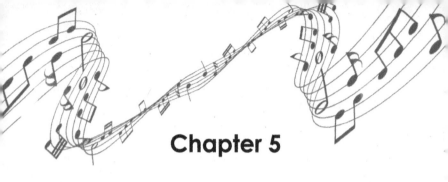

Chapter 5

GUNNAR

Blaire's lips are soft beneath my own, and I slide my tongue over them, coaxing her open.

When she parts those beautiful full lips, I glide my tongue between them, taking what I've dreamed of.

She tastes of peppermint, of beauty. Of perfection. Of the melody and harmony between us. If our voices together had a flavor, this would be it.

The song...

It's a song I've heard a thousand times—a song I like a lot.

But singing it with Blaire gave it so much more meaning.

Not the words even. Not the notes. Not the beautiful melody, and not the vibrant harmony when our voices came together.

It was something different. Something amazing that I've never experienced. We opened up to each other, felt each other. For an instant, we *became* each other.

My thoughts are interrupted, though, when Blaire steps back, breaking the kiss.

The audience is still going crazy with applause, whistles, shouts.

"More, more, more!"

But Blaire, her face a vibrant pink, takes a graceful bow and exits the stage.

I nod to the audience and then follow her.

Sarah grabs both of us, gushing. "Didn't I tell you? The two of you together are magic. Come to my office first thing tomorrow and we'll discuss the logistics. Mary Louise—she's the songwriter—has some numbers that will be perfect for the two of you together." She brings our hands together, draws them to her mouth, and plants a kiss on them. "This is a match made in heaven. My God, I've been looking for the two of you for years. That crescendo in the middle... My God... It was phenomenal."

Blaire's eyes are glazed over. Does she hear what Sarah is saying?

Sarah snaps her fingers in my face. "Gunnar? Did you hear me? This is what's going to put you on the map. Both of you."

My gaze is zeroed in on Blaire's lips. Her dark red lipstick is smudged.

I'm pretty sure it's all over my mouth.

As if she can read my mind, Blaire reaches into her purse, pulls out a compact, and attempts to fix her makeup.

"And that kiss at the end?" Sarah continues. "It cemented the whole thing. From now on, it's Gunnar and Blaire. I've never seen such chemistry. If you can do this with a song made famous by two of the most talented performers in the world, just think of what you can do with something that's written expressly for you. This is going to be huge!"

Sarah's words are intriguing, but I can't stop staring at Blaire's mouth. She's fixed her lipstick, but she can't take away my kiss. Her lips are slightly parted, swollen, and glistening. All I can think about is touching them with mine again.

Kissing her, touching her creamy skin, cupping her cheeks, her gorgeous round breasts. Sliding my fingers over the hard nipples sticking out against the soft velvet.

"Are you hearing me, Gunnar? I need to meet with you both tomorrow, first thing. I'll bring Mary Louise, and we'll start..."

Sarah's words become jumbled.

If I'm not hearing them, I know Blaire isn't.

The guy in tweed approaches us and takes Blaire's arm. "It's time to go. You need your rest."

"Who are you? Her father?" I blurt out without thinking.

He raises an eyebrow and glares at me. "Whatever designs you have on Blaire, you can forget them right now. She has an exciting career in opera ahead of her. She doesn't need to share the stage with some wannabe rocker."

"Wait just a minute," I say. "You can't talk to me like that. You can't—"

Sarah steps in front of me, holding out her hand. "I'm Sarah Leventhal, and I'm a talent agent. I'm not sure who you are, sir, but I think I can take both of these young vocalists to the top."

"Blaire already told me about your idea," the man says. "I'm afraid she isn't interested."

Sarah crosses her arms. "If it's all the same, sir, I think that's Blaire's decision."

Blaire's lower lip trembles, and a need to protect her surges into me. Who the hell is this clown?

"Professor Morgan is thinking about what's best for my career," Blaire says.

"That's right," Professor Morgan—apparently—says. "Blaire is under contract with Opera Livingston. She starts their yearlong young artist program in two weeks."

"We can't plan and cut an album in two weeks," I say.

"What if we can?" Sarah asks. "Are you in, Gunnar?"

Am I?

Can I spend two weeks with Blaire Cavileri without constantly swapping insults?

Yeah, I can do it. Especially if I get to kiss her again.

Maybe Sarah's right. Does it matter if I'm not the next king of rock and roll? Really, I just want to sing, and she's giving me a chance to sing with a beautiful and talented woman.

"Yeah, Sarah. I'm in."

She turns to Blaire. "And you?"

Blaire opens her mouth but then closes it when Professor Morgan grabs her arm.

I absently curl my right hand into a fist. Who the hell does he think he is, touching her like that?

"I'm afraid Blaire is otherwise obligated," he says.

Sarah narrows her eyes. "I think I asked *her*."

Blaire tugs on her lower lip with her teeth, and damn... What that woman does to my body... One thing about being a rocker and performing at the Haven for open mic night—I hardly have a dearth of women throwing themselves at me. I usually go home with a new one every week. Then I make her pancakes the next morning, kiss her goodbye, and never see her again.

So what is it about this particular woman? She's beautiful, yes, but I've been with beautiful women before. Maybe it's her talent. Maybe it's her spitfire personality. She has no problem telling me to go to hell, but for some reason, she freezes up in front of this professor.

And I don't like it. I don't like it one bit.

Finally, she opens her mouth. "I think...I'd like to try it."

Morgan glares at her. "Blaire, it's not a good idea."

She turns to Morgan. "Professor, I have two weeks off. This is a chance to broaden my musical horizons. What can it hurt?"

"You need to rest your—"

Blaire ignores him and turns to Sarah. "Are you sure I'll be able to fulfill my obligations to Opera Livingston?"

"Honestly, I don't see why not," Sarah says. "You don't start there for two weeks, and it's a local company, so you'll be here in town. We'll work around your schedule. I'll give you a call if the plan for tomorrow changes. The industry is one of constant flux, and sometimes things change early in the morning, so keep your phone's ringer on in case I have to wake you up."

Blaire nods, takes out her phone, and switches it off silent mode. And then she smiles.

Blaire Cavileri—my perfect duet partner—smiles.

And the world just became a little bit brighter.

Chapter 6

<u>BLAIRE</u>

"I wish you would change your mind," Professor Morgan says as he walks me to the door of my apartment. "You have so much talent, and you're a future star in the opera world. I hate to see you waste it all away."

I shrug. "I guess I don't consider this opportunity to be wasting anything. Weren't you always the one who told me never to let an opportunity pass by? That the more people who heard me sing the better? Because you never knew when that one person might hear me and take me to the next level?"

He shakes his head. "But your voice, Blaire. It was made for opera. You're made to sing the music written by the great masters. No one writes music like that anymore." He grimaces. "Certainly not this *Mary Louise* person who your new friend Sarah is talking about."

"I don't know what to tell you," I say. "But being on that stage with Gunnar felt... I don't know. I just want to try."

I can't bring myself to tell Professor Morgan that I felt more myself tonight on that stage with Gunnar Healy than I've ever felt—even when I sang the title role in Rossini's Cinderella during my final year at school. The adrenaline rush, the high, the appreciation from the audience. The thrill of singing Cinderella's firework coloratura in the opera's finale. The applause. The whistles and the shouts of brava. It's what keeps me going. It's what keeps me going in this dog-eat-dog world of performing arts. Because it's a tough road. It's more like a mountain with rocks and jagged edges and cliffs. It's scary as hell, and at times my self-doubt plagues me so much that I want to give up.

But then...I perform again. And whether it's for judges in a competition, or producers at an audition, or best yet, for a real audience, I feel alive again.

I love opera. My voice lends itself well to the classical genre, but singing with Gunnar tonight?

It was a new high. More phenomenal even than singing Cinderella.

And that kiss at the end...

I'm still quivering.

I take out my key and unlock my apartment door. "I'd invite you in for some coffee, but I'm exhausted."

He pauses a moment. "I suppose you need to be well-rested to get together with Sarah and that *rocker* tomorrow."

"Well...yes."

He sighs. "There's something I need to tell you, Blaire."

"What is it?"

"Could I come in?"

I sigh. Professor Morgan knows how tired I am, so he wouldn't ask if it weren't important. "I suppose for a moment."

"Thank you." He follows me in.

"I guess I can make some coffee if you want some. Or I could open a bottle of wine, but I won't be having any."

He holds up a hand. "No, no. Don't go to any trouble. A glass of water will be fine. You should have a glass as well."

"Oh, yes, keep hydrated."

He never stops being my teacher.

I walk into my small galley kitchen, fill two glasses with ice and water. Professor Morgan is already sitting on my loveseat. My living area is so small that I only have a loveseat and a recliner. Normally I would sit next to him on the loveseat, but I feel...

I'm not sure what I feel, but I take the chair.

He takes a sip of his water. "Blaire"—he clears his throat—"we've known each other for seven years now."

"We have."

"For six of those years, I was your college professor."

I smile. "You still are, as far as I'm concerned. You know I take your advice very seriously. You'll always be my teacher."

He takes a slow breath in and then sighs. "I suppose that's what I need to talk to you about." He leans forward. "Blaire, I don't want to be *only* your teacher anymore."

I open my mouth as a wave of fear nearly crushes me. "Don't leave me now. I know you're against this thing with Sarah, but I need you. I depend on you, Professor Morgan."

He edges closer to the side of the loveseat—close enough to grab my hand. "Will I ever convince you to call me Corbett?"

"It just..." I rub my arms against a sudden chill. "It doesn't feel right to me."

"I realize I'm twenty years older than you are," he says, "but—"

I quickly rise from the chair, bumping the small coffee table and spilling my glass of water.

"You've nothing to fear from me, Blaire," he continues. "But what I feel for you now is more than just the affection a teacher feels for a student, for his protégé. Somewhere along the way I fell in love with you."

My brain goes haywire. There is no way in *hell* that this man just said that. A man who took me into his studio when I was freshly eighteen, still a child, really. Professor Morgan was always a little more touchy-feely than I was comfortable with, but I've gotten used to it. You have to get used to being poked and prodded in voice lessons. That's part of the deal. He never crossed the line, and I don't believe he'll cross it now.

I hate the idea of upsetting him, of possibly even breaking his heart, but I don't think of him in that way. I never have, and I never will.

"I'm so sorry," I tell him. "But I think you need to leave now."

He pops up from the loveseat and grabs my hands. "Please, Blaire. Don't make me leave. Let me show you how much you've come to mean to me."

I back away, heading toward my door. "I...I don't want to lose you as a teacher. But I'm afraid I don't share your feelings, Professor."

He walks to the door. He cups my cheek, thumbing my lower lip.

It feels all kinds of wrong.

I brush his hand away. "Please go."

He nods and walks out the door without another word.

I close it behind him.

Then I slide, still in my red velvet gown, my back against the door, down to the floor.

I think about Gunnar's kiss.

And I feel like Professor Morgan tainted it in some way.

As if, when he touched my lip, he negated what Gunnar and I shared.

I swallow.

I may have just lost my teacher, right when I need him the most. But he's against the collaboration with Gunnar and Sarah. And there's no way I can share a small studio space with him after he declared his love for me. At least not for a while. We both need some time to cool our jets and move past it.

In the meantime, I'll find another teacher. I'm sure Opera Livingston will have some recommendations.

And before that, I'll meet Sarah tomorrow, and I'll start working on this new project.

I take a shower and get ready for bed. I'm halfway through my skincare regimen when I hear a knock on the door.

My heart skips a beat. It's far too late for company.

I slowly walk to the door. Shivers skitter over my entire body. Why didn't I insist that my landlord install a peephole when I moved into this place?

Another knock. I'm close enough to the door to feel its reverberation.

I ignore it. Whoever it is will get the message. He'll go away.

But another knock, and another. Then, "Blaire, please."
I close my eyes and take a deep breath in.
And I open the door.

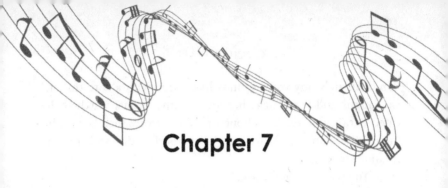

Chapter 7

GUNNAR

I arrive early at Sarah's office.

I spent the entire night tossing and turning, unable to get Blaire's kiss out of my mind.

All I could think about was how her lips felt against mine, how the softness of her curves felt against my chest.

The receptionist gestures me to go on back, and I knock on Sarah's office door.

"Come on in," she calls.

I walk in. Sarah's seated at her desk. On the other side of the desk is a young woman with platinum blond hair and high cheekbones.

"Gunnar, hi." Sarah rises. "Please meet Mary Louise Wilson. She's the songwriter I was telling you about."

Mary Louise Wilson looks more like a Victoria's Secret model than a songwriter. Long curly blond hair and a killer body. She's wearing a leopard-print blazer and a tight black pencil skirt. She rises and holds out her hand. "Call me Ariana."

I lift my eyebrows as I take her hand. No sparks at all, despite how hot she is. "O...kay."

"Ariana Waverly. Sounds better than Mary Louise Wilson." She sticks out her tongue.

Sarah laughs. "I have to agree. From now on, Ariana Waverly will get credit as the songwriter."

"I wish I could sing these songs myself." Ariana riffles through a folio, pulls out some sheet music, and hands it to me.

"Unfortunately, my voice sounds like a frog with a sore throat." She laughs and then turns her focus to me. "I just watched the video Sarah took on her phone of your performance last night. I agree that you and Blaire may be the perfect duo to bring my creations to life."

"You recorded us?" I ask.

"I did," Sarah admits. "I had to show Mary Louise—er... Ariana—that I was serious."

"The two of you together are something else." Ariana gestures to the sheet music in my hand. "Tell me what you think of this."

I look down at the looseleaf paper. Ariana handwrites her songs on staff paper instead of using notation software. Impressive.

The song is called "Catch My Heart," and it's written for a man and woman.

It's a slow pop ballad, and already I can tell the key is perfect for both Blaire and me. I absently sing a few bars. *"Listen to me, babe. You're a world away from me, but in your eyes a spark I see. You're the sunshine in my rain. The calm in my hurricane. Catch my heart, I'm falling for you. Two worlds collide into something brand new..."*

Ariana somehow managed to put into words the feelings I've had since I shared the stage with Blaire. Blaire, a woman who, in terms of her chosen genre, *is* a world away from me. Her angelic voice piercing my brooding rock music is just like golden sunshine peering through the rain. The calm in my hurricane...

And she certainly *has* caught my heart.

"Wow," is all I can say.

"You like it?" Ariana asks.

I put the sheet music down. "It's not exactly rock and roll."

"No, it's not." Sarah smiles. "Not classical either. But I'll be damned if it isn't perfect for you and Blaire Cavileri."

Ariana turns to Sarah. "You said something about Blaire being contracted to sing with Opera Livingston."

"Yeah. She's available for the next two weeks, and then we'll have to work around her schedule."

Ariana twists her lips. "That's a lot of pressure."

"Wait until you hear them sing together, though. In real life, I mean." Sarah glances at her watch. "Where is Blaire, anyway?"

I shrug. "Don't look at me. I don't even know her number."

"I have her number," Sarah says. "I already programmed it into my phone last night. Let me give her a quick call."

Sarah pulls out her phone, puts it on speaker, and taps in a number.

It rings once, twice, three times, and then—

"Help me! Please—"

My heart thuds. Blaire's voice, normally so beautiful and serene, is now quivering in a high pitch, almost screaming.

The call goes dead.

Every hair on my body stands on end as my stomach twists into knots.

Blaire's in trouble.

I get to my feet quickly, the sheet music cascading to the floor. I can feel my heart thundering in my chest. "That was Blaire. It was her voice. We've got to get to her."

Sarah gulps.

"Sarah!" I grip her shoulders, pulling her out of her chair. "Her address. Do you know her address?"

She blinks and then reaches for her purse. "I do, thank God. She wrote it and her phone number on the back of her card after we spoke last night."

I grab the card from Sarah. "Call 911. I'm going to get her."

"Gunnar, you don't even know if she's home."

God, she's right. "Fuck. But I don't know where else to start. Maybe you can trace where her phone is."

"I don't know how—"

"I don't either, damn it!" I rub at my forehead. "I'm going to her place. Call 911 and give them her address. Then worry about the phone."

Blaire's place is only a few blocks away from the studio, so I run like hell. It'll be quicker than getting my car and dealing with traffic.

I run like a gazelle being chased by a lion. I run like I've never run before, my heart pounding against my throat the whole way.

When I finally get to the apartment building, I run inside, find the stairwell, race to the second floor, and find her apartment number.

I pound on the door. "Blaire! Blaire, are you in there?"

"Go away," a deep voice says.

It sounds slightly familiar, but I can't place it.

And then it hits me.

It's the same voice I heard chastising Blaire for her lack of commitment to the classical field. Her music professor. The guy in the tweed. He was against this whole thing.

I think back... He was standing awfully close to Blaire last night. He was finding any excuse to touch her. And he was glaring at me after that kiss.

What if he's obsessed with Blaire? What if—

I pound again. "I've called 911. Where's Blaire? If you've hurt her, so help me God I'll—"

I'll what? She's not mine to protect.

Except that she is.

That kiss last night.

We said more to each other in that kiss than I've ever said to another woman. She may not feel the same way, but damn it, I want to give things between us a chance. I want more from her than just this collaboration.

I want it all.

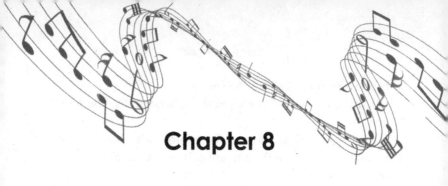

Chapter 8

<u>BLAIRE</u>

My phone is gone.

I had lied when Professor Morgan, with the stench of cheap whiskey on his breath, had forced his way back into my apartment. I told him my phone was in the other room. My plan was to excuse myself to the bathroom when the opportunity arose and then call for help.

But then hours passed, and he didn't let me out of his sight all night.

Then the call came. And my phone wasn't on silent. It blared through my pajama pocket.

I had just enough time to get a few words in before Professor Morgan wrestled the phone out of my hand and threw it out the window.

I didn't even see who was calling. It could have been a robocall. Maybe it was Sarah wondering where I was.

Since then, he's corralled me into my kitchen, the farthest room from the front door. Someone knocked a few minutes ago, but he sent them away. Probably a Girl Scout selling cookies or something.

I take a deep breath in, attempting to calm my jumping nerves. I force myself to look him in the eye. "Let's just talk. It's been hours now. You've just been staring at me. You can't make me feel something that isn't there."

He crosses his arms. "You know why I'm here. I've already told you. I'm in love with you, Blaire. And I know you return my affections. You're just afraid to admit it."

I shake my head. "There's nothing between us. You have to let me go."

He hasn't tried anything. I don't think he's a bad man. Still, I'm frightened, and I want him gone. If only I hadn't opened the door.

He gets to his feet and caresses my cheek gently, sending a chill of horror down my spine. "You're my angel. You always have been."

He hasn't tried to hurt me. He hasn't so much as tried to kiss me. He seems convinced that I want this. That I have some deep-seated feelings for him that he just needs to coax to the surface. We've been at this all night, and my one lifeline is now shattered in pieces on the sidewalk outside my window.

"I've wanted you from the moment you first walked into my studio," he says. "But I'm a professional. I kept an appropriate distance while you were under my tutelage. The whole while I watched you blossom into a beautiful young woman." He grabs a bottle of whiskey from the top of my refrigerator and takes a swig. "For six excruciating years I've waited to tell you how I felt. And then I saw you let Gunnar Healy kiss you, put his dirty hands on you, and I knew I had to interfere. For your sake as well as mine."

God, the kiss.

That kiss...

"I don't know how else I can tell you this, Professor. I'm simply not interested. Now will you please—"

"Shut up!" He throws the half-empty bottle of whiskey onto the floor, shattering it. Amber liquid spreads over the tiled kitchen. I have to jump to avoid a big piece of glass.

The glass is the least of my problems. This man, the man I've entrusted my voice to the last several years, is now behaving violently. And I have no escape. Nowhere to—

I jerk at a pound on the door.

"Open up! It's the police!"

I gasp. Should I be relieved or should I be more frightened?

What will he do now?

Morgan sneers. "Damn it. Now look what you've done."

"I didn't call them."

"No, but you answered your phone. Alerted someone, and they called them."

I gulp.

Then I clasp my hand to my mouth.

A pistol. In his hand. Where did it come from? Where was he hiding it?

He aims at me. "Tell them to go away, or I will shoot."

"I..." My legs don't want to work. Can't work.

"Tell them, damn it." His face goes red.

I slowly walk out of the kitchen and to my front door. I do everything in my power to steady my voice. "Please go away," I yell, my voice shaking. "I am... I'm okay."

"We received a call from a concerned party, ma'am. We also noticed pieces of a shattered cell phone directly beneath your back window."

I stifle a scream as Professor Morgan jams his gun into my shoulder.

"I... I dropped the phone out the window. I was going to head down soon to clean it up. I'm sorry for the trouble, Officer. But you can go."

"He's not going anywhere, and neither am I."

I gasp at the second voice—one with a rock-and-roll edge. Gunnar. Gunnar came for me.

"I'll break down the door myself," Gunnar continues.

Then the door bursts open. Two armed police officers enter, pointing a gun at my voice teacher. "Drop the gun, sir."

Professor Morgan's eyes are wide and bloodshot. "I'll shoot her. I swear it. I'll shoot her before I let any other man touch her."

My heart is going to explode. Tears stream down my face. When did I start crying?

But then, a ray of light appears behind the cop. Gunnar is standing in the doorway.

"Blaire!" Gunnar roars. "You'd best get the fuck away from her, asshole!"

"You can't touch her again if she's gone," Professor Morgan says, ice in his tone.

"Sir, please be quiet," one of the officers says to Gunnar. Then, to Professor Morgan. "If you shoot her, I'll shoot you."

Professor Morgan fixes his gaze on me. "Better us both be gone than have some other man touch her."

"Has he hurt you, ma'am?"

I shake my head, my heart pounding. "Other than frightening me to death, no."

"How long has he been here?"

"Since about eleven last night. He forced his way into the apartment, and then he threw my phone out the window when someone called and I screamed for help."

"Drop the gun," the officer says again.

I wipe a tear from my cheek. "Please, Professor Morgan. I'll do whatever you want. I won't make the album. I won't kiss Gunnar anymore. Please."

"The hell you won't!" Gunnar cries out. He leaps past the cop, straight for Morgan's legs.

A gunshot booms through my apartment. My ears start ringing, and then all sound is muffled. I watch the action unfold like a silent film.

Gunnar is on top of Morgan. The gun is on the floor, just out of Morgan's reach. Without thinking, my heart racing, I get to my feet and snatch the gun.

The cop says something, but I can't hear it. He probably wants me to drop the gun. I slowly back up to my coffee table, gently lay the gun on top of it, and then put my hands behind my head. The cop nods and points his gun at Professor Morgan. He yells something at Gunnar.

Gunnar gets to his feet, and before Morgan can do the same, the cop cuffs him, places his hands firmly on his shoulders, and escorts him out of my apartment.

Gunnar rushes toward me as my legs crumple beneath me.
And then...
Nothing.

Chapter 9

GUNNAR

"Blaire..." I hold her, kneeling, her head in my lap. Touch her soft cheek. "Please, Blaire."

Her eyes open.

"You're okay, Blaire. You're okay."

She flutters her eyes. "Gunnar?"

"Yeah, it's me, baby. You had us all so scared. Sarah is here, too."

"Blaire, are you all right?" Sarah asks.

She doesn't answer.

"We need to get you to the ER," I say.

"She's going to need to make a statement," one of the cops says.

"She can do that later," Sarah says. "Gunnar is right. She needs to be seen by a doctor first."

The cop nods. "Totally understandable. I just need your name, ma'am. Then you can come down to the station later and give your statement."

"Her name is Blaire Cavileri," I say as I help her to her feet. I turn to Sarah. "Do you want to come along?"

She shakes her head. "I think you should take her." Then she turns to Blaire. "I'm so sorry that this happened, Blaire. I had no idea what I was putting into motion when I suggested you partner up with Gunnar."

Blaire shakes her head. "It's not your fault."

"Maybe not. Still, I can't help but feel partially responsible. I know how important this professor was to you."

"All you did was make him show his true colors, Sarah. Better I learn that now. I can always find a new voice teacher."

Sarah nods.

I knew that so-called professor was no good. From the moment I met him, something was off. But it doesn't matter. All that matters is getting Blaire to the hospital.

My God...when I heard her scream through Sarah's phone...

Terror. Pure terror like I've never felt before.

I was terrified of losing something more precious than anything I've ever known.

"Come on, sweetheart," I say. "Let's get you checked out, and once you're feeling up to it, I'll go with you to the police station to make your statement."

"Professor Morgan... I had no idea... That he...felt anything..."

"I'm sure you didn't," I tell her. "It can be hard to see past the façade with someone we've known for so long."

She nods, grimacing. "Thank you. Thank you for coming for me."

I brush my lips lightly over hers. "I'll always come for you, Blaire. You're the sunshine in my rain."

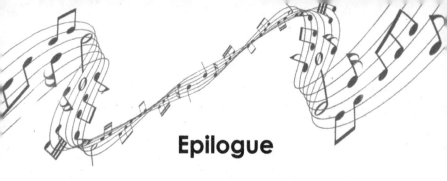

Epilogue

<u>BLAIRE</u>

"Ladies and gentlemen, please welcome to the stage, Gunnar and Blaire!"

Hand-in-hand, Gunnar and I walk onstage to thunderous applause.

We're beginning our tour to promote our album, *Catch My Heart.*

Gunnar caught my heart the day he rescued me from Professor Morgan.

The collaboration has been a smashing success and has put Sarah on the map as an agent and producer. Ariana Waverly is now a sought-after songwriter.

And Gunnar and me?

He's still a rocker at heart, and I'm still an opera singer.

But together...we're so much more.

More than the sum of our parts.

We turn to each other, look into each other's eyes as the band plays our intro.

Gunnar gently kisses me, and then, his lips still only inches from mine, he begins to sing.

THE
NIGHT
WE MET

JILLIAN LIOTA

About the Author

Jillian Liota is a Southern California native currently living in Suwanee, Georgia. She is married to her best friend, has a three-legged pup with endless energy, and acts as a servant to a very temperamental cat.

Jillian writes contemporary and new adult romance, and has had her writing praised for depth of character, strong female friendships, deliciously steamy scenes, and positive portrayal of mental health.

www.jillianliota.com

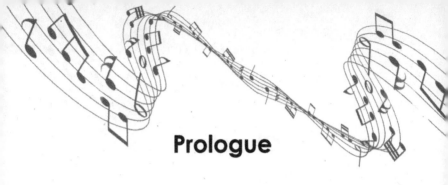

Prologue

<u>MADISON</u>

I'm not sure when I started hearing the music.

Time is funny like that when you're unconscious.

All I know for certain is at some point, in place of the beeps and the quiet voices and the soft footsteps, I began to hear music. A gentle strumming on the guitar and a warm, raspy voice that settled something in my soul as I lay there in my hospital bed, only slightly aware of what was happening around me.

I knew I was hurt. I knew I was tired. I knew I was getting poked and prodded.

But it was a muffled mess.

Except for that voice and the sound of the guitar.

It became what I yearned for.

Day in and day out.

When I finally opened my eyes, I didn't know it would be several years before I would hear it again.

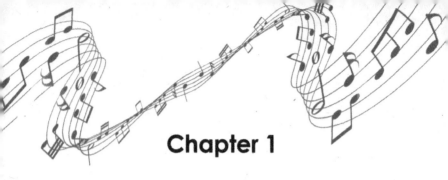

Chapter 1

<u>MADISON</u>

"Are you sure you should be going out? It's late."

I lick my lips and try to school my expression, knowing my sister only has my best interest at heart.

"I'm just going to the gym," I reply, glancing over to where she sits sideways on the couch, her textbooks open in her lap and her legs stretched out in front of her.

She tilts her head to the side, considering me for a beat. "Why don't you call an Uber?"

"It's only five blocks, Avery. I'll be fine."

I want to tell her I'm done with this song and dance every time I go to the gym at night. Or the grocery store. Or out with friends.

But I don't. I never do, and I can't tonight of all nights.

Her face stays slightly pinched, making it clear that my response hasn't alleviated any of her concerns. "Alright, well...call if you need me, okay?"

I give her a tight smile. "Will do." Then I tug the front door open and head out into the hallway, letting out a sigh of relief once I hear the soft thud of it closing behind me.

Freedom.

Much needed, if I'm being honest. The feeling rushes through me once I make it down the elevator and emerge onto the street, the sounds and smells of the city enveloping me as I turn left, heading toward Union Square. I try to remind myself in situations like this one that my sister is looking out for me. She has great intentions and is just worrying because of what happened, but she's my baby sister. I'm supposed to be looking out for her, not the other way around.

I rotate my shoulders and then decide to set the interaction aside like I always do. The reality is that I'm lucky to have people in my life who care about me enough to worry, people who just want to make sure I'm doing okay.

It takes less than ten minutes to get to the gym, and once I've scanned in at the front, I jog up the stairs, heading for the treadmills that overlook the park. Thankfully, the late hour means there are a few available, and I smile to myself, stepping up onto one at the far right.

This is why I like to work out late. Fewer people means I get my favorite spot, and I don't feel pressured to hurry up. This is a busy gym, and on more than a few occasions, I've cut my workout short because people loom around me, waiting for their own chance to hop on the machine.

Not tonight, though.

Once I've tugged my hair up into a loose ponytail at the top of my head and put in my headphones, I click a few buttons and begin a slow-paced jog.

Avery *hates* that I work out late. We've that same conversation on an almost weekly basis since we moved in together, and the frequency doesn't seem to be decreasing in the slightest.

It doesn't matter that it's been three years to the day since the attack that left me unconscious in a hospital bed for weeks. It doesn't matter that I'm on hyper-alert as I walk through the city or that I carry pepper spray now. To Avery, my going out at night alone is something for her to worry about.

Part of me gets it, but another part of me just wants to feel free again, to have that same ease about going out that I had *before*, and Avery's constant questioning makes that difficult. I've tried to put the past behind me, even though it hasn't been easy. Therapy and kickboxing classes have helped me work through a lot of my emotions and fears, and if *I* can move on, Avery should be able to as well.

I bump up the speed on the treadmill, my feet hitting at the same pace as the house music that's made up the majority of my running playlist for years. The heavy bass thumps through my headphones, and I push past my original three-mile goal, feeling like I have the drive right now to go for four instead.

Running is something I've always really enjoyed, though part of why I loved it was because it got me outside. Now, I use the treadmill almost exclusively, though I try not to think about that too hard.

After my attack, I stormed back outside, chin high, completely unwilling to give in to even the slightest bit of fear about being out by myself at night. I'm not sure why running outside is the one thing I've modified in my routine. I wasn't even running when it happened. Apparently, I was out with friends at a bar a few blocks away from the gym, though I don't have any memories of that night.

Regardless, I like to exercise after dark, and now I run at the gym. It's as simple as that. At the very least, I'm sure it gives my sister at least a little solace.

I hit four miles and start my cooldown, my eyes oscillating between the lights of the city outside and my own reflection in the window. Eventually, I power off the treadmill and begin my walk home.

When I get to the corner of Third Avenue, I pause, my eyes snagging on a familiar sign. I should keep walking, should head straight home, where Avery probably hasn't gotten any homework done since I left. But tonight is the anniversary of the night I was attacked, and if there was ever a time to hold my head high and face the past in full, it's now.

So, instead of continuing home, I turn toward Rhythm and Brews. The brick exterior and black wooden doors make the place look almost boring, like so many other New York buildings. Even as unassuming as it is, R&B is a special spot because of the music. Live music seven days a week from 7 p.m. to close. Open mic nights and jazz singers and rock bands. It's an eclectic place, and I've loved it since the first time I stepped foot inside for my 21st birthday.

Though—sadly—I haven't been back. Understandably.

The sound of whoever is playing tonight is loud enough to hear from where I stand 150 feet away, and when there's a break between cars, I jog across the street and push through the wooden double doors before I have a chance to think better of it. The place is packed, and I hover near the entrance for a few minutes, my eyes scanning over everyone and everything. It all looks the same. The same bartenders in all black. Same crowded room and table setup. Same dim lights and a hint of weed and vape smoke in the slightly hazy air.

"Can I get you something?"

I glance at the bartender giving me a friendly smile as she wipes down the bartop in front of her. Before I can respond, the room erupts in cheers as the band finishes up a song.

"I forgot how loud this place is," I say, stepping forward, returning her smile.

She nods. "Tonight especially. KellyKills is up there."

My brows rise in recognition. They're not a global sensation or anything, but even I have heard of KellyKills before, and I hear the lead vocalist speak into the microphone.

"We love performing in this fucking city, our hometown because New Yorkers are the best fucking people in the world."

Another round of cheers goes up, and I shake my head, laughing quietly to myself. Normally, when I used to come to R&B, I picked the quieter nights when the music was in the background. Tonight, there's a full-on concert happening.

"Can I get a water?" I ask the bartender. "I'm only gonna stay for one more song."

She nods, tugging out a highball and filling it with ice.

My head jerks to the side when I hear the guitar begin to strum a melody that's been dancing around in the back of my mind for years.

What...?

"And because you're the best fucking people in the world, in the best fucking city in the world, we're gonna play some new music tonight."

More cheers, but I'm still focused on the sound of that guitar as the chords start over again, repeating from the beginning. My heart picks up pace, a kind of nervous, jittery energy beginning to pump through my veins.

"Did you want your water?" the bartender calls out to me, but I'm already slipping through the crowd, making my way toward the front of the room. It's not a huge bar, but it's large enough to fit maybe 150 people in with standing room only. Everyone's on their feet, their phones high as they take pictures of the almost-famous people on the stage.

"Scotty wrote this song," I hear over the speakers.

"Love you, Scotty!" someone shouts, and the crowd laughs.

I curse my short stature as I continue forward, wishing I could see over the heads of the people around me.

"Scotty wrote this song," the lead repeats, "and tonight, you all are going to be the first to hear it. It's called Wake Me Up."

The melody starts over again just as I slip along the edge of the crowd, finally getting a good vantage point for seeing the four musicians who make up KellyKills where they stand on a small stage barely a foot off the floor. When their lead singer, Shawn, I think his name is, starts singing, somehow, I already know the words.

How do I know this song?

Or, better question...how do they know this song?

I watch, something familiar skittering down my spine and drawing me back to all those nights after I got out of the hospital when I would lie in bed and stare at the ceiling, wondering where the music had come from, the music I could hear as I lay unconscious in my hospital bed.

My family didn't have any kind of explanation. They told me I must have been hearing music over the speakers or someone's phone, but I knew they were wrong. I just didn't have any way to describe it. All I had were the memories of music I couldn't identify, and no matter how much I searched and searched, I couldn't ever find that song.

Now, here it is—though the voice is wrong. I watch the lead singer, mouthing the words along with him, my fingers twitching at my sides.

Then I hear a raspy sound, and my eyes fly to the other guitarist. He's singing in the background, providing the harmony, but I know that voice. I *know* that voice. I listen, hypnotized, unable to look away. A tender spot inside of me feels like it's been opened wide, and it aches...but in the best way.

When the song comes to an end, the crowd goes wild, and the man I've been staring at gives a tiny smile, his eyes flicking out over the crowd as he adjusts his guitar strap around his neck. His head turns, his eyes scanning my side of the room briefly, connecting with mine for less than a second before continuing...

...and then slamming back to me.

I feel like I have to be imagining it when they widen slightly, and his entire body turns in my direction, but I'm not. He stares at me long and hard, and I swallow thickly, a shiver running through me as I wait under his piercing gaze.

Someone behind me moves, bumping me, and I break my connection with the guy on stage. For reasons I can't explain, I take the opportunity to slip through the crowd again, making my way back to the entrance with an urgency I don't fully understand. I'm suddenly desperate to get out of this bar, to get outside where I can breathe fresh air.

When I finally shove through the doors and back out onto the street, I take a long, deep breath and tilt my head back, closing my eyes. It was just too many people. That must have been it. The racing heart and staring at that guy, that had to have been—

"Excuse me."

My entire body freezes at the sound of his voice, and when I turn around, I find the guitarist standing a few feet away, hands tucked into his front pockets. Everything about him feels familiar, but...I don't know him. Right?

He watches me with an intensity I don't understand, and eventually, I manage one word.

"Hi."

His lips tilt up at the sides. "You're here."

I blink a few times, then nod. "I'm here."

"You don't know who I am," he replies after a few seconds, and even though there's no tone in his words to convey disappointment, I can sense it just from the way his shoulders droop slightly.

Licking my lips, I glance to the side before returning my eyes to his. Deep blue. Magnetic. Difficult to look away from for too long.

"I don't," I finally reply. "Should I?"

At that, he takes a step closer and holds out his hand. "I'm Scott," he says. "Scott Kelly."

I also take a step forward, as if my body is compelled to do so, and slip my hand into his. "I'm Madi."

Scott's head tilts to the side, his eyes brightening just a bit. "Madi. Nice to finally meet you."

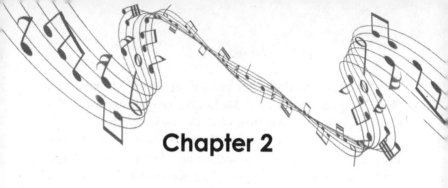

Chapter 2

<u>SCOTT</u>

She's here.

I don't know what I did in a past life to deserve this kind of karma from the universe, but I'll be forever grateful because she's fucking *here*.

Madison.

Or, I guess she goes by Madi. I only ever heard the nurses call her Ms. Madison when I was visiting her at the hospital, and it feels good to learn something small about her that I didn't know before. Especially when she's been such an ever-present question in the back of my mind over the past few years since I found her lying in an alley a few blocks from where we stand right now.

"Finally?"

I tilt my head to the side. "What?"

"You said finally. Nice to *finally* meet you."

At that, l let out an awkward chuckle, having always known if we met—for real—I'd have to explain how I know her. Though I guess I don't, really.

Rubbing at the stubble along my jaw, I try to think over what I should say in response, how to explain to her who I am. What I absolutely don't want is to scare her or bring back any emotions or fears from that night.

She speaks before I do, her beautiful, caramel-colored eyes locked on mine.

"I knew that song. The one you guys played, the new one."

My eyebrows lift in surprise.

"I've been hearing it for years in my head," she continues, "but I've never known why." Madi takes another step forward so there's just a foot or so between us. "Do *you* know why?"

I do. It's because she was the inspiration for its creation. Because I wrote it as I sat in a chair next to the door just inside her hospital room. Because once it was finished, I played it for her every night that I could.

The fact that she knows it—that she's been hearing it in her head—fills something inside of me that I didn't know was empty.

"I sang that song to you when you were in the hospital," I finally say, wondering how she'll respond.

It's not every day you find out some guy sat in your hospital room while you were unconscious, playing music. As much as I know I'm a good guy, she doesn't know me at all. Part of me expects her to recoil, step back in shock, and make a face of disapproval.

What I don't see coming is that smile.

My god.

That. Smile. I've never seen Madi smile before, and it sends a shock straight through me. It's bright and wild and beautiful, better than I ever could have imagined.

Then she steps forward and wraps her arms around my shoulders, her chest flush with mine, pulling me in tight.

"I'm sorry for hugging you without asking," she says, her voice a sweet whisper near my ear. "Especially because I just finished working out. But oh my god, I felt like I was going crazy."

I bring my hands to her back, my eyes closing as I breathe her in, the fresh, citrusy smell of whatever lotion or perfume she's wearing completely at odds with the city. It takes effort to keep my hands braced against her back instead of letting them roam and tug her in closer, which feels so natural.

"I heard that song over and over again, but I couldn't figure it out. I didn't..." She pauses and pulls back so she can look me in the eye. "I thought I made it up. The guitar. The words." Her eyes dip to my mouth for a beat. "Your voice."

The urge to kiss her sweeps through me, but I hold fast. This is a woman who has been through plenty, a woman I don't actually know, regardless of how close I feel to her after the weeks I spent at the hospital and how many times I've thought of her over the years. I've literally dreamt of this moment, wondered what it might be like if we bumped into each other in the chaos of this big world, what I might do or say.

And now, she's here.

Right here.

In my arms.

She brings her forehead to mine and closes her eyes. "Are you the one who saved me?" she whispers.

I nod. "Yeah," I whisper back. "I am."

Madi opens her eyes, and I see they're brimming with tears just before she pulls me back in for another hug. Her hands grip me tightly like she doesn't ever want to let go, and this time, I don't resist the urge to pull her in closer. Holding her in my arms just feels right.

Why does it feel so right?

"Dude, what the hell was that?"

The sound of my brother's voice behind me shatters the intimacy of this moment, and whatever little cocoon we were in evaporates, letting in the sounds of the city and the glaring street lights and the people passing us by.

"You just fucking bailed? We're in the middle of a show."

I turn, releasing Madi. I look at Shawn standing a few feet away, his arms crossed and an irritated expression covering his face. He looks like he could spit nails.

"Madi, this is my brother, Shawn," I say. "Shawn, this is Madi."

He rolls his eyes. "Did you even hear me? You need to get back inside."

"This is *Madison*." My words come out tersely as I stress her name, a name he's very familiar with.

Shawn blinks, and then his head jerks back, realization visibly rolling through him. "*Madison*, Madison?" he clarifies.

As if there could ever be another one.

We were together on the night I found Madison in the alley. He went with me to the hospital and sat with me in the lobby as I waited for an update, covered in blood and dirt from kneeling on the ground and picking her up then holding her as we sped through the city streets. His smile grows wide on his face as he realizes who she is, and he claps his hands together.

"Well, holy shit!" He steps closer and brings her in for a hug, making her laugh. "So glad to see you up and well," he says, moving back and assessing her before looking at me. "Now your little skedaddle off stage makes a bit more sense."

I roll my eyes. "Nobody says skedaddle."

He ignores my comment. "Look, now that you've met while she's conscious, get her number, then get your ass back inside, alright? We're still performing." He winks at Madison and backs up to the doors of Rhythm & Brews. "Nice to meet you, sweetheart."

I snort at his blatant flirting as he disappears back into the bar, knowing the showboat inside him can't keep from doing shit like that.

"Sorry about him," I say to Madison, turning back to look at her.

She grins. "He seems nice."

I chuckle, though it fades when I realize I have to head back in. "I do need to get back to the show, though," I say. "Can I get your number? We're in town for a couple of days, and I..."

"Yes." Her response is quick, and she tucks her chin for a beat and shifts on her feet. "Yes, you can have my number."

We take a quick second to swap information, and once I have her name in my phone, I look at it for a long second.

Madi Ross.

I didn't know her last name before, and getting that next piece of information feels like a treasure. I tuck my phone away in my pocket, already eager to use it and planning to text her as immediately as possible.

"I guess you need to go back in there," she says, and I don't think I'm imagining the tinge of disappointment in her voice.

I nod. It's a struggle for me to step away from her. Part of me can't help but fear I'll lose her again after waiting so long to find her. I reach out and tuck some of her loose hairs behind her ear, then stroke my thumb along the sharp angle of her jaw and chin.

"I'll call you tomorrow," I tell her.

Madi nods. "You better."

I grin.

After a few more seconds of just staring at her beautiful face—her wide eyes and button nose and heart-shaped mouth—I finally do the impossible and go back inside. Once I'm on the stage a few minutes later, I pick up my guitar and slip the strap over my shoulder. I feel distracted as Shawn speaks into the mic. We start the next song, and it takes incredible mental effort to get myself into the right headspace.

But then, over the heads of the crowd, my eyes catch sight of the doors at the entrance opening again, and my heart thuds as Madi walks through and takes a seat at the bar.

She's still here.

Performing like this—with a vibrant audience and high energy—is something I have always lived for, but having Madi here to watch me brings things to new heights, and I play my heart out knowing she's watching. The next hour flies by as we rock out to song after song, focusing on the ones that have been getting the most plays over the past year. It's wild to think back to where I was just a few years ago when Shawn and I were barely scraping by and trying to make a name for ourselves. Now, we're playing sold-out shows and going on tour. It's a dream we fought long and hard for.

When we wrap for the night, I don't take the time my brother does to meet fans or sign autographs. I just want to play, but my brother wants the lifestyle, which works out perfectly because they all prefer Shawn anyway.

Instead, I slip through the crowd, ignoring any attempts to get my attention, and head in the direction of where Madi is waiting, still at the bar.

"You stayed," I say, unable to hide my grin as I approach where she sits, sipping a glass of wine.

Madi nods. "I did."

"Why?"

At that, she tilts her head to the side, her expression growing soft. "I wasn't ready to say goodbye."

I nibble on the inside of my cheek as I consider my words, finally deciding to just say exactly what's on my mind.

"Do you want to get out of here?"

Her lips curve. "Absolutely."

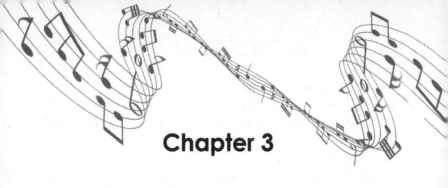

Chapter 3

MADISON

I've been living in New York since I first came here for college. I went from a small residence hall room to a tiny apartment to a studio that I lived in up until my attack. After that, I didn't want to be alone.

Sure, I still storm out of my apartment into the night, refusing to allow the past to rob me of my freedom. But getting hit over the head with a bat, robbed, and left for dead in an alley will make even the bravest person think twice about independence.

I wouldn't ever say this to Avery, but I don't feel safe anymore, not anywhere. I'm always nervous, even if I refuse to let anyone see it, even if I refuse to change my behaviors in deference to that fear. I'm still afraid.

But as Scott and I wander through the city, I've never felt so safe. It feels amazing to hold hands with the man who saved your life.

The doctor said if another hour or two had gone by without medical intervention, I might have had brain damage or lost significantly more blood. Instead, I was kept in an induced coma for a few weeks after surgery while my body did some work to heal itself, and I only had minor cognitive issues for the first several months after I left the hospital.

Now, I'm completely back to normal—minus the fear—and the fact that I get to wander through the East Village with him fills me with a surge of something I can't name. Joy, maybe. Excitement, certainly. But something else.

Maybe it's not that I can't name it; it's that I don't want to.

Because the word flitting around in my head is *desire*, and that can't be right.

Surely not.

His hand is warm and reassuring in mine, and that should be it, but when his thumb strokes gently against the inside of my wrist, a shiver races through me, pooling low in my belly.

I let out a long, steady breath. He's incredibly attractive, and I want to know what it would be like to press my lips against his, to feel his tongue ring as he traces the inside of my mouth.

Another shiver ripples through me.

"Are you cold?" he asks, his voice low as he leans close.

I shake my head, but he's already pulling off his jacket and bringing it around my shoulders. Part of me wants to decline, but I change my mind once I'm wrapped in the smell of him— something warm and spicy and uniquely him.

We don't go anywhere specific. There's no end point in mind. We just stroll aimlessly, sharing our histories, our lives, for hours, and it isn't until we end up at The Battery that I realize we've wandered *miles,* something I haven't done in this city for three years.

Sure, I've walked to work, to run errands, to meet up with friends, but I haven't *wandered.* Not really. Not without a care, not without a purpose or a place to be. And the fact that Scott has given that back to me, tonight of all nights, makes me more emotional than I would ever admit.

Eventually, our feet begin to protest. After I call my sister to give her a brief update and reassure her that I'm okay, we call an Uber to take us to wherever Scott's staying in Brooklyn. He holds my hand as we drive, both of us quiet in the darkness, the city lights fading away as we cross the Brooklyn Bridge, and I realize he has barely let it go since we left R&B hours ago.

Not that I'm complaining.

"Our management company asked if we had opinions about

where we stayed for the couple days we're here," Scott tells me as we walk down the hallway on the 8th floor of a boutique hotel facing the East River. "Growing up in Bushwick, I always wanted a nice city view. So that's what I asked for, and they delivered."

He swipes a key card at the end of the hall and pushes inside. I can't help the way my jaw drops when I see what he means.

"A city view? That is *the* city view," I tell him, laughing.

Through the floor-to-ceiling windows is the iconic skyline, lit up in all her glory. There are only so many places you can get a vantage point like this, and they are almost all way above my pay grade. Getting to see a sight like this is something special.

"And it gets better," he says, smirking as he leads me through the hotel room that's almost as big as my entire apartment and over to a door leading out to a balcony.

We push outside into the cool air of the late spring evening, each of us stepping up to the railing and leaning against it, just taking in the beautiful night and the view in front of us.

"This is amazing," I say, shaking my head.

"It really is."

After a few minutes, I turn and look at Scott, finding him already watching me. I know instinctively that we're going to talk about that night, and I'm relieved. I have so many questions.

"Do you remember anything?" he asks, his voice gritty but gentle.

I shake my head. "Nothing. The whole day is a blur, and then I was in an induced coma for several weeks, so once I woke up, that was kind of a blur, too."

"That must be hard."

Shrugging, I turn my back on the city and cross my arms as I lean against the rail behind me. "Sometimes. For months afterward, I would lie awake and try to will myself to remember something. A sound or a smell, anything. But there was nothing." I pause. "Except for music."

When I look at Scott again, he's looking at his hands where they're dangling over the railing.

"My family tried to convince me I was hearing music from someone's phone or on the overhead speakers, but that never felt right to me. It was so close, and I could hear the words and the voice." I tilt my head to the side. "Your voice, though I didn't know it was yours because I didn't know *you*."

Scott nods then turns to face me.

"Will you tell me what happened?"

He takes a deep breath and lets it out slowly. "Shawn and I were walking to the station when two guys blew past us, almost knocking me over. When I looked down the alley they came from, I could see a pair of pink high heels on the ground next to a dumpster."

"It was 80s night," I tell him, though I only know because my friends told me once I woke up.

"Makes sense." His face darkens slightly as he continues. "I assumed they were trash, but I wanted to double-check, just to be sure. When I approached the dumpster, I found you lying on the ground behind it." Scott shakes his head. "Shawn called 911, but once I knew you were still alive, I picked you up and ran to the street. We flagged a cab and took you to Bellevue."

My heart pangs at the picture of this man holding my bloodied and beaten body in the back of a cab.

"I waited for a long time, both of us did," he continues. "Eventually, the doctor sent us home. They wouldn't give us any information, but I came back a few days later at night and slipped one of the night nurses a twenty. She let me sit in your room for an hour because you were right next to the nurse's station so she could watch me."

At that, I smile. "Was that Taryn?"

Scott nods. "How'd you know?"

I shrug. "She just seemed like the soft-heart type who would let you in against the rules."

"Well, I'm glad she did. I came back as many nights as I could. I didn't want you to be alone."

I was alone. I'd been robbed and had no ID on me. The

only reason the hospital knew my first name was because of the necklace I was wearing with my name on it in silver script. The friends I'd gone out with were people I didn't see often. None of my family lived in the city, and I normally led a very busy life, only calling occasionally. So, apart from Scott visiting, I was completely alone. I was Madison Doe until I woke up and could give them my information.

Of course, my family was mortified that I'd been in the hospital for several weeks and they hadn't known. The next year when my sister started grad school at NYU, we got an apartment together. So now, I'm almost *never* alone. I rarely go longer than a day without hearing from a family member. Sometimes I joke that they have me on a scheduled rotation for check-ins.

Knowing Scott was there, knowing he took the time to come back and make sure I was okay, day after day...warms something in my chest. I *wasn't* alone after all.

"And the music?" I ask, still unsure about that part.

At that, Scott blushes slightly, looking back out to the city across the water. "I read something about music helping with brain function, so I brought my guitar and sang to you a little bit." He shrugs.

I let out a long breath, feeling like this information is giving me a kind of closure I didn't know I needed, a kind of resolution to the trauma I went through. It's wild how connected I feel to Scott and, if I'm reading him right, how connected he feels to me. Just the way he introduced me to his brother, the way he emphasized my name—clearly, they've talked about me plenty.

Though that leaves one more question.

"Why didn't you come when I woke up?" I turn so I'm facing Scott fully, leaning sideways against the rail, then reach out and take his hand in mine. "I would have loved to meet the man who saved my life."

His face pinches. "Shawn and I went out of town for a few days—family stuff—and when I got back, you were gone. You'd woken up, and your parents had you moved somewhere else. I didn't even know your last name, and Taryn wouldn't budge. Said she could lose her job if I went looking for you and mentioned anything about her." Scott shakes his head. "But I wanted to. I wanted to talk to you, wanted to know you were okay."

I didn't know anything about Scott until tonight. All I was told was that a good Samaritan brought me to the hospital, and that was why I walked away mostly unscathed. I wish I had known. I wish I'd known he sat vigil at my bedside whenever he could, even knowing he could get in trouble.

And I wish I could have met him back then. Talked to him. *Thanked* him.

Though, I guess I can do that now.

"Thank you," I say, squeezing his hand in mine.

But he shakes his head. "You don't have to thank me."

"I do, though." I inch closer to him, dipping my head to catch his eyes. "You quite literally made the difference between me standing here, completely healthy, and something that could have been much, much worse."

He squeezes my hand back. "I'm just glad you're okay."

We watch each other for a beat, and then I take a step closer, tucking myself into his side. As if it's the most natural thing in the world, his arm wraps around my shoulder, pulling me close.

His warmth seeps through my clothes, embedding itself into my skin and nestling beneath my bones. I wasn't cold before, but the feeling of being next to him, wrapped in him, warms me just the same.

Our embrace grows long, and I rest my face against his chest, my hands rubbing gently against his back. Scott holds me like I'm precious, and the caring way his fingers stroke down my spine sends that shiver through me again. I tilt my head back, gazing up into his eyes and breathing out a sigh of relief when I think I see the same look mirrored back at me.

Desire.

That idea is back again, and before it can dissipate or be explained away or dismissed, I rise up onto my toes and press my lips to his.

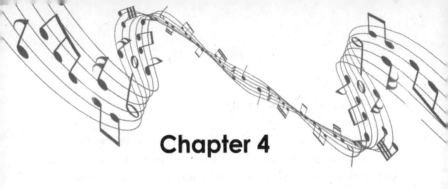

Chapter 4

SCOTT

I only allow myself a beat or two of surprise before I return Madi's eager kiss with my own, my mouth opening and my tongue dipping inside, tasting her sweetness. Not in my wildest dreams did I ever think something like this would happen tonight.

Okay, maybe that's a lie. Maybe in my *wildest* dreams, I could envision a night of passion with the girl who has been on my mind for years, but never in reality. Never like this, never with such a deep, obvious connection that I never could have expected.

From the moment I saw her earlier tonight, there was a sense of knowing her. And I think, just maybe, it feels the same way for her.

Then a thought occurs to me, and I pull away, breaking our kiss.

"This isn't some like...thank you, is it?" I say, panting as if I've run a mile. "Because I would never want..."

"No!" she says, shock in her tone, though it cuts off as she laughs. "Oh my god, no."

A tightness in my chest eases at her reassurance. I didn't think it was true, but I wanted to be sure, even if it made things awkward to ask.

"Good."

"No, definitely not. I just..." She shakes her head and steps back, and I instantly miss her warmth. "Do you feel it? This..." She waves her hand between us. "...connection? Or whatever?"

I nod. "I do."

Her shoulders fall. "Really?"

I nod again. "Yeah."

Madi's smile returns, the brightness of it so relieving.

"Thank god. Because I felt it the moment I saw you tonight, and part of me thought maybe it was just because you're the man who saved my life, but I don't think that's it. I think there's something else, something special. Something..."

Her words trail off as I take her face into my hands.

"It is something special," I tell her, my voice low, my eyes taking in every part of her that I can see. The freckles on either side of her nose and the tiny scar above her lip. The way the hairs at her temples have grown curlier as the night has progressed. The rosy flush on her cheeks.

I don't think it's possible to know you're in love with someone this quickly, but it's hard to categorize the way I feel without using the word love because I love everything about her. I love all these little bits of information I'm learning as I get to know her. I love watching her smile and hearing her laugh. I love holding her close.

But mostly, I love the brightness I can see in her eyes, a brightness this world might have lost if things had been even just slightly different three years ago. The night we met.

Even if we may have introduced ourselves for the first time tonight, we left a mark on each other years ago.

"I'm so glad I found you," she whispers, slipping her hands around my waist before sliding them underneath the flannel of my shirt so they're pressed against my bare skin.

I lick my lips. "And I'm so glad *I* found *you*," I reply, knowing the words have a different meaning when I say them.

Her eyes soften momentarily, then I bring my mouth to hers again. She opens, her tongue twisting with mine, our hands beginning to shift and grab and pull. The softness of the earlier moment dissipates, and the desire I felt before returns with a vengeance. I moan as Madi moves her body, pressing the softer parts of her against the harder parts of me.

"Will you stay?" I ask quietly as I kiss down her neck.

"There's nowhere else I want to be," she answers.

I smile and then bring my lips to hers before leading her inside.

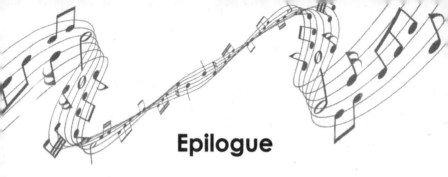

Epilogue

<u>MADISON</u>

I'm not sure when I start hearing the music.

Time is funny like that when you're sleeping so deeply.

All I know for certain is at some point, in place of the air conditioner's hum and the city noise outside the window of our apartment, I begin to hear music. A gentle strumming on the guitar and a warm, raspy voice that always settles something in my soul as I lie dozing in our king-size bed, only barely beginning to rise out of sleep.

I know I'm safe. I know I'm rested. I know I'm warm.

But it's so early.

Except I love hearing that voice and the sound of the guitar.

It's what I yearn for.

Day in and day out.

When I finally open my eyes and see him sitting in his familiar spot next to the fireplace, I smile.

ROCK
ENCORE

KAT MIZERA

About the Author

USA Today Bestselling Author Kat Mizera was born in Miami Beach with a healthy dose of Wanderlust. She's lived from coast to coast, and everywhere in between, but home is wherever her family is. A devoted mom and wife to her wonderful and supportive husband (Kevin) and two amazing boys (Nick and Max), Kat loves to travel the globe with her adventurous, hockey loving family. Greece is at the top of that list. She hopes to one day retire there, spending her days writing books on the beach.

Kat is former freelance sports writer who now writes steamy hockey romance about her favorite fictional teams, the Las Vegas Sidewinders and the Lauderdale Knights. The library of novels she's penned also include sexy contemporary stories about baseball stars, alpha sex club owners, bodyguards, rock stars, and royalty. Regardless of genre, her books about bad boys with hearts of gold will steal your breath, rock your world and melt your heart.

www.katmizera.com

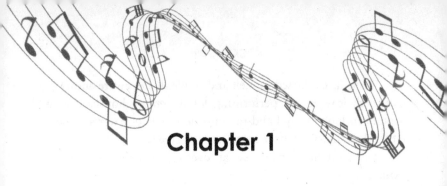

Chapter 1

<u>ROSS</u>

The lights went down and I jogged in place, warming up.

The crowd was loud tonight.

Energetic and excited and ready for some rock and roll.

I caught the eye of my lead guitarist and nodded.

Our drummer was already out there, kicking a rhythmic staccato on the bass drum. The bass player matched his time, punching out deep, low beats that reverberated through the arena.

It was go time.

I ran out on stage and grabbed my mic just as the spotlight hit me.

"Phoenix!" I yelled. "Who's ready for some Ross and roll?!"

Our catchphrase sent the crowd into a frenzy as my drummer counted off.

"1-2-3-4!"

We went right into 'Hot and Hammered', our newest release, and I danced across the stage, my feet moving in time to the beat.

Getting so high so we can't get by
Loving by the lights of the city
Ridin' on the back with your hair in the air
Damn, baby, you look so pretty.

I leaned forward, singing to the ladies in the front row.

But something was wrong.

Their faces started to melt and suddenly the entire audience vanished, leaving me performing for an empty house. I spun around to look at my band in confusion, but they weren't there either. Just lifeless blobs melting into the stage...

I sat straight up in bed, sweat covering my body like a second skin.

Not again.

I wiped my hands down my face, breathing hard, trying to still the hammering of my heart.

God damn nightmares.

I'd been having the same one at least once a week for nearly two decades.

They always started the same, with me living my dream, and ended with the nightmare of my reality.

No amount of therapy, pharmaceutical intervention, or even alcohol stopped them from coming back. The only thing that stopped them was not sleeping, and I could only go so long before that caught up to me.

I got out of bed and padded to the bathroom.

After taking care of business, I washed my face and stared into the mirror.

At forty-two, I didn't think I was old, but my days as a rockstar felt like a lifetime ago.

It had been nearly twenty years since I'd walked away from it all, and most days I considered myself lucky.

Today wasn't one of those days.

Yanking on shorts and a T-shirt, I slid my feet into flip-flops and grabbed my phone and room key. As the tour manager for one of the biggest bands in the world, I didn't go anywhere without my phone. Not even to the john most of the time.

We'd finished a short European tour back in April and taken the summer off to regroup while the band wrote new music and worked in the studio. Now we'd just kicked off what would probably be a two-year world tour with friends and family along for the ride. It was a lot, with a ton of logistics to manage, but I loved my job ninety-nine percent of the time, so I didn't mind.

Except when I didn't get enough sleep.

That tended to make me cranky.

It was currently five thirty in the morning, so the Phoenix hotel was quiet, which was exactly how I liked it. It would give me time to ease into my day, and maybe work through some of the surly attitude I felt coming on.

I wished I'd brought my cigarettes with me, but I'd been trying to quit.

For about a decade.

How's that working out for you, asshole? I asked myself wryly.

I tended to have a lot of solo conversations these days, since I was firmly unattached in my personal life and spent too much time working to cultivate many friendships outside the Onyx Knight organization.

A faint cloud of smoke caught my attention as I rounded the corner to the pool, and I tried to ascertain where it was coming from.

The slight silhouette of a woman caught my attention. She was standing with her back to me, the only time she moved was when she lifted her arm to take a puff of her cigarette. She seemed completely lost in thought, and I hated to disturb her, but the aroma of nicotine pulled me toward her like gravity.

I approached as noisily as I could so as not to scare her.

"Excuse me. Do you think I could bum—" I cut myself off abruptly when I recognized her. "Wynter?"

She turned, a soft smile playing on her lips. "You caught me."

"Is the fact that you're an early riser and a smoker a secret?" I asked, smiling back.

She shrugged. "Harley gets on me about the smoking. It's bad for us, right? I don't know about you, but I was raised in an era where everyone from our teachers to our parents to the advertisements on TV advised us against it."

"And yet, here we are." I plucked the cigarette from her fingers and put it to my lips, taking a long, deep pull.

God, that felt good.

I was probably sending myself to an early grave, but what the hell? I'd already cheated death on a grand scale, so what difference did it make? It wasn't like I had anyone at home waiting for me.

"Why are you up so early?" she asked, watching me curiously.

I shrugged. "Couldn't sleep."

"Same." She took the cigarette back and proceeded to blow perfect little rings above her pretty face.

She had soft, feminine features, with a pert nose, a bow-shaped upper lip, and a heart-shaped face. Her honey-blonde hair was shoulder length, with soft waves that moved when she did, and I could imagine running my fingers through it. It was probably silky and soft. Like the rest of her.

I caught myself before letting my fantasy go any further.

Wynter wasn't a groupie, so she wasn't up for grabs.

She had no business in my fantasies either.

She was my drummer's sister-in-law, and she was in Phoenix on business or something. I'd seen her briefly yesterday when she and a couple of the girls had gotten back from some fancy spa in Sedona. Since she was Tommy's wife's sister, I'd met her on several occasions over the years, but I'd never paid much attention because I didn't mess around with friends and family of the band. Entanglements like that tended to get messy, no matter how careful you were.

Frankly, groupies weren't my thing anymore, so it felt like I'd been impersonating a monk the last couple of years.

Not that I wasn't interested in sex.

I just kept it casual, saving it for the occasional one-night stand on the road.

From what I'd seen of Wynter, she didn't strike me as the one-night stand type.

"I don't sleep anymore," she said, surprising me. "It started when River was born. Then it got worse with my new job. That's when I went from smoking socially, usually just when I was having a drink or something, to craving it all the time. Then I just stopped sleeping more than two or three hours at a time. I've been at this job less than six months and it feels like an eternity."

"Sounds like hell," I said thoughtfully.

I understood what it was like to be in hell.

It wasn't like that with my job, thankfully, but there had been a lot of periods of my life that had felt that way, so I could commiserate.

"Sometimes. But it pays the bills."

"There's more to life than money."

"Spoken like a man who's learned that lesson?"

Now we were in dangerous territory.

I didn't like to talk about the past.

Ever.

"You could say that."

She smiled wryly. "It's okay, Ross. I won't spill the beans."

"Excuse me?" I frowned at her in confusion.

"I know who you are."

Chapter 2

WYNTER

I regretted the words the moment they slipped out. Instead of being shy or surprised that I'd recognized him, Ross seemed almost angry. His silvery-blue eyes turned dark. I could see the fire lurking there even in the limited pre-dawn light, since the sun hadn't come up yet, and I mentally kicked myself. I hadn't been trying to be confrontational, I merely wanted to let him know I understood where he was coming from.

"I'm sorry," I said quickly. "I didn't realize it was a secret. I was trying to be funny, that's all. I apologize."

His face was tight. "The past is best left where it is."

"But you're... *Ross Rocket*." I whispered, as if someone might hear us. "How has no one recognized you? The video for 'Shooting for the Stars' was everywhere when I was a kid. My mom played that album constantly."

"It's been nearly twenty years," he responded quietly, grinding the cigarette into the concrete with his shoe. "I haven't been Ross Rocket in a long time. And I want it to stay that way." With that, he turned and strode in the opposite direction.

Damn.

I hadn't meant to upset him.

Hell, I'd come out here to clear my head after another miserable night of insomnia.

I'd left my extremely demanding job as an emergency room nurse at a Los Angeles hospital and taken a job in the private sector, as the office manager for a busy doctors' practice. I'd thought it would be easy compared to twelve-hour shifts in the ER. Instead, the pressure, along with the insane hours, left me staring at the walls most nights.

The company had sent me to Phoenix for a training conference on some new software, and when I'd seen that Onyx Knight would be in town, I'd reached out to my sister. She'd recently remarried Tommy, Onyx Knight's drummer, and was on tour with the band, so she'd put my name on the list. I'd hoped seeing my sister and hearing live music would be the perfect way to relax and unwind after the week of training, but so far it hadn't worked.

Not even yesterday's spa day had helped, and I'd finally given up on sleep just after four in the morning.

Running into Ross—aka my crush—at the pool had felt fortuitous.

Until I'd opened my mouth and messed everything up.

With a sigh, I headed back inside, undecided about whether I wanted to attempt to get a few hours' sleep or if I should go to the hotel gym and exhaust myself into a nap. Sleeping pills were always an option, but I'd resisted so far. At some point, I might have to give in, but for now, I was taking things one day at a time.

"Wynter. Wait."

I turned in surprise to see Ross heading my way.

I averted my gaze, trying not to stare.

I'd had a crush on him as a kid, watching Ross & the Rockets videos on TV and dancing around the living room to their music. My mother, sister, and I had been huge fans, and it had been something we'd shared until our mother's death a few years ago.

"Hey, I'm sorry about before." He strode over to me, and we came to a stop, facing each other. "No one's ever recognized me before. Not since I started working for Onyx Knight. You caught me off-guard, but I shouldn't have been a jerk. I apologize for that."

"It's okay." I shrugged. "I shouldn't have said anything. Your secrets are none of my business."

"I could've handled it better. And honestly, it's not a secret.

I've just moved on and don't think about it that much."

"That's fair. And I'm sorry too. I shouldn't have blindsided you. My bad."

"Can I buy you breakfast?"

He was asking me on a date.

Casual, platonic, it didn't matter.

My teenage crush had just asked me to breakfast.

Hopefully, I wouldn't sound as excited as I felt.

"Sure." I followed him back inside without doing a little jig and we headed to the hotel restaurant, which had just opened.

Since we were the only people there, they seated us by a window where we could watch the rising sun.

"When did you know?" Ross asked once we had coffee and had placed our food orders.

"Since the first time I met you," I admitted. "As soon as I saw the tattoo on your forearm, I thought it looked familiar, so I found the video for 'Baby's Got My Heart', and sure enough, that was it."

He nodded, absently rubbing his hand over the tattoo. "I forget it's there most of the time."

"And no one else has ever recognized it?" I asked incredulously.

"A few times, but it's more like, hey, that looks like the tattoo from 'Baby's Got' and I usually just laugh and tell them that was my inspiration."

"And the whole thing where your name is Ross and the band was called Ross & The Rockets?"

"What can I tell you? I've done a good job at going incognito. And it doesn't hurt that there's some gray in my hair now, I wear glasses, shit like that."

"Well, I won't expose you. So to speak."

He chuckled. "I appreciate that. It's just... It's not who I am anymore. And I don't want it to become a thing. I like my job and wouldn't want to do anything that might look bad for the band."

"You think they would care?" I asked curiously.

"I don't think they'd be upset, but I don't know how they'd feel about it if I suddenly started getting asked for autographs or interviews. That wouldn't be cool."

"No, probably not." I paused. "Don't you miss it? If nothing else, the music?"

He smiled, though it didn't quite reach his eyes. "Sometimes? I still play a little guitar and write songs, but I write under a different name, so very few people know it's me. I can't do the touring thing forever, so that's my retirement money."

I was suddenly overwhelmed with sadness for him.

Everyone knew the story of the horrific bus crash that had killed the other members of his band, along with Ross's fiancée, the band's tour manager, and the driver. Somehow, Ross had emerged unscathed, and he'd walked away without a backward glance, according to everything I'd read.

Not that I could ask him.

"Go ahead," he said after a moment. "I can see all the questions you don't want to ask. It's all over your face. Let's get it over with. That way, we can both move on."

I flushed, a bit embarrassed at having been caught.

"It's okay," I said. "I've already made a nuisance of myself. We can talk about something else."

He cocked his head. "Tell you what. You ask me any question you want, and then I get to ask you one."

"All right." I took a sip of coffee. "What was your favorite song on the album?" Ross & The Rockets only had one.

"Easy," he said with a faint smile. "The best song on the album was 'City Love'. And ironically, it's the only one I didn't write on my own. We wrote that one as a band and it's always been my favorite."

"That's my favorite too," I said. "I play it in the car on the way to work. Pumps me up to get ready for my day."

"That's nice to hear." He met my gaze. "Somehow, I can picture it. You driving something small, like a Mini Cooper, radio blasting, and singing at the top of your lungs."

I threw my head back and laughed, amazed at his astuteness.

"That's funny. Because I do drive a Mini Cooper, it's bright red, and I absolutely blast the stereo whenever I'm out and about."

"You have long legs for a little car like that," he said lightly, his eyes meeting mine.

Was it dumb that the fact that he'd noticed my legs made me a little giddy?

And why did my heart beat faster whenever he looked at me?

"It's, uh, roomier than it looks."

I was being ridiculous.

This wasn't a date; he was just being nice after how abrupt he'd been earlier.

No matter how giddy my pre-teen heart felt, the thirty-three-year-old woman controlling my brain knew better.

"So, what's your question for me?" I asked as casually as I could manage.

The way I was feeling made no sense.

I'd been around rock stars for years. My sister had been involved with one since she was eighteen and was married to him once again now. I'd hooked up with a guy in one of their opening acts several years ago, and we'd dated for about a year before I caught him cheating on me.

Celebrities were nothing new to me, but Ross was different.

I'd been eleven years old when the Ross & The Rockets album came out.

My mother had played it nonstop for months.

My younger sister Harley and I knew every word to every song.

But while Harley had always been infatuated with drummers, I'd fallen for Ross.

His posters graced the walls of my bedroom, and no one had cried harder than me when we'd heard about the bus crash. It had been so sad. Now I felt a little guilty for talking about it at all.

"Were you surprised to see Harley and Tommy get back together?" Ross asked, surprising me with his bluntness.

"No," I replied honestly. "They've always been in love. They're just finally figuring out how to make it work. Love is complicated, especially for them. Personally, I don't think rock and roll is conducive to true love, but what do I know?"

His eyes were suddenly shrouded. "I can tell you with absolute certainty you're wrong about that, Wynter."

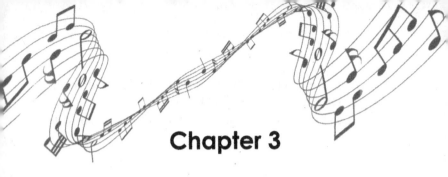

Chapter 3

<u>ROSS</u>

I'd always been a sucker for hazel eyes, and Wynter's were mesmerizing. They were a soft brown, more of a caramel color than brown, and had little flecks of gold in them. When she fixed them on me, I couldn't help but stare.

There was something raw and honest about her, something I really liked.

How long had it been since I'd been attracted to a woman this way? Where I wanted to sit and talk to her, even after she'd said something that annoyed me. It wasn't her fault, though. I kept a low profile for the sake of the band, but it wasn't like I could lie about who I was. Certainly not to someone like Wynter.

"If you believe in love, why are you still single?" she asked after the silence had stretched out a bit.

"I work a lot," I replied. "And when you're on the road as often as I am, only staying in each city a day or two at a time, it's hard to make that kind of connection. I'd be open to it, though."

I'd obviously caught her off-guard because she blinked a few times, as if she hadn't heard me right.

"Why do you look so surprised?" I asked, laughing.

"I guess I didn't think guys in the music business were interested in relationships," she admitted, looking a little sheepish.

"Forty-two-year-old guys who've been in the industry a long time definitely get tired of the game. It would be nice to have someone to go home to." I paused. "You know, if it was the right person."

"Have you ever been married?" she asked.

I shook my head. "Was engaged a long time ago. But you probably know that."

She nodded. "The stories about you are out there."

"After Clara died, I couldn't even think about falling in love again."

"I obviously didn't know her, but if she loved you the way you obviously loved her, then I don't think she'd want you to be alone. That won't bring her back."

"Ten years ago, I would have said you were crazy. But you're probably right."

"I'm divorced," she said after a moment. "Got married right out of college. It was a disaster. Most of the time, I wonder if I'm better off on my own. But once in a while, I think about falling in love, maybe having a kid." She lifted her coffee cup, holding it in front of her mouth with both hands.

"I think about it too, but I don't know how realistic it is considering what I do for work. What kind of dad will I be on tour for two years at a time?"

"The guys in the band seem to be doing it," she said softly.

"Yeah, but they're multi-millionaires. I make a respectable salary, and I have plenty in my retirement fund, but I can't afford to bring a family on tour full-time. And it wouldn't be fair to my wife for her to be stuck in a hotel room with a baby while I'm off doing what I do."

"I think where there's a will there's a way." Her eyes met mine. "If you really want something, you can make it happen. And every good relationship takes compromise."

God, she was pretty when she was pensive.

Was that why I was staring at her like a lovesick teenager?

"So." I cleared my throat, trying to find something else to talk about so I didn't blurt out anything stupid, like, "Will you marry me?" It might be time for me to find a lady to take my mind off the one in front of me.

Right?

"You're a nurse, right?"

"I am. Although I'm currently in a managerial position." She made a face.

"Not your thing?"

"I spend all day putting out fires between the employees. Two nurses who don't like each other. Computer system goes down. Patients on the phone freaking out about billing issues. Everything falls to me, and none of it is nursing or actually caring for patients, which was what I loved. I thought it would be easier than emergency medicine, but it's not. It's just a different kind of hard."

"Can you go back?"

"I don't know. I'm considering doing a travel nurse thing, where I just take short-term jobs all over the country. The pay is fantastic, and I'd get to see places I've never seen before."

"So you'd be a road warrior like me."

"I guess."

"Not conducive to getting into a relationship, though," I pointed out.

She wrinkled her nose. "Ugh. Why you gotta rain on my parade? I almost had a plan."

I laughed. "You know what they say about the best-laid plans."

She stuck her tongue out at me, and of course, horn dog that I was, my thoughts went to all the other things she could be doing with that tongue.

I really needed to get my mind out of the gutter.

"I'll figure it out," she said after a moment. "I've only been at this job six months. I'd like to give it a year. At that point, I'll reassess. They've promised me a secretary. If that happens, I might be happier."

"Life is short," I said softly. "If the job is making you miserable, don't stay. Yes, you have to make a living, but you're skilled. Nurses are in high demand, from what I've read online, so don't torture yourself at a place that makes you so unhappy you don't sleep."

Her face softened as she nodded. "I keep thinking that maybe there's something wrong with me, that two jobs in a row made me miserable, but you're right. I'm skilled. I'm employable. I shouldn't have to put up with stress-induced insomnia. So thank you. I needed to hear that."

"Believe me, I know what it's like to be miserable. Avoid it at all costs."

"You're sweet, Ross."

If I was smart, I'd ask her out and get it over with. If she said yes, we could spend a little time together and see if the spark went beyond the sexual attraction. She was smart and beautiful, two things I loved in a woman, and there was no doubt she liked me. The only question was whether she liked Ross-the-forty-two-year-old-tour-manager or if she was simply infatuated with Ross-the-has-been-rocker.

Before I had a chance to say anything, my phone buzzed.

It was a text from Devyn, our bass player.

> **DEVYN: Can you come up to the room? Kingston may not be able to sing tonight.**

"I'm sorry," I told Wynter, waving to get the waitress's attention. "I have to go. Something's going on with Kingston."

Kingston was the band's frontman.

"Oh no. Is he sick?" She looked up with concern.

"I don't know. All Devyn said was that he might not be able to sing tonight."

"Maybe I can help?" she said, quickly getting to her feet as I signed my name on the ticket so breakfast would be charged to my room.

I hesitated but then nodded. "Sure. Thanks. Let's go."

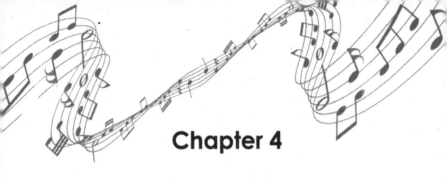

Chapter 4

WYNTER

I wasn't a doctor, and I was certainly no expert in anything to do with vocal cords, but Kingston's throat looked red and inflamed. Without tests it would be impossible to know what was wrong, but there was no doubt something was going on. He said he felt okay, except for the sore throat.

"I think you should go to an urgent care," I told him after I'd given him a cursory examination. "If nothing else, to rule out strep. Because if that's what it is, you'll infect the whole crew."

"Agreed." Devyn gave him a look as she pulled out her phone. "I'm Googling now, looking for one nearby."

Devyn was the band's new bass player, and she and Kingston had become a couple. She'd been hired after the death of their original bassist—Carter, whom I'd loved dearly—and I'd been worried about how she would fit in. However, she was an incredible musician and she and Kingston were adorable together. I'd known Kingston for years and hadn't been able to picture him settling down, so it made sense that when he did it was with another musician.

"I really don't want to go to an urgent care," Kingston muttered, making a face.

"If you have strep, you'll need antibiotics," I said.

"It could be something worse," Devyn said, still scrolling on her phone. "And there's a place about two miles from here. Go get dressed. We need to get this over with."

Kingston got up with a grimace. "Yes, dear."

"I'm calling for an Uber, so don't mess around!" she called after him as he padded into the bathroom.

"Christ." Ross had his hands on his hips. "What do we do if it's strep or laryngitis or some other throat thing? This right here is why I wanted a backup band. Depending on what they say, we may have to cancel the show."

"Let's not stress until we have to," I said quietly. "It might be okay. A lemon juice, brandy, and honey concoction could help too. Not to mention hot tea and a bunch of other things that could get him through the show."

"The rest of us could do extended solos," Devyn added. "He could also let the crowd sing the choruses on the bigger hits, which limits how long he has to sing for each song. We have options."

"Those things aren't going to fill a ninety-minute set," Ross said.

"Maybe we cut the set shorter tonight," Kingston said, coming out of the bathroom and putting an LA Dodgers baseball cap on his head. "I don't know what else to do."

"Go find out what's going on first," I suggested. "Then we can come up with a backup plan."

Ross and I followed Kingston and Devyn into the elevator and down to the lobby.

"Let me know!" Ross called after them as they headed outside.

"What happens if you cancel the show?" I asked curiously.

He made a face. "Honestly, it's not the end of the world, but fans really dislike it, and we have to either refund everyone's money or reschedule at the end, which we all hate to do. It can be a scheduling nightmare, you know? That's why I like to have an opening act. We've had injuries and illnesses before, and had someone from the opening act fill in. Crimson Edge is joining us in Salt Lake City, but their guitarist had a death in the family, so they're delayed for another week." He paused. "It's weird because King never gets sick. I think he had the flu once about six years ago and he did the show on a stool, with a hundred-and-three fever. He's hardcore. But when his voice is impacted, it's a whole different thing."

"Well, I'm sure you know the lyrics," I suggested lightly. "You could sing."

He stared at me, those gorgeous gray eyes of his narrowing into slits. "I thought we already had this conversation?" he asked quietly.

"We did, but this is different."

"It's not. The last fucking thing I'd ever want to do is get up in front of an Onyx Knight crowd. Can you imagine the headlines? It would be a disaster."

"But why? I understand that what happened to your band and fiancée was horrible, but hiding away your talent and the man you are doesn't make that tragedy go away. Why are you hiding the man beneath a façade?"

"*This* is the man I am," he said, irritation lacing his voice. "There's no façade, Wynter. I'm not twenty-one anymore. I'm not a rock star. And I'm definitely not up to filling in for Kingston Knight. I'm just a guy approaching middle age with a job to do."

"How will you know if you're up to it if you don't try?"

"So I can humiliate myself in front of twenty thousand people? That's a hard no."

"But—" I tried again but he cut me off.

"You need to let this go, Wynter. Seriously."

"You're right. I'm sorry." I said the words, but they frustrated me.

"I've got things to do. See you later." He turned on his heel and practically speed-walked back toward the elevators.

I was a jerk for pushing him so hard.

I didn't even know what my end game was.

It didn't change anything in my life if he ever performed as Ross Rocket again, so it shouldn't have mattered so much.

But it did and I was trying to understand why.

Maybe it was because it seemed like he still had so much to offer, both personally and professionally, yet he seemed determined to hide his talent.

The truth was that it was none of my business.

And I had a feeling any chance I'd had with him had just walked away.

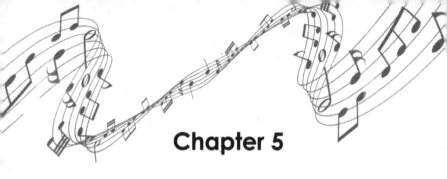

Chapter 5

ROSS

It was a busy morning as I tried to come up with a plan for the band.

The most obvious option would be to postpone the show and add it to the end of the tour.

The issue with that was that we had a full schedule with a European leg set to begin at the tail end of the US leg, but the dates weren't set in stone yet, so adding on could become problematic. Plus, it took months to prepare for their world tours. This was their first major tour since Devyn had joined the band, and she added a slightly different dynamic, so there were details to sort out that had nothing to do with the music itself. Putting any major changes into place now could add a level of complication no one needed.

I made a handful of phone calls to people I knew, but no one was available to drop everything and come to Phoenix for the night, which left me back at square one.

After lunch, I knocked on Tommy's door, hoping we'd hear something from Kingston sooner rather than later. Devyn had texted that the wait would probably be a couple of hours, so we still didn't have any answers.

"Hey." Tommy opened the door looking like he'd just woken up.

"It's after one," I told him, arching a brow. "And we didn't even play last night."

"Well, we didn't play music," he said, pouring himself a cup of coffee. "That doesn't mean Harley and I didn't go out."

I chuckled. "She still asleep?"

He shook his head. "No. She was up with River and took him to the playground." He looked at me over the brim of his cup. "You want a cup?"

"Nah, I'm good." I sank into a chair by the window.

"Still no word from King?"

"The place is busy, so they're still waiting."

"We leave for soundcheck in a couple of hours," he pointed out needlessly.

"I don't know what we're gonna do," I said, "but we'll have to decide in the next hour. If we're going to cancel, we want to do it before people actually leave for the show."

"It's going to depend on how long it takes King," he replied. "I hate to cancel, but not much we can do if he can't sing."

"I tried to find a singer, but no one was available."

"I can sing a couple of songs, but I don't have his register," Tommy said thoughtfully. "Devyn and Z sing a little too, but not enough to carry us, and I don't think Kellan has the range to pull off a whole set either."

"It might be best to just call it," I admitted. "And not even bother making it up at the end since we don't have much time."

"I hate that for our fans," Tommy said. "Especially since this is the first full tour since Carter."

It was hard to think about the bass player we'd lost, but Devyn was amazing and the band's new album was killing it.

"It's a new era for us," I said quietly. "You're all married now, with women and kids on tour... It feels different."

"It's good, though, don't you think?" He cocked his head curiously.

"Well, it doesn't change a lot for me. Except, you know, not having to check the IDs of the groupies now that all you boys are wifed up."

"You almost sound jealous."

"Nah. It's not easy to be in a relationship with what I do."

"That why you're still single?" he asked.

"Well, that and the fact that it's hard to meet nice women who want to be with a guy who's on tour for two years at a time." There was no reason to deny it.

"Wynter's single. And she's a very nice woman."

I hesitated.

She was definitely a nice woman, but her infatuation with Ross & The Rockets bothered me, so I didn't know if it would work out.

"She knows who I am," I blurted out. "Or, you know, who I used to be."

"Oh." His eyes widened. "Shit."

I'd exaggerated when I'd told Wynter that no one knew who I was.

The band had done a full background check before hiring me, and when they asked about it, I'd simply let them know I wasn't interested in talking about or reliving the past. They'd taken me at my word, and it never came up again.

"What'd you tell her?"

"The truth. That it was my past and I didn't want to talk about it."

"She's wonderful," he said slowly. "She deserves someone who'll love her and take care of her emotionally. I don't think she's worried about you being on tour."

"I barely know her," I protested.

"Yeah, but you think she's hot, right?" He grinned and I chuckled.

"She's beautiful," I agreed.

"So, you're interested." It was more a statement than a question, and I hesitated before nodding.

"Is the problem with her specifically or just where you are in life?"

"The bigger problem is that she brought up the Ross Rocket thing again when Kingston said he might not be able to sing. *After* I'd asked her to leave it alone."

Tommy's eyes snapped to mine, but I immediately shook my head. "No fuckin' way, man. I haven't sung in years. Even if I wanted to—which I absolutely do not—my voice is in no shape to do an Onyx Knight set."

"What about a third of a set?" he countered. "If King can sing some, and I can do one or two..." He let the question linger unanswered, but I continued to shake my head.

"Me getting up in front of a crowd like that would reopen wounds that have barely healed," I said firmly. "It's not happening. Please don't ask."

He put up his hands in mock surrender. "Okay, okay. It was worth a shot."

Just then my phone buzzed, and I saw a text from Kingston.

"They're back," I told him. "He wants to meet up in his suite."

Tommy got to his feet. "Let's go."

Chapter 6

WYNTER

I'd spent the afternoon reading in my room and I looked up when I heard my phone buzz, indicating I had a text. I reached for it, surprised to see a text from my sister.

> **HARLEY: Heading for the venue for soundcheck in thirty. If you want to ride over on the bus with us, meet us in the lobby. We won't come back to the hotel before the show, so be prepared to hang out at the arena until after.**

I quickly responded.

> **ME: Getting dressed! See you downstairs.**

I was surprised they were still going to do the show because Kingston's throat had looked like it would really hurt to sing, but what did I know? I was only a nurse. Kingston had the money to get the best medication and medical advice available. This couldn't be the first time he'd gotten sick in a twelve-year career.

No matter how strongly I wanted to tell him not to risk

damaging his vocal cords, I had to learn to keep my opinions to myself. That kind of thing got me into trouble at work sometimes too. It was like I cared too much.

And in my experience, people rarely appreciated it.

That was a big part of the reason why I'd been considering going into travel nursing. I wouldn't be in one place long enough for my mouth to get me into trouble, and the money was so good I'd be able to save up the down payment for a house quickly.

At least, that was the loose plan I'd come up with.

I was thirty-three and still living with my sister. I'd initially moved in to help her with River, and then I never left. I'd assumed I would wait until I met the right guy to think about something more permanent, like buying real estate. But now she was back with Tommy, and I felt like a third wheel.

It was time to grow up.

I didn't need a man to be the best version of myself.

Or even a more stable version.

I shook off my maudlin thoughts and focused on what to wear.

I'd brought black jeans, a lace-up corset that showed plenty of cleavage, and black boots to wear for the show, so I quickly pulled them on. Since I hadn't known whether or not I would be going anywhere tonight, I'd done my hair earlier but hadn't bothered with makeup. Now I wasn't sure whether to go all out with my heavily layered rock and roll face, complete with false eyelashes and black lipstick, or to just keep it simple.

Ross was mad at me, so he wouldn't pay attention to my makeup, and since I didn't have a lot of time, I opted for the basics: foundation, bronzer, a little eyeliner, and a couple of coats of mascara. Mauve lipstick rounded out my look and I stuffed my room key, ID, some cash, and the lipstick into my crossbody purse. It was my favorite, small and comfortable for a rock concert, and I draped it over my shoulder as I walked out of my room.

To my surprise, Ross was just coming out of his room across the hall.

He looked like he was in a hurry, so I smiled as I caught his gaze and our eyes met.

"Hey."

"You riding over to the arena with us?" he asked.

"Yeah."

"Cool." He didn't say anything else as we walked to the elevator and rode it down to the lobby.

Ugh.

He was almost definitely mad about earlier.

"You look nice," he said as we stepped out of the elevator.

Okay, maybe not *mad*-mad.

"Thank you." I bit my lip shyly.

"Ready to go?" Tommy waved and we moved toward the exit, where the bus was waiting and we appeared to be the last two to arrive.

Ross and I followed him outside and up the steps.

"How are you feeling?" I asked Kingston as I sat down.

"He has laryngitis," Devyn replied, holding up a hand to stop him when he opened his mouth. "He called his doctor back in LA, who told him not to talk at all until the show. I've had him drinking tea with lemon and honey all afternoon, and this other concoction the doctor suggested. He hasn't spoken a word since this morning and he's hoping his voice will last long enough to get through most of the show."

Kingston typed something on his phone and showed it to Devyn, who read it aloud. "You all need to plan for extended solos so I can sing less, and I've switched up the set to songs where I either sing less or are easier on my voice. And I'm not doing soundcheck either."

Everyone nodded.

"I can sing 'Not Going Away'," Z said. He'd written the power ballad for his wife, so he sometimes sang it live anyway.

"And I'm down to sing 'Shiny Pieces'," Tommy added. "It's from the first album—no one will notice if I screw up the lyrics."

"I beg to differ," I said, laughing. "It's one of my favorites."

They all grinned at me, and I sat back, listening to them discussing the set and their plans to compensate for Kingston's limited singing ability. It reminded me of other days, when Tommy and Harley had first gotten together, and we'd spent almost every night of the week listening to them rehearse or play live around Hollywood.

We'd all known they were going to be big, but we'd never imagined how big. Or how fast it would happen.

I'd loved being able to watch it happen, even though it had slowly destroyed my sister.

"You look melancholy all of a sudden," Ross said quietly as we walked down the long hallway toward the underground backstage area of the arena.

"I was just thinking about the early days, when we used to hang out and party on the bus during their first tour. Before things took off."

"I wasn't around yet," he replied thoughtfully. "I came on for their second album and tour. And they were already big by then."

"It was a crazy time. I was in college, but Harley and Tommy were together, so I spent almost every free night watching and listening. There were so many good times. It was enchanting. I had to stop coming around as much after they got divorced, and I've missed the magic that surrounds them. As someone on the outside looking in, I can't imagine what it's like to see something you wrote suddenly become a household name. Like writing some random words and then seeing millions of people sing them."

"It's pretty magical," he agreed, looking away.

The faraway look in his eyes made me long to touch him.

Comfort him.

Say or do something to make that pain go away.

But he didn't want that comfort, at least not from me, and I'd already pushed it enough.

If I wanted to be his friend, and I really did, I had to keep my mouth shut and mind my own business.

That was all there was to it.

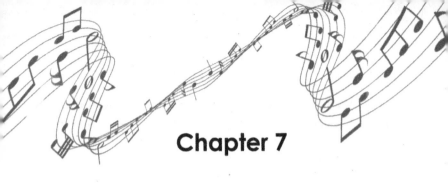

Chapter 7

ROSS

Onyx Knight was typically a well-oiled machine. Everyone, from the band to the crew to support staff, knew their jobs and did them well. Unless there was a technical problem or something broke unexpectedly, we were prepared for almost anything. I had to keep an eye on things from start to finish, but once they hit the stage, all I had to do was watch. Their techs knew how to handle broken strings or if the sound went out or anything else that might go wrong. The sound and light guys had this down to a science, and most arenas had capable, efficient staff to make sure things went smoothly.

However, no one could do anything about Kingston's voice.

All we could do was hold our collective breath and pray for the best.

He definitely wasn't himself tonight.

His energy was fine, but he was singing much lower registers and his voice had already cracked a few times.

And this was only the third song.

I couldn't imagine him getting through ten.

Not to mention the two-song encore.

Their normal set was sixteen, with a three-song encore.

They'd scaled way back tonight, but I was nervous.

Kingston jogged off stage when Z started to sing 'Not Going Away', and the look he gave me was worrisome.

"I don't know how much more I've got," he admitted, his

voice hoarse.

"Drink this." I handed him the concoction Devyn had instructed me to have ready for him at any point in the show.

He took a few sips and closed his eyes.

"This isn't good," he whispered. "I may not be able to finish."

"Do we need to cancel the tour?"

He met my gaze guiltily. "We might. The doc said it'll take at least a couple of weeks for me to be back to a hundred percent. And we've got back-to-back shows for months..." He didn't have to finish his thought for me to understand how difficult this could be.

"We'll figure that out later. Right now, you have to get through maybe four songs? We can sub in some covers and let the other guys sing them."

He took a breath, looking at me intently.

"Or...you could."

I stared at him.

What the fuck was happening?

I'd been with the band nearly ten years and they'd never asked anything like this of me.

I'd been clear from day one that my life in the spotlight was over.

We'd *agreed* it would never come up again.

They knew the story.

They supposedly understood how painful it was for me.

They fucking *knew* I couldn't do this.

Not for him, not for the band, not for anyone.

"We don't have to tell them who you are," he said, his lips close to my ear since it was hard to hear anyway. "Just our awesome manager helping out because I have a cold." That was the story he'd told the audience at the beginning of the show. Laryngitis would bring out every couch warrior doctor on social media, so it was easier to simplify things.

"I can't."

"You can. And it's time. If you ask me, you need this more than I do."

Wynter had hinted at the same thing.

I glanced over to where she was watching the show, her body swaying in time to the music. She looked beautiful standing there, and I watched her for a moment, wondering what she would say if she could hear our conversation.

She caught my gaze and cocked her head curiously, a faint smile playing on her lips. I'd been a dick to her today, going hot and cold like a fucking faucet on speed. She shouldn't have pushed me so much, but I could have been more gracious.

Especially since I was planning to ask her out.

Instead, I'd used her pushiness as an excuse to avoid doing something I hadn't done since Clara died. I'd gone out with a handful of women, had sex with more than I could count, but I'd never asked a woman out with the intention of starting something. Or at least seeing where it could go.

I'd been hiding under grief and pain and myriad other emotions to avoid emotional entanglements.

And I'd done the same thing with my music.

It was easier to hide than to face my grief again, or to remember everything and everyone I'd lost.

What Kingston was asking was too much.

It was.

Wasn't it?

I was still looking into Wynter's beautiful eyes, and suddenly, I wasn't sure about anything.

Devyn, Z, and Kellan had come off stage, leaving Tommy to do his drum solo, which might last three or four minutes if he pushed it.

And now they were looking at me too.

As if they'd planned this.

"I can't," I said finally.

"You can," Kingston said firmly. "You can do anything you put your mind to."

"Stop talking!" Devyn admonished him, smacking his arm.

He gave her a look and she turned to me, the question in her eyes impossible to miss.

"Not you too," I groaned.

"We promised him we'd never bring this up," Kellan said.

"This is different," Z pointed out. "We couldn't anticipate running into a situation like this."

"I haven't sung like that in over a decade," I interjected. "I don't know what shape my voice is in, even if I wanted to."

"It can't be worse than Kingston going out there and losing his voice completely," Devyn said.

"Come on, man. This is important." Z lifted his hands in a helpless gesture.

"There could be a nice bonus in it for you," Kellan added.

I gritted my teeth, trying to calm the roaring in my ears. "You know this isn't about money. Jesus."

"This isn't part of your job description but we're a family here," Kellan said. "We're there for each other. Aren't we? It's only a couple of songs."

Only a couple of songs?

They had no idea how much they were asking of me.

It was so much more than a couple of songs.

Yet there didn't appear to be a way for me to say no.

Because Onyx Knight was my family, the only one I had these days. My parents had passed away several years ago, I had a brother I only saw once or twice a year, and that was about it. So, these guys were important to me beyond the fact that they were my employers.

"I'm not sure I know all the lyrics," I hedged, looking from Kingston to Kellen and back again.

"I still have all the lyric sheets from when I first joined the band," Devon said turning to her guitar tech and motioned him over. "Pete, do you still have my lyric sheets?"

He nodded and ran toward one of the supply cases rooted around until he pulled out a stack of papers and brought them to us.

"Look at me," I said, motioning to my ratty jeans and T-shirt as I realized this was going to happen. "I'm not stage-ready."

"So you'll do it?" Kellen asked, his eyes sparking with excitement.

They were all watching me expectantly.

How the hell could I say no?

"And what happens if I fuck it up?" I demanded. "My voice isn't trained for this anymore."

"Doesn't matter," Kingston said, before grimacing and holding up his hands to Devyn, who glared at him.

"Here." Pete pulled a leather vest out of one of the supply chests. "Tommy wears this sometimes but he gets too hot. It should fit."

"Take your shirt off," Devyn instructed, motioning for me to hurry up.

Thank God I spent a lot of time at the gym.

I pulled on the vest, thinking I looked ridiculous, but Devyn grinned. "You look awesome."

"What song do you know the best?" Z asked.

My mind momentarily went blank.

Did I know the full lyrics to any of their songs?

I had to think fast because Tommy's solo was almost over.

I caught him looking in our direction and he seemed to understand something was happening, because instead of winding down, he picked up speed again.

These guys really were amazing.

I owed it to them to make this work.

Two or three songs would save the show and Kingston's voice.

"Probably 'Judgement Call'," I said after a few seconds. "And 'Break Your Promise', but we're saving that for last, right?"

Z nodded. "Yeah. So let's do Judgment, then 'Symphony of the Broken'. Devyn can sing that one with you while King plays piano."

"I can do the background vocals on that one," Kingston said, before quickly clapping his hand over his mouth and backing away from Devyn.

"You guys suck, you know that?" I stared at them.

"You got this, bro." Pete nodded and clapped me on the shoulder. "Ross Rocket is in there somewhere. You just gotta dig deep."

Christ.

Had everyone known all along and just pretended they didn't?

What did that mean?

Was I the asshole for trying to pretend to be someone I wasn't?

The irony didn't escape me, but I didn't have time to contemplate any of that because Tommy was winding down for real this time.

It had been eighteen years and seven months since I'd last performed.

Now I was about to sing in front of 19,698 people.

I was either going to faint or puke.

Chapter 8

ROSS

There was a little scrambling as the crew adjusted the set list and found me a wireless microphone.

And I just stood there, trying to distinguish the past from the present.

Almost nineteen years since I'd been on stage and yet, there was no stage fright.

There were ghosts instead, ricocheting through me in the form of memories.

So many fucking memories.

Clara standing in the wings, leaning up to give me a good luck kiss before the show.

My old guitarist, Joey, flipping me off before grabbing his guitar and running on stage.

Rambo, my bassist, grinning as he pulled off his shirt and picked up his eight-string.

The roar of the crowd as they chanted.

Rockets – Rockets – Rockets

The strobe light moving back and forth across the audience, highlighting their excitement. The full house. The fact that we were on our way to the top.

"You ready?" Kingston gripped my arm, forcing me to look at him. "You got this, man. I'll introduce you as—"

"No." I cut him off, shaking my head. "If I'm going to sing, I'm going to be who I am. And I *am* Ross Rocket."

He smiled. "Yes. Yes, you are."

Then he turned and ran back onto the stage, leaving me frozen in place.

A warm hand on my arm made me look down and Wynter smiled, her eyes dark with excitement and compassion and support. That was the best way to describe how she was looking at me.

"Go out there and own it," she said softly. "For one night, take back everything you lost. And no matter what happens, you'll always have one fan waiting right here." She leaned up on her tiptoes and pressed a soft kiss on my cheek.

Damn, she was pretty.

"Will you go out with me when this is over?" I asked spontaneously.

"I will."

I pressed my lips to hers, firmly, letting her know I meant it.

Our eyes met for a fraction of a second and then it was time for me to go.

"...tonight we have a very special guest helping us out on vocals—anyone remember Ross Rocket from the one and only Ross & the Rockets?" The crowd went wild as Kingston introduced me, and whether it was because Kingston seemed excited or genuine interest in seeing me perform again, I would never know, but it was enough to propel me forward.

'Judgment Call' was a hard rocking tune with lots of energy that would get the crowd on their collective feet, so I motioned to the set list and Tommy started tapping the snare drum.

"Phoenix." I lifted my arms in the air. "How the hell are you? Is it hot in here tonight or is that just Onyx Knight?"

The crowd responded with an energetic bout of screams, and a lacy black bra landed at my feet.

Well, that hadn't happened in a while, so I scooped it up and twirled it around my finger. "I think it's time for a judgment call!" I launched into the opening lyrics and found they came easily.

Onyx Knight was talented. No one achieved their level of success by being mediocre, and they definitely didn't do it by being shoddy musicians. They were professional and smart, making it easy for me to fumble through the first few bars. I knew the music, the lyrics, and the songs, but this was different. Being front and center for a band like Onyx Knight took me to another level.

Another time.

And then the memories came, whiplashing through my heart and bouncing off my soul.

A quick glance to the wings and Clara was there.

Swaying in time to the music, her smile huge.

For the briefest moment in time, it was as real as I was, but when it faded, there was no pain, no melting, no nightmare.

This time, when I looked back, Clara had morphed into Wynter, fingers laced together against her chest, as if she were so nervous, she was praying.

Luckily, even though my brain might have been terrified, the rest of me knew what to do.

The rest of me remembered the beat, the moves, the music.

And when 'Judgment Call' ended, we went right into 'Symphony of the Broken'. Devyn had written that one, and we sang it together, harmonizing as if we'd done it a million times before, while Kingston wowed everyone on the Baby Grand piano he played.

It was riveting, even to me.

As the song came to an end, Kellan came up behind me, yelling in my ear, "Let's do 'Shooting For the Stars'. We know it. You know it. The crowd will know it."

There was no time for me to say no, because Tommy was already pounding out the all-too-familiar opening bass drum rhythm.

Had they somehow planned this?

Something that I'd buried so deep I'd almost forgotten it was there exploded out in a torrent of emotion that was impossible to describe. Sadness, excitement, guilt, longing, and a touch of nostalgia hit me like a physical blow. But instead of letting it take me down the way it might have even a few years ago, I leaned into it.

This was the magic of rock and roll, and if I was only going to experience it one last time in my life, I was going to give it everything I had.

So I did.

I ran back to the front and raised my hands over my head, clapping them together. "Who's ready to shoot for the stars?"

To my complete shock, the crowd went nuts.

They fucking remembered.

Of course, they fucking remembered. You're Ross Rocket. Show them how it's done, brother.

Joey's voice was clear as day, even though he'd been dead for nineteen years.

I felt another pang of nostalgia, but I grinned as I shook it off.

I'd miss Joey later.

Right now, he was next to me.

They all were.

Joey and Rambo and Dixon.

My friends, my bandmates, my brothers.

Tonight, I'd do this for them.

For Wynter.

But most of all, for me.

Ross and Roll, my brother.

EYES
ON
YOU

LAYLA REYNE

About the Author

Layla Reyne is the author of *What We May Be* and the *Agents Irish* and *Whiskey, Fog City,* and *Perfect Play* series. She writes sexy, intense LGBTQIA+ romance featuring highly competent adults in kitchens, sports arenas, car chases, and other high-stakes situations. Whether it's adrenaline-fueled suspense, rival athletes, vampires and shifters in alt-realms, or love mixed with mouth-watering foodie goodness, queer folks finding happily-ever-afters is guaranteed. You can find Layla online at www.laylareyne.com, on social media @laylareyne, or in her Facebook reader group—Layla's Lushes.

www.laylareyne.com

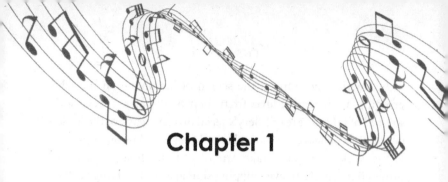

Chapter 1

Gino couldn't believe the words on the paper in his shaking hands. He read the first paragraph again, a third time, before looking up at the man across the breakfast table from him.

His husband. His best friend. In the morning light, the tear tracks—old and new—glistened on Bennett's ruggedly handsome face. A face Gino knew as well as his own after thirty years together. Had never seen in such wretched sorrow before.

Gino gulped, unstuck his tongue from the roof of his mouth, and forced out words around the lump in his throat. "You want a divorce?"

Bennett flinched. Closed his eyes and lowered his chin, face angled away. Another tear slid over the hard lines of his face and disappeared into his morning scruff. Prickly brown and silver hairs that Gino had felt under his fingertips last night when he'd kissed him goodnight.

"I don't know." Bennett's voice was as ragged as Gino's insides felt. His body looked it too, shoulders slumped beneath a threadbare band tee, nothing artful about his messy brown hair, hazel eyes bloodshot when they opened and met his again. "But I do know I've never been this fucking tired, G. I feel like fucking roadkill, and we haven't even started the tour yet."

"That's fair," Gino said as he tossed the divorce papers onto the table. "Rehearsals have been a bitch and the logistics for this tour are complicated. But how does that translate to divorce?"

He cut his gaze to their kitchen island covered in the arena stipulations their manager had sent over last night. "Because I can't remember the last time I spent more than a few hours in bed with you." Tapped the screen of his phone on the table, bringing up dozens of texts from their bandmates. "Because I'm so tired of taking care of Ellery's serial broken heart, of the broken hearts Roscoe leaves in his wake, of Miles and Mason's twin spat of the week, that I can't take care of you, much less myself." He slumped in the chair, eyes slipping shut again as he hung back his head. "Because I barely remember the taste of you, the feel of you beneath my hands. Because I barely remember me."

"Baby." Gino slid from his chair and onto the floor between Bennett's spread knees, circling his husband's shoulders and pulling him into an embrace.

Bennett fell the rest of the way off the chair and into his lap, hugging him back with the same desperation Gino felt, his grip like a drowning man's. It scared the shit out of Gino; so did Bennett's words. "We made it. You were right five years ago when you wouldn't let us quit. Our shelves are decorated with awards, our walls with platinum records, but somewhere in the rise, I fell. I lost myself, and I lost you and us too."

His last words were barely a whisper, swallowed by his quiet, tired sobs. Gino held him tighter, his husband's hot tears seeping through his own tee, searing into his soul. Into his heart that still—would always—belong to Bennett York. "You're right here, B. Right here with me. I'll get us back, I promise."

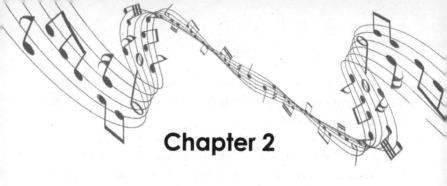

Chapter 2

Bennett woke sometime later in bed, the sun's warmth on his face, a Gino-shaped space heater at his back. He eked open his eyes and stared outside their bedroom windows, watching the ocean lap gently against the horizon. God, he loved their home; their own little oasis by the sea, midway between Los Angeles and San Diego, equidistant to work and family. They hadn't escaped here enough the past five years, gone more days than home. He missed it, same as he missed the weight of Gino's arm over his waist and the brush of his lips on his nape.

A satisfied sigh slipped out, and Gino's arm around him tightened, tugging him closer. "How long have I been out?" Bennett asked.

"Most of the day."

He'd guessed as much, given the distance between the sun and the waves. Guilt snaked through him, stealing the warmth Gino and the sun had imparted. He closed his eyes and moved to roll away. "You don't have to stay."

Gino held him tighter, hand splayed over his abs. "I'm not going anywhere."

Bennett's gulp was loud in the quiet room, his "I'm sorry" scratchy and painful to his own ears.

"Don't ever apologize for how you feel." Using the arm around his waist, Gino shifted him onto his back. "Especially not to me. But I do need to understand it better."

Opening his eyes, Bennett stared up into the warm brown ones that had been his world for three decades. Hurt and pain—confusion—swirled there, and he hated that he'd been the one to cause it. He opened his mouth to apologize again, but Gino's fingers lightly skimming over his face, smoothing the lines of his forehead, stopped him.

"I get that you're tired, that you're burned out," Gino said. "I heard you. But why did you think divorce was the answer?"

He tangled his fingers with Gino's. "Handing you those papers was one of the hardest things I've ever done." Just remembering it made his stomach roil and his eyes refill with tears, made his breath hitch and his voice scale several octaves higher as he spoke. "I didn't mean it as an ultimatum. I wouldn't. I don't want you to think I'd manipulate you like that."

"Shh, shh, shh," Gino coaxed, fingers squeezing his. He lifted their joined hands to his lips and kissed Bennett's knuckles. "I don't think that. I know you better than that."

Bennett lowered their hands to his chest, and when his pulse was slightly less frantic, when the panic had ebbed enough to breathe in time with Gino's calmer breaths, he started again. "It was the only exit ramp I could see. The only way to give you the freedom to go forward with the band and the music you crave while also taking back some freedom for myself, away from the band."

"Babe, open your eyes."

Bennett hadn't realized he'd closed them. When he opened them, Gino's brown ones, wet at the corners, stared back with fiery conviction. "There is no music for me without you." The hand in his slipped lower, Gino's thumb skating over the barely-there scars on Bennett's wrist, the ones hidden by the tattoos that decorated his arm from shoulder to fingertips. "And if I didn't walk away twenty years ago, I'm not walking away now."

Bennett's relieved sigh wobbled as he turned into Gino, burying his face in his warm, inviting chest, his ear pressed over his pec, the rhythm of his husband's heart steady. The music that had kept him going that awful night on the bathroom floor in a shitty Knoxville motel. So far away from home, from everyone who loved and accepted them, from who and what they'd wanted to be. Decades later, they'd drifted again, and with all the distance life had put between them, it hadn't occurred to him that Gino still loved him like that. That he'd be willing to step back with him.

Gino dropped a kiss on the crown of his head. "Can we table the divorce discussion for now?"

Bennett breathed another measure easier and nodded.

"Do you still want to do the tour?" Gino asked.

That heavy weight was still on their shoulders. "We made commitments—to the band, the crew, the label, all those promoters and venues. We can't just cancel."

"It happens. We wouldn't be the first."

"I want to play our songs." He spread a hand over Gino's chest, bracing for impact, for Gino's reaction to his next words. "One last time."

He jolted, as Bennett expected, but a cleared throat later, he asked, "What do you need to make it bearable? To make it the farewell tour you want?"

Gasping, Bennett drew back and gazed again at his husband. Conviction shone in his eyes, expression unwavering. "Are you for real?"

He laughed, and the gentle rumble was even better than the music of his pulse. "Yeah, babe, I'm for real. Tell me what you need to put one foot in front of the other, to get behind that mic and be the sexy, fierce front man of Middle Cut everyone is there to see."

"I think they're there to see the sexy bassist."

Gino smiled. "Let's both be honest, they're really there for Roscoe."

Bennett laughed out loud, the last thing he expected on a day that had started so awful. How their beefy drummer with his knotty nose, grizzly smile, and missing canine tooth had the entourage he did would forever be a mystery. Maybe it had something to do with the flannel or being an ex-hockey player, two things Bennett, being from San Diego, knew little about.

Gino gave him a soft shake, refocusing his attention. "What do you need, B?"

He rolled onto his back and considered this new possibility, a different road than the freeway he'd thought was the only option. A slower, more scenic route they could drive along at thirty-five miles per hour instead of their usual breakneck speed. "I'd like to enjoy the places we visit, maybe stop at some new ones along the way. Not do three nights on the same stage, then dash to the next. And if we have to sacrifice any cities, I don't want them to be places we've never played before. I want to go to those places and explore."

"Not gonna argue about a couple days off in San Francisco with you." Gino shifted down onto the bed, draping himself along Bennett's side, arm over his waist, head resting on his shoulder. "What else?"

Fingers carding through his husband's chestnut hair, Bennett remembered a time when it was longer, when their lives and shows were simpler. Not easier—those were the days of cup of noodles and bad coffee—but the music, and playing it with each other, was the center of their world. "Do you remember that charity gig we played in Santa Cruz when we were nobodies?"

Gino laughed. "We were like six-point font at the bottom of that show poster."

"It was one of the best sets we ever played."

"Your beat-up old Martin, my upright bass from high school. Was that the night we found Roscoe?"

Bennett nodded. "He played piano with the group before ours. You told him to stay there on the bench and keep up."

"You want to go back to the trio? Or just you and me?"

He shook his head. "No, I like our fuller sound now, but I want to do it simpler. Acoustic, like we did for that show. Stripped down and laid bare. That's what I want to leave our fans with. The real us."

"Anything else?"

"I'm sure that's enough turmoil for you and Gavin to sort." Their manager wouldn't be happy, but he was their friend first. He'd met them at that same show all those years ago. He'd get it, even if it did make his life a temporary living hell. "Do apologize to him for me."

"I told you, no apologies. But I want you to do something for me too." He picked up his hand again, thumb skating over the scars once more. "Call Britt. Make an appointment. Don't reschedule it." He chuckled at how well Gino knew him. He'd already rescheduled three times with his therapist. His laughter died, though, when Gino added, "And ask her for a referral to a couple's therapist." He wound their fingers together. "I'm not giving up on us."

This time Bennett lifted their joined hands, lips lingering over Gino's knuckles, hope infusing his words for the first time in he couldn't remember how long. "I don't want to give up on us either."

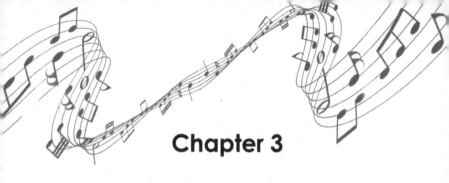

Chapter 3

"For the health of ourselves, our bandmates, and our crew, we're making some changes to the upcoming fall tour. Gavin, if you will please."

Bennett had to give Gino credit. Over the past week, he'd moved heaven and earth to make the tour Bennett needed happen. As their manager went over the shows that had been cut, mostly second and third nights in the same city or shows in towns where they'd played numerous times before, Bennett wondered if the sea of reporters could tell his insides were as rough and tumble as the ocean had looked that morning under a dark gray sky, a rare summer storm rolling in. Did they have any idea that under his usual leather and denim, he felt as fragile as Gino's mom's fine china? Hell, the only things holding him together today were the hour-long call with Britt that morning and Gino's hand wrapped around his on the table.

"Will there be more dates announced to make up for the canceled ones?" a reporter asked once Gavin finished going over the details.

"Will there be a back half of the tour?" another shouted.

"I'll take that one, Gavin." Gino leaned forward in his chair, the lines of his shoulders and back tense. Did the reporters see beneath *his* jeans and tee that he was as strung tight as his upright bass? Probably not, distracted as everyone was by the sexy smile that made fans swoon. "Yeah, so, I've never lied to y'all, and I'm not gonna start now." Wasn't that the truth. One of their early labels had suggested they keep their romantic relationship a secret. That same night, Gino had called his mother and told her to do her worst with the wedding. And Liz had—they had their nuptials at her Rancho Santa Fe mansion, big and ostentatious, the opposite of under the radar, their truth out there for everyone to see. And today, Gino was bearing more truths. "Bennett and I have been on the road for more than two decades, and these last five years, man, they've been incredible. Beyond our wildest dreams, and we are so very grateful, especially to our fans. But things lately have been hard. We've been rehearsing for the new tour, and we're realizing we're not twenty-somethings anymore. Hell, we're closer to fifty than forty at this point. We're tired, and we hurt, in our joints, in our minds, and in our hearts."

Bennett swept the room with his gaze. Long faces, some angry ones too, but the latter were outnumbered by understanding expressions and nods of commiseration.

"We need to slow down," Gino said. "We need to go at a pace that makes sense for us." Then lowered the hammer. "So we can go out on top."

Eyes grew wide and hands shot up, the earlier reporter getting in the first, most obvious, question. "Are you saying this is a farewell tour?"

"I think if someone wants to see Middle Cut, they should do it this tour."

Internally, Bennett cringed just thinking about the secondary market price for tickets.

"To that end," Gino said, "Gavin has some new ticket opportunities to tell you about. Thanks for your time today." With that, Gino tugged him up by the hand, and they exited the stage while Gavin explained they would be adding more fan club tickets, plus lottery seats and passes at each remaining show. Those were Gino's stipulations, and Bennett didn't disagree.

Same as he hadn't disagreed with informing the rest of the band first, none of whom had stuck around for the press conference. Bennett wasn't surprised. "Do you think they'll stick with us through the tour?" he asked when he and Gino found a quiet hallway.

"I hope so," he said. "It's not what any of us expected, but it will do us all good to remember what we love about making music."

"You don't have to sugarcoat it, G. This is my fault."

Gino drew him closer, pushing up his sunglasses so he could meet his eyes, surely seeing the misery Bennett couldn't hide. He skated a thumb beneath his left one, catching the tear before it fell. "We've been going a hundred miles an hour since we broke through. Thank you for being the one who recognized we need to slow down. To remember what we love about it."

He dropped his forehead onto Gino's shoulder. "I hope you still feel that way when the shitposting starts on social media."

Gino's big hand on the back of his neck was as warm and comforting as his "Fuck 'em." He squeezed and drew him closer. "We've earned the right to do things our way."

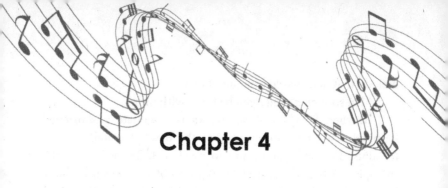

Chapter 4

Gino couldn't say how long he'd been sitting behind the hotel bar piano when Roscoe slid onto the bench beside him. He reeked of booze and sweat, his flannel and undershirt drenched, his mop of hair wet, but his eyes were sharp and assessing. "Aren't you supposed to be asleep?" he asked, specks of glitter shining on the leftover knot of his nose, the bridge broken numerous times over. "Big day tomorrow."

Gino tossed his pen atop the sheet music he'd been scribbling on and shifted sideways, giving his drummer a glaring once-over that was likely belied by the laughter in his voice. "And where are you just getting in from?"

"Maybe I was already here," he drawled in his honeyed Southern accent. "Maybe I just came downstairs to check on you." He dragged a hand through his damp hair, depositing more glitter where it didn't belong, and Gino lost the battle to his laughter.

"Or *maybe* you forgot your room key when you went to the rooftop club and came down to the lobby to get a replacement." And maybe Gino had insisted on staying in *this* hotel because said club was on the premises, and Roscoe couldn't end up somewhere he wasn't supposed to be the night before their first show and cause Bennett to spend all day tomorrow searching for him.

Not the meditation Britt had recommended before each show.

"How's Bennett?" Roscoe asked, uncannily reading the direction of his thoughts.

Gino shifted forward again, fingers resting atop the keys. While he preferred to perform with the bass, he had always composed best at the piano. "Asleep," he said as he struck up the melody that had chased him out of bed.

"I'm sure he'd prefer you be there with him."

Maybe? They'd had six weeks to negotiate a shortened, stripped-down tour, to get used to the new setup and set lists, to adjust Bennett's meds, and to meet with Trish, the couple's therapist Britt had referred them to. That last one had finally happened the day before yesterday, and it had wrung them both out, leaving them tender and tentative with each other.

"Should we be worried?" Roscoe asked. "We—you guys—are clearly making some big changes."

"We're working on it."

"For what it's worth, he's looked better during rehearsals."

Gino had noticed that too. Bennett's easy manner with the acoustic guitar, the easier time he had moving around the less cluttered stage, the easier set of his shoulders and easier breaths that led to the deeper, richer tone of his voice. Clear signs Bennett felt better about the direction of things. But what about the rest of the band? Was it easier on them too, beyond telling Gino what he wanted to hear? "How's the rest of the band doing? With the acoustics and the farewell of it all?" While Roscoe was their wildest, most unpredictable bandmate, he was their drummer, the keeper of the rhythm, the glue that held Middle Cut together.

"Surprised, bummed, but excited for this tour. It's fun to change things up. For me, it's the first time playing a full tour acoustic. I got off the ice, plugged in, and here I am." He wiped his hands together in a that-was-that gesture, more glitter raining between them. Roscoe was a musical and athletic prodigy, the latter taking him to the NHL, the former offering a second career after the first was cut short by injury.

"Do you think you'll do more acoustic stuff after this tour? It's what caught mine and Bennett's attention about you in the first place."

"Dunno." He shrugged. "I'm gonna spend some time at the cabin in Asheville, then maybe see what gigs I can pick up between there and Nashville."

"You know you can write your ticket anywhere." Gino clasped his shoulder. "Any band would be lucky to have you."

He quirked a bushy brow. "But will any band put up with my shit the way you and Bennett do?"

"That's something only you can answer. But do you think maybe you can tone it down for this tour? For Bennett's sake?"

"Was already planning to."

Gino replied with a raised brow of his own.

"I get to have some secrets too. Speaking of, what's that?" He jutted his chin at the sheet music atop the piano. "New song?"

"Maybe."

Roscoe grinned. "Writing? On the farewell tour?"

"Melodies won't stop coming." He shrugged, helpless when it came to the muse that had tossed him around for a lifetime. "It's like there's space now without the pressure."

With a nod, Roscoe peeled his flannel down his arms and off, balled it beside him, then righted himself, fingers tickling the keys. "You want some help? That way you can get back to your husband sooner."

"Won't say no to that."

"Where are we?"

Smiling, Gino drew the sheet music closer, pointed a line-up from where he'd left off, and started playing on the bass end of the keys.

Roscoe listened once, twice, then seamlessly added another layer of melody atop Gino's, flourishing right past where Gino was stuck and dragging him into the next verse. Roscoe shot him a sly smile and a wink. "Keep up."

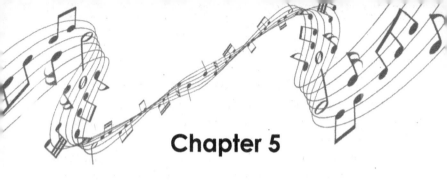

Chapter 5

Their third show was in Wilmington, North Carolina, at an outdoor pavilion by the river. It was their first time playing the venue, their first time back in Wilmington since their breakout record, and Bennett had the crowd—and Gino—eating out of his hand.

Gino couldn't take his eyes off him. Had never been able to when Bennett York was on stage. Ever since their junior year of high school when Bennett had auditioned for the holiday musical by rocking out to eighties hair metal. Didn't win him the role, but the way he'd thrown himself into it, the way he'd hit notes even while screaming, the way he'd worn a pair of thrift-store leather pants, had won him Gino's heart right there on the spot. His leather was designer now, the wrinkles around his eyes deep like his voice, his music more rock and bluegrass than metal, but Bennett was as utterly captivating as ever.

And judging by his wide smile as he ate up the stage, strumming his guitar, growling out lyrics, he was loving it. Gino hated that it had taken him too long to see Bennett hadn't been, that Bennett had had to take such drastic measures to get his attention, but he had, and they were making steps in the right direction. Like scheduling extra days between the Wednesday show in Atlanta and the one tonight, spending those extra days at an oceanfront cottage in nearby Hanover, keeping their video call with Trish yesterday afternoon, then walking hand-in-hand along the beach last night before having their bandmates over for dinner, the six of them plucking away at their instruments until after midnight not because they had to but because they wanted to. Some of those new riffs had made appearances in tonight's show, and everyone on stage, Bennett included, had grinned wider for it.

He was still smiling when he caught Gino's hand as they headed into the wings for a breather, the rest of the band jamming on stage, Roscoe and Ellery in a strings versus percussion face-off with the twins egging them on with their horns.

As soon as they were behind the curtains, Gino wrapped Bennett in his arms. "You good?"

His smile faltered. "Why? Did I miss—"

Gino silenced the doubt with a kiss, one that started firmly in you're-perfect land, softened into you-taste-so-good territory, heated into I-want-to-kiss-you-all-night vibes, before ending in the I'll-hold-you-to-that-promise place. Gino rested his forehead against Bennett's, catching his breath. "You're incredible out there, B." He unwound his arms from around his waist and squeezed his leather-clad biceps. "You look good. Relaxed." He pulled back far enough to catch his gaze. "I'm just checking in."

"I'm good," he said, hazel eyes clear and bright. "This feels better. Feels right. How's it feel for you?"

"Amazing." Except for that thread of guilt that snaked through him like an off note he couldn't quite shake.

Bennett noticed. "But . . ."

Gino straightened and raked a hand through his hair. "But it feels like we should have been doing this two tours ago. Like I should have caught on and fixed it sooner."

"Hey." Bennett clasped his chin between his thumb and forefinger and tilted his face back down, forcing his gaze. "Remember what Trish said. You don't get to blame yourself either. We learn, and we move forward."

"Mr. Morelli," came the voice of one of their roadies behind them. "Got that delivery for you."

"Delivery?" Bennett said.

The roadie handed Gino a poster tube and the marker he'd asked for before disappearing back into the sea of folks scurrying backstage to make sure the remainder of their show went off without a hitch. "A surprise for you," Gino said. He'd worried Bennett might need a pick-me-up by the end of their first week touring. Turned out he didn't, which made this gift all the sweeter. "When we talked that day in bed . . ." He didn't need to say more, Bennett's features tightening for a second before he seemed to steel himself and nod, understanding Gino meant the day that had started out like hell but ended with them turning a corner. "You mentioned that show in Santa Cruz we played, and it gave me an idea." He popped the plastic off one end of the tube, then held it out to Bennett. "Something else I'd like to put on our walls when we get home."

Bennett wiped his hands on Gino's jeans, then turned the tube upside down and shook it, the poster inside sliding out into his hands. He unrolled it, then laughed out loud, the sound musical and full of joy, and that note of guilt snaked through Gino again— why hadn't he noticed the laughter missing?—but he couldn't dwell on the past. He could only do better going forward, giving Bennett what he needed, including more joyful things to laugh about. His hazel gaze roved over the concert poster from that charity gig long ago, fingers doing the same over all the signatures on it, before landing on MIDDLE CUT on the second to last line in teeny tiny print. When he glanced back up, his smile reached all the way to his eyes. "How did you get this? And all the signatures?"

"Magic." And Gavin making *a lot* of phone calls for him. He held out the marker to Bennett. "Will you sign it for me, Bennett York? I'm your biggest fan." He batted his eyelashes and puckered his lips, and Bennett gave him a laughing smack of a kiss before turning him to use his back as a signing surface. The swoop of his signature, another joyful laugh, was music to Gino's soul. When he turned back around, Bennett's smile had softened and his eyes heated back to I-want-to-kiss-you-all-night vibes. "I take it there will be more posters coming?"

He brought their foreheads together again, lips brushing. "For that giant grin on your face? Hell yeah, baby. Hell yeah."

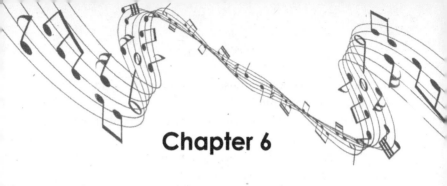

Chapter 6

Posters were great; band members who showed up on time, ready to play, were even better. After two months on tour, Bennett had more than a few of the former, Gino gifting him one every Saturday night. Reliable band members, however, had become scarce the past week.

The wheels had begun to come off last week in Chicago. Roscoe had gone to a hockey game the night before the show and had missed the morning band meeting. Ellery had taken that as his cue to flake out of the press call and sound check for the midweek show in Madison. And then the twins had gotten so drunk in downtown Pittsburgh after the show last night that Gino had had to leave their bed at two in the morning to sweet talk a local bar owner out of pressing charges. No doubt that had cost an arm and a leg, between paying off the bar owner and anyone who'd witnessed Miles and Mason's shenanigans.

Which Bennett still didn't know the full extent of. Gino had given him minimal details—*They're idiots, they're fine*—when he'd returned to bed just before dawn, wrapped an arm around his waist, and drifted back to sleep. There were no salacious news stories this morning either. Nothing in the local press or in the usual gossip rags about two of Middle Cut's band members causing a scene. In fact, there hadn't been a single bad behavior story all week, no web alerts other than for rave reviews of their shows, and come to think of it, Bennett hadn't received any SOS texts lately either.

He darkened his phone screen and set the device face down on the mattress beside him. "How have you kept everything out of the press this week?" He raised his voice so Gino in the hotel bathroom could hear him.

"Been working with Gavin and the extra handler we hired for this tour."

"We hired a what?" He briefly ran through the roadies on tour with them in his head, landing on the newest member of the crew. "You mean Erica? The blond in the SF Giants gear who's always directing us which way to go after the show?"

"That's her. She's a junior publicist in Gavin's shop. Damn good." Gino emerged from the bathroom, travel kits in hand. He'd insisted they get the hell out of Steel City and on to Boston before any more trouble found them; Bennett hadn't disagreed. Sure, there was a restaurant in town they'd planned to try tonight, but hush money only went so far. He dropped their kits into their luggage, redirecting Bennett's mind from where it had wandered. "It's not your job to babysit the band," Gino said. "It was wearing you down. You didn't need that."

Bennett snagged his nearest wrist and drew him closer, between his spread knees. "It's not your job either." He tugged Gino down to kneeling on his level so Bennett could get a good look at his face. In the morning sun, the bags under his eyes were dark and that little vein at the edge of his hairline was bulging with tension. Bennett gently coasted his fingers over it, then into Gino's hair, carding through it softly, causing Gino's hitched shoulders to lower and his eyelids to flutter closed. A couple of deep breaths later, Bennett asked, "Did you tell them to text you and not me?" Gino's silence was answer enough. Bennett pulled him into his arms. "Thank you for sparing me that, but you don't get to make my life better by making yours hell. We share the load."

"I can take a little more if it means improving your mental health. You're enjoying yourself and this tour. You've been remarkable on stage, B. You've seemed better offstage too. I don't want to risk that. I can't risk you."

He was rambling, his voice escalating like Bennett's had that day months ago, and every muscle under Bennett's hands had gone tight again. He needed to rest, he needed to relax, he'd needed that dinner out tonight, more than Bennett had realized when he'd agreed to forgo it. But maybe they could have dinner someplace else even more special.

He drew back and cupped Gino's face with both hands, thumbs swiping over his cheeks. "We have an extra day now, right? Before the show in Boston?"

Gino nodded.

"Get Gavin and the handler on the phone. You're taking the night off."

"But—"

Bennett covered Gino's mouth with his, shoved his tongue between his husband's lips, and only came up for air again when Gino surrendered. "You get to enjoy this tour too. And tonight, I'm taking care of *you*."

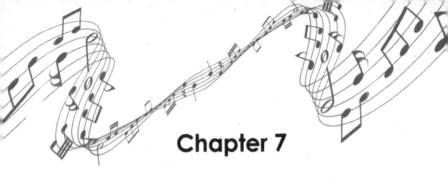

Chapter 7

Bennett drowned the last of his garlic fries in the leftover white wine broth from the bowl of mussels he'd devoured, then likewise devoured the soaked-in-delicious fries. He couldn't have asked for a better dinner or better company to enjoy it with, Gino smiling around another bite of his lobster mac and cheese before slowly drawing the fork from between his lips. Bennett shifted in his seat, wishing like hell his tongue—or other parts of his anatomy—were the tines of that fork. "Quit teasing me."

"No," his husband answered with a sexy leer. He scooped up another bite and repeated the whole excruciatingly erotic torture.

This entire day had been an excruciating exercise in foreplay. Of his own doing. The runaway trip to Martha's Vineyard, the day spent cruising around the island in their rented convertible, the date night out at Chess, the award-winning restaurant Bennett had caught his foodie husband eyeing online last week. After a day of sun, food, and wine, the tension that had been weighing Gino down had noticeably lifted, and his cheeks were pink, his smile wide, and his eyes sparking with heat.

He looked like his sexy self again, which had been Bennett's intention, along with thanking Gino for sparing him the chaos of the past week. And for making the first two-thirds of their tour more than bearable. To his surprise, Bennett was enjoying himself.

Were there bad days among the good?

Sure, several the past week with their misbehaving bandmates.

Or that first week on tour when he and Britt had been dialing in his meds, a slight increase in one causing him to tip over into the floaty, nauseous place he hated. Gino had sat by his side in the hotel bathroom that night, the two of them plotting how to spoil their niblings that were due next month, Gino distracting him through the worst of the leveling out.

Or the week before last, at the show in Baltimore, when it had taken Bennett an extra half hour of meditation to make it on stage. He'd needed a second set break later, another breather, but to the fans, it was the Middle Cut show they came for, and to Bennett, it was manageable. It hadn't set off a spiral or drained him for days after. Even if it had, there'd been two days built into the schedule for recovery. Gino was listening, was taking him seriously, was supporting his mental health and fighting for them. Bennett wanted to fight for them too, to show his appreciation and to continue the work of reconnecting, something they'd talked a lot about with Trish.

Gino's knee knocked his under the table. "Where'd you go?"

"Was just thinking about the past two months."

"You doing okay with everything?" He waved a hand in the air. "This past week notwithstanding."

"Better than." He finished his wine, set the glass down, then reached across the table for Gino's hand. "Thanks to you, *especially* this past week."

Gino tangled their fingers together. "You're putting in the work too." Hand in his, Gino scooted to the chair beside him and nuzzled into the crook of his neck. "Thank you for tonight. It was the escape I needed, and the food was incredible."

"You deserved it."

Gino hummed his agreement. "We deserved it."

"You know," Bennett said, voice lowered, "you keep doing that, and you're gonna get us kicked out of here before dessert."

"And you do not want to miss dessert tonight," came a Southern voice from behind them. The giant bearded chef who'd earlier introduced himself as Miller Sykes appeared beside their table. He slid two snifters of what smelled like the peatiest scotch to ever peat—Gino's favorite—onto the table. "Colby's doing huckleberry pie with creme anglaise gelato."

"Maybe we can box the pie to go?" Bennett said from over Gino's head.

"Nuh-uh," Gino said, straightening as he patted his thigh. "I'm gonna enjoy this scotch, that pie, and this view"—he jutted his chin at the moonlit Nantucket Sound out the floor-to-ceiling windows by their table—"with you a little longer."

Bennett groaned in frustration, and the chef chuckled. "I cockblocked my husband the first time I brought him here too," he said as he cleared their plates. "But don't worry, the dessert will do nothing to dampen the mood." He threw a blue-eyed wink their way, then headed back to the kitchen.

Bennett waited until he was out of earshot to grumble, "The big burly bear better not be bullshitting."

Gino's smile graced the underside of his jaw. "Someone's alliterating." He dropped a line of kisses to the spot behind Bennett's ear that made his whole body shiver. "And horny."

"Very." He dipped his chin to whisper in Gino's ear. "I need to get back to the hotel and fuck my husband."

"Don't worry, baby." Gino palmed his length under the table. Stroked. "I'll make sure you come tonight."

Before Bennett could clarify that Gino would be the one coming first, Miller reappeared at their table, no longer the picture of winking hospitality. Instead, his brow was creased below his plaid bandana and his eyes were wary, his hand shaky as he held a phone out to Gino. "Mr. Morelli," he said. "It's the FBI for you."

Gino's eyes grew wide, and Bennett cursed. "Fuck, what'd Roscoe do now?"

"Is there somewhere private we can take this?" Gino asked as he stood.

Bennett rose behind him, and they followed Miller to a small office off the kitchen. Miller shut the door behind them, and Gino clicked the phone over to speaker. "This is Gino Morelli."

"Gino, it's Levi." Bennett nearly collapsed with relief. Gino practically did, catching his weight between Bennett's side and the desk covered in children's books. "Fuck, Levi," Gino said to his cousin. "The chef said it was the FBI."

"Well, both your and Bennett's phones are going straight to voicemail, so Marsh had to track your asses down, and we couldn't chance the call being ignored."

The urgency in Levi's voice, the reference to his cyber agent husband's efforts to find them, the distinct hospital sounds in the background, had Bennett firming his position at Gino's side. "What's going on, Levi?" he asked.

"June's in labor."

"She's not due for another two weeks," Gino said. "Is she okay?"

"Vitals are holding steady, but this isn't going to be easy, especially not with twins. They may have to do a C-section."

"Fuck, we were supposed to be back on the West Coast for this." Gino had missed his baby sister's wedding a couple years back when they'd been on tour in Europe. They'd planned this tour so as not to miss the birth of her twins. Boston was their last show before heading west.

"Well," a deep Texas drawl—Levi's husband, Marsh—said from the other end of the line. "Your future niblings have other ideas, and sweet-as-pie Juney is spitting nails."

"Let's go," Bennett said, already pulling Gino toward the door. "We'll get a private jet out of here or Logan. Perks of being a rock star."

Gino pressed Mute and tugged him back by the wrist. "But the Boston show tomorrow ..."

"Can be rescheduled."

"But that's more stops, will you be—"

Bennett's heart pounded into his ribs as he rose on his toes and kissed him quiet. He truly was the luckiest man alive, and at that moment, he'd never loved his husband more. "I'll be fine, G. Family first, let's go."

Chapter 8

Gino rocked in the chair by the hospital room window, enjoying the warm midday sun and the warm bundle of joy in his arms, softly singing his newborn niece to sleep.

"That's a new one," June said from the bed where she was nursing Rachel's twin, Riley. "The song."

"Just something I've been noodling," he replied, and excitement sparkled in her blue eyes, causing Gino to divert his gaze out the window, guilt crawling its way up his throat. She was happy for him, always so supportive, and yet he'd failed his baby sister again. It had been five in the morning by the time they'd made it back to San Diego, only to have Marsh greet them at the airport curb with news that June was resting in recovery after a thankfully uneventful C-section. "I'm sorry I wasn't here in time."

"You could've just lied and said you made it. You were here when I woke up. I would've never known."

He chuckled, causing little Rachel to open her eyes and blink up at him. "Except you can always tell when I'm lying."

"Well, you're here now. That's what matters." She shifted Riley in her arms, closing her robe and holding him against her shoulder to burp. "How are things?" she asked as she patted his back. She was barely eight hours into motherhood and a pro already, all that babysitting she'd done for the rest of their siblings and cousins serving her well. "You had all those tour changes, and we didn't get to talk before you left."

"Juney, you don't need to worry about me right now."

"Humor me." Being the baby made June the most easygoing of them, and being closest to their FBI agent cousin made her an excellent observer and a not too shabby interrogator. Or maybe that was just their mother coming out in her. "How are you and Bennett? How's the tour going?"

"We're good, and the tour's going really well. Best in a long while."

"I heard you're playing acoustic."

He nodded.

"So, then, what about all that farewell tour talk? If things are going so well . . ."

Before Gino could answer, Levi appeared in the doorway. Suspiciously solo. "Where's Mom?" Gino asked.

"Where's Rick?" June asked on his heels.

Levi wandered into the room and perched on the end of June's bed. "Bennett drove your husband to fetch In-N-Out for you." June practically swooned. After she'd come to in recovery, the first words out of her mouth were *Where are my babies?* followed in short order by *I need a double-double after that.*"

"And Mom?" Gino said.

"Marsh took her to get those kouign-amann pastries they both like so much."

"At the bakery near your place?"

He nodded. "They're gonna pick up David too."

Gino saw where this was going. "That bakery is farther away than the closest In-N-Out."

"Exactly," Levi said with a wide grin, one Gino had wondered if he'd ever see again on his widowed cousin's face. He didn't know Marsh that well yet, but he knew the hacker cowboy made Levi happy again after losing the first love of his life, and Levi's son, David, was wild about him too. That was good enough for Gino.

June was certainly a fan, sighing happily as she rested back against the propped-up pillows, Riley on her chest. "I love your husbands."

"I won't tell Rick you said that," Gino said as he handed Rachel to Levi, everyone's laughter stirring both newborns. It took a few coos and chords and Levi swapping places with him in the chair for the munchkins to settle back down, but once they were quiet, Gino asked his sister, "Does the early delivery complicate anything at work for you?"

"The lab had a game plan in place. Just accelerating it a smidge." She was a principal scientist at a biotech company in town. "I'll need to do a lab call sometime next week, make sure everyone's on the same page, but with the product officially launched, it's mostly in commercial's hands at this point anyway."

"How's work for you?" he asked Levi next.

"Not shot at or almost run over this week," he said with a smirk and a shrug. "Will count that as a win."

June balled up a tissue and chucked it at him, then turned the inquisition back on Gino. She nudged him with her toe. "Don't think we missed you dodging my farewell tour question."

He glanced again out the windows, at his sunny hometown, then around the room at his growing family. "It's for real," he said with a nod. "Not saying we won't play a charity gig here or there, but this is it."

"How do you feel about that?"

"How do you know it wasn't my decision?" The nearly identical Morelli brow lift on June's and Levi's faces—the same their mothers had long ago perfected and wielded on all of them—made him laugh out loud. "Fine, yes, it was Bennett's call, and initially I panicked. Middle Cut has been our life for more than two decades, the music for three, but the music doesn't stop just because Middle Cut stops touring. Hell, we've been doing fewer shows this tour and the music is even better. There's space for the music to grow again," he said, explaining to them what he had to Roscoe at the start of the tour. Two months in and five new songs later, it was without a doubt the truth. But that wasn't the only thing growing. "And there's space for me and Bennett to grow too, together and individually, even at our ripe old age."

"I feel the same."

Gino twisted where he sat on the end of the bed and spied his husband standing in the doorway, wearing his favorite smile. The one that had appeared more and more often on this tour. The one he'd do anything to keep, for both their sakes.

He held out a hand, and Bennett stepped the rest of the way into the room, twining their fingers together and moving into the circle of his arms. "Touring like this . . ." Bennett mused. "I'm not ruling it out in the future, but I want to take some time for us and our family too."

Gino couldn't disagree, not sitting here with the love of his life and his family. Especially not with the warm San Diego sun on his face and the smell of home in a red and white paper bag filling the room, Rick carrying in June's In-N-Out behind Bennett.

"Just so long as you understand," June said around a mouthful of fries. "You're on birthday party entertainment duty."

"Free concerts!" Rick said, holding his hand up for a high-five with Levi.

June waggled her brows. "And more babysitters."

"Sounds perfect," Bennett said as he dropped a kiss on his head.

Gino stared up into his husband's happy, hopeful hazel eyes. "It does."

Chapter 9

It was almost ten when Bennett turned the key in their front door. An unexpected visit home but no less welcome. Standing a second longer on the porch, he inhaled a giant gulp of salty sea breeze, then stepped inside, flipping on lights as he juggled the box of leftover pastries Marsh had sent them home with.

Gino entered behind him and rolled their luggage to the foot of the stairs. "How many hours have we been awake?"

Bennett groaned as he set the pastries on the kitchen island. "I lost count somewhere around thirty-six." In truth, they were closer to forty-eight with only catnaps randomly stolen over the past two days.

Gino's arms circled him from behind, his chin resting on his head, the two of them staring out the windows at the moonlit Pacific, the lights of tankers and oil rigs twinkling far off in the distance. "We'll just have to sleep for the next day and a half to make up for it."

Tipping back his head, Bennett kissed the underside of Gino's scruffy jaw. "We have to be in Seattle tomorrow." He chuckled at Gino's heavy sigh and turned into him, burying his face in his chest.

Gino dropped a kiss on his crown. "We can resch—"

"No, we'll make it," Bennett said, glancing up and seeing the worry in Gino's eyes, realizing he'd misconstrued Bennett's need for closeness. It wasn't distress driving him into the warm embrace. It was contentment, pure and simple, after spending the entire day celebrating new life with their family, with those who had welcomed him with open arms these past thirty years. And now he was home, in the place he loved most, with the person he loved most in the world, and he wanted to share that peace and happiness with him. Something that had seemed impossibly out of reach just a few months ago. "We'll get a good night's sleep in our own bed, then catch a flight up in the morning."

Arms tightening around him, Gino started walking them toward the stairs. "Something else I'd like to do with you in our bed first."

Bennett liked the sound of that.

Liked the sound of the knock at their door a whole lot less.

"Awfully late for visitors," he said.

Brow creased, Gino released him and crossed back to the door.

Bennett couldn't see around him, but the distinctly Midwest "Yo, G-man, welcome home!" clued him in to their visitor's identity. He grabbed a pastry out of the box, then moseyed over to Gino's side. "Hey, Casey," he greeted their neighbor.

Casey was a walking SoCal stereotype. Blond hair, sun-kissed skin, blue eyes, and a big smile, and if you saw him at sunrise or sunset, a wet suit hanging from his waist. This late at night, he was in board shorts and a tee, the latter advertising a surf gear company. "Didn't expect you guys back for another couple weeks," he said.

"Brief detour," Bennett said around his bite of kouign-amann.

"June had the twins," Gino explained.

"Oh, yay, congrats, dudes." He extended his fist for bumps, each of them returning one. "Well, I was just bringing this over." He held out the stack of mail in his other hand, then ducked back out the door to bring in a large box. "Figured you might want this package sooner rather than later."

"You figured right," Gino said, and Bennett glanced up to see his husband smiling wide. It wasn't a poster tube, obviously, but Bennett wondered if it might be another memento like the ones Gino had been gifting him all tour long. "Thanks, man."

They made plans to catch up with Casey for coffee in the

morning before heading to the airport, then closed the door and locked up behind him. Not a minute too soon, Bennett's curiosity killing him. "What's that?" he said, gesturing with a sticky finger at the box.

"A surprise for you," he answered, grin impossibly wider, as he picked up the box and carried it to the table. Light, then, whatever was inside, despite the size. "Was going to give it to you after our last show in San Diego."

"But Boston is gonna be our last show now."

"So, I'm guessing by your logic, you think you should open it now."

He rose on his toes and pecked his husband's lips. "You know me so well."

Gino lightly shoved him toward the sink. "Wash your hands first, pastry monster. You and Marsh together are dangerous."

They were both still laughing when Bennett returned to the table, box cutter in hand. "Is it a *framed* concert poster?"

"Not exactly," Gino said as he plopped into one of the chairs. "And be very careful with the knife."

Bennett nodded, then carefully sliced through the tape at one end of the box. He set down the cutter and slowly drew out the bubble-wrapped, framed something, foam bumpers on each corner. He popped those off, then ran a finger under the piece of tape keeping the bubble wrap secure. Inside was definitely a framed picture of some sort, wrapped in butcher paper with a kitchen twine bow.

Pausing, Bennett glided his fingers over the thick brick red paper, remembering his dad, remembering how Middle Cut had come by its name. Gino's hand landed on his back, a comforting, commiserating weight, no doubt remembering the same, remembering all those afternoons they'd practiced on the loading dock of the butcher shop Bennett's late father owned. The other businesses at the industrial park where it had been located loved the free music; the neighbors where they'd each lived, not so much. "I miss them."

"I know you do, baby. They were good people."

Good people who'd had Bennett in their forties. They'd passed a few years back, ten months apart, his mother first from cancer, then his father from a stroke. More likely a broken heart—the pair never could be apart for too long.

Bennett understood that, even better now than he had several months ago. Giving Gino those divorce papers had been the last thing he'd wanted. In retrospect, it probably would've broken him for good if Gino had taken those papers, signed them, and left. But if that was what Gino had needed, Bennett would have given it to him. Would give him the world.

And his heart, forever.

"Open it, babe," Gino said, rubbing his back.

His hand was shaky as he untied the ribbon and peeled back the paper, and he was glad for Gino's swift reflexes; his husband surged to stand beside him when the picture inside was revealed, when Bennett gasped and tears instantly filled his eyes.

"How?" was all he could manage around the lump in his throat.

"Pays having FBI agents in the family, especially when they're friends with a bunch of hackers and bounty hunters."

Laughter escaped past the lump, the thought of Levi and Marsh leading a team to find a beat-up, yellowed sketch of the primal cuts of a pig, with Bennett's red crayon OINK scribbled in one corner.

This precious, assumed-lost memento once again in his hands.

"You remember that day?" Gino asked.

"Like it was yesterday. We were at the shop, doing history homework, and I looked up at this picture over Dad's counter and said, *The band is called Middle Cut.*"

"And that was that."

"And that was that," he repeated as he skated his hands over the sketch he'd drawn.

Until Gino carefully slipped it from him and set it on the

table. He twined their fingers together and lifted their joined hands to his lips. "Middle Cut was there before our first tour, and it'll still be there after this last one. It will always be where we are." He lowered their hands over Bennett's heart. "Because it's right here."

Bennett leaned forward, returning the kiss to their hands, then to his husband's lips. Their love, their music would be right here with them, always.

FOREVER MINE

M. ROBINSON

About the Author

M. Robinson is the *Wall Street Journal* and *USA Today* Bestselling author of more than thirty novels in Contemporary Romance and Romantic Suspense. Crowned the "Queen of Angst" by her loyal readers, you'll feel the cut of her pen slicing through your heart as your soul bleeds upon the words of her stories with each turn of the page.

Most notably known for the Good Ol' Boys, M's newest venture has graced her with the #1 Bestseller on Apple Books with Second Chance Contract. The Second Chance Men are powerful, intelligent and will sweep you off your feet and leave you weak in the knees— every woman's wildest dreams.

M. lives the boat life along the Gulf Coast of Florida with her two puppies and real life book boyfriend, the inspiration for all her filthy talking alphas, Bossman.

When she isn't in the cave writing her next epic love story, you can usually spot her mad-dashing through Target or in the drive-thru of Starbucks, refueling. Yes, she's a self-proclaimed shopaholic, but only if she's spending Bossman's money.

www.authormrobinson.com

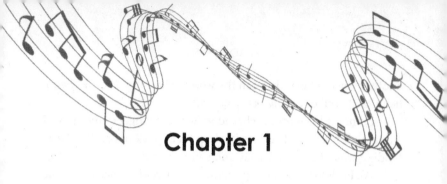

Chapter 1

HAYLEY

"Shit," I whispered to myself, looking around. Hoping I'd find a sense of direction on where I'd come from. I must have gotten lost, ending up by a waterhole.

"Well, look what we have here," someone whispered from behind me, causing me to stumble back against a tree as he caged me in with his arms around the sides of my head. "I haven't seen you before. I'd remember such a pretty face and banging body," he rasped too close to my face, smelling like liquor and weed. "What's your name?"

I didn't recognize this guy, and the longer I stood there, the faster my heart began pounding against my chest. "Hay-ley," I replied, feeling much more vulnerable than before.

"Such a beautiful name, for such a beautiful girl. What are you doing all by yourself in the woods, babe? Don't you know you can run into a bear or a wolf?"

"Ummm ... right. I need to go back." I sidestepped him to leave, but he blocked my advance.

"You don't need to leave. I'm here now."

My eyes widened. "I want to leave." I went to move again, but he wouldn't let me.

"Naw, I'm not done with you yet."

"Catch a clue—I'm not interested."

"I bet I can make you interested."

"If you don't let me leave, I'm going to scream."

I turned my face as he leaned in to kiss me while the sound of another voice echoed through the woods, shouting, "Frank! Leave her alone! You're scaring her, you jerk!"

I'd never been more relieved to hear a stranger's voice than I was at that moment. I released a deep breath I didn't realize I was holding when he backed away and spun around.

We both looked in the direction of where the voice had come from. There was a tall, stocky guy with dark hair standing a few feet away from us. I couldn't make out who he was yet. It was too dark out.

"Mind your own business, Joshua. This has nothing to do with you."

Walking toward us, he grinned, looking in my direction before nodding to Frank. "You want to stay here with him?"

I peered back and forth between them, sputtering, "Umm ... no."

Joshua laughed, smirking wide.

It was Joshua Co. He was one of the most popular guys in our school. I couldn't help but smile back at him, feeling relieved he was there with me now. This was the first time he'd ever said a word to me. I didn't even think he knew I existed.

The reassuring expression on his face kept luring me in. When he caught me staring at his defined arms and broad chest, I blushed and looked back at Frank.

"Oh, I see," Frank chimed in. "You want to hang out with him instead? Is that it? Because I'll tell you right now, he doesn't do girlfriends."

Yeah, so I've heard.

Joshua chuckled.

"I said that out loud, didn't I?"

He laughed again before nodding to Frank. "You can go now."

"Screw you, man." With that, he spun and left, leaving Joshua and me alone.

Now I was nervous for a whole different reason. I knew all I needed to know about him. His reputation preceded him wherever he went. It didn't matter what county we were in, everyone knew who Joshua was. It had been that way since I'd moved here in middle school. Guys like them were all the same, every last one of them. Acting like they were hot stuff and owned every place he walked into.

The worst part was that girls fed into their lines, cocky smirks, and no care attitude. Through the years, I'd heard enough to know I needed to steer clear of Joshua, and the fact that he was looking at me in the way guys did in romance movies was unsettling. As much as I didn't want him to have an effect on me, when one of the most popular boys in our school was devouring you with his gaze, you couldn't help but feel affected.

With an overconfident arched eyebrow, Joshua narrowed his stare at me, and I swallowed hard. I watched as he continued making his way over to me, one assertive stride after the next.

Slowly, I licked my lips, my mouth suddenly becoming dry. Out of nowhere, it felt as though I was under some spell I couldn't control or begin to understand. His gaze immediately followed the movement of my tongue, and I found myself taking a step back while folding my arms over my chest and trying to stand my ground.

"Ummm ... thanks," I expressed, wanting to break the awkward silence. "You kind of saved me just now."

"I do what I can. Hayley, right?"

"You know who I am?"

"Of course I know the name of one of the prettiest girls at our school."

My heart beat faster, and I couldn't help but notice how much he towered over me. He was tall, much taller than my five-foot-three frame. He was probably a little over six feet with dark hair and intense green eyes that had a hint of blue running through them. His chiseled jawline and facial hair only added to his sexy allure.

Not to mention he didn't look his age. He looked older. It was probably easy for him to buy booze or sneak into clubs which I knew he did with Julian. At least that was what everyone at our school gossiped.

Joshua was unfazed, standing there in all his glory as I tried like hell to ignore his muscular build as he took me in.

"Are you checking me out?" I blurted, mentally chastising myself.

The one time I needed to sound calm and cool, and I couldn't pull it off. Not with the way he was staring at me.

"Would you like that?"

"No."

"That's not what your body's telling me."

"Well, you can't read my mind."

He gave me a sexy smirk, making my eyes roll.

"Fine. Try me."

"I don't want to embarrass you more than I already am."

"I'm not embarrassed," I shrieked, clearing my throat, my voice giving me away.

"Just remember you asked for it." He stepped toward me, leaving no room between us. "You're shocked that I know who you are, which is funny because I've actually asked around about you, but from what I've heard you're messing around with your best friend."

I gasped. "I am not."

"You didn't let me finish. I don't think you're messing around with David because you don't strike me as the kind of girl he'd be interested in."

He was right. I couldn't argue with him there.

"You don't date. You've never had a boyfriend. So that tells me you're either waiting for Prince Charming, or you have no interest in getting hurt. Which, let's face it, we're in high school, and the odds of a guy breaking your heart are very likely. Especially since you have no experience—"

"I have experience."

He smirked. "I bet you've never been kissed."

My mouth dropped open. "Yes, I have."

"Hmmm ..." He thought about it for a second. "I call bullshit."

"I totally have."

"Alright. Then prove it."

I shrugged. "It was with this guy from another school."

"You mean the guy you just made up?"

"I'm not making him up. His name was Joseph, and he was the best kisser. We actually made out a lot. We couldn't get enough of each other."

"Right ..."

"Stop with the snide comments. I'm not lying."

"Like I said, prove it."

"I just did. I told you his name was—"

"I said prove it, not make up lies."

"How am I supposed to prove it then?"

I never expected what came out of his mouth next. Never in a million years did I imagine one of the most popular guys in our school would challenge...

"You can prove it by letting me kiss you."

Chapter 2

JOSHUA

"Are you for real?" she asked, completely caught off guard by my challenge.

I knew she was full of shit. I'd been asking around about Hayley McKenzie since middle school when she walked into my science class with a turquoise backpack. It was the first thing that caught my attention about her.

What girl in the sixth grade didn't have a pink or purple backpack? So naturally, I was instantly drawn to her, being that turquoise was my favorite color. I was going to ask her to be my science partner, but David beat me to it, and they'd been inseparable ever since. His head was so far up her butt, I was surprised he could still get around with as many chicks as he did on a monthly basis. Supposedly, they weren't into each other.

Although I couldn't blame him if he was into her. She'd never been touched by anyone, and every guy at our school wanted to try to get with her just to say they were her first.

It was immediate, the desire to want to help her.

Protect her.

The second I saw her start walking into the woods alone, my feet moved on their own. I'd developed a protective quality to watch over those I loved, and there was a gravitational pull to protect Hayley at that moment. I was surprised David had left her alone long enough to get lost in the woods. He was by her side all the time. It was really annoying, and since we were by ourselves for the first time since she'd walked into my science class all those years ago, I was going to use it to my advantage and kiss her.

Be her first kiss.

The longer we stood there, the more I craved to be in her life. It was the weirdest thing. I'd never experienced any-thing like it before. Maybe that was why I wanted to kiss her, knowing that to a girl like her ...

It would mean something.

The truth was I was over it not meaning anything to me as well. There were only so many times I could hook up with a random chick. I was born and raised in this small town where everyone knew each other. I was almost sixteen, but felt much older. Wiser.

"Want to touch me?" I teased, smiling. "Make sure you're not dreaming?"

"So is this how it works?" she asked with amusement in her tone. "You save girls from jerks and then make your move?"

"Don't mind Frank. He's not much of a gentleman."

"And you are?"

"I mean, my mom did raise me right, and I have a little sister I need to protect."

"From guys like you?"

I placed my hand over my heart. "Ouch."

"Oh please ... you don't fool me with your witty comebacks and amazing cheekbones. I know all about you too."

"Oh, so you've been asking around about me, Hayley?"

"Hardly, but everyone knows about you, Joshua."

"I don't care what everyone knows. I want to know what you know."

"I know that you're one of the most popular guys at our school."

"Yeah, that doesn't mean shit to me."

"I find that hard to believe."

"Wow. You must think very highly of me?"

"I don't think anything about you."

I touched my heart again, looking down at my hand. "Am I

bleeding? Or do you want to dig that dagger a little deeper?"

She giggled in that girly way that usually annoyed me, but coming from her it didn't. It was cute.

"So what else do you know?"

"That you're with a lot of girls."

I laughed, I couldn't help it. She was adorable. "How much longer do you plan on stalling? You could just say I'm right and you're a liar, and then you wouldn't have to pretend like you're unaffected by my awesome personality."

"I'm not stalling." She shook her head. "I just don't have to prove anything to you either."

"You're the one who said I didn't know what you were thinking, and I just proved to you that I do. Like right now, you're thinking how much you want me to kiss you, but you're worried I'm going to know that it's your first kiss by the way your lips move with mine, so I'll ease your mind since I'm a gentleman, and tell you that all you have to do is follow my lead. I'll do all the work." I winked. "You're welcome."

"Ugh! You're unbelievable. You know that?"

"Oh, I know. I'm especially unbelievable at kissing, which you're about to find out for yourself, Hails."

"Hails? You have a nickname for me now?"

"Would you prefer I call you sweetness?"

She arched an eyebrow. "Sweetness?"

"Yeah, I know you're going to taste as sweet as you look."

"Dude! You just have a witty comeback for everything, huh?"

"What can I say, pretty girl? You bring out the best in me."

She smiled, a real smile that time as she tucked her hair behind her ear. I instantly reached over and pulled it out to tug on the ends of it, letting my fingertips graze her cheek.

"Is this one of your moves?"

"Do you want it to be?"

"I have no interest in being another one of your girls."

I grinned. "Jealous?"

"You wish. I'm not one of your cheerleaders."

With a hard edge, I replied, "That you aren't."

"Why do you want to kiss me anyway?"

"Can't a friend just help out another friend?"

"We're friends now? When did that happen? I don't even like you."

Calling her bluff, I narrowed my eyes at her. "That really hurts, Hayley."

"You're so full of it."

"And you're beautiful."

"I don't know if I should be offended or flattered that you're hitting on me."

"If I had to choose, I'd prefer the latter."

"Well then, thank God you don't."

"That sassy little mouth of yours is really fucking cute."

She was gorgeous. The girl didn't even have to try. She was naturally stunning. I just stood there in awe of her. There was something about the way she was looking at me that truly had my mind reeling with what her lips would feel like against mine.

"I guess letting you kiss me could be like a thank you for saving me."

"I didn't save you. I protected you."

"What's the difference?"

"You don't need saving, Hayley. You're a survivor all on your own."

Her face paled, understanding I knew more than she assumed I would. I didn't know what was worse. Her pretending like she didn't want me to kiss her, or her wanting me to. I couldn't help noticing the look in her eyes. They spoke volumes, roping me in, taking hold of my mind, and not letting go. I was so fucking conflicted. The effect she was having on me, and we'd only just spoken for the first time.

What was happening?

As if reading my mind, she changed the subject. "Frank's going to talk smack. You know that, right?"

"Good. Let him run his mouth. It will keep other jerks away

from you too."

"But not you?"

Unable to hold back any longer, I coaxed, "I'm going to kiss you now, Hayley."

I waited a couple of seconds for her to object, and when she didn't, I leaned forward, closing the small distance between us. Wanting to touch her skin, my hands reached up and grabbed ahold of her cheeks. The smell of her assaulted my senses as I softly claimed her lips, laying my mouth right on hers. Her eyes tightly shut, her breathing hitched, and her arms fell to her sides. Right from the start, I could tell she had no idea what she was doing.

Her lips were smooth against mine, and I could feel her heart drumming so fast against my chest. The desire to ruin her for every other guy was as real as the feelings I was experiencing toward her.

Slowly, I parted my lips, pulling her in closer, and she followed my lead, matching the same rhythm I'd set. My tongue touched her lips before she did the same, leaving the craziest sensation in her wake. I pulled back my tongue, and she understood what I wanted, what I sought. She gently slid hers into my eager mouth.

My tongue did the same as hers, turning this kiss into something more than I thought it would be.

I was losing myself in her.

From her lips to her eyes, to the sounds she was making.

Words couldn't describe what was happening at that moment between us. The feelings she stirred with each stroke of our tongues. Feelings I didn't think were possible to experience. That I didn't even think existed.

I didn't want to stop kissing her.

It was surreal.

Consuming.

And I wanted more.

When another soft moan escaped her mouth, I pecked her lips one last time before gradually pulling away. Already missing her touch. Incoherent thoughts ran rapidly through my mind.

I was grinning down at her as her eyes fluttered open, not removing my hands from the sides of her face. My infatuated stare hadn't changed—if anything it was worse.

Murmuring against her lips, I rasped, "Like I said, you've never been kissed until now. Until me."

Chapter 3

HAYLEY

It was the annual back-to-school carnival in Fort Worth, and everyone from our small town was there to celebrate the end of summer. Usually, I avoided this fair like the plague, but Joshua was insistent on us going and wasn't taking no for an answer. Since that night on the lake two months ago, we'd spent almost every day together when I wasn't with David.

I could immediately tell that Joshua didn't like our friendship, not that I could blame him. We were best friends, and with all the rumors about us, I knew he had concerns but hadn't mentioned them yet. I was aware it was coming, though.

Joshua and I were getting closer, and the more time I spent with David, the harsher his tone would become when he'd call me to hang out. The second I said I was with David, it was like night and day with his voice. He was biting his tongue, biding his time to bring it up, and I'd be lying if I said I wasn't doing the same when it came down to asking him what we were doing and where this was going.

This was the first time I had these deep, intense feelings for a guy. Don't get me wrong, I loved David, but it wasn't like that between us. It was like a sister loved a brother, and the feeling was mutual. But you wouldn't think that with the way Joshua and David treated one another.

David was as protective over me as Joshua was. He'd already warned me about Joshua, saying he was going to hurt me. Joshua had the worst reputation with girls, and everyone knew it.

He was a huge player, and David was simply being a good friend, wanting me to steer clear of him. As much as I was worried that he would hurt me, I couldn't stay away from him. There was something about the way Joshua looked at me, talked to me, made me feel that I couldn't ignore or push away.

He made me happy, triggering butterflies in my stomach every time we were together. I never wanted our time to come to an end. It was getting harder to hide my real feelings about him, and a huge part of me knew he was aware of the effect he was having on me.

Once I stepped out of Joshua's truck at the fair, he waited for me by the hitch of his truck, extending his hand when I got close to him. I cocked my head to the side, raising an eyebrow. He was going to hold my hand in public, and since we always hung out alone, I was a little caught off guard by his gesture. This only confused me further as to where our relationship was going. The more time we spent together, the more I realized how much of a romantic he truly was.

"Let's go show off my girl, huh?" He grinned while I grabbed his hand.

I tried to keep my amused expression to myself as he tugged me toward him. We walked hand-in-hand into the carnival, strolling past all the rides until we were by the water. The fair was next to Eagle Mountain Marina, and he led us down to the docks.

Joshua loved the boats. He was always talking about them, saying how much he wanted to own a yacht one day. When we reached the end of the boat slip, he stepped over the railing onto a gorgeous yacht.

"Whoa. I'm not down for breaking and entering."

He grinned again. "Don't you trust me?"

"Not if we get arrested for trespassing."

He laughed, nodding to the front of the boat. It was only then that I noticed there was a blanket spread out on the bow. He winked, pulling me onto the yacht.

"Wow," was all I could manage to say as I slowly turned in a circle, taking in my surroundings.

The sun had just set, and every star shined bright above the water. I took in the blanket and picnic basket that was perfectly placed in the center of the bow.

"Is this another one of your moves? Do you bring all your girls here? I can see why you get laid as much as you do." I chuckled to no avail, taking in his stern expression. "What?"

"Sweetness, let's get one thing straight, alright?" He placed his finger under my chin to get me to look up at him, and I did, anxiously waiting for what he was going to say.

"Anytime we do things together, it's the first time for me too."

I shyly smiled, his words warming my heart. Making me feel like shit for what I'd said before.

"If there's anything important you need to know about me, it's that I don't do anything I don't want to. But with you ... I don't know how to explain it, Hayley. I was drawn to you from the first day you walked into my science class in sixth grade."

"What?" I jerked back. "You remember that?"

He smiled. "The girl with the turquoise backpack."

My eyes widened. "Turquoise is my favorite color."

"It's mine too."

"I didn't know you even knew who I was back then."

"Of course, I knew. I was going to ask you to be my lab partner, but your best friend beat me to it."

"Oh."

"Oh? Is that all you can say?"

"Depends. Are you going to say something mean about David?" I blurted, unable to hold back.

He cocked an eyebrow. "So you've noticed that I don't care for him?"

"I mean, anytime I say I'm with him, your tone immediately turns sour." I shrugged. "Do you not like him?"

"I'll answer that question after you tell me what he thinks about us hanging out."

I swallowed hard.

"I think you have your own answer built in your question, Hayley."

"We're best friends."

"So I've heard."

"He's just trying to protect me. You don't have the best reputation, Joshua."

"David needs to mind his own fucking business before I do it for him."

"Whoa." I raised my hands. "Where did that come from?" I lowered my eyebrows, confused by the turn of events. Instinctively, I peered down at the makeshift picnic he had made for us ...

For me.

"I don't want to fight. Especially after you planned this beautiful picnic. I still don't know if we're going to get arrested, but you know, it's the thought that counts."

He laughed, throwing his head back, and I took the opportunity to ease his mind.

"You have nothing to worry about when it comes to David. I promise. But if you wanted to get to know me back in sixth grade, why wait till now?"

"You're always with David."

"So?"

"I don't like to share."

"Then why now?"

"Honestly ... I don't fucking know. I saw you at the bonfire party, and you looked upset walking into the woods by yourself. I followed you before I even realized what I was doing. It's the effect you have on me. I lose all sense of control when it comes to you."

I smiled, and my chest seized. He'd often express the sweetest things. Still, I couldn't just open my mouth and be sincere with him, tell him what I felt, because every last insecurity that was buried deep within my bones would consume me, bordering on the point of pain.

The truth was I was falling for him. I was only sixteen but felt much older. Mature beyond my years. It had always been that way for me, having to grow up fast and mostly alone. You don't realize how much of your childhood affects the person you become, the person you are. How memories shape your life, your feelings, and most importantly your *love*.

"Do you mean that?" I asked, my heart beating fast.

"Here's another thing you need to know about me, Hayley. I don't say anything I don't mean. Since we started hanging out, I find myself doing all sorts of shit I've never done before, and I don't want it to end."

"You don't?"

"Do you?"

I shook my head.

"Words, sweetness. I need to hear you say it."

I took a deep breath, admitting, "I like being with you too, Joshua. Although I can't say I noticed you in science class in sixth grade. I was a mess back then. I didn't notice a lot of things. It's why David is my best friend. He's the first person to ever want to get to know me, and I learned a lot about myself through our friendship."

"What's that?"

"I have a hard time letting people in, and when push comes to shove, I do the pushing and shoving. I guess it's how I survived my mother. You know?"

"I know." He was weighing his words. I could tell by the expression on his face.

"Just ask me, Joshua."

"Alright. Well, what about me? You want to push me away too?"

"Yes ... no ... I don't know. I don't want to get hurt, and I know you definitely break hearts, but at the same time, I like being around you. These last two months have been fun, and I like you. A lot."

He smiled wide. "I like you a lot too."

Hearing him say those six words meant everything to me. I

could feel my guard coming down more and more with him, and for someone who had suffered so much abuse as I had, it was a hard pill to swallow.

"How about I promise you I won't hurt you, if you promise me that you and David won't have sleepovers anymore. Deal?"

"You've heard about that?"

"Amongst other things."

"I can assure you that most are made-up lies. We've never kissed, we've never even held hands. Sure, we've had sleepovers, but he stays on his side of the bed, and I do the same. We don't cuddle if that's what you're imagining. It's not like that between us. I don't feel for David what I feel for you when we're together. The love I have for him is just brotherly."

My heart dropped when he jerked back, and the expression on his face quickly turned somber, then he bit out ...

"You love him?"

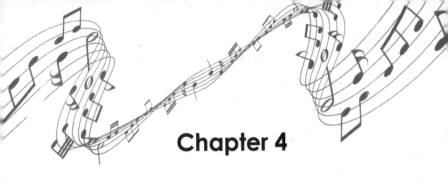

Chapter 4

JOSHUA

I eyed her skeptically.

"You know there's a difference between loving someone and being in love with them, right? I love David, but I'm not in love with him, Joshua."

It'd been three months since Hayley turned my world upside down and two months since we'd started hanging out.

I held her hand.

I kissed her lips.

I listened to everything that came out of her mouth as if she was telling me the world's biggest secrets.

I didn't so much as try to get her to make out with me. Being around her was enough. It was all I wanted. To be with someone, to really be with them on a level other than physical, was something I'd never experienced before. Something I never had, and I didn't want it.

The bullshit.

The emotions.

The ups and downs.

After our first talk in the woods, I'd hung out with a couple of girls, trying to forget about Hayley to no avail. I couldn't stop thinking about her, and anytime a girl attempted to kiss me, I instantly turned my face. Feeling like I was cheating on Hayley which didn't make any sense.

At that point, we'd had one conversation, but it felt like the deepest connection I'd ever had with anyone in all my life. I didn't understand any of it. The need to be around this girl was throwing me off-kilter. I thought about her constantly—the next time I would see her, talk to her, hold her ...

The list was endless.

Our connection was easy, we didn't have to work at it. It wasn't a burden or a struggle to be with her like it sometimes was with other chicks. I used to get bored the minute the sex stopped, moving on to the next.

Not with Hayley, though. I wanted more. Our dynamic flowed seamlessly, our conversations, our chemistry, our *friendship*. Another thing that was new to me was being friends with a girl I was hanging out with. I never cared to get to know them. They were a means to an end.

It was simple.

Now I was in a dynamic I couldn't get enough of. One of the things I adored the most about her was the subtle looks she would give me when she didn't think I was looking.

She came into my life like a breath of fresh air, and I breathed her in like a man who was suddenly on death row. Unable to fight against her pull. Every time I was with her I was lost in us. I never expected to fall for her. I wasn't even looking for anyone, but there she was, this girl with such a force, such a drive. It was so powerful that I never stood a chance.

"Did you hear what I said, Joshua?" she questioned, bringing me back to the present. When she'd just told me she loved another guy.

"I heard you."

"Do you believe me?"

"You haven't given me a reason not to. I don't want to talk about David anymore."

"Good." She smiled, and it lit up her entire face. "I'm starving."

For the next hour, we ate dinner on the bow and talked about nothing in particular.

I watched the way her lips moved.

The way her hair blew in the wind, framing her face.

The way she laughed with her whole body, feeling it deep in my bones.

I especially watched the way she looked at me as I swept her hair away from her face. She didn't say a word, but her eyes spoke for her. The way she affected my mind and heart was terrifying, but it was so real.

So consuming.

She felt it too. That much I knew.

Breaking the strong connection that held both of us captive, I cleared my throat and stood up, bringing her right along with me. Something came over my senses, and I reached for my phone in my pocket to hit my playlist. Once I found the song I wanted, I set it down on the ground next to our makeshift picnic, which I'd made just for her.

With the music, the boat rocking softly, and the bright moon shining above our heads, I spun her into my arms before holding her close to my chest. Taking one of her hands, I placed it on my shoulder then intertwined the other with mine, placing it near my heart.

Her face conveyed so many emotions in a matter of seconds, and I paid attention to each and every one. She placed the side of her face on my chest, and I knew what she was trying to do, but it didn't matter because I already felt everything she was trying to hide.

"Tell me something you've never told anyone," she uttered out of nowhere.

I thought about it for a second. "I want to be a doctor."

"What?" She gazed up at me. "Really?"

"Mmm-hmm."

"Wow. You're just full of surprises, huh?"

I peered deep into her eyes. "Sweetness, you have no idea."

HAYLEY

After we cleaned up the boat which I learned was actually his parents', Joshua grabbed my hand and led us back to the fair where it felt as though all our classmates were in attendance. Girls were looking at us, more like glaring everywhere we went. I was at the fair with Joshua Co, and it was a big deal in and of itself.

There we were, holding hands throughout the carnival, and he didn't do this. He wasn't this guy who was winning stuffed animals and kissing my lips every chance he had.

It was as much of a shock to me as it was to our classmates, the open affection he was showing me. He wasn't trying to hide the fact that we were hanging out.

When my eyes shifted to the photo booth by the trees, Joshua didn't hesitate to take me over there.

I smiled, knowing he was doing this for me.

"Come here," he ordered, sitting me on his lap once the curtain was closed and no one could see us. We were both facing the camera in front of us.

"You feel good on top of me, sweetness."

"I thought you didn't like taking pictures?" I asked, trying to calm my racing heart.

"I don't," he whispered in my ear from behind me. "I'm doing this for you."

I smiled wide, my stomach fluttering.

We took five pictures in different positions. The first was with us facing the camera. His arms were around my waist, and his face was nuzzled in my neck. I could feel his breath on my skin, igniting tingles to stir down my spine.

The next one he started tickling me, both of us laughing like fools as the camera clicked for another photo. The third picture was a funny one, where we were both sticking out our tongues. The fourth photo caught me by surprise, as Joshua spun me around so that we were now facing each other.

I gasped when I realized I was straddling his waist, making him grin. Pulling back my hair, he kissed my lips, and the next two images were just of us kissing.

He rasped against my lips, "I'm going to like taking pictures with you."

Everything was perfect.

He was perfect.

"Come on." He stood us up. "Let's go on the Ferris wheel. It's my favorite ride. You get to see the whole town from the sky, and there isn't anything like it."

I opened my mouth to say something, but nothing came out. I didn't have to wait long until he kissed my lips. His mouth felt different this time. It was soft, tender, caring. I didn't know how long we kissed. All I knew was that my reckless thoughts were fading into the background, and I was consumed by the way he was able to bring me peace.

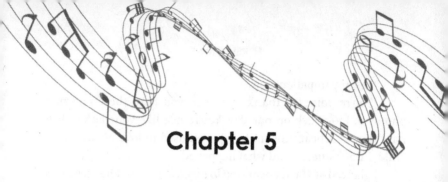

Chapter 5

JOSHUA

"Congratulations! We're so proud of you guys! Just one more picture!" Mom celebrated, much to my annoyance, but I played nice for her.

We had just graduated from high school, so it was the least I could do.

"Honey," Dad reasoned. "You have like three hundred pictures already."

"I know, but our babies are growing up."

"Oh, honey ..." Dad pulled her into a tight hug.

Hayley beamed, looking at my parents adoringly. I knew she admired their marriage. She loved being around them any chance she could get.

"Okay, okay," Mom surrendered. "Just a few more of Joshua and Hayley."

I smiled and threw my arm around my girl as I tugged her toward me.

"Smile. Oh, come on, Joshua, smile!"

"I am smiling," I griped, unable to take much more, my face fucking hurt from smiling so much.

"You guys look so nice! Now give her a kiss!"

I did.

"Joshua!" Mom chastised. "There are children around! Don't grab her butt!"

Hayley giggled, pulling away from me.

"Great, are we done now?"

"Yes, my impatient son."

"You're going to thank me when you have these amazing photos to look back on one day. You're just like your father. You have the most beautiful smile too. You used to love pictures as a child. I don't understand what happened."

I glanced at Hayley, wanting to smile for her, but her gaze was captivated by someone behind me.

"Babe, you oka—"

"Mom," Hayley announced out of nowhere, making my body snap around to the woman who was suddenly walking toward us.

All eyes flew to her mother. My gaze went back to my girl.

"I love you so much." I kissed all over her face, her mouth. "I love you. I love you. I love you."

Our eyes locked, both of us trying to focus and take each other in.

"I need to ask you something." I asked.

My eyes widened.

The rest proceeded in slow motion. Especially when we're standing there at graduation.

I kept thinking I found the love of my life.

She knew what was coming ...

Big.

Huge.

Ugly tears.

I didn't hesitate, pulling away and looking profoundly into her eyes. All I saw was my future, with her as my wife.

I made my choice, it was her.

It was always her.

So I spoke with conviction ...

"Marry me, sweetness."

HAYLEY

Did I want to marry him?

I inhaled a deep, solid breath while he held onto my grasp. Joshua always went from zero to a hundred and this was just another one of those circumstances. He didn't half-ass anything ever.

One thought would occur while the next one was forming.

I did love him ...

Did I want to be his wife?

Everything was changing at a moment's notice and I was hanging on by a very thin thread that felt as if it was going to snap any second.

"Have you lost your mind?!"

"Actually, for the first time in my life, I'm thinking pretty fucking clearly."

"Joshua, you're insane!"

"Insanely in love with you." He pulled out a ring box from the inside of his jacket.

"Joshua ..." I warned, my voice laced with unease.

"What?" he played coy.

"Joshua ..."

"Don't you want to open it?"

"No."

"No?"

"What's in it?" I asked.

"You know what's in it, Hayley."

Since I wasn't moving from the spot I seemed cemented to, he opened the box for me. As soon as I saw the three karat princess cut diamond ring shining bright against the sun, I loudly gasped and my hands shot to my mouth.

Fervently shaking my head, I yelled, "Oh my God! I can't believe you. I don't even know what to say to you."

"A yes would be great. I want you to be my wife because I love you. I'm done playing games. I want you in my life forever and I'll do whatever you need to make that happen. It's really quite simple."

I placed my hand on his chest. "I think I'm having a heart attack."

He chuckled, "Hayley ... That's your reply? What about everything else I just said?"

"You're not making any sense and if you took a second to think about that, you'd realize it."

"Quite the contrary. I'm completely rational."

I didn't move.

I didn't speak.

I was barely breathing.

He grabbed my hand, kissing the palm for a couple seconds. Allowing his lips to linger on my skin before he declared, "I've loved you from the moment I set my eyes on you. There is no me without you. I love you. You're mine, Hayley. You've always been. Now," holding up the ring, he repeated, "marry me, sweetness."

My mouth was wide open. "I ... I ... I don't know."

"Well." He cocked his head to the side. "At least it's not a no."

And I couldn't hold back any longer, I shouted ...

"Yes! I'll marry you!"

CONNECTED

BECCA STEELE

About the Author

Becca Steele is a *USA Today* and *Wall Street Journal* bestselling author of new adult romance. Her books have been translated into multiple languages.

Becca resides in the south of England with her family. When she's not writing, you can find her reading or gaming. Failing that, she'll be watching Netflix or making her 500th Spotify playlist.

www.authorbeccasteele.com

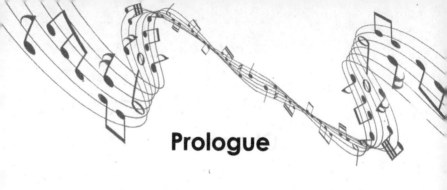

Prologue

BREAKING NEWS

After months of speculation, Mizar Records confirmed today that they have parted ways with American boy band Morningside. Lead singer Troy Ramirez has reportedly negotiated a solo deal with the label, but as for the remaining members, we have yet to see. Felix Prince, Timothy Hill, and Joe Garcia have all posted statements to their respective social media pages (read their statements in full below), but as for Jay Bowman...who knows? Morningside's notoriously private singer deactivated his social media accounts when the split became public, but we have been unable to confirm any further information.

Our inside source tells us that there were rumors of a growing rift between former teen idol Troy Ramirez and the rest of the bandmates prior to the announcement, and coupled with Morningside's declining album sales, Mizar Records were keen to strike a new deal which would allow them to focus solely on the band's most bankable star.

We are unable to verify if the rumors are true, but with today's announcement, we say there is no smoke without fire.

Our hearts are broken.

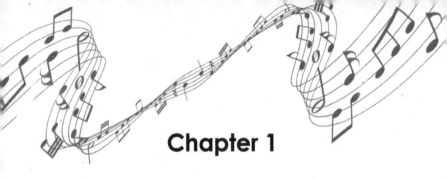

Chapter 1

CURTIS

A soft note echoed in my wake as I brushed past the cymbals, crossing the shop floor to the wall display of guitars. Tuned was quiet today...it always was, for that matter, and I loved that it allowed me to disappear into my own world for four hours at a time. It gave me time to think, away from the noise of London Southwark University, and away from my band, the 2Bit Princes.

Not that I didn't love being a part of the band, but I also needed my downtime, and my part-time job in this quiet little south London music shop was the perfect way to unwind. I flexed my wrists, going through the range of hand exercises I'd discovered on a YouTube video a week earlier. As the 2Bit Princes' drummer, my hands were kind of important. Okay, yeah, they were for all the band members, since everyone played an instrument, but hand exercises were my new thing. I continued to rotate through the range of movements in between arranging the guitars in a more aesthetically pleasing way—not that there was anything wrong with the way they were displayed, but there was only so much I could do with an empty shop on a Monday afternoon.

Humming along with the music that was playing softly through the speakers, I lifted my wrists—

"What are you doing?"

I spun around at the voice, my heart pounding out of my chest.

It was *him*. He was back, for the fourth time in two weeks, and this time, he was actually speaking to me, rather than shooting me sideways glances before disappearing from the shop without buying anything.

"Sorry, that was rude. It just came out. Excuse me. Let me start again." The stranger ran his hand through his dark, overgrown hair, tugging his full bottom lip between his teeth as he scuffed the floor with the toe of a battered Converse shoe. "I saw you doing that—" He paused, waving his hands in the air, and I smiled. "—thing with your hands."

My smile widened. This guy was so cute. No...he was hot, even in his nondescript ripped jeans and faded T-shirt, with hair that desperately needed a trim. But from the first time I'd set eyes on him, I'd been unable to look away. His face was fucking gorgeous. Perfect, symmetrical lines and angles, soulful, deep blue eyes, and a mouth that was made for kissing...among other things.

Calm down, Curtis.

When he'd first walked into Tuned, I'd felt like there was something vaguely familiar about him, almost like déjà vu, but I was positive he hadn't been in the shop before. And now I'd heard him speak with that sexy American accent, I was betting he was a tourist.

"I was doing hand exercises. I'm a drummer. Can I help you with anything?"

The guy flashed me a tentative smile, revealing a glimpse of straight, white teeth. Shoving his hands in his pockets, he shrugged. "I'm not sure. I'm, uh, going to be in England for a while, and I thought about playing the guitar?" It came out as a question.

"Okay. Acoustic?"

"A drummer?" he asked at the same time, stepping closer to me.

"Yeah. I'm in a band. The 2Bit Princes. We mostly do local gigs, but we're getting a decent following on our social media. We play covers, as well as our own original stuff."

"Yeah? That's cool." He was right next to me now, those deep blue eyes fixed on mine. This close, I could feel the heat radiating from his body, and I caught the scent of something fresh and beachy. Delicious. He shot me another smile, and my stomach flipped.

"It's great. You should come and hear us play sometime. We have a gig on Saturday, if you're still here then." Fishing for information as well as casually inviting him to spend more time with me? I was so smooth.

Turning to face me fully, his gaze trailed down my body, then back up to my face. As if he realized he'd been caught checking me out, his eyes widened, and he coughed, rubbing his hand across his jaw. "I'll be here for a while. So yeah, I'd like to see you play."

"You would?"

Biting down on his lip, he nodded, then moved away, breaking our connection as his gaze slid toward the display of guitars. "I guess you should tell me more about your band. What kind of music do you play? It's not...pop, is it?"

I gestured at myself. "Do I look like someone who plays pop music?"

"Looks can be deceiving," he said softly. "I wouldn't be able to tell by looking at you. You look like...uh...you look...you look good."

My cheeks flushed, and I busied myself with rearranging the guitar display for the tenth time, doing my best to ignore my hammering heart, which was far too excited by this cute American boy. "Not pop music. Like I said before, we play a lot of covers—mostly Britpop and indie rock—as well as our own music. If you come and see us on Saturday, you'll see. We're playing at the Rose and Crown pub in Southwark. We'll be onstage somewhere around eight-ish, I think."

When I glanced back at him, his own cheeks were flushed, and he was grimacing. "Sorry. I don't know how to do this. This is all new to me."

So fucking cute. Maybe teasing him would help to put him at ease. "What is? Talking? Britpop?"

Shaking his head, he ran his hand down the strings of one

of the guitars on the wall. "Being me. Fuck. Sorry. That sounded weird. I should just—I should go."

With that, he spun on his heel and bolted from the shop, leaving me alone.

Chapter 2

JAXON

Three months. That was how long I'd been in England, away from the USA and everything I'd once thought was important to me. It had been a huge change, but one I desperately needed. When I'd stripped the famous platinum blond dye from my hair and let it grow from the short, styled cut to its current overgrown mess, it was as if I became invisible. Losing my perma-tan—which had come from a bottle, anyway—and dressing in nondescript, casual clothes had completed my transformation.

My dad lived in the UK, and when I'd proposed a change of scenery so I could lie low and work out what I wanted to do with my life, he'd been nothing but supportive. And so, here I was. At first, I'd stayed with my dad in his house in the city of Manchester, and then I'd relocated to his work crash pad in London, alone and with no one to answer to for the first time in my life.

Going from everyone knowing my name to no one knowing my name had been freeing. If I'd still been in NYC, I might have been recognized, but here on the other side of the pond, Morningside had never reached the heights of fame we'd experienced in the US. I'd gone from Jay Bowman, boy band member and headache for my management team to Jaxon Messier, another anonymous American tourist in London. Bowman had been my stepdad's surname, and when I'd reconnected with my dad, when everything with Morningside began falling apart, it had only seemed right that I reverted to Messier. My stepdad had never had much interest in me, anyway, and it felt almost fraudulent to keep using his name.

Being in charge of my own life was a huge adjustment, but I was determined to make it work. I'd been in the band since I was sixteen. I was now twenty-two, and already fucking jaded by my experience in the music industry. Sick of being told what to do, how to dress, how to act. My life had been micro-managed for years. When the label had called us into a meeting and broken the news that they were dropping us after months of tension between Troy and the rest of the band, I'd felt nothing but relief.

Once, I'd had everything, but now I was my own person again. And I was still trying to wrap my head around just who Jaxon Messier really was.

The guy in the music store hadn't recognized me. I was confident about that. I'd been in there three times before I'd finally gathered the courage to talk to him, having seen no recognition in his eyes. It could've gone a lot better, though. Without my pop star persona to hide behind, I'd floundered. Tonight, I needed to rectify that, to leave him with no doubt that I was interested in him.

The way he looked intrigued me—a combination of bad boy and boy next door. With a lean build, soft mid-brown hair, expressive hazel eyes, and symmetrical features, he could have almost passed for a member of Morningside at first glance. That was until I noticed the tattoos, the piercing at the top of his ear, and the matte black nail polish on his fingers. He'd given me what I was sure was a heated, suggestive look from beneath his thick lashes as he invited me to watch his band play, and my heart had skipped a beat at the thought that he might actually be interested in me. Not Jay, famous boy band member. Me.

The thing was, although our management team hadn't actively discouraged my bisexuality during my time in the band, it had been strongly suggested that I keep it quiet. So, I'd felt the pressure, and other than a few discreet hook-ups accompanied by NDAs and a whole lot of fucking stress just to get laid, I hadn't had a chance to explore my attraction to men. To go on a date with someone—not even a guy—without the paparazzi getting wind of it was almost impossible with my level of celebrity.

It sounded like I was complaining, but it hadn't been all bad. Far from it. Money, fame, the knowledge that on the rare occasions I posted something on social media, I'd instantly get hundreds of thousands of likes and comments. It was a rush. It was addictive. It had been everything I ever wanted, once.

But it was no longer my life.

So, here I was, outside the Rose and Crown pub, dressed in my most nondescript clothing. I could already hear the band inside, playing a song that sounded vaguely familiar. Probably one of the songs my dad liked to play when I'd been crashing with him after the band split.

"'Scuse me, mate."

I jumped at the voice close to my ear and moved aside so I was no longer blocking the door. Two men brushed past me and entered the pub, and squaring my shoulders, I followed them inside.

Despite the limited interior space, there was a large crowd surrounding the raised stage that immediately drew my attention. My gaze slid past the bleached-blond lead singer who was growling into the mic, to the drummer, a wide grin on his face as he tapped out a rhythm with his drumsticks. Dressed in a tight T-shirt, the muscles in his tattooed arms flexing with his movements, and his hair tousled and damp with sweat, he was gorgeous. Sexy. Mesmerizing.

Tearing my gaze away from him was difficult, but I needed to blend in. Making my way to the bar, I ordered a pint of IPA, keeping my voice low and talking to a minimum. Although I was almost certain I was incognito here, my accent would stand out in a room full of patrons with various London dialects. While I waited for my pint to be poured, I glanced around me, taking in the tired, faded decor of the nondescript British pub. Over in the corner of the pub, away from the band and the crowds, two guys were seated close together in a high-backed booth with a battered wooden tabletop. They were holding hands under the table as they talked quietly, staring into one another's eyes, too caught up in each other to notice their surroundings.

That was what I wanted. Maybe if I was lucky, I'd get a taste of it.

I edged through the crowd until I was close to the stage and made my way to the side of the room, leaning back against the wall. From my vantage point, I had a great view of the 2Bit Princes, away from the crush of people. I tapped my feet along with the music as the band went through their set list, playing songs that were vaguely familiar, and others I'd never heard before.

They were good. There was something about them—a magnetism that was impossible to authentically replicate. You either had it, or you didn't.

A cheer went up from the crowd as the band launched into what was clearly an old favorite, and one I recognized from my dad's playlists. Half the World Away by Oasis. I found myself singing the lyrics, swept up in the music along with everyone else. This was on a miniature scale compared to the sold-out arenas where we used to do our shows, but watching Morningside must have felt something like this. The camaraderie of being surrounded by people all experiencing this shared moment, feeling the music deep in our souls. It was an incomparable high, and I was so glad I'd come tonight. Even if nothing happened with the hot British guy, I'd have this.

* * *

The lead guitarist was busy winding up a long cable at the side of the stage when I approached. "Hi. Is, uh—" Fuck. I didn't know his name. "—your drummer around?"

He glanced down at me, his brows lifting. "Curtis?"
Curtis.

"Yeah. He invited me here tonight. I thought...I just wanted to say hi."

"He did? Yeah. Of course, he did." A smirk curved over the guy's lips. "Give me a second to finish putting this away, and I'll find him for you. In fact—" He paused, glancing across the stage, and sighed. I followed his gaze, my eyes widening as I took in the unexpected sight of the lead singer making out with a dark-haired guy, right in the middle of the stage. The guy in front of me clapped his hands together. "Huxley! Get your mouth off your boyfriend and get this shit packed away! Cole! Make yourself useful."

They broke apart, and the dark-haired guy grinned, throwing up his middle finger.

"Can't take them anywhere." The lead guitarist turned back to me. "I'm Tom, by the way. The sulky-looking blond guy's Huxley, and the one who had his tongue down Hux's throat is Cole. He's Huxley's boyfriend and our unofficial roadie. The guy who looks like a Viking is Rob, our bass guitarist and keyboardist."

"Nice to meet you. I'm Jay—I'm Jaxon. Or Jax, if you like." The way my former nickname had almost slipped out...I needed to be careful. Despite the friendliness of this guy and the vibes that I got from Curtis, the fact was, I knew nothing about them. And there were those who would seek to take advantage of me and my music connections.

"Alright, Jay Jax Jaxon, let's find Curtis." He straightened up, flashing me a smile. "Wanna come with me?"

"Sure." Ignoring my suddenly racing heart, I climbed up onto the stage and followed Tom out through a side door and down a short corridor. There was another door, propped open, leading out into a small parking lot where a van was waiting, already filling with the band's equipment.

Tom came to a stop next to the van. "Curtis! You out here?"

There was the sound of scuffing footsteps, and then he appeared.

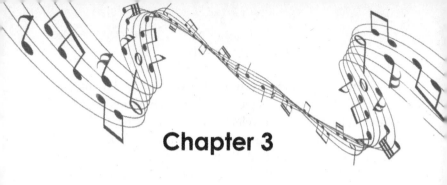

Chapter 3

CURTIS

I stopped and stared, my mouth falling open. *He came.* The guy from the music shop. Just as unassumingly cute as I remembered, biting his lip as he shot me a cautious look.

Tom cleared his throat, amusement dancing in his eyes. "I'll leave you to it. Have fun."

When he disappeared, I stepped closer to the guy, a smile spreading across my face. "You came." From the way he'd run out of the shop, I hadn't thought I'd see him again. But here he was.

"Yeah...well." He shrugged. "A stranger in a music store invited me to watch his band play. I had nothing else planned, so I thought I'd check it out."

"Yeah? What did you think?"

"You were good. Really good. I...it's different from the music I usually listen to, but I liked it. You were good."

"You already said that." Closing the final bit of distance between us, I leaned against the side of the van, trying to act casual, even though my heart was pounding.

"Yeah, well, I meant it. And..." He audibly inhaled, his chest rising with the movement. "I wondered if you wanted to celebrate a successful show by letting me buy you a drink?"

My smile widened. "I'd like that."

He grinned, relaxing, and then held out his hand. "Yeah? Maybe we should start by exchanging names. I'm Jaxon, or Jax, if you prefer."

My breath caught in my throat as I curled my fingers around

his, his palm warm against mine. Fucking hell, I shouldn't have been this affected by a simple handshake. "Hi, Jaxon. I'm Curtis." Releasing his hand a little reluctantly, I inclined my head towards the door. "I need to finish packing up our equipment, but if you don't mind hanging around, I'll be free in about twenty minutes. The pub's closing, but there's a bar not too far from here with a late license."

"Need any help? I'm stronger than I look." Raising his brows, he flexed his biceps. "See?"

I laughed. "Okay. Come on. I'll introduce you to the others."

* * *

Somehow, we'd managed to find seats in a tiny, hidden corner of the busy bar, which was a miracle, considering it was the weekend and we were in central London. Even better, we were seated on a small loveseat that was not designed to hold two grown men, which meant we were plastered together, Jaxon's thigh a hot, delicious press against mine. My pint was gathering condensation on the table in front of us, but I ignored it for now, far more interested in the guy sitting next to me.

"So," I began. "When we met, you mentioned you were going to be here for a while. Based on your accent, I was thinking you're American, but I guess I shouldn't assume..." I trailed off, hoping he'd volunteer some information about himself. I didn't want it to seem like I was interrogating him, but it was always a bit awkward at first, getting to know someone completely new.

He sighed, staring into his drink as he traced patterns in the condensation on his glass. "Yeah. I'm American. And British. My dad's a Brit, and I have dual citizenship, but this is the first time I've been here since I was a little kid. I was...uh...living in New York City until recently, but I decided I needed a change, and here I am. As for how long I'll stay, I don't know for sure, but I like it here. I needed...a break, I guess, and my dad has an apartment in

London he uses for work, so it was as good a place as any."

I nodded. "That makes sense. What did you need a break from, or is that too personal? Sorry—tell me to back off if it seems like I'm prying."

"You're not." His lips kicked up at the corners. "Believe me, having someone want to get to know me and not just assume they already know me is a novel experience."

What did he mean by that comment? I didn't have time to think about it because he continued to speak.

"I needed a break from...life, I guess. A career change. A chance to experience something new and different. Like a, what's it called...a gap year? I never had the chance to backpack around Europe, so this is my substitute."

"That sounds good. I never took a gap year, either, but I always thought it sounded fun. One of my friends went backpacking across Southeast Asia and then on to Australia and New Zealand. To tell you the truth, I was a bit jealous, seeing all his updates. The furthest I've managed so far is Greece." Lifting my pint to my lips, I swallowed a mouthful of cool cider. So good. I was the band's drummer, not a singer, but I always ended up singing along with the setlist, and a chilled cider was the perfect way to soothe my throat after a gig.

"You've never been to the US?" Jaxon turned his head, and our eyes met, and the intensity of his gaze made my breath catch in my throat. Fuck. He really was so hot.

Holding his gaze, I placed my pint glass down. "Not yet. But maybe I could take you sightseeing here, and then you could return the favor one day. Or repay me in another way."

His eyes widened, and then, after a long moment where I held my breath, he smirked at me. That smirk did things to me. Things that weren't appropriate in a public place, but fuck it, you only lived once. Before he could respond, I leaned forward, sliding my lips across his, and kissed the smirk right off his face. He gasped, but then his hand came up to curl around the nape of my neck, and he opened his mouth to me.

That first slide of his tongue against mine was electric. I reached out, gently cupping his stubbled jaw as we kissed, slow and deep and so fucking good. I never wanted it to end.

When we drew apart, he stared at me, his mouth open. "Wow," he said eventually, breathless, dragging a hand through his hair. "Yeah. Wow." Picking up his pint, he downed a third of it in one go, and I noticed his hand was shaking. For my part, I was feeling just as shaky as he was. That had been an *incredible* kiss. It felt like we'd connected in that moment, on a level I'd never experienced before. We didn't even know each other, and I was reeling.

Picking up my glass again to give me something to do while I gathered myself, I cleared my throat. "I'm glad I didn't misread the signs."

"No, you didn't." A disbelieving laugh fell from his throat. "I can't believe that happened."

"Me neither." I wanted to kiss him again, badly, but he still seemed a bit shaken up, and I didn't want to push him for anything. Instead, I leaned back in my seat. "You said you needed a career change. What were you doing before? I'm still not sure what I want to do after I finish my degree. The dream would be to be the full-time drummer for the 2Bit Princes and to make enough money from it to live on, but the chances of that happening are probably one in a million, or something."

Thanks to our close proximity, I felt the exact moment his entire body stiffened, right when I mentioned his career change. Fuck.

"Sorry. You don't have to talk about it."

He took a deep breath, and then his hand landed on my arm. "I like your tattoos," he murmured, his cheeks flushing as he adjusted his tentative grip, his fingers lightly stroking over my skin. "Uh...yeah. I'm not ready to talk about that. Not yet. Sorry."

I placed my hand over his, and he stilled, his gaze flying to mine. "You don't have to apologize. I just want to get to know you, but you don't owe me anything, okay?"

"You're incredible. So different from anyone I've ever met."

His voice came out as a whisper. "I think...I think I'd like to kiss you again."

"Yeah?" Leaning in, I smiled. "I'm not going to stop you."

We alternated between talking and kissing, our drinks forgotten, as I told him about my experience as a uni student, and he shared little crumbs of information about himself—things like his favorite colour, his star sign, a place in New York that did the best pizza he'd ever had in his life, the tourist spots he'd already visited in London. When I pulled my phone from my pocket to check the time, I was shocked to find it was almost three in the morning.

"Bloody hell. How is that the time?"

Jaxon glanced down at my screen and laughed. "I guess we were enjoying each other's company so much, we lost track of time." His laughter died away, and he licked his lips, his eyes darkening as we stared at one another. "Want to continue this back at my place?"

I knew exactly why he was inviting me back to his, and it wasn't to continue our conversation.

Instead of replying, I stood and tugged him to his feet. He laughed as I dragged him out of the bar and down the street.

"Hey, wait up. We're going in the wrong direction. I think."

I stopped, turning to see him grinning at me, his eyes sparkling in the glow from the street lamps. Fucking gorgeous. Pressing him up against the wall we were standing against, I dipped my head to his ear. "Sorry. Why don't you show me the way?"

His body shivered against mine, and I heard his breath hitch. "I think I need you to show me the way."

Drawing back, I stared at him, incredulous. "Are you saying what I think you're saying?"

The corners of his lips curved into a wry smile. "I'm saying I'm not all that experienced when it comes to...uh, men, and you seem...like you know what you're doing."

Fuck. I lowered my head again, kissing up the side of his

throat as he pulled me closer. "I'm gonna take such good care of you."

"Yeah," he whispered, grinding against me. It was so fucking hot, and I was rapidly losing the ability to think.

In between kissing and getting my hands all over him, I managed to say, "No pressure, either. Whatever you want."

"Curtis. Fuck. I want you."

The sudden sound of loud conversation close to us had us springing apart, panic flaring in Jaxon's wide eyes. I stepped back, running a hand through my hair as I exhaled harshly, trying to compose myself. How had we both managed to get so carried away that we'd forgotten where we were? Not that I necessarily minded a PDA, and we were outside a gay bar that had seen way more action than our kisses, but Jaxon was clearly uncomfortable. The sooner we got back to his place, the better.

"Let's go. How far is your place? Do we need to get a taxi? It might be quicker to get an Uber than wait for a black cab."

He tugged his phone from his pocket, frowning down at the screen. His hair was falling into his eyes, and my fingers itched to brush it back. I shoved my hands into my pockets instead.

"Uber," he said. "It's a lot further than I thought." Then, he glanced up at me, the nerves that had been there only moments ago melting away. Moving closer, he lowered his voice, shooting me a heated look from beneath his lashes. "Too far when all I want is to get you alone."

I was in complete agreement. "Yeah. Uber. Now."

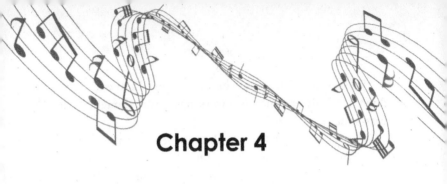

Chapter 4

CURTIS

When we slid into the Uber, the driver greeted us, and then did a double take, grinning as he eyed Jaxon. "Mate, has anyone ever told ya you look like that singer Jay Bowman? Course, ya don't have the right hair, but if ya did..." He trailed off, shaking his head. "My missus is a big fan. It'd make her day to have a real celebrity in here."

Next to me, Jaxon had gone very still, and when I looked at him, I saw his jaw clench, his throat working as he swallowed hard. "Have you ever had anyone famous in here?" His voice sounded different—softer, his accent less pronounced. He ignored the driver's question, and I had nothing to add because I had no idea who Jay whatever was.

The driver began recounting a story about the time he'd driven a daytime TV presenter to the Emirates stadium for a football match, and bit by bit, Jaxon relaxed next to me. When the driver fell silent, I leaned over to him, sliding my hand onto his thigh, just above his knee. Time to get back on track.

"Has anyone ever told you that you look like—" His body went rigid again, his wide-eyed gaze flying to mine. I lightly squeezed the tense muscle of his thigh, dipping my head to his ear. "What I was going to say was, has anyone ever told you that you look like someone I want to do bad, bad things to?"

He huffed out a soft laugh. "Does that line normally work on people?"

Pressing a kiss to the skin beneath his ear, I smiled. "Honestly? I don't normally use lines. Is it working on you, though? That's all I care about right now."

His hand covered mine, sliding them both higher up his thigh. "You don't need to use any lines with me. I'm a sure bet."

"Good." I kissed lower, then nipped at his jaw. He groaned low in his throat.

"This is..."

"This is what?"

"Different."

Raising my head, I met his heavy-lidded gaze. He was so fucking gorgeous, all turned on, and I couldn't wait to get him alone. "Different good?"

"Very, very good," he confirmed. His lips curved upwards. "I'm about to find out just how good, I hope."

As if on cue, the Uber slowed to a crawl, and Jaxon tore his gaze away from mine, blinking as he turned his attention to the driver. "Uh, it's the building on the left with the black door." I shivered at the sexy rasp in his voice. What was it about this man that made me want him so badly? Yeah, he was gorgeous, but no one had ever managed to get me this worked up so fast, had never made me feel like I needed them so badly.

When we made it inside his flat, we were on each other the second the door closed behind us. I had no idea what his flat looked like, or even where we were. My entire focus was on Jaxon, hot, hard, and hungry for me.

It wasn't an exaggeration to say it was the best night of my life.

* * *

"Morning." I squinted against the sudden brightness as I stepped over the threshold of Jaxon's kitchen. Remaining in the doorway, I waited. I wanted to take my cues from him, because as much as I liked this guy and wanted to see him again, it might have only been a one-night thing for him. One epic, hot night, that I knew we'd both be feeling the effects of for at least the next day or two—

Jaxon turned around, and I gasped. Not only feeling the effects...there was visible evidence, too.

"Admiring your handiwork?" He smirked at me. "Come on in. Want a coffee? I'm running low on food supplies, but there's a cafe close by that does awesome breakfasts."

He didn't want me to leave. My smile was helpless as I crossed the small kitchen to stand in front of him. I traced a fingertip over the marks I'd left on his neck. "Sorry, I didn't mean to go all vampire on you."

"Have you checked a mirror?" Tugging me into him, he pressed a soft kiss to my lips, and whoa. Butterflies. A whole horde of them. "We were both attacked by a rogue vampire."

"Yeah?" I kissed him again. "At least we match, I guess."

When we broke apart, his cheeks were flushed, and I could feel the evidence of his arousal against my thigh. I was in the same state, and with both of us only wearing boxer briefs, there was no hiding it. He pressed closer, dipping his head to my ear. "Mmm. New plan. Forget the coffee. Let's shower, and then I'll take you out to breakfast."

I tilted my head, a shiver running through me as he kissed down the side of my throat. "If by 'let's shower' you mean we're showering together, I like this new plan."

In reply, he flashed me a dirty grin, grabbed my wrist, and pulled me towards the door.

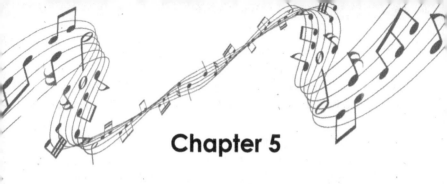

Chapter 5

CURTIS

"You know, we've been dating for three months now, if we count our first date as the first time I came to watch your band play."

I came to a stop at the foot of the Millennium Bridge, St Paul's Cathedral behind us, and turned to Jaxon, a smile spreading across my face. "It's been three months already?"

"Yeah." Sliding his fingers through mine, he led me over to the side of the bridge, down the steps, and stopped next to the river Thames. Releasing my hand, he leaned in, giving me one of his soft kisses that gave me fucking butterflies every time. "I was thinking it was time to make things official."

"Official, how?"

His lips curved upwards. "I'd like to officially call you my boyfriend."

Boyfriends. I wanted that so badly, but there was still so much I didn't know about him. He refused to talk about the events that had led him to come to the UK, or his previous career, changing the subject every time I brought it up. He didn't have any form of social media, either, so I had no clues about his recent past. I didn't want to push him, but I also couldn't help feeling like he just didn't trust me enough to share important parts of his life with me.

But then again...there was so much I *did* know. I knew he was kind and generous, and he was so easy to talk to. Aside from the off-limits subjects, we could talk for hours about anything and everything, and we'd shared so much with each other. Tom and

Huxley had been teaching him to play the guitar, too, and he'd started penning song lyrics in a battered notebook he'd taken to carrying around with him, matching the lyrics with guitar chords and coming up with simple melodies that he played for me as he sang. His kisses were so fucking addictive, and the sex was out of this world. But waking up next to him, seeing him all sleepy and vulnerable with his arm slung over my chest, was my favorite thing.

The truth was, I was falling for Jaxon Messier hard and fast, and I'd be a fool to give him up. I just had to hope that eventually, he'd realize he could trust me with everything there was to know about him.

"Boyfriends." Turning to face the river, I leaned my elbows on the low stone wall. The water glittered in front of me, and on the other side of the Thames, I could make out the Tate Modern with crowds of people milling around outside, enjoying the mild weather. "I'd like that."

His arms slid around my waist, and he placed a kiss on the nape of my neck. "Good. Then it's settled."

Tugging my phone from my pocket, I unlocked the screen and held it up. "Selfie to document the moment. Just for us—I won't share it anywhere."

He hooked his chin over my shoulder, pressing a kiss to my jaw as I took the photo. "Sorry. I know... Fuck, Curtis, I know I'm—"

Twisting my head, I cut him off with a kiss. "It's okay. I hope that one day you'll be able to trust that I'd never—"

"I do trust you. I think I trust you more than anyone, other than my dad. It's just...there are so many things I want to tell you, but I don't know how."

Turning to face him properly, I wrapped my arms around his shoulders. "Jax, listen to me. I'm not putting any pressure on you."

He sighed against me. "You're incredible."

"So are you," I reminded him softly. "I like you so much. You know that, right?"

A cool breeze ruffled his dark hair, blowing it across his forehead as he nodded. "Yeah. Yeah, I do."

* * *

After our conversation, Jaxon had been extra attentive, taking every excuse to touch me as we made our way across the bridge and through the Tate Modern, and the smile had never left his face. The butterflies in my stomach had developed into a swarm, and now we were strolling along the riverside with his fingers wrapped around mine, I'd never felt happier.

My life was so good. I got to be a drummer in a band with people I'd clicked with from the moment we'd first played together, I was doing well in my degree course, and I loved living in London.

But Jaxon? He was the delicious icing on the cake. Something I hadn't even known was missing until I had it. A man who had connected with me right from the start, and who had rapidly become such an important part of my life.

"Jay Bowman!"

The high-pitched screech from our left made me jump, but it was nothing compared to the effect it had on Jaxon. His entire body froze, his fingers stiffening in my grip, his eyes turning wild and panicked before he took a deep, shuddering breath and shuttered his expression.

"It is you! Isn't it? You disappeared, and no one knew where you'd gone, and omg you're in disguise, right? We won't say anything, we swear! We love you! Troy sold you out! No, Mizar did! They didn't deserve you!"

The breathless excitement from the teenage girl clutching her friend's arm, both staring at Jaxon in complete awe, had my gaze swinging between the three of them, my brain scrambling to make sense of what was happening.

That was when Jaxon ripped his hand away from mine, gasping like he couldn't get enough air in his lungs.

He ran.

* * *

Back in my student house with my bedroom door locked behind me, I opened my laptop.

It took me less than nine minutes to gather the evidence.

Jaxon Messier. The man I'd been seeing for the past three months. My official boyfriend of less than a day.

He wasn't who he'd told me he was, after all.

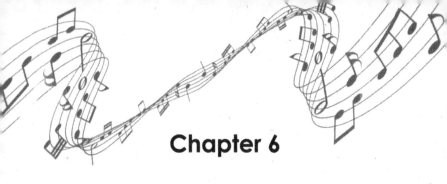

Chapter 6

JAXON

Burying my head in my arms, I let the tears finally fall. *Fuck.* I'd ruined the best thing that had ever happened to me. I was completely alone in my cold, empty apartment, and I only had myself to blame.

There was no way Curtis wouldn't put two and two together. He was clever—the only reason I'd managed to hide who I was from him without outright lying was because he genuinely didn't know or care about Morningside. And that fact was unsurprising, given that he didn't really listen to pop music, not unless it was playing in Revolve, the gay club we'd been to a few times where Cole, Huxley's boyfriend, worked part-time as a bartender. Add that to my previously mentioned fact that Morningside had never been popular in the UK, and...yeah. I'd let myself become complacent. I'd originally put off telling Curtis about my past because we didn't know each other, and there was no way I'd ever give a stranger that kind of information about me, even if he was cute. Then, the more time I spent with him, the harder it became to tell him I'd been hiding something so big from him.

I'd been meaning to tell him before we made things official, but I'd been so scared that he'd leave me, and now... Now, I'd fucked it all up, anyway.

Dragging myself upright, I scrubbed a hand across my face. Nausea was churning in my stomach, but I forced myself to climb to my feet, making my way into the kitchen, where I downed a glass of water with shaking hands.

What was I going to do?

There was no one I could talk to who'd understand my position—

Wait, no. There was one person. The one member of Morningside who'd stayed in touch with me, the one guy who'd been a true friend rather than just a bandmate.

Picking up my phone, I called Joe Garcia.

"Jax! Hey, man, it's good to hear from you. How's London? Rainy? Does everyone eat cucumber sandwiches?"

I huffed out a laugh, my mood already improving. "Hey, Joey. Sorry to disappoint, but it hasn't rained yet this week, and I haven't seen anyone eating cucumber sandwiches." Pausing, I thought for a moment. "I did see a tuna and cucumber sandwich in my local convenience store, though."

"Gross. You've got to try it. For me?"

"I can't make any promises." Taking a seat at the kitchen island, I rested my elbows on the smooth wooden surface, staring out of the window at the rooftops of the houses across the street. "Listen, are you busy? I could use some advice."

The teasing tone immediately disappeared from his voice. "What's up?"

As quickly as I could, I detailed everything that had happened with Curtis. Joe already knew that I was incognito in the UK, but I'd avoided mentioning Curtis in our infrequent conversations. As I spoke, I realized I'd been trying to keep the two parts of my life separate, as if they existed independently of each other. It could never be sustainable, and I should've had a plan in place sooner, rather than burying my head in the sand.

When I finished speaking, Joe cleared his throat. "Yeah, you fucked up, man."

"I—"

"Not in my eyes. In *his* eyes. He...he's a normal guy. He has no idea what it was like for us, ya know? If I'd been in your position, knowing how you shy away from the spotlight—or have done over these past couple of years—then I probably would have done the same. But you need to speak to him and make him understand what it was like for you." He sighed. "If he means something to you, then you need to fight for him."

"Thanks. That's...that's surprisingly insightful."

"I'm not just a pretty face. I was the brains of Morningside."

"If you say so." We both laughed and spent another fifteen minutes talking, catching each other up on our lives. By the time we ended the conversation, I was feeling much more positive.

If Curtis would let me explain, hopefully, I could make him understand.

* * *

"We're giving you one chance, and you'd better not fuck it up." Huxley stared me down, his arms folded across his chest as he glared at me.

"Hux. Calm down. We don't even know what happened," Cole said, before turning to me and clearing his throat. "But just so you know, if you make things even worse for him, you'll have me to answer to, as well as the rest of the band. Okay?"

I nodded. "H-how is he?"

Huxley jabbed one black-tipped finger into my left bicep. "Unhappy. Fix it."

"That's why I'm here." Curtis hadn't been answering my calls or texts, so in desperation, I'd gone to Revolve when I knew Cole had a bartending shift and put myself at his mercy. Thankfully, he'd taken pity on me, and he'd arranged for me to come to the recording studio the 2Bit Princes had use of once a month. Their session was over, but Cole had told me they'd come up with a reason for Curtis to stay behind. They were placing a lot of trust in me by letting me do this, and I appreciated it more than they would ever know. "Thanks. I appreciate you giving me this chance, and I'm going to do everything I can to fix it."

Cole's expression softened. "Good. We like you, and you

make Curtis happy, and I really don't want to have to fight you. I did enough of that with this one." He jerked his thumb towards Huxley, who rolled his eyes.

"Yeah, let's not revisit our past history."

My brows rose. "You two fought?"

Wrapping his arm around his boyfriend's waist, Cole nodded. "It took Hux a while to fall for my charms."

"What charms?" Huxley muttered, but when Cole pressed a kiss to his cheek, he smiled, and it transformed his face. He glanced over at me, then at the door Cole was propping open with his foot. "Go on, then. He won't be waiting around forever."

Right. "Yeah. Thanks, guys."

"Second floor. Hopton Studios," Cole called after me as I entered the building.

Breathing deeply, attempting to calm my racing heart, I made my way up the stairs.

When I entered Hopton Studios, I almost collided with the very person I'd come here to see, sidestepping him at the last second. Curtis came to a sudden halt, staring at me with wide eyes before they narrowed. "What do you want? How did you get in here?"

"I..." This was so hard. Licking my lips, I began again. "I wanted to explain. I can't and won't force you to listen to me, but I'd like a chance to explain. Please."

He sighed heavily but stepped over to a large couch that was placed against the wall, taking a seat at the far end. "Okay. I'll hear what you have to say, but I'm not promising anything else."

Relief coursed through me, and I joined him on the couch before he could change his mind.

"I guess from your silence that you found out about—"

"About the fact you gave me a false name? That the person who'd just asked me to be his boyfriend had a whole different identity as a fucking pop star? That—"

"Curtis!" Before I knew what I was doing, I was sliding across the couch to him, placing a hand on his knee. "It wasn't like that.

I never lied about who I was— Fuck, okay, I didn't tell you about Morningside. But I'm me. I'm Jaxon Messier. That's my real name."

His gaze slid down to where my hand rested on his leg and his jaw tightened, but he didn't comment on it. "The things I read online said your name was Jay Bowman."

"Yeah." Running a shaking hand through my hair, I attempted to gather my thoughts. I'd never felt so exposed, so stripped back. Jay had been a persona to hide behind, but he no longer existed. "When I signed my contract with the record label, I was sixteen, and at the time, my mom called me Jay as a shortened version of Jaxon. She didn't like Jax. So, uh, other people called me Jay too. Bowman is my stepdad's surname. Our band was having problems...we were... Fuck. I signed an NDA, but I need you to understand. We'd been having problems for a long time, and it soon became clear to me that my mom was only interested in Jay Bowman, not Jaxon, and my stepdad didn't—he didn't—" My voice cracked. There was a sharp intake of breath from Curtis, and then his hand covered mine, so gently, his thumb stroking over my skin.

"Take as much time as you need."

My gaze flew to his, and the hostility that had been there when he'd first seen me had disappeared. It gave me the courage to carry on, to bare myself to this man I was falling for.

"My stepdad wasn't interested in me. Not like, anything bad, but he was apathetic, I guess. My mom, too. I was feeling so alone, and I didn't know who else to turn to, so I reached out and reconnected with my dad. He was so supportive, right from the beginning, and I wished...I wished I hadn't left it so long. He was the parent I'd always wanted but hadn't known I had until things were falling apart." Tipping my head back, I blinked away the wetness threatening to spill over my lashes, willing myself to stay strong and get the words out. "He flew out to New York and stayed with me for a while, and after experiencing his unconditional support, I decided to change my name. Messier was on my birth certificate, and I reclaimed it. Then I came to the UK, stayed with my dad for a little while, but eventually I wanted—no, needed to be alone. To learn how to be me. Jaxon Messier. It probably sounds crazy, but I wanted to get to know myself. I'd been caught up with Morningside for so long, and I'd never had a chance to be an adult and just...just do my own thing."

"It doesn't sound crazy." His voice was soft. "I can't imagine what it was like for you, but I can understand you wanting to find yourself. It must have been a lot to deal with, especially if you'd been in the band since you were sixteen."

Turning my hand under his palm, I slid my fingers between his, so we were properly holding hands. "I don't want to sound ungrateful, because I did enjoy being in the band. At first, it was everything I'd ever dreamed of, but I guess I became jaded. Tired of being 'on' all the time. I started becoming more reclusive, I guess, outside of everything we were contracted to do. Troy—he was the lead singer—wanted a solo deal, and the rest of us wanted out. Our popularity was waning, and I think by the end we'd all had enough."

Curtis met my gaze again, and this time, I could see the hurt he'd been trying to hide. "I understand why you didn't tell me who you were at first. We were strangers, after all. But why not tell me after? You asked me to be your boyfriend, Jax. You said you trusted me. But that clearly wasn't true, because you kept all this from me."

I swallowed around the lump in my throat. "I do trust you. The more time I spent with you, the harder it was to say anything. I'd been hiding this huge part of me, and then more and more time passed, and I didn't know how to tell you. I didn't want to lose you." Blinking rapidly, I bit down on my trembling lip. "But I lost you, anyway."

"*Jaxon.*" Releasing my hand, he wrapped his arm around me, pulling me into him. "You didn't lose me. I shouldn't have ghosted you, but I needed time to think. I was angry and hurt, but look." Gripping my chin, he stared into my eyes, and it felt right then as if he saw me. Me. "When you asked me to be your boyfriend, I told you I wouldn't put any pressure on you. I understand what you're saying to me, and although I'm not going to lie and say you didn't hurt me, I can understand why you did what you did. But would you have ever told me?"

"Yes." My voice came out as a choked whisper. "I was going to tell you before I asked you to be my boyfriend, but I was so scared you'd leave me. I know it was wrong, and I wish more than anything that I could turn back the clock and do it differently. I just...I didn't know how to tell you after so long. But I swear, I would have told you. I hated hiding it from you. *Hated* it. I trust you, and I know you wouldn't betray my trust, but I was just so scared that I'd lose you once I told you the truth." Against my will, a tear fell from my lashes, and he reached up, gently catching it on his fingertip.

Leaning forward, he brushed a soft kiss over my lips. It was over before it had really begun, but it was enough. It was hope.

"Okay," he said. "Let's try this again." Clasping my hand, he shook it. "I'm Curtis Ward. Uni student and drummer for the 2Bit Princes."

A tremulous smile spread across my face. "Hi, Curtis. I'm Jaxon Messier, previously known as Jay Bowman. Former member of US boy band Morningside, and potential future songwriter."

His smile matched mine. "Songwriter, huh?"

I shrugged as casually as I could. "Maybe. We'll see."

"We will."

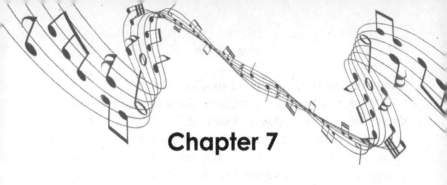

Chapter 7

CURTIS

"I don't get your obsession with cucumber sandwiches. Tell him, Neil." Eyeing Jaxon's phone screen with a sigh, I glanced from Joe's smirking face to Jaxon's dad, Neil, who was shaking his head.

"Sorry to disappoint, but I've never had one either. A chip butty, though—you can't go wrong with that."

Joe's brows lifted. "What the fuck is a chip butty?"

Arms wrapped around my waist from behind, and then Jaxon's cheek pressed up against mine as he grinned at his phone. "You'll find out if you ever come and visit us."

"Can your weather compete with Cali?" Joe panned his camera to show a view of golden sand and crashing waves.

"That doesn't count. You're on vacation. New York—where you actually live—has more rain than London, so try another argument." Jaxon gave a mock sigh, tilting his head to press a kiss to the side of my jaw. "He doesn't know what he's missing out on."

"Guess what? The joke's on you because I have a flight confirmation on my phone that says I'll be arriving at Heathrow next month for a five-day visit to see you and meet Curtis in person. You gonna be there to meet me?" Joe's smile disappeared when Jaxon cleared his throat uncertainly. "I'll do what I can to stay under the radar, but maybe we should forget you meeting me and have our reunion somewhere private."

Neil waved at the screen to get our attention. "I need to show my face in the London office sooner or later. It's been a while. Give Jax the details and I'll meet you inside the airport. The boys can wait in the car. Does that sound good to everyone?"

We were all in agreement, and after a few more minutes of conversation, Jaxon ended the video call.

"How do you feel about seeing Joe again? Are you worried about publicity?" I asked as Jaxon released me, crossing the lounge to his guitar. Picking it up, he sank down onto the sofa. After quickly tuning it, he began gently strumming the strings, humming under his breath. In the two months we'd been officially back together, I'd noticed him doing this when he wanted to think something through.

Eventually, his fingers came to a halt, and he carefully placed the guitar down, leaning it against the wall, and then slid down into a reclining position, stretching out across the full length of the sofa. He held out his arms, and I went to him, letting him pull me on top of his body, with my head on his chest and our legs entwined.

"I've made my peace with it, mostly. Yeah, there probably will be photographers somewhere, especially because Joe's still in the limelight, but I'm not interesting anymore."

I kissed his throat. "You're very interesting to me."

He laughed against me, stroking his hand down my back. "I'm glad to hear it. You're very interesting to me, too. You know that, right?"

Raising my head, I nodded. He reminded me enough. Okay, it was a little daunting to know that he'd been a famous pop star in the past, but I knew he liked me for me. I knew *him*. And the upside of getting to know him without the knowledge of Morningside, back when I'd thought he was just another tourist in London, was that I'd had no preconceptions about him. He knew I liked him for him, too, not because of his status.

"Good." His fingers traced circles across my shoulders before sliding up into my hair. "Realistically, I know there will be some interest, because of who I was, and there's also the fact I haven't been seen in public for so long. Joe told me his new publicist has some contacts in London, and it might be good to get something set up with them. Let PR handle it all." He smiled. "I'm honestly not worried, though. I feel stronger now. Much more sure of myself and of who I am. And I can handle anything, as long as I have you by my side."

"I'll be with you, Jax. Whatever you need to do, I'll support you through it."

"Did I ever tell you how fucking incredible you are?"

Shifting forward, I tugged his lip between my teeth. When I released it, I watched with satisfaction as his eyes darkened, his tongue swiping across the place I'd just bitten, leaving his lips looking shiny and so kissable. "Once or twice, but if you want to give me a physical reminder, I wouldn't say no."

He pulled my head back down to his, speaking against my mouth. "Mmm, it's like you read my mind."

Our mouths met, and then it was a blur of lips and teeth and hands, and bodies sliding together. When we were both sated, still wrapped in each other's arms, with sweat cooling on overheated skin and our heart rates slowing, Jaxon looked at me, his expression so serious, but so soft it made me melt inside.

"I love you, Curtis."

My breath caught in my throat as I stared back at him, seeing the truth shining from his eyes. It took me a minute to reply, but when I did, I meant the words with everything I had.

"I love you, too, Jax."

His arms tightened around me, his throat working as he processed the things we'd said to each other. With a soft sigh, he pulled me back to him, kissing me slowly and deeply.

It made my head spin, thinking of how we'd reached this moment. A moment I wanted to freeze in time forever, because surely nothing could ever top it.

Everything between us had been so unexpected, but so right.

We'd begun this as strangers in a music shop, and we'd connected instantly. Now, here we were, two people from two different worlds, who somehow fitted together perfectly.

Epilogue

EXCLUSIVE INTERVIEW

Reclusive songwriter Jaxon Messier and his partner, drummer Curtis Ward, invite Tempo magazine to share afternoon tea with them in London...

Jaxon Messier, 24, formerly known as Jay Bowman, one-fifth of US pop band Morningside, greets me politely as he seats himself at the table alongside his partner, Curtis Ward, 22. He asks if I drink tea, and when I tell him yes, I do, he proceeds to serve the entire table, pouring the fragrant brew into delicate bone china cups. This formal tearoom in a smart hotel in Knightsbridge is an incongruous setting for the former pop star and his drummer boyfriend, and I ask why this particular location was chosen.

Messier glances at Ward, and they both laugh. Messier tells me he has an ongoing joke regarding cucumber sandwiches with his former Morningside bandmate, Joe Garcia, 23. As he speaks, he waves a hand toward the stand of miniature sandwiches to his left, artfully arranged over three tiers.

"We heard the cucumber sandwiches here were the best in London, so we had to come," he tells me, as Ward snaps a photograph of the display.

As we help ourselves to the sandwiches, Messier and Ward rate each filling. They persuade me to join them, and together, we rank the sandwiches from best to worst (best—roast beef and horseradish, worst—cucumber). In between rating the food, they pepper the conversation with anecdotes about their lives together, constantly touching and teasing each other.

I mention how at ease they seem in my presence, despite Messier's notoriously private persona. Messier shrugs with a wry smile. "Yeah, it's a little weird, right? I guess Curtis has that effect on me. He makes me able to be myself, no matter who's around."

Ward cups a hand around his mouth and leans in as if he's preparing to tell me a secret. "He's making me sound like it's all me, when really, it's all him. But if you want to give me the credit in print, I can't stop you." Giving me an exaggerated wink, he adds, "Just don't ask him about my bad habits. I wouldn't want to tarnish my reputation."

When Messier elbows him, he laughs and tells me he has a habit of leaving wet towels on the bathroom floor— something Messier has been trying to cure him of since they moved into their Shoreditch flat eighteen months ago. As far as bad habits go, this one seems fairly mild, and I tell them so. "See?" Ward says triumphantly, and Messier sighs, insisting we must be in cahoots.

Our sandwiches are replaced with a selection of miniature cakes, and when we've filled our plates, the conversation veers towards Messier's highly anticipated upcoming collaboration with multi-award-winning north London grime artist, ZW. When I ask him how the collaboration came to be, he shrugs modestly. "It was pure luck. He somehow found my music channel and heard one of my songs, and got in touch to ask if he could sample it for one of his tracks. Things snowballed from there."

Ward shakes his head, smiling, and tells me that Messier is too modest. "Anyone would be lucky to work with him. He's so f**king talented, and he doesn't even realize just how amazing he is."

I ask if the two of them have any plans to collaborate in the future (Ward is the drummer for up-and-coming London indie rock band, the 2Bit Princes). They laugh again and say they have no plans to, and that they've made an agreement to keep their careers separate. From the glances they exchange, though, I wonder if that may change one day.

We switch from tea to champagne (we're celebrating Messier's collaboration, apparently), and when Messier refills my flute, he tells me he's been feeling nervous about this interview. When I say that I, too, have been a little apprehensive, given the pressure of being one of the scant handful of journalists allowed to interview him since the dissolution of Morningside, he relaxes.

Ward squeezes his arm and mouths, I'm so proud of you. *Messier leans in and kisses his partner's cheek. "I love you,"* he says, and Ward's entire face lights up.

"I love you, too," he replies, and we all smile.

IDOLYZE

RACHEL VAN DYKEN

About the Author

Rachel Van Dyken is the #1 *New York Times, Wall Street Journal,* and *USA TODAY* Bestselling author of regency and contemporary romances. When she's not writing you can find her drinking coffee at Starbucks and plotting her next book while watching guilty-pleasure TV.

She keeps her home in Idaho with her Husband and adorable sons. She loves to hear from readers!

www.rachelvandykenauthor.com

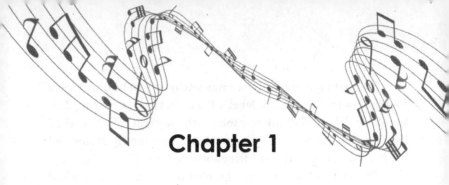

Chapter 1

<u>LYRIC</u>

Sometimes it's not about the talent that performs in front of your eyes, it's the people behind it who should be given trophies, the ones you walk by on the street and assume, project, disdain, and ignore.

Sometimes, the ones who should be called celebrities aren't the figureheads you imagine, but the artists that wrote that small little chorus that saved you when you were young. Staying Alive, Staying Alive.

That song by the Bee Gees.

My dad was a huge fan of anything from the seventies, and that song, the one I clung to, was also the one that he met his demise with.

Dark?

You have no idea, but I still play it over and over again when I need to focus, when I need to write and create.

The darkest moments in our lives don't have a hold on us, sometimes, they just barely keep us.

Alive.

* * *

"One more time." Annoyed that it was his seventeenth try, at the very least, I knew my response sounded short. I spoke without even looking up at the talent in the room. At that point, I refused to even say his name out loud so he wouldn't see the twitch in my eyes through the thick glass every time I finished begging him to actually do a moderately good job and stop acting like an ass.

It wasn't even that his voice was pitchy or that he didn't seem to care about my time or the label's. It was that he was wearing dark sunglasses like he'd drank way too much the night before, smelled like he was born in a club full of fruity cologne and cigarettes, and his clothes were so wrinkly I felt another eye twitch coming on.

Oh, and he was late for the studio time his label booked for his new album, a fresh new look for a washed-up singer who couldn't keep it in his pants four divorces in. Good luck to lady number five sitting behind me sipping milk, yes milk, from a straw while posting selfies to social media.

Her legs didn't reach the ground and, for a second, I had to suspend disbelief that he would bring a nineteen-year-old into the studio post partying all night to show off a song he barely knew the lyrics to.

Absolutely ironic, since my name's Lyric. Thanks to my musician dad, his sense of humor, and, in his opinion, manifestation, it was all I had.

Almost every single artist I worked with commented on it as if I hadn't been hearing it since I could understand words.

Most were genuinely kind, but there were some I actually wanted to punch in the face. Like Axel is any better, you asshole? We all know you were born a Peter!

And I swore on my parents' graves that if one more celebrity walked up to me and said they identified as younger, I would pull my hair out.

Yes, I, too, identified as a twenty-year-old. I also identified as a billionaire, and oftentimes identified as Taylor Swift's bff—Okay, that was only one time, and nobody should blame me for that.

Jaz didn't move when the music started again. It was upbeat, kind of nostalgic of nineties hip hop with a bit of a smooth transition into a sick hook of a chorus that I knew would grab people immediately—if he could just get the words and fix his pitch. How could he end every single note so sharp? I would even take a flat. Auto-tune could only work so many wonders.

He shook his head, cleared his throat, and then grabbed his

bottle of water, only to start choking and throw his headphones off.

Oh.

Perfect.

"Jaz?" I asked again. "Do you need a minute?"

He kicked the stool, it barely missed the wall and rolled to the side of the keyboard. "This is complete bullshit! I'm not doing it. I'm not feeling it, I don't like it, it's shit music, to sell shit albums, to make shit money, it's all shit!"

My producing partner, Gerald—a great name, I know— leaned over and shoved his black-rimmed glasses back up his nose. He was wearing a Star Trek shirt with Spock holding hands with Yoda. Ah, when worlds collide and all that. "I think that was at least four shits with a bullshit, does that mean five, or do we keep it at four and separate the different uses?"

I kicked him in the leg under the table.

Wincing, he rubbed his leg. "I was genuinely curious!"

"Five shits." Jailbait yawned and stood behind us, setting her milk back on the table. "I'd just group them all together at this point. I'm out, he's about ready to have a breakdown, and he has a massage later. I'll have his manager reschedule." She waved her impressively long purple-nailed hand at us, went into the studio, grabbed him by the wrist, and started walking out.

"They just don't get me." I was already at DEFCON one since he jumped into an immediate aegyo look, which basically meant pouting and looking cute in front of her when minutes ago he looked ready to trash the entire studio.

"Yes." She patted him on the back softly. "Nobody does."

I was out when he started to sniffle, then looked over his shoulder and glared at us. She kept rubbing his back and walked him out while I stared at the tossed stool, the empty space that would no longer be filled, and all the higher-ups' headaches that I would possibly have to take the fall for despite everyone knowing that Jaz was the worst to work with.

I tilted my head, spun my chair around twice, and then faced

Gerald while I said, "I think this one might stick."

The sarcasm was thick with that one.

He tapped a pencil against his chin. "It's weird when we root for the young ones versus the first gens. Let's be honest, they do tend to be getting smarter...should we blame TikTok or thank them? I get so confused these days."

I grabbed his black beanie and jerked it off of his head, then slammed it against his chest. "Pull the song."

All I got from Gerald was a slow blink from his Bambi-brown eyes. "I'm sorry, did you just say to pull the song?"

"He's not right for it; the label won't like it even if he tries his best, let's toss him what he wants or at least try to convince them to go in a different direction." I didn't say that I liked the song too much to let someone who didn't respect the music sing it. It was my least favorite part of the job, watching someone perform something I wrote only to have absolutely zero respect for the artist—I could at least have respect if they were really talented, but if they were imposters with a god complex, it was like handing over my favorite child and hoping they didn't lose it when they had trouble even remembering where they last left their keys.

Gerald let out a sigh. "At this point, I think the label would be happy just to get some sort of track for his new single rather than him showing up like this. I'll go back to the list of tracks they liked and choose something he can do in his sleep. The rap in this would have destroyed him anyway, he either speeds up his words or slows them down, there is no in-between."

I groaned. "Because he's not a rapper, he's a singer who wanted to expand and thinks he's a rapper. I swear if he talks about how hard growing up was one more time, I'm going to smack him back to Brentwood."

"Private school shits can be so shitty." Gerald joked. "See, two more shits, we might hit our quota for the day." He stood. "Hang in there, let's just give the song to someone else, appease everyone for the time being, I'll call his manager and figure it out...not a big deal, since technically we were doing them a favor." He stood and checked his phone. "And there's the final shit, I'm leaving. Oh wow, best timing ever, have fun!"

I frowned. "Fun? Why? What's happening? Why are you sweating?"

He grabbed his black jacket and bolted from the studio. The door closed quietly behind him.

No words followed, only a very long pause which had me questioning what would happen next.

Happy Monday?

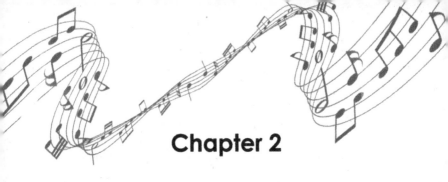

Chapter 2

LYRIC

Once Gerald left, I just shook my head and went back to the song I'd been working on and listened to the rap again, then turned it off and tossed my headphones onto the table. My frustration was strong with that one. It wasn't just the attitude, it was that it was a really good song, and he wasn't here for it, and I was sick and tired of working my ass off at weird-ass hours only to have an artist come in drunk.

They weren't all like that... I wasn't stupid, I was just tired, maybe? Jaded a lot? Depressed a bit, and my anxiety was constantly through the roof. The labels put so much pressure on us, and while we often worked as a team with the other writers, I craved a moment to shine. To see my song performed at a musical award ceremony, so I told myself it was okay to skip meals, I lied and said it was fine that I got three hours of sleep and smiled when I got yelled at.

Then there were always the amazing team members that would come in with coffee and a hug or those who would sit with me and complain, yay for NDAs, or even the artists who were genuinely incredible human beings who worked their asses off the same way we did.

That was life in any industry, quite frankly. I knew that, but it didn't make it any easier.

"It wasn't good," I said under my breath after listening to the shit rap for the thirtieth time and shutting it off in frustration. "It won't get better."

"It might, though?" A deep male voice sounded, followed by the quiet shut of the door, a damning shut.

Why did that voice sound familiar? The smell? Even the way the door softly closed. I was used to the loud walking and perfume or cologne to cover the smell of weed.

This was fresh.

The smell.

The quiet sound.

"Sorry. You have to book the studio time, did you walk into the wrong one?" What was with man buns these days? His jet-black hair was pulled into a messy bun on his head, and I was pretty sure we were wearing the same brand of baggy black cargo pants.

His loose Supreme white shirt was different from my black hoodie, but still...

He looked vaguely familiar, but I was too tired to really think too much about it until he walked in closer and sat in Gerald's chair, spinning toward me like he owned the place. "Nice to see you."

See me? As in he'd seen me before?

All the air left my body. Muscles spread down his forearms. Why would the universe punish us like that? He was fit, like super fit, and his face was chiseled like he'd found a doctor who knew how to shape like *the* David. I looked down at his fingers as they gripped the chair and swallowed. Oh God, the veins in his arms.

They moved as if his body was so jacked and hydrated that they had to wave when exposed.

Gerald poked his head in again. "Sorry to interrupt the silence, but Hi"—the guy in the chair spun around and shook his head—"this artist is from an incredible K-pop group. He just got back from the military, treat him right, or you'll probably be fired." He laughed. "No, but I'm serious. I can't fake laugh anymore, it hurts my soul too much. He's here to record one of your demos, the one that dipshit..." He looked over his shoulder.

"Sorry, thought I heard a noise and didn't want to have to carry his puke again. Don't ask. Anyway, he's going to record the last song you were working on, he hand-picked it, called up the label and studio, and booked you last minute, have fun kids." He shut the door before I could yell that I needed food, to pee, and a shot of tequila. I'd been working for over twelve hours already with a rapper who was not, in fact, a rapper!

The oddly familiar random K-pop dude leaned in, but I didn't make actual eye contact. "My bandmates are coming in a week, but I'm performing my solo and hopefully a new song for the group for Award Season. So you see..." He grinned at me like he knew me. "...it's a win-win!"

I waved him off. "Listen, I don't have you anywhere on my schedule." I grabbed my phone from my pocket just when my mentor and boss poked his head into the studio.

Another knock sounded while Gerald interrupted yet again. "Sorry, just had to add...be nice to Hills, he just got out of the military, maybe eat some candy? Get that blood sugar up?" I almost threw something at him when I realized.

Hills?

Why did that sound familiar? Hills, Hills, Hills.

The Hills are Alive...with the sound of.

Shit.

I forced a smile as Hills turned and stood. "It's cool, man, sorry I got here a bit early."

"Oh, she doesn't mind." Gerald waved me off.

She does, she one hundred percent does. "Plus, we just had an opening, stay as long as you want." Or leave, buy me ramen, a hot dog, beer, seven shots of espresso, a puppy, just don't stay any longer.

He checked his watch. "Looks like she has around two free hours, go over the tracks we discussed, and when the rest of the group comes in, we can start planning from there. We don't have a lot of time, but I know you've been listening to all of the demos that have been sent to you for the last few months, so it should go pretty quickly. You know the label's still against your plan of debuting your song before the group's, but it might add in some excitement, so they gave you the go-ahead. Make it great, text me if you need anything. You're in good hands."

I almost gasped. As if this random stranger ever touched my hands.

Hills, was it? He got up and moved toward Gerald. Up until this moment, he'd been the best mentor.

Ugh, don't, just don't.

Don't do it, don't do the bro slap on the back.

Gerald's hand moved.

Hills didn't dodge.

Ah, and the heavens rejoiced at two more bros being bros while I had to sit and watch.

I turned back toward the soundboard, gently set my phone down on some free space next to my already half-empty Americano with its pitiful lack of ice, and stared straight ahead as the door clicked shut.

I smelled his cologne again, like a wave I couldn't escape; it was clear like vanilla but had a bit of a spicy edge to it as well. He was warm, too, not that he was touching me, but he was close enough that I could feel the heat emanating from him. "So, should we start?"

No. I wanted to scream. I hated when this happened with VIPs—when I had no heads up, and no say in anything.

Grinding my teeth, I clicked on the file of the song we'd just used. "Sure." I hoped my smile was sweet, demure. "If you can make this song work for you, then I'll work with you, if you suck balls and waste my time, then you walk. Deal?"

He suddenly stood, sending his chair spiraling backward toward the couch. "So, you want me to nail it, and only then I get the supreme pleasure of working with you, Lyric? Did you want me to do it blindfolded, too? Should I play all the instruments and lay the track myself, no not enough time, how about a compromise? I'll do the rap part first and I'll do it better than the last guy that was in here."

I snorted, should I clue him in that the last guy was drunk off his ass and most likely floating into the universe while touching both stars and grass at the same time? "Yeah, be my guest—that's the hardest part, and something tells me you're not the main rapper in your group." It was a guess. Seriously though, why did he look so familiar? Had every single person I'd worked with in the last three and a half years suddenly melted together into one giant person?

I finally looked at him, really looked at him, our eyes locked. I counted the seconds, one, two, three.

The smirk.

I gasped and nearly fell out of my chair. Hands shaking, I bit down on my lip to keep myself from asking all the vulnerable questions, the explanations—no, the excuses.

"Ah, so she does know who I am." He winked. "Whiskey really doesn't taste the same after you, or was it maybe after the military?"

He could rap.

He could use his tongue—*voice*, I meant *voice*, very well.

His hands played the guitar like I'm assuming he played every other person the way he played me.

* * *

"Just one song." He'd teased after we wrapped up after a late night. "Come on, we'll write it together. It could be a hit."

"They should all be hits." I was a bit drunk and a lot high off the way he moved around the room, finally spreading out on the couch in the corner. "Come on, Lyric, we're practically best friends now."

I rolled my eyes. "We met this morning."

"It was three in the morning, and now it's three in the morning the next day, so technically, we've known each other for at least two days."

"Wow, someone's reaching."

"Reach for the stars." He fell back against the couch, and his black joggers fell low over his hips, making his grey shirt ride up across his abs. His Yankees hat, too, had fallen off his head. *"They always tell you it's possible if you work hard enough, and then you realize the industry is full of liars with perfect smiles."* He jerked up to a sitting position. *"Do you think it's the veneers? Should we blame those?"*

I burst out laughing. "Does it matter that I had braces for five years?"

"Oh." He shot to his feet. *"Well, that means you win, it means you're a natural."* He leaned down next to my chair. *"I'm manifesting it."*

"What?" I leaned forward. His hair was short and messy against his head, his brown eyes were bright and innocent; they matched mine. *"What are you manifesting?"*

"Us," he said it so simply, like he was making a promise to the universe. *"And, of course, the hit song we just recorded. I can't wait to show the rest of the group."*

"Ah, and I can't wait to meet this new crazy talented K-pop group. Be proud, you guys only debuted a little while ago, and you've already managed to get on Billboard." I leaned forward and crooked my finger. *"Be honest though, was that merch?"*

"Wow!" He fell back on his ass. *"Shots fired, and no, that was all organic, incredible talent from the lead singer."* He pointed at himself.

I got up and stumbled onto the ground, nearly kneeing him in the balls. "That wasn't on purpose."

"Even if it was..." He wrapped his arms around me and spun me onto my back, pinning me to the floor. *"...I'd be okay with it because now I have you."*

"Do you, though?"

"May I?" he asked, oh God, he asked.

I opened my mouth and shut it, then opened it again like an idiot. "Nobody can know."

"Who would find out that I kissed the words, the lyrics from Lyric right out of her mouth?" His thumb spread across my bottom lip. "Hmm?"

Everyone, was what I said in my head.

What ended up coming out was. "Nobody."

"Good." He leaned down and tugged my lower lip between his teeth while sliding his hand down my side. "Still okay?"

Why was it sexy that he asked?

Why did I care?

He wasn't taking advantage, and I wanted him, he'd been brilliant during our session, and once I found out who he was, I was so intimidated I wanted to puke.

The new golden voice of K-pop.

I nodded. "I want this."

"Good," was all he said before tugging at my shirt.

* * *

But it hadn't been good two days later, after more moments together, when I was met with a sticky note from him on my computer that said, "Sorry, management wants us back in Seoul."

I'd been in LA at the time with our sister label, so I had no choice but to stay, and it was good for me because TMZ, for the most part, didn't cover them.

MINE: the biggest up-and-coming K-pop group with their gorgeous singer. I didn't have to look, and I refused to. I stuck to celeb tabloids, and I'd kept my head down.

Until now.

Finally, I found my breath and managed to get words through my teeth. "It took me a while to see through all the bullshit and muscle, but I think I just managed. Get in the booth."

Still shaking, I spoke up. "You'll have the eight count before you jump into—"

"—I got it."

Arrogant as ever.

More beautiful than before.
Fuck.

Chapter 3

<u>HILLS</u>

I was told she'd be hard to work with and that she'd been busy post-award season. Then again, post any award season, everyone was busy. Most people had no clue that by the time November came, you were shit out of luck in the industry when it came to work, books included. It's like everyone took a huge hiatus until February and then scrambled to get content out the minute all the film festivals were done. For musicians, it was a bit different since we were working on things behind the scenes for promo and marketing. Even having a solid plan, it was hard as hell to get ahold of people and even when you did. It was even harder to hear back from them unless it was a major deal.

Yay for execs taking a two-month-long fucking vacation while the rest of us worked our asses off and prayed they'd give us good promo for our next song, good marketing, money, placement, and time. Oh look, skiing in Sun Valley again, nice, must be nice, how's the powder, oh and about the title song for our next mini album, I was thinking...

Yeah, good luck with that.

Basically, when I got back from the military, everything was dead, so I had one choice: go skiing with everyone else, order some chicken and beer in Seoul, or fly over to LA and lay down some tracks that might not even make it on our album. The rest of the guys weren't out yet, so I could at least tease a bit and promote our next album, which was set to release, get this, in two months. Most got out in two weeks.

So we had that long to record. The K-pop industry was a different breed. I'd grown up in Chicago and moved over to train with my label when I was thirteen and had no idea what I was getting into.

School, vocals, dance, testing, repeat.

Thankfully, it didn't take long for me, but I saw way too many friends burn out and leave after years of trying to get their debut with a group, and even then, some of the ones that did debut fizzled out after one album. So much was involved in the factory that was K-pop. Then again, they had the formula down because when it went right, they saw nothing but dollar signs.

I wouldn't really call myself a social media stalker, but a friend of a friend had used one of Lyric's songs, and I'd been following her since getting out of the military. Then I just couldn't look away, and by the time I realized what I was doing, I was already landing at LAX and driving to the studio she worked at.

It may have been a one-night stand, but she had no idea why I ghosted her. But you can't really walk up to the girl you walked away from after you became famous and say, oh hey, our thing wasn't about getting some ass, and you're super talented.

I had to prove myself.

Make sure she remembered me—remembered us most of all. I just hoped she wouldn't be offended when I showed her everything.

The scars.

The bleeding.

The vulnerability that felt shameful in society—saying I need help, I'm sad, I'm anxious, I'm not okay—all of those words that made you want to scream at the world and beg for your soul to be set free—these were the things I was dealing with when I met her.

My savior.

But people can't save you.

You can only save yourself.

And you can only hope you're strong enough to do it.

Especially knowing how horrible people in the industry could be—specifically one that didn't want you dating anyone but your fans. Idols were called idols for a reason.

So I studied her songs, I felt them, and then I convinced the rest of the guys I'd get her and her team for our next album. We didn't want to be forgotten after being out of the scene for two years, but we also wanted to show a more mature side of ourselves.

And she had that. She felt that.

Would we still be relevant?

Would people forget us?

Would it matter in the long run if the music was complete shit anyway?

No, even if we failed, we needed to show it all: the good, the bad, and the ugly; isn't that why music transcends languages, orientations, worlds?

Because it hits different.

I wanted to be known for that, and I know the other guys did too.

I cleared my throat. "Ready?"

She stared at me, black headphones on, eyes staring straight through me. Her hair was longer, blonde with shots of pink in it, and her makeup was perfection despite the fact I could still see some dark circles under her eyes.

High on caffeine. Typical.

Low on food. Also typical.

Her eyes blinked away. "I'm starting you in like I said, eight counts into the rap. You have the lyrics in front of you, want me to play the demo first or—"

"—I've got it, I heard the butchering earlier." I grinned.

Her lips twitched. "Sure, yeah, okay, go for it, Hills." The music started, and then she stopped it. "Seriously though, you told me your name was Johnny."

"Hills." I nodded. "Johnny Hills. It's my middle name. My stage name is Hills."

Most K-pop artists had them.

"Oh." She exhaled like it was a relief I didn't lie to her. "All right, let's go, I'll let you do your thing."

The song was fast coming in, the melody had shifted from the chorus down into the third rap, which would go into the main killing part and bridge into the, whoa, okay, there was a lot going on. I didn't get to hear all of it when I listened to the demo, and since I wasn't in the booth, I didn't actually hear him do the rap, I just assumed it was shit when he walked out and swayed against each wall down the hallway until he finally made it to the elevator only to hit the down button then the up button and stumble against his girlfriend for the seventh time.

Wasted.

Messed up.

I focused as much as I could while Lyric tapped her bare nails against the headphones and nodded at me.

I took a deep breath and dove headfirst into it, kind of the way I dove headfirst into her, without thinking of the ramifications.

"We are the stars that shine
We are the stars that shine
You by my side
We break the walls that bind
Leave everything behind
Be the star so bright
The star that's always been mine
Cuz you're the only way to make things bright
Leave the world you say behind
Driving me insane
Help me find the way while begging me to stay
Follow you anyway
Girl, follow you anyway."

I was too slow on the last part.
My voice cracked at least twice.
She stopped recording.

It was too eerily silent in that booth.

I gulped at least twice when she looked up at me and tossed her headphones onto the table in front of her. "Again."

Yeah, I could have guessed that.

"And jump into the chorus when you're done, do you need the replay of the demo?"

I almost said no, ma'am, like I was in the military. "No, I'm good." I was just rusty, and it wasn't helping that she was right in front of me the girl that got away, the one I walked from in order to protect my own career, her heart, the one I wasn't careful with when she was the most precious person in my world.

She hit the music again without warning, pulling her headphones back onto her face. Her hair stuck against her pink lipgloss while she stared me down.

Why was that so sexy in the first place?

I locked eyes with her, I did the rap, and then I went right into the bridge.

"Exploding in the air.
Catastrophe awaits.
Come dive with me inside.
Destiny's the only way."

She stopped the music again.

Shit.

"Again."

Was she a fucking general or something?

I knew I killed that last part.

Maybe that was the whole point, torturing and killing me.

I nodded and started again.

And again.

And again.

Two hours later, *again* was my least favorite word, and she somehow looked cheerful over the fact that I was seconds away from throwing instruments around the booth.

A cymbal, God, even a cymbal, would give me stress relief.

The song stopped again, abruptly.

Her finger had to be sore from all the times she slammed it down. But there was no way she was finished with me. She was a sadist. "Good."

That. Was. It?

Good?

Good?

Just good?

My jaw dropped. "Is that your idea of a compliment?"

"Is that your idea of singing?"

Oh shit, I took a deep breath and looked down, not trusting myself to keep calm. "I'm more than good."

When I looked up, all I saw was a shrug and a small smirk.

I narrowed my eyes, then I went for it. I stomped out of the booth, marched toward her chair, and pulled her against me. "Admit it."

"What?"

"You missed me, and I'm more than good."

She licked her lips and stared up at me. "Mildly better than good, and I didn't even remember you until now."

"Lie." My nostrils flared. "I know I messed up, but I also know that the minute I met you I'd be leaving you for at least eighteen months. You can't blame me for panicking when I had one of the best moments of my life after, mind you, growing up as a trainee who's told he's going to basically get blacklisted if he gets involved with anyone."

Her smile grew a bit. "Probably not a good idea to hook up then in a recording studio as your first act of rebellion."

"No." I laughed. "Probably not my best moment."

"I did."

"What?"

"Miss you. I missed you. And you hurt me. And you're better than good, and now you're going to have another hit album, especially if I'm on it, and then you'll walk away again. The good ones always do, want to know why?"

"Tell me."

"Because of the music." She nodded, her eyes glistened with tears. "The music is always number one, and I don't blame you for it, but I don't want to live my life as number two."

"But..." I tilted my head and leaned in. "Couldn't it be a tie?"

"What?"

"Music, love, can't it be a tie? Why does one have to lose out when they're always better together?"

"Two powerful things like that are terrifying, don't you think?"

I sighed and grabbed her hand; it was as soft as I remembered. "I'm not sure it's worth having if you aren't scared. I'd rather be afraid than not feel anything."

She tried to pull her hand away, but I didn't let her. "And you think this is going to somehow go differently than before?"

"Of course," I said, without a shadow of doubt. "I'm older, I've lost my touch, so I'm going to need a lot of direction." I stood and pulled her to her feet. "Maybe it's time to stop fighting so hard and just give into the fear. Life is about more than sitting in this chair and creating dreams and melodies for other people."

"Did you practice this speech before walking in here?"

"I literally wrote it down on my hand." I teased. "And then I forgot all of it after seeing you. I wanted to sweep you off your feet and ended up falling a bit harder; maybe I'm out of practice."

She rolled her eyes. "You know you can't just walk into a studio and seduce the writer after almost two years, it doesn't really work that way."

"Seduce?" I frowned. "I just wanted to be your friend. I'm sorry, did I miscommunicate?"

"You ass!" She laughed. "Be honest, why are you here?"

"I ran," I admitted. "The minute I was done with the military. I ran home, I showered—don't worry, I made sure to practice this speech in my head—and then I ran to you." I shrugged. "Gerald helped."

"Of course he did. He's a romantic like that."

"So?"

"Dinner." She shrugged. "Buy me dinner first, then we can talk."

"And the song?"

She leaned up and wrapped her arms around my neck. "It's yours."

Her hands dropped too fast, she turned even faster, and I was once again feeling like I was chasing something I would never catch, no matter how hard I tried.

It wasn't an obsession.

It was something deep, something that I couldn't stop thinking about the entire time I was gone. I knew that I walked away first in order to keep myself from hurting while I told myself it was the best for her and her career.

After all, what good would it do to have the media find out that an up-and-coming producer and guy from one of the biggest K-pop groups in the world hooked up?

She would have never made it.

They would have destroyed her.

It was easier to destroy us, hoping that later on, I could possibly salvage what was left after she made a name for herself.

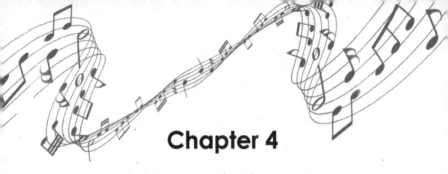

Chapter 4

LYRIC

I would be lying to myself if I didn't at least admit how much I'd thought about him and what happened between us.

It hurt.

When he left, it hurt bad, but I didn't want to be clingy, and I definitely didn't want to be the sort of fangirl to just chase after him when clearly, he'd needed his space. By the time he and his group blew up and he found out he'd be enlisting within the next year, I'd all but convinced myself to forget about him. I stopped checking the news and only focused on the songs. I did hole up a bit and just decided that my only job was to write for musicians, and they all looked and felt the same when they came into the studio.

Some were incredible, others were into themselves so much I wanted to offer them an extra mirror just in case theirs broke.

Being in LA was a breath of fresh air, something I'm sure a lot of people wouldn't agree with...but for me, it was just far enough away from Seoul that unless they dropped a new song, I didn't see anything about him.

While K-pop was blowing up, it was still easy to avoid in the States. I kept my head down, and I wrote.

I just never expected him to come back.

Specifically for me.

For songs, I knew it was probably inevitable because I was good at what I did, but for me?

I wasn't sure how much I could trust him, just like I wasn't sure if he would stick around again.

We walked out to the elevator.

He hit down.

I looked away.

And then his hand grabbed mine. "What sounds good?"

My heart thudded against my chest. "Huh?"

"Food?" He smiled down at me, his long black hair covering part of his face, his smile open, friendly, happy.

Before, he'd been a bit more closed off.

Now he seemed...relaxed almost.

Warm.

Content. That was the word. Content.

"Chicken," I finally said once the doors closed. "At my apartment. Let's just catch up and order chicken."

"Chicken." He repeated. "Very sexy, I've always dreamed of having chicken with you after a long night at the studio dropping beats."

"Never say dropping beats ever again if you ever want to get laid."

He burst out laughing. "Noted."

"Ever."

"Got it."

"Ever again."

"So, chicken..." He pulled me closer, wrapping an arm around me. "...let's do that, and once we're done, I'll tell you why I walked away, why I left, why I abandoned one of the only relationships I should have stayed in. I'll tell you I thought I was protecting you when really, I think I was afraid. I'll tell you that I didn't want to get involved with someone who had so much potential and was blowing up. How I was scared about the netizens going insane over us hooking up, and then I'll tell you I was being a dumbass. Sound good?"

Stunned, I couldn't move. "W-what?"

"But chicken first." The doors opened. "Always chicken first."

I had no choice but to follow him out while he blatantly held my hand, while people walking by saw, while security smiled at us, and while a car was already pulled up for us.

He still didn't let go of my hand.

I smiled and jumped into the car.

He drove.

"Address?" he asked.

"Are we doing this?"

"The chicken? Yes. The sex, no, sadly not. I kind of want to do things backward this time let's eat first, talk, catch up, and then I'll take you against the nearest hard surface—in a very respectful do-I-have-permission sort of way—before it turns into *Fifty Shades*, as it should, where I use my teeth, rope, and create our own fantasy."

I laughed again. "Something's unhinged in you."

"You..." He pulled into traffic. "I've had a lot of time to think about you."

"I hope it was miserable."

He shook his head. "No, it was everything."

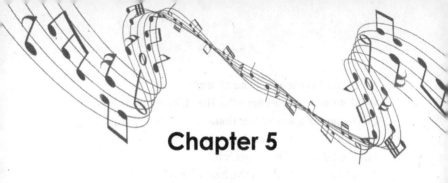

Chapter 5

HILLS

One Year Later

"Stop panicking!" I pulled Lyric against me and kissed her hard on the mouth. She moaned and deepened the kiss, her tongue soft, flicking against my lower lip.

I growled and pulled away.

She pouted. "What?"

"Not the time. I can't perform like this."

She looked down and grinned. "You'll be fine."

"Famous last words." I adjusted myself. "But seriously. It's your song, and I have to do it right and stop looking at me right now or I'm going to walk away."

"Never again, you said." She winked. "And you'll do great."

It was my first performance with the group since returning from the military, and, of course, it had to be the music awards of all places. I'd already nailed my solo performance, but this felt different, harder, because I had more people I could let down.

I'd sweat so much leading up to it that I was afraid something was physically wrong with me.

The song hit number one in over thirty countries, the album held strong on Billboard at number one for three weeks straight, and our Spotify listens were absolutely insane.

Not to mention our music video had hit sixty million views in under a week.

The pressure was on.

And she'd written half the album.

We'd moved in together after the chicken.

I'd proposed a week after that.

And life was chaotic and messy.

I looked down at her stomach.

About to get messier in the best of ways.

We ignored people who speculated on our relationship, who wanted the worst for us when we'd only ever wanted the best for others, for the world, through music. And when it got hard, I just thought about her forcing me to sing a damn near perfect song again and again.

Again.

It was my least favorite word for so long.

Now it was my favorite.

Again, meant more. It meant her.

Again was all I needed to hear for the rest of my life.

"You're up." She winked. "Again."

I cracked up. "Yup, again." I leaned in and kissed her across the mouth. "And again, and again. Love you."

"Love you too."

THE ROAD TO YOU

MEREDITH WILD

About the Author

Meredith Wild is a #1 *New York Times, USA Today,* and international bestselling author of 22 novels. After self-publishing her debut novel *Hardwired* in 2013, Wild used her ten years of experience as a tech entrepreneur to form her first publishing imprint, forging relationships with major retailers, and becoming one of the first indie authors to become fully stocked in brick-and-mortar bookstore chains nationwide.

Both traditionally and self-published, Wild's books have hit No. 1 on the *New York Times* and *Wall Street Journal* bestsellers lists. She has been featured on CBS This Morning, The Today Show, the *New York Times, The Hollywood Reporter, Vanity Fair, Publishers Weekly,* and *The Examiner.* Her foreign rights have been sold in over 23 languages. She resides in Florida with her partner, children, and many furry companions.

www.meredithwild.com

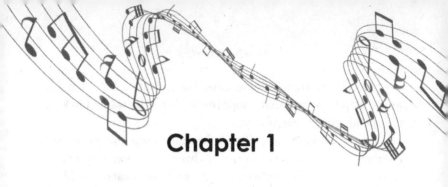

Chapter 1

BARON

"Mr. Porter?"

Baron hummed absently, his focus on the blueprints spread out before him.

"You have a voicemail from Sam Westwood. It's about the theater."

He hummed again. The Westwood Theater was a near daily pain in Baron's ass, one he didn't need today. *Today* he had to sign off on the final plans for renovating the co-working office space in the theater's neighboring building, yet another expensive but soon-to-be lucrative project that would revitalize the downtown.

"It's the roof," she continued.

Baron lifted his head. Casey was posted at the desk on the other side of the office, her chin propped on her fist.

"Shit," he muttered. "Tell me it's not bad."

"I wish I could. I guess there's a bunch of new leaks from the storm that blew through over the weekend."

"Call one of our contractors. See what it'll take to patch things up."

Casey shook her head. "Sam already talked to someone. They're saying the whole roof needs to be replaced."

Baron sat back in his chair and stared out the windows that faced Dupont Street. Years ago, he'd fallen in love with this little beach town. He saw more than a hidden gem along the coast that he could enjoy on his free weekends. He saw potential. He'd snatched up whatever property he could on the beach. But the downtown was the ticket to transforming Cape Haven from a forgotten dot on the map to a place that a sophisticated traveler wanted to visit and spend money year after year.

Smack in the middle of that downtown was the Westwood Theater—a cornerstone of the town's history. He was only able to acquire it after Sam Westwood made sure the theater would be preserved. Baron had been in the middle of several negotiations at the time, and the nostalgia of breathing new life into the old building eventually won out.

"Should have known," Baron muttered.

Casey lifted a questioning eyebrow.

Baron shook his head. Seemed like every emotional decision he made in business lately came back to haunt him. The theater was becoming the epitome of a real estate money pit.

Baron gathered up the blueprints into a tidy pile, rose from his desk, and threw on his jacket. "I'm going over to check it out. Tell Sam I'm on my way."

CORA

The sky was blue, but a brisk winter wind whipped through the leafless crepe myrtles that lined Dupont Street, blowing the last of their fine pink and white petals across the braided blanket where Cora sat. She wasn't living on the street, per se, but it had been a long time since she'd had a place to call home. She shivered and cradled her guitar against her chest a little tighter. She flexed her fingers to draw some warmth back into them, then began strumming an easy, familiar tune—a melancholy one she'd written as a teenager.

She'd had a roof over her head then and a warm bed to sleep in, but Cora wouldn't trade her life now for that one, cold fingers and all. She was happy enough to be singing on the sidewalks from town to town, living off the kindness and generosity of strangers.

When she'd left home for good, she'd soon realized how much good was in the world.

A couple walking hand in hand stopped briefly in the middle of Cora's song before dropping some bills into her basket.

She thanked them and thought of a woman she'd met two towns back who'd given her the fingerless gloves she was wearing now, after Cora had been singing her heart out in the damp cold, her voice quivering as her body shook to regain its warmth. She'd made enough that day to put herself in a motel for a night before getting back on the road.

And the road brought her to Cape Haven late last night, the closest town she could find before the gas needle on her Honda Civic went to zero. It was a pretty town. Clean beaches and lots of new homes built on stilts along the water, protection against the fierce storms that hit the coast every year at random.

"There's no busking here, you know."

Cora's meandering thoughts came to a grinding halt as she sat in the shadow of the man before her. She blinked up at him, noting the messiness of his brown hair and the stubble along his jaw. He was dressed well, in crisp blue jeans and a thin, black jacket.

"I'm sorry?"

He cleared his throat and a little line formed between his brows. Something in her gut told Cora that this man might not be the first in line to extend kindness to strangers. His clothes were expensive, his shoes polished leather. His wrist glimmered with a thick watch. Of course, she'd often felt that the people who had money were that way because they didn't give much away. But what did she know...

"There's no busking. No street performing here in Cape Haven without a permit."

"I didn't know that," Cora said, setting her guitar to the side and rising to stand. They weren't exactly eye to eye—he was much taller than her five-foot-four frame—but she could look into his better while standing. They were dark blue and stormy like the water in the Gulf this time of year.

"You should probably find another place, then," he said without feeling, even though his eyes wandered over her the way hers did him.

Cora tucked her hands into her jacket pockets to warm them. "I've been here all day, though. No one's given me any trouble about it. Just singing a few songs."

The man sighed and glanced down the mostly empty street. "It's off-season. You're not likely to get many people passing through until the weekend anyway."

Cora's smile faded a little. "I'm just trying to get enough for gas, and then I'll be on my way."

His frown deepened. He seemed more worried than annoyed now. "Where are you headed?"

"California. If my car gets me there."

The man paused, then pulled his wallet out and handed her a hundred-dollar bill. "Here. This ought to do it."

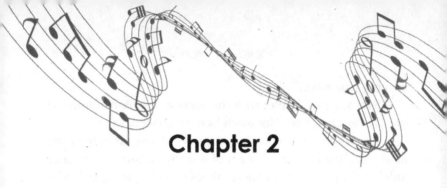

Chapter 2

BARON

The girl was young and far too pretty to be traveling across the country on her own. Baron didn't know where she'd come from, but he was surprised by the trust in her eyes and the easiness of her smile. Maybe the world hadn't hardened her yet. But it would...

He left her behind as he pushed through the double doors of the theater and called for Sam. He was on the stage, rearranging a series of paint buckets that were presumably collecting rainwater. Baron cussed aloud and assessed the wet towels strewn around the floor.

"What the hell, Sam? How long have you known we needed a new roof?"

Sam threw his hands up. "Since this morning, Baron. Not like it's been a big secret. It's an old building. Old buildings need new roofs. Especially any one within a mile of this coast. It holds on until it can't anymore."

Baron sighed and scraped his fingers over his scalp. "How much is it going to cost?"

Sam shrugged. "Buddy of mine says he'll do it for fifty."

"Fifty thousand? That's not friendship. That's robbery."

"It's a commercial property, and there's no shortage of jobs for them around here. He doesn't need our business, but we need a roof."

Baron paced in front of the stage. "I need a roof. This falls on me now, remember?"

Sam stopped fussing with the buckets to look Baron in the eye. "I'm aware of that. Not much I can do about it, can I?"

A year ago, who knows how Sam would have taken the same news, with the financial burden of it solely on him. The theater didn't belong to him anymore, though. Sam was tasked with operations and whatever maintenance he could manage on his own. But the rest was on Baron's shoulders now.

"What about the shows this weekend? We can't lose the revenue."

Sam sighed. "Hoping things dry up a little by then. Should be all right."

Baron held his stare, hoping his "employee" who had lately become more of a friend could understand the increasing gravity of the situation. "We had to deal with the plumbing fiasco last month. The insulation needs to be redone come summer. The energy bill on this place is giving me a heart attack. What's next, Sam?"

Sam wiped his hand over his face. "I don't know," he murmured. "I don't know."

"I agreed to help you save this place, but it's like keeping the Titanic above water here. I appreciate that it's important to you, but at what cost? You know this isn't anywhere close to a profitable venture for me—"

"You bought up half the downtown, Baron. You own like a quarter of the town's waterfront at this point. You're going to make your money back, believe me."

"Doesn't mean this makes any damn sense. Throwing money down the drain that I could spend on literally anything else to help this town."

Sam stabbed his finger through the air. "This is a historical treasure—"

"This is a dilapidated building with dwindling promise at best. Even without the repairs, we're in the red."

"It's off-season..."

"It's a failing proposition. One I should have never agreed to."

Silence fell between them with Baron's admission. He'd never said it aloud before, but they both knew the strain of the theater was eating away at Baron's hope for the place. He dragged his foot across the dull red carpet.

"Sam, I hate to say this, but if things don't turn around here soon, I'm going to have to make some hard decisions."

Sam frowned and stepped off the stage to stand a few paces from Baron. "Hard decisions like what? You can't shut it down. We agreed—"

"I agreed not to renovate in a way that would dramatically alter the visual integrity of the theater. I agreed not to turn it into something else—a Banana Republic or an office building. I didn't agree to keep the roof from falling in."

Sam stilled, and the air between them grew thick with the quiet truth. Perhaps letting the theater fall into disrepair was never something Sam had considered, but the look in his eye said he was taking it seriously now.

"You would do that? After everything..." Sam worked his jaw. "I thought we were friends."

"We are. I just..." Baron glanced up at the entrance, at the decorative balconies and the architecture that made the theater a place he'd wanted to save once upon a time. His emotions were coming into play again, and that was what had gotten him into this mess to begin with. "It's just business, Sam."

CORA

"Everything good, honey?" The red-haired waitress stopped to refill Cora's iced tea.

Cora swallowed her last bite and groaned. "This is the best cheeseburger I've ever tasted."

The waitress, whose name tag read Dee, laughed. "Then you should try our key lime pie. Best one you're going to find in the

Panhandle."

Cora smiled and wiped her mouth. The cheeseburger and fries should have been filling enough, but the emptiness in her stomach never really seemed to ease since she'd been living on the road. Pie sounded amazing, but she needed to save the rest of her money for gas.

"No, thanks. Maybe next time," she lied, knowing she'd likely never grace this town again. Not if her California dreams came true anyway.

Dee leaned in, her elbows bent on the counter. "You might as well, honey, because that fine gentleman in the corner booth is paying for your meal anyhow."

Cora spun on the diner stool to see who Dee was talking about. The fine gentleman was the same very fine, not-so-nice guy who'd shoved a hundred-dollar-bill at her to leave town not thirty minutes ago.

"Why?" Cora muttered, but Dee had already made her way to the pie display and was plating up a big piece for her. "Who is he?" Cora asked when Dee returned.

"His name's Baron Porter. He is a big deal in this town. Big property developer from Atlanta, but he's been down here for the past few years trying to build things up. They call this the 'Forgotten Coast,' because every time we seem to find our footing, something knocks us down. Weather, economy. Oyster industry isn't what it used to be. We can't get by without tourism now. Porter may not be a local, but most of us wouldn't have a job without everything he's doing."

Cora ate her pie, silently regarding the man in the corner who seemed totally engrossed with his phone. No doubt he'd taken pity on her earlier, singing on the streets for gas money. But she'd learned to check her pride long ago, accept the unexpected blessings that came her way, and pay it forward whenever she could.

Having cleared her plates, she rose and made her way to Porter.

"Hi," she said. "I wanted to thank you for lunch."

He lifted his gaze from his phone. "You're welcome."

Cora nodded, unsure of what else to say. He hadn't exactly been friendly to her before, but something made her want to linger a little, maybe to peel back another layer of this man who had become a bit of a contradiction in her world.

"Well..." She picked absently at a tear in the leather booth. "Thanks again. For the money too. You didn't have to do that."

"Sorry. I was kind of a dick earlier. Cape Haven has like three cops, and no one's going to bother you here. I just have spent an unusual amount of time studying the town's ordinances, and sometimes my mouth works faster than my brain."

Cora grinned at his self-deprecating apology, one she would have never expected from him. "I accept your apology."

He traced the edge of his water napkin, folding and unfolding the corner of it. "You travel alone?"

Cora nodded, sensing his concern. A skeptical part of her considered that Porter could be a creep, but none of her instincts were telling her that he was. So far those same instincts had kept her safe and guided her to help when she'd needed it. "It's not as bad as you think. Most people are happy to help."

"There are also a lot of bad people out there looking to take advantage of someone like you."

His words felt like a punch to the chest. Heat rose to her cheeks. "Someone like me?"

"Yeah, someone like you. A pretty girl with an innocent smile who thinks there's a lot more good in the world than bad."

She nodded slowly. "You may be right. Maybe I've just been lucky so far."

"You're a long way from California."

"If I can sing my way there, I suppose it was meant to be. If not..." She didn't want to think about the alternatives right now. Settling down with some regular job, living paycheck to paycheck, and giving up on her dreams wasn't something she was ready to entertain yet.

"Don't get me wrong, you can sing." Porter paused, rubbing his fingers across his lips. "There's actually an open mic at Marty's down the street tomorrow night. You should come."

Cora smiled. For this earlier coldness, Porter was quickly revealing a softer side. A side that genuinely worried about a stranger's safety. A side that wanted to maybe spend a little more time with her? "Thanks. I love the stage, but I need a real gig. I can't afford to stay that long if I can't make a little money too."

"You ever wait tables?"

She laughed. "Of course."

"Then let me talk to Marty. He's always short-staffed on open mic night. Run some drinks for him, and you can still perform. You never know... Maybe you'll land a real gig once people hear you sing. Never know who'll be in the audience. A couple places around here do live shows from time to time."

Cora lifted a brow. "Yeah?"

He held out his phone. "Here, put your number in. I'll text you after I talk to Marty."

"I'm Cora, by the way." Cora punched her name and number into his phone and handed it back to him.

"Cora Clark." He studied the screen with a little smile, his fingers moving over the keys. "I'm Baron Porter."

Her phone dinged with a smiley face from an unknown number. She responded with a wave emoji. "Your reputation precedes you, Baron. I've already heard you're the hero this sleepy little town needs."

His cheeks colored, like he was uncomfortable with the praise. "Maybe," he muttered. "I'll see you tomorrow, then."

She waved goodbye and stepped out onto the streets that had warmed a little with the afternoon sunshine. Her day had taken some unexpected turns, no doubt. So many pieces of her journey so far had. On the surface, Cape Haven didn't seem like it was brimming with potential for someone like her. But Porter seemed to have the respect of a lot of people here, so maybe staying one more night was worth a shot.

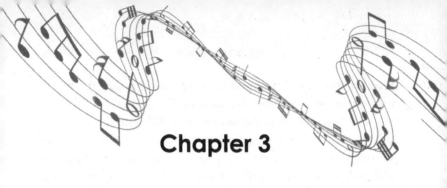

Chapter 3

BARON

Baron had no business getting involved in this girl's foolish journey across the country. Cora wasn't looking to be saved, but she'd welcomed his help when he had offered it. Hell, she had two thousand more miles to cover. Then what? Not like crossing the border into California had ever made someone's dreams come true. Who knew what troubles lay ahead for her.

And what was Baron doing but delaying the inevitable? He'd all but told her to get out of town the minute he saw her. Now he was giving her reasons to stay. Making arrangements so that she could afford to.

After a quick exchange with Marty confirmed that he would indeed be short-staffed tomorrow, Baron texted the details to Cora and returned to the pile of work that was waiting for him at the office.

The next morning, he woke early with the sunrise. He didn't need coffee to set his brain whirling through the events of the previous day and all he had in front of him. He was wired that way. Focused on the task at hand always, like too much idleness might break the spell of his success. Most of Baron's life was about forward motion, creating momentum, and identifying the problems in a plan before they could compromise his work.

He stepped out onto the sand in front of his house and started on his morning run. The beach was empty save a couple locals who had the same early routine as he did. Baron should have been thinking about blueprints and meetings and choosing the best of three quotes for a new roof, but he kept drifting to Cora.

The two of them could not be more different. She was open and trusting—too trusting, in fact. He didn't usually have that problem. Something about her goodness and inherent kindness fascinated him, though, until all he could think about was seeing her again at Marty's tonight. He wanted to hear her sing again, and hell, if he wasn't thinking about ways to help her stay longer.

Fried seafood baskets and beach gear stores wouldn't be enough to make Cape Haven what he wanted it to be, ultimately. The town needed art and culture and more talented, free-spirited people like Cora to give it texture and soul. Maybe she could be a part of that and save herself weeks of tribulation getting to California where too many dreams went to die.

He slowed his run at the beach access pier that led back to the main road. He took his shoes off to feel the sand and the too-cold waters of the Gulf lapping the shore. He wasn't a spiritual person, but he subscribed to the grounding medicine of the ocean. This was usually the most peaceful part of his day, when he felt most like himself, and every morning was a reminder of why he'd chosen this place to be home.

After a few minutes, he scaled the wooden steps and was rinsing off the sand at the outdoor showers when he heard a beautiful sound—a woman singing. He knew that voice already like a song he'd committed to memory. It was Cora. Singing her heart out. In the pier bathroom at six o'clock in the morning.

Baron followed the sound to the entrance of the restrooms, catching his breath from the run and this new concerning discovery. Cora wound down her song and was humming when he called out her name.

There was a moment of silence before she peaked her head around the cinder block barrier to see him standing in the doorway.

"Baron?"

With wide eyes, he lifted his hands. "What are you doing

here?"

Her expression froze, as if she'd been doing something she wasn't supposed to. She'd had the same look on her face yesterday when he'd told her she was violating the town ordinances.

"I...um, I was just taking a shower." She walked closer, a faded beach towel wrapped around her body.

He shouldn't have been thinking about how perfect she looked, with her bright-blue eyes and her dark-blond hair in wet streaks over her tanned shoulders. Or her thighs peeking out from under the towel that he suddenly wanted to rip away so he could take in all of her. Every sweet, delicious inch of her...

"Why..." He cleared his throat and forced himself to a more decent line of thinking. "Where exactly are you staying, Cora?"

"Staying?" Her voice was high, like a child caught in a lie.

"Where did you stay last night?" He said each word slowly, quietly demanding that she offer up the truth. A truth he truly didn't want to hear, because then he'd have to do something about it. And he would do something about it.

Cora nibbled at her lip and stared down at her bare feet. "I stay in my car sometimes, you know, when money's tight. It's no big deal."

"Your car? It can get close to freezing around here this time of year."

"I have a really good sleeping bag. Someone actually gave it to me—"

"Not to mention you're a target for people who may not have the best intentions. You have special victims unit written all over you."

She winced. "I do?"

Baron sighed and sliced his fingers through his hair. "Can I offer an alternative, at least while you're staying in town?"

Her lips parted, like she was afraid to take him up on his offer.

"I own a bunch of rentals here in town. Most of them are empty with it being off-season. I can set you up in one."

Cora shook her head and wrapped her towel a little tighter. "I don't usually say no to a helping hand, but you've already done too much, Mr. Porter."

"Baron."

"Baron... I... I'll be fine in my car, I sw—"

"Completely out of the question. Not to mention another violation of town ordinances. This one I'll enforce."

Cora's face broke with a smile. "Mr. Rules is back, I see."

Baron's shoulders relaxed, maybe from the sight of her smiling and hopefully relenting. "Please accept, and we can end this conversation and have a coffee. I really need a coffee right now."

Cora lifted a shoulder. "I guess so. Give me a few minutes to get ready."

Ten minutes later, Cora emerged dressed and bundled in her puffy jacket. "My car is over there." She pointed twenty feet away to the sole car in the beach access lot, a patchy red Honda sedan. "But can I follow you?"

He could read the embarrassment in her eyes. Of course she didn't want him to see inside her car, where she was storing everything to her name. "No need. The place is right down here. I was walking back that way anyway."

CORA

"This is too much." Cora let her coat slip off her shoulders as she walked toward the wall of windows facing the sunrise stretching over the Gulf of Mexico. When Baron said he had rentals, she was imagining small apartments, maybe not that unlike the motel room she'd gotten used to staying in. Nothing in her imagination could have dreamed up the pristine beach house he insisted was hers to occupy for as long as she was in Cape Haven.

"It's nothing. I'm not earning anything on this place right

now anyway. I trust you'll take care of it."

"I will," Cora rushed to say. "I'll clean up after myself before I go. You'll never know I was here."

He waved his hand. "Make yourself at home."

She sighed with wonder, getting lost in the breathtaking views and the immaculate furnishings. "I'm not sure I'll know how. This place is incredible."

Baron came closer and held out the key. "I'm happy to help," he said, his voice thoughtful. "Really. And I'm looking forward to hearing you sing tonight too. This town has no idea what's about to hit it."

Cora's fingers brushed his as she took the key in her hand. The gift. A luxury she wasn't sure she deserved. She looked into Baron's eyes, compelled to thank him again, but when she saw the look he returned, the words died in her mouth. She couldn't deny that she was attracted to this man. The energy radiating off him now told her he felt it too, even if he wasn't acting on it.

He exhaled a shaky breath and stepped back. "I'll let you get settled in, then. I'll see you tonight."

The distance between them suddenly felt wrong to Cora. She trusted that Baron wasn't the type of guy who would push himself onto a woman or coax her into intimacy she didn't want. And that made her feel even safer in his presence. After all, he'd seemed concerned about her safety from the start. Maybe rightly so. As independent as Cora tried to be, knowing he was looking out for her felt good. Really good. And it made her want to be even closer to him, wrapped in the heat of whatever fire was hiding behind his eyes.

Hours later, after a long soak in the tub and a nap in the rental's fluffy king bed where she'd slept better than she had in weeks, Cora dressed for her shift at Marty's. Not knowing the staff's dress code, she went with black jeans and a tight white top. She tied her hair back into a loose braid and applied a little makeup, something she rarely did these days.

As she walked into town, any nervousness she may have

had about waitressing at a place she'd never been faded. She was consumed with thoughts of Baron. He'd be there too. Maybe tonight, unlike this morning, he'd actually make a move. Maybe she'd never see him again after tonight, but that's how life went sometimes. He'd be a memory, and maybe he'd remember her too.

The night sped by quickly. The event was surprisingly well-attended, and the crowd seemed lively for a Tuesday night. Marty was friendly and helped her out whenever she needed a hand. Bringing drinks to tables wasn't too complicated, though, and most everyone she waited on was pleasant to talk to. Many asked about her, having identified her as someone new in a sea of locals.

When the emcee called her name, though, her heart sank. Because as the hours had ticked by, the one person she really wanted to be there was missing. Baron was nowhere in sight. She shouldn't care so much. Not after their brief interactions. He'd done enough for her after all—more than enough. She picked up her guitar from beside the little stage and tried to tamp down her disappointment.

He'd probably realized being in her life was a slippery slope. Despite his hard exterior, Baron was a generous soul, and Cora had a hard time saying no when she needed the help. Maybe the attraction that hummed between them was a distraction he didn't need right now. And maybe she didn't need it either. She needed to focus on her dreams and where life would take her next.

With that thought center in her mind, she took the stage and adjusted the microphone to her height. She'd weighed the different songs she might sing tonight, but she always changed her mind depending on how she felt in the moment. Tonight, with a little sadness on her heart, she picked a song about hope. It was one that was born on the road. It was a little unpolished, like her, but maybe performing it in front of the crowd would make it shine.

She sang about the loneliness of the road that led her far from home, about the silver linings she'd found when she was down on her luck, and the dream that she still held fast to...a dream of sharing her songs with the world. And when the song was done, silence fell inside the little cafe bar. When she looked up, she almost didn't notice the loud applause and shouts for more, because Baron was standing next to the bar, his body far but still squared to hers, his eyes dark with an emotion she couldn't quite name.

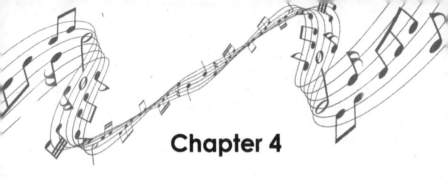

Chapter 4

<u>BARON</u>

Cora was breathtaking in every way. Baron literally struggled to take in his next breaths after hearing her perform. If he didn't already have a sense of her heart and her sweetness, her performance alone would have brought him to his knees. Her voice seemed to sweep into his soul, carrying him into her song's story, one that was fraught with heartache and hope.

When Cora walked up to him after playing one more song for the eager crowd, he didn't think it through. He slid his hand behind her neck and pulled her to him, hovering his lips above hers for a few painful seconds before she lifted on her toes and joined them in a kiss. Inside the brief connection, he found out what he'd been wondering nearly since they'd met—how soft her lips were, what she tasted like, and how right she might feel with her body pressed to his.

When they parted, the air hummed with a promise of more.

The promise was held in her misty eyes and the wild beating of his heart. This wasn't over. Not by a long shot. But he was moving too fast. He'd invited her into his beach house hours earlier. Now he wanted her under him, wanted his name on her lips...badly. He took a step back, trying to get ahold of himself. To break the spell she had over him, at least for a little while.

He cleared his throat and glanced over the bar where the crowd was beginning to thin. "Can I buy you a drink?"

Cora tapped her fingers on the glossy countertop, as if she

was deciding. He felt it then, instant regret at having pushed her too far too fast. But when she spoke again, her voice was steady, her words sure.

"Actually...if it's okay with you, could we go back to my place? I mean...your place. The place I'm staying." She laughed and put her hands on her cheeks, which were growing darker.

Baron met her smile, and relief flooded him. "Sure. Are you all set here?"

She nodded. "Marty told me I could take off after I played. I can pick up the rest of my tips tomorrow."

"Perfect. Let me get this for you."

Baron picked up her guitar, and on the walk back to the beach house, Cora slipped her cool hand in his. She felt small and delicate, and all over again he worried about the journey before her and all the dangers that might lie ahead.

Once inside, Baron made his way to the gas fireplace in the living room and switched it on.

"This is heaven," Cora moaned, stretching her fingers out to absorb the heat of it. She glanced up at Baron, a smile playing at her lips. "I wouldn't mind that drink now actually."

The property managers for the house always left a couple complementary bottles for guests, so Baron knew where to find them. "Red or white?"

"Red would be great."

"Red it is."

By the time he finished pouring two glasses, Cora had curled up on one of the comfy couches. Baron joined her there and swirled his wine like he was in the habit of doing.

"What should we toast to?" she asked.

He pursed his lips a moment before lifting his glass. "To all your hopes and dreams, Cora."

Her smile was slow and sad, and Baron wasn't sure why.

"Cheers," she said before sipping the deep-red wine.

"You were incredible tonight. I had no idea..."

"I was emotional tonight. That helps. I get really lost in the moment, and when I snap out of it, I just hope the audience likes what I've given them. It's like going into another world for a little while."

Baron could understand why she'd want to. The life she was living was far from comfortable, but she'd chosen it in search of a dream. Still, he wondered how much she'd sacrifice in the name of that dream.

"How about you? What's your passion?" Cora snuggled a little closer, tucking her socked feet under his thigh.

Baron ran his hand over her calf, enjoying the familiarity, the easy intimacy that had developed between them. He was relaxed, happy even, being this close to her.

"My passion," he mumbled. "I work. I work a lot."

"I could have guessed that about you. Seems like you have a lot of projects in the fire. Has it always been like that?"

Baron took another swallow of wine, collecting his thoughts. "Yes and no."

"Tell me." Cora traced her fingers along his jaw, drawing his gaze to hers. "I want to hear."

He'd tell her, but he wanted to kiss her first. So he did. The wine married with the taste of her, making him want to taste the rest of her. Every inch of her perfect body. She giggled when they pulled apart.

"Stop trying to change the subject."

He pulled in a deep breath and began. "I've been driven for almost as long as I can remember. I think sometimes a person can be like that from how they're raised. It was always hard to please my dad, but I never stopped trying. Until he died eight years ago. Everything changed for me. I tried to work through the grief, pick up where he left off, but I couldn't do it. Something had shifted, and I needed to give it space. Needed to grow from it, learn whatever I could from this new hole in my life."

Cora softened her shoulders and clasped Baron's hand gently. "I'm sorry. That's a terrible thing to go through."

"We all have to face it eventually."

"What happened then? You took a break?"

"I did. I took almost two years off. I traveled, I sulked, I let a lot of things fall to the wayside. I dabbled in things that I wouldn't have made time for before. I became kind of unrecognizable to the people around me who knew me as someone who just worked constantly."

"And here you are..."

Baron chuckled. "Working, right? I was raised to push the limits of what I could achieve. But I realized that even if that had a lot to do with my dad, it was also a big part of who I was. Who I am, inherently. I slowly started to get back into work, but I took projects on for reasons that meant something to me, that reflected my values, not his. And I started taking better care of myself. I'd work hard, but I'd rest. Take breaks. Find balance with other areas of my life. I'd never done that before. I was the poster child for burnout."

"How do you stay balanced here with so much on your plate?"

Baron swirled his wine again. "The beach grounds me. The people too. They make it all real. Human. It's easy to get wrapped up in facts and figures. The paperwork and fine print. But these people's livelihoods depend on the choices I make every day. So I try to make smart ones. Not everyone always agrees, but I really want this place to succeed. I've invested a lot of money into Cape Haven, but I've also put a lot of heart into it."

"I'm beginning to see that. They're lucky to have you."

Baron shrugged and brought his glass to his lips.

"I'm lucky too. You've been kind to me when you had no reason to be."

He shook his head. "That's not true. I have every reason to be kind to you. You radiate it to everyone around you. How on earth can a man not return that kind of gift?"

"That's sweet of you to say," she said, setting her wine glass aside.

"I have to know..." Baron brought her hand to his lips, kissing the back softly. "Were you born under a lucky star or something?

You're one of the purest people I think I've ever met."

Cora laughed sadly. "I don't know about that."

"I do. I deal with people constantly. It feels like a big part of what I do. You're different."

"I don't know. I probably shouldn't be so trusting. I was forged in fire, I guess. Not the best home life. But you can let the world turn you into an ugly, hateful person, or you can keep trying to look for the good. The seeds you water are the ones that grow."

CORA

"You're wise, young traveler," Baron murmured, lacing their fingers together lazily.

She had yet to see this side of him, so relaxed and unguarded. And honest, baring the hurts of his past to her...little more than a stranger.

But she cherished his vulnerability because she sensed he shared it with so few. Now her heart was twisting in her chest, and her skin singed every time he touched her. And she counted herself lucky to be someone who was getting to know the new Baron Porter.

Cora carefully lifted herself to straddle him, bringing their faces close. "Wise...and blessed...and..." She tapped her finger gently on his lips, falling into a heated vision of those lips other places on her, lighting her up everywhere.

Almost as if he could read her thoughts, Baron silenced her with a kiss unlike the others. This one was deep and possessive, hungry. He set his glass on the table with a clatter and settled his hands on her waist firmly. "And?"

Cora rolled her hips, creating friction between them, communicating with her body what she was hesitating to say with words.

"And very much wanting to be with you right now."

"Are you sure?"

Cora lowered to nibble on his ear before whispering, "I haven't been able to think about anything else."

Baron lifted to his feet, bringing Cora with him. The master bedroom's bedspread was rumpled from where she had napped earlier, and Baron laid her down onto it before turning on the bedside lamp.

"I want to see you. Every inch of you, Cora."

She licked her lips anxiously. "I want to see you too."

The next moments were a blur of mouths and tearing clothes away. Cora lay bare on the bedspread, staring into the eyes of a man she couldn't imagine wanting more. She slid her fingertips over his scalp as he dragged searing kisses across her flesh. He was handsome already, but under his clothes, he was lean and toned with a dusting of hair across his tan skin. She couldn't have drawn a more perfect man in her mind than the one who was moments from making love to her.

And the minute their bodies joined, she knew that's what this was. He was loving her and she was loving him, as deeply as the moment allowed. As strongly as the connection that had already developed between them. The deeper he rocked into her, the louder she cried his name and the more visceral that truth became. Ephemeral and intoxicating. And she truly never wanted it to end.

But he was Baron Porter, real estate mogul who owned half a town, and she was traveling on a hope and a prayer, straight out of his life come morning. She scored her nails over his shoulders, lost herself in the depths of his savage kisses. And he made love to her like a man who never wanted her to forget this moment...their moment.

The waves crashing on the shore mingled with their ragged breaths as they came down from their own crest. Baron's hand found hers, drawing it over his chest, where she could feel his heart pounding the same rhythm as hers. Already she wanted more, even as exhaustion was tugging at her. She didn't want to let him go.

When he lifted onto his elbow and gazed down at her, she couldn't stop herself from asking... "Stay?"

He held her stare for a moment, seeming to search for something there. Then he nodded and kissed her reverently, like Sleeping Beauty in reverse, because the moment he curled his body around hers and swaddled them together in the blanket, she fell sound asleep.

When the first light of the morning filtered into the room, Cora stretched her arms and legs, reveling in the buttery soft sheets and the warmth of the room. Until she realized that the warmth she was missing was Baron's. He was no longer beside her, and the tangle of sheets and her clothes strewn around the room were evidence of everything they'd done last night—when they were as close as two people could be.

She sat up and combed her fingers through her messy hair. She went to the kitchen still naked, feeling a little drunk on the memories. Replaying the dirty things he'd whispered in her ear heated her cheeks as the coffee maker brewed loudly. She'd never had a lover like Baron. For a man who held his feelings so close, he seemed to unleash it all in the bedroom.

Cora finally found a sweater and walked around the house sipping her coffee, finding no trace of Baron's things. The wine had been corked, the glasses washed, the pillows on the couch straightened.

He was gone. The moment...their moment...had passed.

The memories of their incredible night began to recede, gradually taken over by Cora's reality. The road that lay ahead. So many unknowns. She decided to take a long shower. There, she let the tears flow, tears that she'd held back for weeks. Then she pulled herself together and packed her bag. She went from room to room, cleaning and tidying. She changed the bed linens and started a load to wash, leaving no trace as she had promised.

When there was nothing left to do, she forced her feet forward, her heavy bag slung over her shoulder. Leaving the key on the counter, she let herself out, saying goodbye to the house, to

Cape Haven, and the memories she'd made here.

She had one stop to make on her way out of town. She'd forgotten to ask when Marty's opened, but she'd hoped it would be early so she could pick up any extra money she'd earned the night before. When she knocked on the locked door, though, no one answered. She sighed and decided to explore the town a little more. She stopped in a few tiny galleries and read the menus on some of the restaurant windows, something she wouldn't normally do since she could rarely afford a meal anywhere nice.

But she felt more alive than she had in a while. The sadness of leaving...the bliss of being in Baron's arms...the energy of singing in front of a rapt crowd... She felt everything just a little more deeply today, and she wasn't ready to give up the richness of it all. The good and the sad. So she dipped into the diner for a late breakfast and was happy to see Dee serving the counter again. She ordered a hungry man's breakfast with water, hoping it would give her the calories she needed to get to her next stop.

When she cleared her plate, she ventured back over to Marty's. The door was open this time, and she found Marty sitting at a two-top table with a bunch of paperwork in front of him.

"Hey, thanks again for helping out last night," he said, handing her a small envelope of cash.

Cora didn't bother counting it but hoped it would be enough to take her to Mississippi, maybe as far as Louisiana.

"I'm glad I could help. It was a great crowd too. Is it always like that?"

"It's starting to be. We couldn't draw folks out for much other than high school football games until recently. Baron's started up all kinds of community events to get people driving in from the nearby towns though. I guess we just needed the right kind of entertainment. And you sure delivered. Wow."

Cora smiled. "Thanks, Marty. I had a lot of fun."

"You should join us next week. Same time. You've got a job if you want one too."

As tempting as staying here for one more week was, it wouldn't bring her any closer to her dreams. "I wish I could, but I'm getting back on the road today."

"Oh yeah? Where to?"

"California maybe? Or who knows..."

He answered with a half-smile and a grunt, like he wasn't too impressed by Cora's plan. She was starting to question the plan herself.

Leaving Marty's, she inhaled the salty air and made her way to her car.

"Cora, wait."

She spun in the direction of the voice she'd probably never forget. Baron was walking briskly toward her, worry in his eyes.

"Baron. Hi."

"You're not leaving, are you?"

She let out a weak laugh. "Well, yeah. It's time, you know?"

"You weren't going to say goodbye?"

"You left, Baron. Which is fine, but—"

"I came back. I run in the morning. I always do. But I didn't want to wake you up, so I showered at my place before coming back. And you were gone."

"Oh," she whispered, hating the heartbreak that was starting to creep in. Somehow it was easier to think that he was done with things between them. That he was ready for her to move on to.

"You don't have to leave yet, right?"

She shook her head, tears burning hot behind her eyes. She could stay, but she shouldn't. Nothing would get better by staying. More nights in Baron's bed would only bind her heart tighter to his, and neither of them needed that. "I have to go."

"But what's the rush? You can stay at the house—"

"I can't keep living off your generosity, Baron. It's not fair. Not to you...and—" Emotion seized her throat and assaulted her thoughts. "I broke down this morning. Because I realized that with everything you've done for me—the money and the house and getting me that gig at Marty's—for the first time in a really long time, I could set down so much of what I've been carrying around. The stress, the worry, the not knowing what to expect, or if I'm making the right decision. And being with you last night, feeling safe..."

Tears streamed down her cheeks. She tried brushing them away, but she could feel that she was falling apart all over again, this time in front of Baron. As if walking away from this place wasn't going to be hard enough already.

"Baron, you're a good man. And this time I've had here has been the greatest gift. I'll never forget it. I'll never forget you."

"Cora," he whispered, drawing her close to kiss the wet streaks on her cheeks. "Baby."

She sighed into the contact, the strength of his arms, the surety of Baron Porter and the life he so masterfully held together. If she could spend forever this way, she probably would. But forever with Baron was a foolish hope, a loftier dream than the flimsy ones she was already clinging to.

"I have to go," she said, stepping away and breaking the contact while she still had a shred of willpower.

Baron's eyes widened with panic. "Wait. Give me five minutes."

"I can't—"

"You said you can't stay unless you have a gig, right?"

She sighed, studying his features. His eyes were pleading, but there was something else there. Determination.

"I did say that, yes."

"I have a gig for you."

She rolled her eyes, trying to reach for irritation, anger, anything that would make getting in the car easier. "I don't want to be a cocktail waitress for the rest of my life."

"Okay, how about headlining your own show?"

She winced. "What?"

He pointed past her to the old marquee above the theater. "That's the Westwood Theater."

"I know." She'd spent most of yesterday outside it, singing for strangers. So what?

"And I own it."

She rolled her eyes again. "I'm happy for you. Also not surprised."

"And I'll be completely honest with you. It's struggling. The building is falling apart, and the ticket sales are shit. But I figure that's mostly because the guy I have running it—god love him—has no business sense and the talent around here is slim pickings."

"What does that have to do with me?"

"Perform. Put a set together. Let me advertise it and put some shows on the calendar.

"How can I let you pay me if you're losing money on the place? You've been too generous already."

"All business is risk anyway. I'm willing to take a chance on you and your voice, the same way any producer out in California is going to have to if you want a big break. That's the way it works, right?"

"I...I guess."

"It's an opportunity, that's all. You do with it what you will. But maybe this could get you closer to those dreams of yours."

Baron closed the space between them again, taking her hands in his. "What do you say? Give the theater a chance. Give us..." He swallowed and looked down at the sidewalk before meeting her eyes again. "Give us a chance."

Cora's lip quivered as more tears fell. Tears of happiness, tears of hope.

"Do you mean it?"

He palmed her cheek, touched her nose with his, and took her mouth in a slow, perfect kiss.

"If you leave right now, Cora, I'm going to have to follow you to California, and it's going to mess things up for a lot of people here."

She smiled, her heart tightening at his words. "I couldn't take their hero away from them now, could I?"

He smiled. "Then say you'll stay."

Leaving home for the road had taken all the courage Cora

could muster, but somehow it seemed like a small step now. She was about to take a different kind of leap into a future with Baron, in this little town that had stolen her heart in a way too. As sure as she knew a brighter future lay ahead, she knew now that Baron was a part of that future.

She lifted up her keys and twirled them around her index finger. "You want to show me the theater?"

Baron's eyes brightened. "You'll stay?"

She nodded with a grin. "I'll stay."

WORDS
LIKE
STARDUST

JULIA WOLF

About the Author

Julia Wolf writes sexy rockers, broken billionaires, and badass heroines with sass and snark. She's a firm believer in happily ever afters, no matter how rocky the road is to get there.

Julia lives in Maryland with her husband and three crazy, beautiful children. When she's not writing romance, she's reading it. Some of her favorite things are, in no particular order: goats, books, coffee, and Target.

www.juliawolfwrites.com

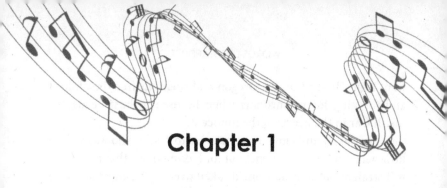

Chapter 1

<u>MARCO</u>

"Diversify your assets, man."

Never, not in a million fucking years, not even when we were breaking laws and living free, did I ever think I'd one day be receiving those words of advice from my boy, Amir.

But we weren't twenty years old, hitting the books hard after classes at Savage U by day, partying even harder at night. That was almost a decade ago, and while Amir might've pulled some all-nighters with his newborn daughter, his partying days were long behind him.

By the nature of my business, I spent my nights surrounded by debauchery. Owning nightclubs meant my waking hours were mostly after dark, and my body had become accustomed to being rattled by booming bass.

"You're not going to want to live that lifestyle forever, and you're getting up there, old man."

"Fucking geriatric," I agreed.

Amir huffed a laugh. "Check out where you can invest some money in a different market. Something adjacent. Music?"

"You're telling me you think music is less volatile than the club scene?"

"Let me do some research. Zadie'll look over the accounts. We'll get back to you."

Amir had been my boy since we had dirtstaches and no game. Luckily, we'd both grown up, though in different ways.

Amir broke away from the less-than-legal side of his life and went legit. He left Cali for Oregon and spent his free time hiking and foraging for mushrooms when he used to bust heads and instill fear in the hearts of the innocent.

He was a family man now, married to Zadie, who was a sweet little accountant with a penchant for baking treats that made eyes roll straight out of heads. She'd taken over my business accounts a couple years back, and she had terrified me ever since. Zadie Vasquez wouldn't hurt a fly, but she'd rip me a new one if my books were a mess.

I wasn't anywhere near settled down.

But I'd listened to my boy, which was how I'd ended up at Ocean Studios, an independent music studio in NYC used by big names in rock music.

Rock 'n' roll. What the hell do I know about that?

I was here as a potential investor. Ocean was looking to expand to the West Coast, which was my home base. Zadie did her due diligence, and she felt like it was a good investment for me, but I wasn't sold.

Night clubs, I knew. I could sink my teeth into the vibe, spend time in each of my clubs, and feel at home, but I was a fish out of water here. If I had my partner, Ivan's wife, Evelyn, by my side, she'd give me her unfiltered opinion of the tunes this place put out. Boohoo for me, I was on my own this time around.

I'd had a week to haunt the halls, sit in on recording sessions, and really get the feel for this kind of business. It'd been a good few days. Interesting, to say the least, but I was still trying to decide whether my green would stay or go.

The Seasons Change were on the last day of recording their next album. I'd heard of them but put a gun to my head, and I still couldn't name a single one of their songs.

They were cool, though. Chill to let me sit in the last two days and watch the mayhem. I had a seat in the back of the studio while Iris, the lead singer, scream-sang a song about true love. The rest of her band—Callum, Adam, and Rodrigo—were rapt, nodding along with her lyrics. In fact, everyone in the room was enthralled, fully focused on Iris, giving me a minute to look them over.

I liked that the crowd was diverse. I wasn't the only Black guy in the room. That was a checkmark for me.

Everyone I'd seen so far was tattooed and artsy-looking. I stood out in my suspenders and button-down, but when I was doing business, I dressed for it.

The only other person who stood out in this room was the girl in the corner. I'd first missed her sitting there yesterday because she was so quiet. She wore an oatmeal-colored cardigan, tortoiseshell glasses, and jeans, so her style wasn't exactly eye-catching, but she was. In my line of work, women were flamboyantly gorgeous—all skin, tits, hair, ass. This girl was all kinds of subtle.

Her dark brown hair was cut in a shoulder-length bob, thick bangs curtaining her forehead. Her body was covered from neck to ankle, and there was no hint of her shape beneath her ugly-ass sweater, but I had a feeling there were curves there—and lots of them.

But her face. Face was stunning.

Smooth, olive-toned skin, deep brown eyes and dramatic brows, high cheekbones, and angular jaw, with plush, dusky lips as the crown jewel of her features.

She nodded along to Iris's singing, those pretty lips moving with the lyrics.

She must have felt me looking at her. Eyes slid my way, but as soon as they connected with mine, they jerked away. A flush rose on her cheeks.

Hmmm.

Seemed like Pretty Girl was shy.

My pondering over her was cut short when Rodrigo, The Seasons Change's drummer, spun around in his chair to face me.

"You in for tonight?"

I cocked my head. "What's tonight?"

"Grabbing some dinner and going out to celebrate. Nothing late or crazy. All of us have homes we're jonesing to go back to, but we can't let this accomplishment go unrecognized."

I rubbed my chin, contemplating. "Everyone going?"

He shrugged. "Everyone's invited." He pointed to Pretty Girl. "That includes you, Lena. Don't even try to hide. I'll find you."

Pretty Girl shrank slightly. "I-I won't hide."

Ah, pretty voice, too.

I wanted to hear more of it.

"I'm in."

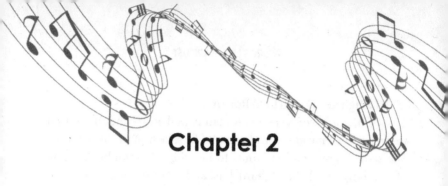

Chapter 2

<u>SELENA</u>

When Iris Adler handed you an edible, you took it and said, "Thank you, Mother," even if your intention for the evening had been to curl up with a mug of tea and a book.

Iris wasn't my mama, but she was an absolute goddess of rock. My idol. The fact that she liked me too still boggled my mind, and even more mind-boggling was that I'd co-written three songs with her on TSC's last album, solo-written two, and I was on my way to having my lyrics in just as many songs on their new album.

Since Iris found me online four years ago, my safe, calm, quiet world exploded. A golden award statue, a dream career, and an entirely new lifestyle later, and here I was. Out to dinner with Iris and the band like they were regular people. The hell of it was, they kind of were. I'd known goofy, sweet guys like Rodrigo back in school. Quiet, mysterious men like Callum had sat at the bar I used to tend. Friendly golden retriever types like Adam were neighbors. I even occasionally ran into stunningly beautiful but shockingly nice and funny girls like Iris at sample sales or grabbing coffee.

After four years in their orbit, I didn't quiver in their presence.

But I was still me. Selena Cruz from Queens. The girl with the stutter and big ass—though only one of those was seen as a fault around here, and it wasn't the size of my ass.

"I get the sense you need this, honey bunny," Iris whispered.

"Your senses are t-t-tingling." I popped the proffered weed gummy into my mouth. "Thanks, girlie."

She winked and punched my shoulder lightly. "Anything for

my main squeeze."

I laughed. "D-don't tell Ronan that."

"Oh, don't worry, Lenie. Ronan is well aware that if he tried to get between me and your lyrics, I'd forsake him in a heartbeat." She sighed, pressing her hands to her cheek, no doubt thinking of her huge, Irish bodyguard husband. "No one else can turn emotion into art like you do."

"Th-thank you."

I wanted to say more to her, but the irony of my life was while I had a gift with words, I couldn't easily get them out of my mouth. Only when I sang, but unfortunately, life wasn't a musical.

I took a bite of my juicy, southern-fried chicken sandwich, probably making a mess of myself. My lips were saucy, hands greasy, but it was delicious. I moaned at the crispy saltiness on my tongue.

That was when I felt eyes on me.

His eyes.

The suit who was hanging around the studio this week was watching me from across the table. Today had been his second day sitting in on TSC's recording session, and he'd been as unobtrusive as a man who looked like that could be.

Keeping my face tilted down, I peeked at him and accidentally met his assessing gaze. My stomach plummeted like I was going over the edge of a rollercoaster.

This man was too slick, too cool, and far, *far* too good-looking to be my type.

He had the tall, dark, and handsome thing down pat. Easily six three or four, he was leanly muscled and wore his finely tailored clothing like it was made for him.

His rich, earthy brown skin was silky smooth. I bet he lathered himself in expensive lotion morning and night. His black hair was buzzed almost to the scalp, and I wondered what it would feel like to drag my hand over it.

Well, I'd never know. It was frowned upon to touch the heads of strangers, and this man wasn't going to be around long enough for us to become acquainted.

Iris elbowed me. "Did you get introduced to Marco?"

I shook my head and swallowed my mouthful of food. "N-n-no, I didn't."

"Let's rectify that, honey bunny." She put her hand on my shoulder and beamed, revealing the cute gap between her front teeth. "Marco, this is Selena. She's an absolute genius who never gives herself enough credit, so if she tries to deny it, don't believe her."

Marco swept his deep brown eyes over me and bit down on his plump bottom lip. My goddamn soul evacuated my body, then rushed back in, not wanting to miss a moment of this man looking at me like a piece of cake. With sprinkles.

"Hello, Selena. Nice to meet you."

Marco's voice was like butter, so smooth it slid over me.

But now he was looking at me, waiting for a reply.

So I waved because I was certain if I tried to speak, I wouldn't be able to get a word out without stuttering.

He stared at me expectantly, which I got. It was common courtesy to reply with words, but he had me tongue-tied more than usual, and the edible hadn't kicked in enough to mellow my anxiety.

I mouthed, "Nice to meet you too," hoping it was good enough.

Iris squeezed my shoulder. "You two can get to know each other at our next stop."

Marco raised a brow. "You're taking me to a second location?"

She laughed. "You only need to be concerned about that if I'm kidnapping you, which I'm not. I already have one tall drink of water at home. I have no use for another."

He chuckled. "Glad we got that settled. How about you, Selena? Is there a husband waiting up for you, too?"

I shook my head, wishing I could channel some Iris Adler. She made it look so easy, and it probably was for her. In my head, I was spunky like her. I had all kinds of comebacks on the tip of my tongue, but I couldn't force myself to even try to say them.

"Well," he huffed. "That's cool. For the record, I don't have a husband either."

"Wife?" Iris asked.

"Nope. Too damn early to settle down. I'll give it a few more years," he replied.

Iris wiggled her fingers, showing off her wedding band. "Do I seem settled to you? Say no, because I'm not. Being married is fucking fun."

He slowly crossed his arms and leaned back in his chair. "Why is it that the marrieds always try to get the singles joined up? My boys do it, too. 'When you gonna settle down, Marco?' and 'Time to let a woman make an honest man out of you.'" He focused on me. "Do your married friends try to get you to join them?"

I lifted a shoulder, but if I didn't speak soon, it was going to get weird.

"No," I murmured.

His eyes lit up. "Ah, she speaks. I was wondering if I should take it personally that I couldn't get a word out of you. Now it's my mission to get another one before the night's over."

Iris patted my leg under the table and bumped my shoulder with hers. She knew my issues with speaking to new people, and she was always trying to draw me out because she wanted the world to know me like she did.

This was why I loved her and why she drove me nuts.

Luckily, love was the stronger emotion.

"G-good luck," I whispered.

Marco shot me a mischievous grin. "We're going to have fun tonight."

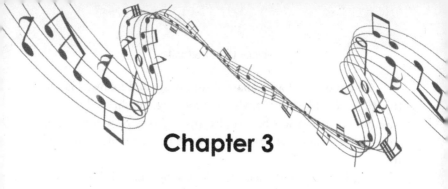

Chapter 3

<u>MARCO</u>

Karaoke?

They had to be fucking with me.

I expected our next stop to be a club, not some direct-from-Tokyo karaoke bar. If not for the pretty little mama I was trying to entice from her cocoon, I would have gone back to my hotel room for the night. Karaoke was *not* my vibe.

"Aren't you guys tired of making music?" I asked Adam, TSC's guitarist.

"Nope. Earlier was work, this is for fun. But lemme tell you a secret, Money Guy: all of it's fun." He slung his arm around his fly-as-hell wife, Adelaide. I'd met her earlier in the week when I sat in during another artist's recording session. She worked at Ocean Studios as a producer but not for her husband's band. I guessed work and pleasure didn't mix.

I cocked a brow. "Were you told to talk me into investing?"

He chuckled. "Nah. I couldn't give a shit where you sink your money. I mean, it would be cool to have the option of recording out in California from time to time."

"There are plenty of studios in Cali," I pointed out.

"Not like Ocean." Adam winked at his wife. "I'm a loyal guy."

She squeezed his cheeks. "Like a sexy golden retriever."

He wagged his brows at me. "Did you hear that? My wife thinks I'm sexy."

She let go of his face to tug on his hand. "Come on, sexy. It's our turn to sing."

He put on a hat and a pair of sunglasses and followed her to the stage. Not like anyone who was looking couldn't tell who he was, but the crowd was buzzed, happy, and very New York. They weren't bothering this band. They were out for their own good time.

While the two of them got their song on, I slid down the bench to have a chat with pretty Selena. She was flipping through the songbook and sipping a girly pink drink.

I peered over her shoulder at the book. "Are you going to sing?"

Her head jerked up, brown eyes wide and alarmed. "I-I...yes."

"Really? You strike me as too shy to get up on stage in front of everyone."

She shrugged.

I tapped her shoulder. "You give this thing a workout around me. Might want to switch up which shoulder you shrug so they don't become off balance." I poked my finger at a song. "I dare you to sing this."

She tilted her head my way. "And i-i-if I do?"

"You want something in return?"

She nodded eagerly.

"Hmmm." I tapped my chin. "You sing that, I'll sing the song of your choosing."

Her eyes narrowed. "P-p-promise?"

The more I heard her speak, the more evident her stammer became. It didn't put me off wanting to talk to her in the slightest, and now I was kind of hoping this was the reason she'd been reluctant to respond to me.

"I swear." I made an x over my heart. "But I don't think you're going to do it, so I'm not too worried."

She pressed her lips together in a sassy little smirk and shoved the songbook at me. "Watch."

Striding to the stage, she swayed her hips, which was a contradiction to the shy girl she'd been showing me all day. And when she got there, she spoke to the guy running the music. He looked at her for longer than I would have called 'friendly.' My stomach rocked while watching their interaction. There was no reason for me to feel any kind of way about this pretty girl talking to other people, but I did. Those were words I wasn't getting.

My heated thoughts were quickly interrupted when Selena unbuttoned her cardigan and slipped it off her shoulders. She tossed it on a nearby chair and smoothed her hands over her tank.

Selena was *built*. Dear god, was she hot. Big, round tits, a nipped waist, and hips that looked like the perfect place to rest my hands. Then she turned around to face the stage, and my tongue about rolled out of my mouth. Ass like a fairytale. Too good to be anything other than make-believe.

When Adam and Adelaide stepped off the stage, Selena took their place. She approached the mic like she already owned it, clutching it with both hands.

The music began, and moments later, Selena's voice burst from her lungs and shot through me. Powerful and husky, she sang "Umbrella" like she was Rihanna's more talented cousin.

No stuttering or hesitation, she owned the stage. Someone moved to the bench beside me, but I couldn't tear my eyes off Selena.

"She's incredible, isn't she?" Iris murmured.

"Yeah."

"She won't listen to me and sing professionally, but she should."

Either that or become my own private songbird and give me that voice every night before I tucked myself in bed.

Iris went on. "She's a behind-the-scenes kind of girl. Her mind...the lyrics she writes...she is amazing."

I tore my eyes from Selena for a second. "She's a songwriter?"

"Mm-hmm. I write some of my own, but Selena has elevated my lyrics to another level. I love how she thinks. It's beautiful."

Selena swayed her hips during the chorus, and I followed them like a ticking clock. Back and forth, back and forth. My tongue darted out to wet my upper lip, but I wished it was her body I was licking instead.

Iris had planted the idea in my head, and now I wanted to hear Selena's thoughts. When I had a chance, I'd look up some of the songs she'd written. Get to know her musical mind.

Selena and I had yet to exchange many words, but I already knew I wanted more. My gut told me I needed to get to know this woman in the short time I had left in the city.

The second Selena's song came to an end, I released the breath that had been caught in my throat.

Selena beamed at the applauding crowd, showing her pretty white teeth. She blew a kiss, then scurried off the stage.

I was on my feet and crossing the bar before I knew I'd decided to go to her. Meeting her in the shadows, I helped her put her sweater back on, only dragging my knuckle along the soft skin of her shoulder for a moment.

"You blew me away, Selena."

She spun around to face me, still grinning, mischief dancing in the golden flecks in her eyes. "You're next."

For a second, my mind went filthy, but I quickly pulled myself together and remembered the promise I'd made. I would have rather gotten my foot run over by a semi, but I gave my word. No backing out.

"I'm ready. Did you pick a song for me?"

She nodded. "W-we're doing it together."

My brow popped. "A duet?"

"Mm-hmm. That okay?"

"Yeah, mama. That's more than okay. If I'm going to make a fool of myself, then I'm taking you with me." I scratched my jaw. "Although you look so good up on stage, you're probably going to make me look even worse. On second thought, maybe I should go solo."

Her mouth fell open. "I—"

I chuckled. "Kidding. I'm not doing this without you. What song did you pick for us?"

Her smile returned, though it was smaller. "'Don't Go B-b-breaking My Heart.'"

I leaned closer and chucked my knuckle beneath her chin. "I couldn't if I tried."

Chapter 4

<u>SELENA</u>

At the end of the night, I hugged all my friends. I'd see them again soon, but it wouldn't be as intense as the last couple of weeks in the studio. There was nothing like the bond formed in the trenches of recording an album.

I'd miss them, but I had some big changes coming, and I'd be too busy to get down for long.

My rideshare was the last to arrive, and Marco volunteered to wait with me.

He leaned against the building beside me, kicking one foot up. "I had a lot more fun tonight than I expected."

My mouth hitched. "Y-y-you didn't think you w-w-would like karaoke?"

"Nah. And I can honestly tell you there's not a chance in hell I'll be going back unless you're there, taking the stage."

My stomach fluttered a little bit with nerves, but more from excitement. Marco wasn't exactly who I'd pegged him as. He'd gotten up on stage with me and let himself be goofy. I really loved that he was able to drop his cool-guy facade and laugh at himself.

For the rest of the night, he'd been by my side, making a game of guessing the song people would choose based on their style. His picks were off the wall, and maybe it was due to the edible, but he had me crying from laughter.

I raised my eyes to his. "That could happen."

He turned to the side and slowly lifted his hand to slip his fingers beneath my hair. "Could it?"

He brought his face to mine, hesitating right before our lips touched. My heart thrashed as I tipped my chin back and closed the breath of space between us.

Nipping at my bottom lip and pulling it between his, he tasted my mouth. I flattened my palm against his chest and leaned into him, my knees already weak.

He banded his arm around my waist and pulled me closer, deepening the kiss. I whimpered when his tongue breached the seam of my lips and came into contact with mine. His tongue curled and slid, taking his time inside my mouth.

I opened wider to him, and he tasted like ice and vodka, like thrills and warm nights by a fire. Comfortable yet so incredibly exciting, my head was spinning.

My phone buzzing in my bra brought me back to Earth. A loud, beeping horn cemented me to the ground.

"Crap," I muttered. "My ride's here."

His arm stayed tight around me, and he drifted his hand down to the upper curve of my ass. "I need a ride, too. We're headed in the same direction."

"Are we?"

"Mm-hmm. We should be environmentally conscious and share."

I looked into his heated, deep brown eyes, and I was certain I didn't want the night to end yet.

So I slipped my hand in his and pressed a quick kiss to his lips. "Let's go, then."

* * *

He kissed me all the way back to my place. Hands in my hair, lips on mine, kissing soft and sweet. As much as I wanted to climb onto his lap and feel his body against mine, I also liked how respectful he was in the car.

Once inside my apartment, all that flew out the window. He

shoved my cardigan off my shoulders and pressed me into the nearest wall. Erection thick and hard against my hip, he palmed my breast and licked up the side of my neck.

My head fell back, eyes fluttering closed, as I gave myself over to this experience. I wasn't naive enough to not understand this would most likely be a one-time thing, so I wanted to soak up every detail. His scent, the sounds he made, how his body felt under my hands.

I yanked his shirt over his head, and mine followed. His abdomen was bumpy under my fingertips. The boxes of muscles flexed as I trailed over them and around to his sides, digging into his narrow hips. Marco was gorgeous everywhere, and the man could kiss me brainless. I was so giddy with anticipation I had to stop myself from bouncing on my toes.

Toe bouncing was not sexy or cool, and I wanted to be sexy for this man.

Eyes on mine, he reached around me to unhook my bra. The straps fell down my arms, and he drew them the rest of the way off. With the barrier gone, he groaned like he was in real pain.

"Fuck, mama, you're gorgeous."

He kissed my chest and trailed lower, giving my sensitive parts his full, undivided attention. I watched him, not wanting to take my eyes off him.

But I was impatient. I wanted my mouth on him, his taste on my tongue.

"Come with me," I rasped. "Bed."

He followed me to my bedroom, his hands on my hips, his mouth on my neck, and as soon as we entered the room, he spun me around to face him again, covering my mouth with his.

He groaned, vibrating my lips with his desperate sounds that sent heat straight to my core.

Breaking his mouth from mine, looking down at me, he panted. "I can't put into words how good you feel. I need to see more of you. Can I have you? All of you?"

I nodded eagerly. He could have asked to shave my head, and

I probably would have agreed with how turned-on I was.

"Take me."

We might only have tonight, but I wouldn't regret following my heart and being with Marco. He was treating me like he was lucky to be with me, and I'd keep these memories close, always, especially the ones that hadn't even happened yet.

* * *

We tangled together in my sheets, skin on sweat-misted skin. His hot mouth on my neck, and lower, *lower*, bringing me so much pleasure I had to beg him to stop, even though I never wanted him to.

He whispered that I smelled and tasted like heaven. That he never wanted to leave this place, and he could live and die between my legs.

Then he climbed over me, his eyes on mine. I reached for him and kissed him—hard. How had his mouth become so familiar in such a short time? No one had ever made me feel this comfortable, especially not a man like Marco.

We rolled, and I took my chance to taste him too. I kissed my way across his chest, loving the smoothness of his skin. I rubbed my cheek against him, his heart pounding against the surface.

"You're driving me crazy, mama. Love how you're touching me. Don't stop."

I met his soft, needy gaze, the frantic edge in his request giving me a shot of satisfaction. "Okay."

A beat of hesitation, then his mouth hitched like he was so fucking pleased with me. "Sexy, Pretty Girl."

"Sexy, beautiful man," I whispered.

I could have teased him, but I had no desire to. I wanted to take him in my mouth, so I did.

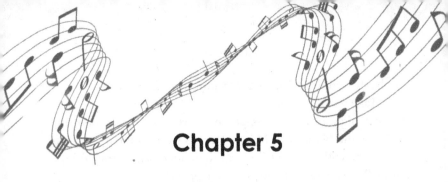

Chapter 5

<u>MARCO</u>

I hoped I'd given Selena half of what she was giving me. Pretty Girl wasn't shy when it came to taking care of me. She made me feel like she wanted to give me everything. To pleasure me exactly how I wanted. Needed. I was going to finish before I was ready if she wasn't careful.

It wasn't just her mouth making me quickly lose myself in her. It was everything about her. Her honey and cream scent. How fresh and addictive she tasted. Her equal fervor to touch me everywhere. The shape of her body. Holy shit, the shape of her body.

I hadn't gotten my fill of looking at her. Exploring those curves and sinking into her softness. I would. Before this night was out, I'd make sure I didn't miss a thing.

But even as I thought it, I knew one night wouldn't be enough to know every secret corner of this woman. I would barely have time to explore the surface.

Grunting with frustration, I tugged on her hair. "Come up here, pretty. I need more of you."

With a naughty light in her eyes, she crawled over my body and pressed her plush curves against me. She grazed her fingers over my jaw and traced my bottom lip.

"I want you," she whispered, sure and clear.

"I don't know if I'll live if I don't have you." From the visceral need I had to draw her into me and keep her there, I believed it in that moment. There had never been anything like this for me before. This connection, this deep, deep desire.

She was right there with me. We moved together as I slid into her. Her eyes on mine, my hands on her face, her hips, her legs. Kissing, so much fucking kissing. Lips like dreams. Hopes like feathers floating over our joined bodies.

Hoping for what, I couldn't say. Not yet.

My mind was on her. On my pretty girl, who writhed beneath me and saturated my senses. We were two rolling waves, crashing into each other again and again.

Until we broke, clawing and panting. Her legs wrapped around me, my fingers tangled in her hair, our mouths fused.

And then we fell, still wound around each other. Blinking, disbelieving what just happened. Two people who weren't even aware of each other's existence forty-eight hours ago, experiencing something soul shaking.

"You felt that, didn't you, mama?"

She nodded, her eyes wide. "W-w-what is it?"

"Don't know." I stroked her hair off her damp forehead. "Never had it. Didn't know to look for it."

"I—me neither." She ran her hand over my head and sighed. "Are you h-h-hungry? Thirsty?"

"What a good little hostess you are. You gave me the best sex of my life, now you want to feed me?"

She nodded, giggling softly. "Best of mine, too."

"Yeah, I know."

Her brow rose. "Y-y-you do?"

"Yeah, Selena, I know. There's no way possible you've had anything better than that with someone else. That was chemical, my body reacting to yours. That's solely between you and me."

She narrowed her eyes. "Maybe."

I gave her ass a gentle smack. "Admit it."

Squealing, she rolled away from me, but I followed, clamping down on her shoulder like the rabid dog she'd turned me into.

"Fine, fine," she cried. "I admit it!"

"Mmm." I kissed the spot I'd bitten and rubbed my lips against it. "That's right. Now feed me, mama. I need my energy because I'm nowhere near done with you."

* * *

I didn't get a good look at Selena's pad until I wandered out to the kitchen after her. It wasn't at all what I would have expected if I'd spent time thinking about it.

She had a wall of windows and a balcony with a view beyond it. The ceilings were tall, the space airy. Walls were a sleek gray, furniture stylish and lush.

This wasn't some boho studio. Nah, this place was legit. I would have crashed here if I lived on this coast, and I was the type of man who was accustomed to the finer things in life.

While she whipped up something to eat in nothing but her tank and underwear, I pulled out my phone to look her up. It gave me pause that I didn't know her last name, but I didn't let that stop me. Typing in Selena plus songwriter was enough to get hits.

A lot of hits.

Selena Cruz had many fucking credits to her name and gleaming gold awards to go along with them. She'd written songs for most of the popular musicians out there, not just The Seasons Change.

The luxurious apartment made sense now.

The woman I was spending time with was a powerhouse. A success in her industry by anyone's standards.

And yet she was a dichotomy of shy and confident. Maybe equal parts both, and when I thought about it, I *liked* both sides of her. I'd definitely never met another woman like her.

I leaned against the kitchen entry, taking her in. Her back was to me, so I let my gaze linger on her round cheeks peeking out of the bottom of her underwear before drifting up to her silky hair, tangled in a nest at her crown. That shot a pleased thrill to my belly, knowing I'd been the cause of that mess. Yeah, I liked that.

"How old are you, Selena Cruz?"

She peered at me over her shoulder as she cooked something on the stove. "Twenty-six," she mouthed, not saying the words aloud. "You?"

"I'll be thirty in a couple months."

"S-s-still twenty-nine, though."

"Mm-hmm." I approached her, leaning a hip on the counter beside her. "I like your optimistic look on things. I'm over here prematurely kissing my twenties goodbye."

She smiled and pointed her spatula at the pan. "Eggs?"

I frowned at what she was cooking. "That looks like a whole lot more than just eggs." I slid my hand around her waist. "Whatcha cooking, mama?"

Lips rubbing together, she hesitated, and I felt her gathering herself. "It's a quick Spanish tortilla. My abuela gave me her secret shortcut."

Her stutter was there, but I wanted her to keep talking. To feel comfortable enough with me not to let anything stop her from expressing herself.

I kissed her shoulder. "Honored you're making your abuela's recipe for me. She alive?"

She shook her head. "Died a few years ago."

"Sorry about that, but I'm glad you have her recipe."

Turning, she rubbed her nose along my jaw. "A lot of them." Using her spatula, she pointed at a small wooden box. "They're in there."

"You trust me to look?"

She arched a brow. "Are you going to steal them?"

I chuckled. "Nah. I wouldn't know what to do with them. I'm not what you'd call a chef. But I'm going to look at them because I love this kind of thing. Generation after generation, passing down secrets."

I thumbed through her recipes, warmth permeating my chest at her abuela's handwriting and the splashes of food on the well-worn cards. This was history here.

By the time I'd gotten through looking at all of them, our

midnight breakfast was done, and Selena was dishing up slices of tortilla on plates.

We sat at her kitchen bar, my hand on her bare thigh, her shoulder bumping mine.

I took a bite of my tortilla and chewed, savoring the salty eggs and potatoes. "This is legit, Selena. Abuela knew what she was doing."

Her giggle was sweet as sugar. "She did."

I speared another bite, then another, enjoying every single thing about these stolen minutes. It bothered me more than it should have that that's all they were. Moments that were mine, but only until I was forced to give them back.

"I looked you up," I told her. "You're a big fucking deal, huh?"

A flush rose on her cheeks, so pretty I wanted to scoop her up and take her back to bed. But not more than I wanted her words.

"I don't know about that."

"You are. I feel pretty foolish for not knowing exactly who you are. Iris said you write music for her, but she didn't say you've written for a lot of other people, too."

Her shoulder lifted, and I had to suppress a groan. I'd thought we were past the shrugging stage.

I grabbed the underside of her stool and swiveled her to face me. She yelped, her brown eyes going wide with surprise.

"Marco!"

I took her face in my hand, stroking her silky smooth cheek with my index finger. "You've made me curious, Selena. And the thing about me is when I'm curious, I don't stop until my mind is sated. Talk to me, tell me everything."

Her mouth fell open. "I—"

I kissed her parted lips. "Let's start small. Tell me the story of how you met Iris Adler."

"Online."

"Go on."

I was on the edge of my seat with no plans of sitting back until I knew everything about this girl.

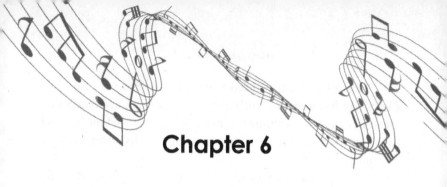

Chapter 6

<u>SELENA</u>

Marco expected me to talk, and the thing was, I wanted to talk to him.

"I d-d-don't talk a l-lot." My teeth dug into my bottom lip. "I'm s-sorry."

Grabbing my hand, he brought it to his lips. "I get that about you. I'm about to say something that's probably impolite, but I'm the kind of person who lays my cards on the table."

I nodded. That was exactly my impression of him.

"I heard your stutter the first time you spoke to me, Selena. It's not a secret you're hiding from me. If I had to guess, it's the reason you don't like to talk openly."

My head burst into flames, and I wanted to curl into a ball of embarrassment. It was stupid, really. This man had seen every inch of me. He'd been inside me. Why the hell was I still so ashamed of something I couldn't help?

"O-okay," I whispered.

"No, listen." He pressed his lips to my knuckles. "I heard it then, but after a while, I stopped noticing it. When you talk, it's just you talking, and I want to hear every fucking thing you have to say. I mean that, Selena."

He proclaimed it with such adamance I had no choice but to believe him. He wanted my words, even if they weren't perfect, and that was something I couldn't shy away from. I didn't want to.

So, I spoke like I didn't have a stutter. I wove my story around him with perfect threads, drawing him closer to me.

"When I was little, I used to get so frustrated because I had a lot to say, but it never came out right. So one day, my abuela told me to write down everything in my head. She assured me it didn't have to be perfect or even make sense, but I needed to let it out, or I would burst at the seams."

Marco nodded along with me, his gaze wholly focused on my lips, my expression, my eyes. His body was attuned to mine as he stroked my cheek and held my hand against his chest.

"I still have my old notebooks stored in boxes." I smiled faintly. I'd have to dig those out when I had the chance. "I filled them one after another, first with streams of consciousness, then they began to take form. Stories, poems, and lyrics. I sang them in whispers to my abuela, sometimes to my close friends. Everything that I'd locked away for so long began to explode out of me. Words like stardust, showering all over the pages of my notebook. Then, my friends encouraged me to share my writing, so I set up a couple social media accounts. I read the poetry and sang the lyrics."

"You don't stutter when you sing," Marco filled in.

"No. Not when I read either." I smiled, unsurprised he'd noticed. "Sadly, I don't live in a musical."

"You could be a star, Selena. That could be you, center stage."

I shook my head. "I've never wanted that. It's enough to get the words out."

"That's how Iris found you?"

"Yeah. She slid into my DMs."

He chuckled. "Did you know who she was?"

"I'd heard of her, but I had a hard time believing it was really her. Then she gave me her number, and when she answered with 'Hey, honey bunny,' I almost fainted."

He laughed a little harder. "I bet you did. That's wild."

"It was, but Iris is cool. She made me feel like her best friend from the start. I've worked with a lot of people now, but she's my favorite. Iris had written some incredible lyrics, and our styles just mesh, you know? It's like our brains are on the same wavelength when we're writing together."

"Is it like that with everyone?"

"I don't write with others. Only Iris. The rest, I go solo."

"Hmmm. Has anyone asked to cowrite with you?"

"Of course, but..."

He dipped down, his eyes latched on mine. "But that involves a lot of talking?"

"It does. It's easier for me to talk through my lyrics, except with a few select people."

He never looked away. "I like the hell out of talking with you, Selena."

I rubbed my lips together, nervous from his sudden intensity. "You're easy to talk to. You make me forget it's hard sometimes."

With a groan, he rose, dragging me against his chest and sliding his fingers through the side of my hair. "You are incredible. Never want you to stop giving me your stardust."

Then he kissed me, speaking to me in a whole different way but just as effectively.

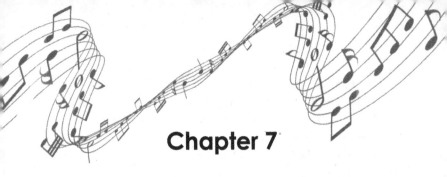

Chapter 7

<u>MARCO</u>

My suitcase was packed.

This was the stage I was normally antsy to go home, but not today. After my night with Selena, I was in no rush to cross the country. I couldn't hold off on my return, though, not even if I wanted to more than anything.

I had a club opening in LA I needed to oversee. Being physically present was necessary. Otherwise, I might've tried to convince Selena to allow me to work from her swanky-ass living room for a week or two so I could have my fill of her.

But even that didn't feel true. A week or two would have just left me even more bereft, not cured of this sudden, inexplicable ache in my chest.

I picked up my phone and checked the time. A text from my boy, Julien, was waiting for me.

> **Jules: You're coming back tomorrow, right?**

> **Me: Yeah, unfortunately.**

> **Jules: Unfortunately? I thought you'd be chomping at the bit to get back here so you can oversee your kingdom.**

Jules and I went as far back as Amir and I did. For a long time, we'd been the three musketeers, then we graduated from college and the two of them turned into family men. I didn't begrudge them that. They'd found something they had been looking for and treasured the hell out of it. My family life had been just fine. Mom and Dad were still married, and I had a couple nephews from my older sister. I wasn't pining or needing to fill the void. Not the same way they had been.

But I had this ache square in the center of my chest. It intensified when I thought of getting on a plane tomorrow. Never seeing Selena again.

Me: I met a girl. Selena.

An instant later, Jules called. I had to laugh at his speed.

"What's up?" I answered.

He exhaled. "Jesus, I was convinced your phone had been stolen. A girl, Marco?"

"I meet girls."

"Oh, I know you've never had a shortage, but you've also never said those words to me. 'I met a girl.' As if she's important. So, you're going to need to explain Selena to me."

Sinking into the leather chair near the floor-to-ceiling windows, I kicked my feet up on the desk. "Selena Cruz. She's a songwriter. Genius. Sexy as hell. The kind of pretty that stops you in your tracks, combined with the kind of sweetness that I see you and Amir getting from your wives, but I've never had directed at me." I groaned. "Lives in New York."

He went quiet for a beat, but I could hear his gears turning. "You've met a woman you feel strongly enough to tell me about, and it sounds like you're going to let geography stop you from pursuing her. Is that right?"

"We had one night together."

"All right. Then why are you telling me about her?"

I rubbed my face, frustrated with him for seeing the truth even when we weren't sharing the same space. This was what I got for keeping him around for so long. He knew me too well for me to get anything by him.

"Because it was special, and I feel like a prick for even saying those words, but it's true."

His whooshing breath vibrated my ear. "There's nothing wrong with recognizing you had a connection with someone."

"There is when she lives on the opposite coast from me."

"Planes exist."

I dropped my hand to the side. "Which I'm frequently on for business. You know this, Jules."

He made a disgruntled sound. "I do know. I see ghosts more than I see you."

"Right. So this thing with Selena, it's going in the memory banks. If I try to do some kind of long-distance thing with her, I'll end up breaking my heart or hers. Or, fuck, both."

"Marco..." he uttered. "You're talking about your heart. That means something."

I squeezed my eyes shut. "I'm talking about it breaking, man."

"You've never cared about that before."

"That was—" I couldn't let myself say it.

"Before Selena."

Count on Jules not to let me off the hook.

Fucking Julien.

* * *

My mind was still on my conversation with Jules when I knocked on Selena's door. I only had a few more hours left to spend with her, and the last thing I wanted was to be stuck thinking about the end of everything.

She opened the door with a grin on her pretty face. "Marco Rider," she purred, leaning her head against the side of the door. "You're here."

I stepped into her, dipping down to brush my lips over hers, and it *hurt*. This was the first and last time I'd get to show up at her door and kiss her hello.

"You're here too, looking like a dream, mama." Her hair was pulled back with a red bandanna, forties-style. Cuffed jeans hugged her thick thighs, and a white T-shirt snuggled up with her tits, exposing a slice of her golden abdomen.

Gorgeous.

I already knew for a fact I'd never find another woman more beautiful than Selena Cruz.

She took my hand, pulling me into her place. Regret weighed my feet down, but I followed her.

This was it.

A beginning and an end.

It wasn't like me to get philosophical. Normally, I didn't get caught up in my feelings, but this ache. This fucking ache.

Selena bounced on her toes, and it was adorable. But it killed me that she was happy-go-lucky while I was trying to hold my cracking chest together.

"Okay, here are our choices: my favorite hole-in-the-wall down the road, or we order in. I'm too trashed to cook, and I packed most of my pans anyway. What do you think?"

I blinked at her and then the boxes behind her. Her living room was now lined with cardboard boxes. Stacked high, they were clearly marked with the contents in big, bold letters.

"You packed?"

She laughed and looked back at the boxes behind her. "Yes. I could have let the moving company do it, but I can't stand the idea of someone else having their hands all over my things, you know?"

I furrowed my brow. "Let's back up a step. You're moving? Why would you leave this pad? If I lived on this coast, I'd be all over it."

Her hands went to her hips, and the furrow in her brow matched mine. "Well...wait, what do you mean?"

"Just that I like your place, and I find it hard to believe you're going to find one better."

"Oh, well." She crossed her bare feet. "My new place isn't anything like this, but I'm looking forward to living in an actual house after a lifetime of apartments."

"You're leaving the city?"

"Marco." She brought her hand to my chest. "I know I told you I was moving...didn't I?"

I shook my head slowly. "This is brand new to me." Snagging her around the waist, I tugged her against me. "Tell me about it, mama. Where are you going?"

The corners of her plush lips curved like she had a naughty secret. It pulled me in, wanting her lips next to my ear, sprinkling her stardust.

But what she said out loud, in plain, direct words, was more than magic.

"The thing about writing music is I can do it anywhere, but most musicians live in LA. I've been traveling back and forth the last few years, but I got tired of the long flights, plus I'm ready for some sunshine."

My blood roared in my ears, and my arm tightened around her. "You're moving to LA?"

"I really thought I told you." She tilted her head as she looked me over. "I didn't tell you I'm moving next week?"

"Not at all. I think I'd remember you were moving to my city." I dropped my hand to her ass, squeezing her firmly. "Then I wouldn't have been tearing myself up at the prospect of never seeing you again."

"I'm sorry," she said softly. "But I kind of like that you were tearing yourself up over me. You like me, huh?"

I gave her a light smack. "I thought you were a sweet girl. Now I know you're nothing more than a sadist."

"I'm not, I promise. I'm just really into you, and now I'm thinking you're really into me too."

I pressed my lips to hers. "Yeah, I'm into you. But you need to work on your communication skills, mama. You *definitely* didn't mention your move to LA. Where I live."

"It isn't possible you didn't hear me?"

"No, Selena." I nipped at her bottom lip. "It's not possible. Because if I'd heard you tell me you were about to move to my town, I would have been here helping you pack so you could get there sooner."

She curled her arms around my neck. "I'm going to work on that since I really could have used some help today."

I rocked my hips into her soft tummy. "I need to be inside you more than anything right now."

"Yes, please."

She led me to her bedroom, and it was even more incredible than it had been last night. We moved together, eyes locked, smiles on our kissing lips. She rose over me, showing me all of her. Curves and valleys I'd have time to explore because this was the beginning, not the end.

We kissed, and then she slid her lips next to my ear. "I can't wait, Marco. I can't wait to see you in the sunshine. I can't wait for all of it."

Words like stardust...

Epilogue

SELENA

One Year Later

My stomach fluttered with anticipation and a little bit of nerves. This was my first anniversary with anyone, but more importantly, it was with the love of my life.

One year for everything to change.

It started when Marco walked into a recording studio. When he heard me speak and asked for more. Since that day, he'd never stopped asking.

We moved in together a month ago officially, but unofficially, I'd barely lived in my little bungalow since touching down in LA. Now we had a place we'd chosen together, a house with a little yard and an orange tree.

We were busy in our careers, but we enjoyed being together so much that we made it a priority to find the time. I went to his clubs with him. He let me bounce lyrics off him when I got stuck. We both invested in Ocean Studios West, and so far, it had been a wise decision.

Marco and I were good for each other. This much I knew down to my bones.

I'd never spoken to anyone as much as I spoke to him. With him, the words came easy, and not just conversation. I wrote lyrics day and night. He had freed up a part of my creativity that I hadn't known existed before I fell in love with him.

I pulled into our driveway, butterflies dive-bombing my belly.

It was always this way when I came home, another sign I was in the right place, with the right person.

Jumping out of my car, I slung my bag over my shoulder and rushed to our front door. Before I could even put my hand on the knob, Marco was there, tugging me into our home.

His mouth covered mine in a deep, lingering kiss, teasing my tongue with his. He dragged his nose along my jaw to the side of my neck, where he inhaled, and slid his fingers through the back of my hair.

"Happy anniversary, mama."

"Happy anniversary, my love."

He finally stepped to the side, revealing the living room. He'd lit candles, maybe a hundred of them, and placed them randomly around the room.

"Wow," I breathed. "This is...baby, this is beautiful."

"I wanted something special for us. Firsts don't come around often, but I plan to give you a lot of them. First anniversary, first love, first house together. We'll have many more." He slipped my bag off my shoulder and took my hand in his. "I had some idea of how tonight would go. The order of things. But I can't sit through dinner to do this."

"What?"

But my heart knew, and it was thumping inside my chest with the promise of forever.

Marco faced me, and then he dropped to one knee, still holding my hand. Tears welled in my eyes, but I willed them away so I could experience every second of this in sharp focus.

"Selena Cruz, the prettiest girl I've ever seen." Marco cleared his throat and rubbed his thumb over my ring finger. "You've given me everything I didn't know I was missing. Made me happier than I thought possible. Took me for who I was and made me want to be better. I will keep being better for you for the rest of our lives, if you'll have me. Will you marry me, Selena?"

I nodded, unable to get any words out at first. But I wanted him to hear me. To reply to the beautiful things he'd said to me.

"Yes, Marco. Yes, yes, yes. I will marry you with my whole heart because I know you will keep it safe and take care of it like you always have. Yes."

He slipped the ring on my finger and wrapped me in his arms, his face pressed to my stomach. There we stayed, shaking, tears slipping down our cheeks, not saying a single thing.

For once, words weren't needed.

His arms around me and mine around him said it all.

We were in this together.

Forever.

MusiCares helps the humans behind music because music gives so much to the world. Offering preventive, emergency, and recovery programs, MusiCares is a safety net supporting the health and welfare of the music community.

Founded by the Recording Academy in 1989 as a U.S. based 501(c)(3) charity, MusiCares safeguards the well-being of all music people through direct financial grant programs, networks of support resources, and tailored crisis relief efforts.

For more information please visit: www.musicares.org.